# VERMONT ESCAPE

## MARSHA R. WEST

This print version is published by MRW Press LLC and released September 2014

VERMONT ESCAPE was e-released in by MuseItUp Publishing

14878 James, Pierrefonds, Quebec, Canada, H9H 1P5

Cover Art © 2013 by Charlotte Volnek

Edited by Rosalie Skinner

Copyedited by Sarah Champoux

Layout and Book Production by Lea Schizas

First eBook Edition *July 2013

***DEDICATION***

*To my wonderful husband, Bob. You have backed me in everything that I've ever wanted to do. From the time I said I want to write a book until VERMONT ESCAPE's e-release was approximately six years. You never complained though you must've wondered what was taking me so long. Now, you've encouraged me to take the road to self-publish the print version. Thank you. I couldn't have done this or any of the other endeavors without your love and support.*

# ACKNOWLEDGEMENTS

Thanks to Charlotte Volnek, my cover artist for the e-version as well as this print version. You captured the essence of the book. Thanks to the folks at Formatting Faries.com who saved me tons of time and frustration. Thanks to Jerrie Alexander for holding my hand through the scary process of publishing a print version of this book.

I've been fortunate to work with four excellent critique partners on VE. Jerrie Alexander and Jeannie Guzman, you brainstormed with me, nagged me, and told me the truth about my writing even when I didn't want to hear. (They have had input in all six of my books.) Denise Cohen worked with me on-line for a time on this book. Her input, too, has been important. Renee Jones was my third (in person) Critique Partner. She was even more of a grammarian than Jerrie and Jeannie. Thanks for loaning me your good eye. Through difficult times of self-doubt, y'all believed in me. "Thank you" is not near good enough.

Kaki Foster, you're the only person to read every one of my books. You've been a long time good friend, and I appreciate your encouragement more than I can say. So glad I can put a print book in your hands. The late Emily Seat, a beautiful writer herself, also encouraged me. Thanks to three people who loaned me parts or all of their names and professions: Gene Miers, Melinda Smith, and James Russell.

Thanks to Klaran and Andy Warner who introduced me to beautiful The Woodstock Inn. Margie Lawson, you showed me how to fix what Jerrie and Jeannie said was missing from my writing. Your packets and the time on the mountain with you and the Stellar Scribes made the difference between a good book and publication. Many, many thanks.

Thanks to the most generous people in the world, the community of romance writers, especially those in North Texas RWA. I have to single out Cindy Dees. I learned the "save the cat" rule from you.

Thanks to my daughters and sons-in-law for their support.

Though this is the print version of VERMONT ESCAPE, it would be remiss not to recognize the folks at MIU who published the e-version of this book: Lea Schizas, publisher; Rosalie Skinner, content editor; Sarah Champoux, line editor; Charlotte Volnek, and the supportive family of MIU authors.

Lastly, thanks to Charles Ireland, who gave me the idea for the first book I ever wrote and started me on this journey.

You've heard that it takes a village to raise a child. Well, it takes a small town to get a book published. I am indeed fortunate to have such an excellent small town.

Any errors or mistakes are my own.

# CHAPTER ONE

*Wednesday, April 25*

Jill Barlow reached for her make-up kit and brushed against the one thing she'd done her damnedest to avoid. Her heart rate tripped into overtime.

It was the package she'd received days after her dad was murdered. That was one month ago, but she couldn't face opening a reminder of the nightmare.

Pictures of her vigorous father mixed with recent images of his closed casket. Nausea hit. Again. Damn. Why would someone blow off her father's head? She hadn't stayed to find out. She'd run.

She'd pushed herself on a four-day drive from Texas to Vermont. Emotionally and physically exhausted, all she wanted to do now was unpack her pajamas and climb into bed. Habit required she clean and moisturize her face. Habit provided comfort when life was chaotic. Habit could get her through the worst. Or not.

She removed the package and dropped it onto the bed in her Woodstock Inn suite. It lay on the white coverlet like a scorpion.

Sweat drenched her palms. Hands propped on her knees, she leaned over and drew in needed oxygen. A minute passed, and then she straightened.

"Okay, open this. Every time you come across the thing, you implode, morphing into a quivering mass of mush." Two years since her husband George was killed. Now a second murder, and Dad was gone. No wonder she'd lost the battle against stress and babbled out loud.

Despite the bravado of her words, her hand shook as she reached toward the potential time bomb. Bile rose in the back of her throat.

"I'm forty-nine, and I'm acting like eighteen and talking to myself again. Daddy probably sent me a nice piece of jewelry." She used her manicure scissors and slit through the tape. Holding her breath for a moment, she released it in a whoosh, and then flipped open the flaps. Her heart fluttered like a bird caught by a cat. She drew in needed oxygen. Inside, nestled a small box. A relieved sigh escaped. Had to be jewelry.

Jill withdrew the box and raised the lid. Pulling out tissue revealed the contents. A flash drive.

"What in the world?" She removed the device.

*Jill* written in Dad's distinctive script on a folded white piece of paper.

Her heart jammed against her throat. The stationary in her unsteady hands wavered like a leaf caught by a zephyr. She opened the sheet.

*Dearest Jill,*

*I hope I'm able to answer any questions you have. If I'm not around, arrogance got me killed. You need to get out of Texas.*

*You told me how much you loved Vermont when you visited after George's death. Go there. With me out of the way, you, Ellen, and Ethan should be safe.*

*I sent the original information on Greg Richardson and the actions of the consortium against me to an FBI agent. You know how responsible I feel for George's death.*

*This copy is for you. I didn't want you to be shocked when the news about the arrests hit the papers.*

*However, if I'm dead, the bad guys won, kitten. Use your own good judgment. Destroy this or not. Your choice.*

*You and the kids are everything to me.*

*Love, Dad*

Jill's whole body quaked. Tears slid down her cheeks before they became a gushing waterfall.

Sobs gagged her. She stumbled into the bathroom where she threw up. Finally, she stopped and collapsed on the cold tile floor.

The sobs changed to whimpers, and then became short hiccups. She had to stop crying. To catch her breath. To stop hurting.

Holding onto the counter with clammy hands, she pulled herself up. Weeping willow legs offered little support, and she leaned against the cabinet. She rinsed her mouth. The cold water she splashed on her cheeks stung. She looked up.

Mirrors didn't lie.

Grief hurt. The last two years showed on her face.

What should she do?

Jill stumbled against the overstuffed chair in the small suite and made for the door. To think, she needed to walk. She dropped the key card in the pocket of her slacks. Rapid strides carried her down the lengthy hallway. Flowers in a large vase at the far end marked her goal. Their sweet scent provided a contrast to the turmoil in her mind. No other guests appeared to interrupt. She chewed over the problem of what to do with the flash drive.

She'd suspected the gambling syndicate was responsible for the murder two years ago of her husband, George, but the Fort Worth police found no hard evidence. A month ago when her father was shot, evidence didn't provide any solid clues for the Austin Police Department or the Texas Rangers.

What should she do with the flash drive? If her father gave the original to the FBI, and it contained evidence as he claimed, they should've investigated. An agent should've contacted her. But no one did. Didn't they investigate? If not, why?

A lightning streak of fear zinged through her heart, and sorting through all the options shot pain through her temples. Jill spun on her heel at the end of the hall and made for her room. She slid the plastic key card into the slot. The soft click clarified her decision. She'd stash the device in a bank safe deposit box and not look at the information that got her father killed.

His note lay on the desk. One word jumped from the page.

Vermont.

"Well, Daddy, I'm here. Let's hope you're right."

* * * *

*Thursday, April 26*

Tall and slim, Jill's transplanted Texas friend Karen wore her curly brunette hair tied back in a long bushy ponytail. Fine lines outlined her eyes and grooved her thin cheeks. Jill considered her friend an earth-mother type.

They ate breakfast in the inn's restaurant, chatting like schoolgirls catching up after summer break. Because of phone calls and social media, it seemed no time had passed since they'd been together.

"Did you get hold of Ellen and Ethan after you arrived last night?" Karen raised the cup to her lips, and blew before taking a sip.

"Yes, after I unpacked I called them." Warmth spread around her heart. The twins checked on her every day during her trip north. They'd become the care-takers. Even though they were grown with their own careers, Jill couldn't deny her maternal desire to protect them from everything connected to their father and grandfather's deaths.

"I'm sure they must've been worried about you on the road by yourself." Karen took a bite of bacon.

"They were concerned." Not a subject she wanted to pursue. The blueberries in her pancakes burst on Jill's tongue with their combination of sweet and tart. "We just don't get anything this fresh at home."

"Texas Bar-B-Q sings to my taste buds. I always make a point to eat it a couple of times when we visit family." She leaned forward.

It was obvious Karen had a scheme on her mind.

"I hope you're planning on continuing with your volunteer work." Karen lowered her voice. "Because we've some great organizations in town, any of which could use your skills and experience."

"I don't know what I want to do."

"Well, I have no doubt we'll find something worthwhile." Karen's voice had the confidence of someone who hadn't endured incredible loss.

"Let's hope so." Jill slung a brown sweater around her shoulders and scooted out the chair. "Okay, time to get this show on the road."

Karen stood and then glanced down. "I'm glad you've worn comfortable shoes."

"Comfortable shoes?" A chuckle burst out. "I learned my lesson last time when you walked me to my knees."

So much had happened since then, yet so much was the same.

They left the inn and headed across the village green. "I can't get over how much this place looks like a movie set." Old buildings. Ancient trees. Fragrant baskets of colorful flowers hanging from light posts. All gave the town its picture postcard charm.

"First stop is the bank," Jill said.

After opening her account and placing the flash drive in a safe deposit box, Jill drew in a deep breath. The clean air washed through her. She puffed out much of her anxiety. The little bit of technology had weighed her down. A dull headache, plaguing her since she'd read her father's note, lessened a degree.

Tires screeched, and the two women paused at a corner. Horns blared. Jill's heart rate jacked up, and her hand flew to her mouth. "Oh, my gosh," she yelled, not the calm person she pretended to be.

A man dashed in front of the car, waved to the driver, and scooped up a small, fluffy white dog. He hurried up the street. Yips faded away. "The pup and his owner were lucky," Jill said in a shaky voice. The hand on her chest quivered with fear at how close the car had come to smashing the dog.

"The pooch belongs to Anne Phillips. Whenever her son is home, he spends part of his time catching the run-away."

"Well, that's nice of him." Jill gulped another calming breath. "If the dog makes a habit of escaping from the house, I'd probably decide it was safer to keep him inside."

The light changed, and they crossed the street.

"Jerrod has suggested as much to his mother. Anne doesn't comply, and Princess skips out. He's a good son. Unlike Mitch." Karen almost huffed.

"Who?"

"Long story. Not now. Now is for fun."

They walked on with an occasional stop to window shop.

Karen looped her arm through Jill's. "Tim and I are so sorry for your loss. We hated that we couldn't get there for the funeral." Her voice shook with emotion. "Your dad was a sweetheart."

Jill nodded and tightened her jaw against the loss never far away. "Thanks. Your support means everything."

"I'm glad you decided to come." Karen gave Jill an extra hug.

Jill cleared her throat. "You helped so much last time. I figured I'd give you another chance at putting me back together."

Karen blinked away tears and squeezed Jill's hand. "You're staying longer this time, right?"

Jill nodded. "You know a good real estate agent?"

"Sure thing. Mark Jennings' office is down the street past Anne's store." Karen grabbed Jill's arm and dragged her to a stop.

"What's the matter?" Jill's heart jumped into her throat. She had to get a grip if she wanted to others to believe she was okay, trustworthy, normal.

"We'll stop by her shop. She must be there. It's the only time Princess gets out." Karen threw an arm around Jill's waist and hurried them along. "Anne told me to be sure you looked her up when you arrived."

Jill's conscience tugged at her, raising the specter of a returned headache. She hadn't told Karen everything. Damn, she couldn't risk mentioning Richardson or the gambling consortium and certainly not the flash drive.

Because Karen knew everyone in town, they stopped often to introduce Jill. When Karen discussed a piece of business for the Historical Society's gala with a board member, Jill smiled at the reminder of her old life in Fort Worth.

Pain wound its way through Jill's chest to the back of her throat. She swallowed hard. How could she have a good time with her father recently murdered and George gone? Curling her fingers tight into her palms, she straightened her shoulders and stuffed her feelings deep inside. That's what both men would expect of her. She could almost hear them say, "carry on."

"I'm sorry." Karen grinned in apology. "We get into a discussion whenever we run across each other. Drives Tim nuts. We're almost to Anne's store."

"Seems like she talked about selling when I was here before."

"Yeah, but I don't know how hard she tried. It was only a month ago I saw the 'For Sale' sign."

Windows full of rainbows and sparkling crystal caught Jill's attention.

"We're here." Karen pushed open the door.

The tinkle of chimes welcomed them, accompanied by a delightful aroma.

"Anne, look who I've got with me." Excitement filled Karen's voice as though she was about to give the storeowner a long anticipated gift.

"Mother, you've got to fix the fence or hire someone to babysit this little girl or sell the store so you can stay home. You'd be upset if chasing after you gets her killed."

The man's deep voice reverberated in Jill's chest, sending a tremor along her spine. Her gaze snapped to his face. His eyebrows canted down. One hand scratched behind the dog's ears. Clearly a dog lover and a man who cared about his mother. He never looked in Jill's direction, focused instead on concluding the business about his mother's pet.

"Princess is very determined, Jerrod. You know I've fixed the fence several times." Anne's smile made up for the lack of a welcoming one from her son. "Forgive me, we're being rude. Jerrod, this is Karen's friend from Texas, Jill Barlow."

The man handed the dog toward Mrs. Phillips, but she didn't reach for the pooch.

He frowned, as though not at all happy about his mother ignoring her responsibility for the dog. Perhaps his displeasure spilled over onto Jill, because he scowled.

Maybe the beard added to the impression of gruff disinterest he gave. Jill granted him the benefit of the doubt, but his behavior struck her as odd.

"Nice to meet you, Mr. Phillips." Jill extended her hand. His fingertips had a slight roughness, and a tingle zapped her, almost like she'd experienced a mild, static electricity shock, but the floor wasn't carpeted.

"Ms. Barlow." He sent a nod in her direction and turned to Karen with a warm smile. "How's Tim?" From his tone, Jill knew he was speaking to a good friend.

"He had a cat surgery this morning," Karen said, "but I skipped out." She barely squelched her chuckle.

"It's nice to see you again, Mrs. Phillips." The woman didn't appear any older than when Jill met her on her last visit.

"Oh, you must call me Anne."

Jill glanced around. "I'm surprised you haven't sold the store. It's a wonderland in here with rainbows bouncing everywhere. Makes me smile. Not much does anymore." She cleared her throat before going on. "Seems to be a great opportunity. Unless you're losing money."

"No, we're quite successful. People come from all over to purchase our glass collections." Anne ignored her son who stepped away from them, still holding the darling Lhasa Apso.

Karen grabbed hold of both of Jill's hands. "Why don't you buy Crystal Rainbows?" Her pitch rose with the enthusiasm of a reformed smoker. "You've been wondering what you'd do here. This would be perfect."

"What?" Jerrod pivoted toward them. His expression and tone told Jill what he thought of the proposal. He appeared horrified.

"An excellent idea, Karen, but let's not rush Jill. She needs time before making such a decision. However, I can make you a very good deal, my dear." Anne's eyes sparkled like those of a mischievous small boy who'd discovered a treasure. Jill's gaze flicked around the store, drawn to the reflections from the sunlight hitting the beautiful cut glass.

She didn't say no outright, and she should have. Liking crystal and glass didn't provide credentials for buying and running a store. The word stuck in the back of her throat. A rainbow lighted on her outstretched palm. Almost like a butterfly. Against all rational thought and for whatever reason, Karen's idea resonated within Jill.

"Mother, you can't be serious." Jerrod took his mother's arm and tugged her aside. He lowered his voice, but his words carried.

Anne pulled free. "I'm fairly certain of this, Jerrod. Woodstock can tolerate two Texans living in our small community. Jill's not deciding today. And you don't want the store, so you can't complain about whom I sell it to, can you?"

"Don't do anything rash until we talk more." His mouth flattened into a straight line, defying argument.

"You'll scare her off. Go work on your contract."

One sharp shake of his head and Jerrod leaned to kiss his mother on the cheek before plopping the dog in her arms.

"Thanks for rescuing her again, son."

Jerrod nodded to Karen and Jill. "Ladies." His deepened pitch sent butterflies twirling in Jill's stomach.

Anne smiled with obvious love at her son but shooed him out anyway. The door again offered its calming ring. "I apologize if Jerrod was less than hospitable." She walked toward Jill. Waves of energy radiated from the woman. The sun shone on her white hair, contrasting with the warm watermelon shade of her mid-calf linen skirt and matching shirt. Her enthusiasm was infectious. The idea of buying the shop teased Jill. "He's an outstanding lawyer, and I brought him up to be much more polite than he displayed just now." Ann ran a hand under her dog's chin. "My letting Princess get out has left Jerrod a little miffed."

"Why isn't he in Montpelier?" Karen turned to Jill. "He's an assemblyman, which is what we call our state legislators here."

"I see." He wouldn't have the job long if he weren't friendlier to his constituents.

"He drove down to help a client." Anne's broad smile spoke of pride in her son.

Evidence of this kindness to his client and his efforts to save Princess contrasted with his treatment of Jill. She'd heard the natives tended to be insular, and that probably accounted for his standoffish behavior.

Well, she didn't need, nor did she want, any more politicians in her life, despite that silly tingle. She rubbed her palm on her pant leg.

"Jill, why don't you come to dinner at my house this evening? Karen, you and Tim, too. Give us a chance to get to know each other better, maybe discuss a possible sale. You're interested, aren't you, dear?"

Jill's gaze traveled again across the sparkling glass counters. The rainbow reflections soothed her. After taking a deep breath, she released it slowly. She'd have to remember to ask what gave the store the delightful aroma.

Karen and Anne both stared at Jill, their eyebrows raised. Question marks floated above their heads.

"Thank you for the invitation to supper, Anne. I accept."

"Great." Karen clapped both hands together.

"Very good, my dear." Anne's tone and nod suggested her satisfaction with Jill's agreement.

"Maybe we'll talk business, maybe not. My accountant and attorney will have my head for even considering a deal when I've only just arrived." Jill spread her arms and shrugged her shoulders. "I can't explain, but I confess the possibility is intriguing."

Was she nuts to want to make this town her new home? Maybe, but she did want that. She sought the healing she'd gained in her short visit after her husband's death. Her throat tightened. Of course, then her father was alive. Maybe after two losses, she'd never gain any peace.

"Oh, my gosh." Karen squealed, grabbed Jill around the waist, and then spun them in circles. "You're really staying."

Jill nodded and Karen squealed even louder. Jill's insides warmed at the giggles pouring out of the three of them.

Their delightful company was in contrast to the earlier frostiness of the bearded Jerrod Phillips, however ruggedly handsome he was with that square, whiskered jaw. She'd ignore the little sexual spark his touch and voice aroused in her. She'd not experienced that exciting rush since her husband's death.

Regardless, Anne's son came across as unfriendly and rude, even for a Yankee.

\* \* \* \*

Jerrod nodded to people he passed while he made his way from his mother's store to his home office. The slam of the door behind him worked off some of his frustration.

"What the hell is Mother thinking to consider selling the store to someone she's just met?" His family had been hurt enough by a Texan. Yeah, yeah, this one was a friend of Karen's, who'd turned out to be a great wife to Tim. She was the exception that proved the rule.

Jerrod walked directly to the kitchen, opened the coffee can, and prepared a second pot. Who was this friend anyway? Small. No more than five-feet-two inches. A stiff wind would blow her away.

He flipped through the newspaper while he waited for the coffee to perk. After filling a cup, he sipped at the steaming, dark brew.

The newcomer popped back into his mind. Did she know anything about running a business? His mother would regret selling to someone who might ruin the store's reputation. He'd check out this woman and make sure his smart, but sometimes emotional, mother didn't make a mistake.

Carrying a refilled cup, Jerrod walked into his study. He dismissed the visitor and his mother's store from his mind and focused on a contract before him.

In the middle of the afternoon, he took a break and hit the streets of Woodstock, speaking to acquaintances.

"Hey, Harold. How's the ice cream business going?" He stopped by a tiny store with a service window facing the sidewalk.

"Great, Jerrod. Got your favorite chocolate almond on special today. Can I tempt you?"

"You know you can. One scoop in—"

"A sugar cone." The older man's crinkled lines spoke of the many times he smiled during his life.

"That's why you do so well, Harold. Customer service."

The storeowner handed Jerrod his order. After licking around the edge to keep the ice cream from dripping down his cone, Jerrod gulped two healthy tongues-full. "Wow. Ate too fast." He rubbed the bridge above his nose. "Brain freeze."

"You always do that." A customer behind him spoke with a gravelly voice.

"What?" Jerrod turned, not surprised to see who crowded close.

"Hurry and pay. You're making me wait." Jack Hardwick slapped Jerrod on the shoulder and leaned an elbow on the counter.

"Sorry. Here you go, Harold." Jerrod handed over a couple of dollars.

"Hey, Sheriff, what'll you have?"

"Peppermint, Harold, two scoops in a waffle cone. Skipping out on the assembly, are you, Jerrod?"

"Just today. Writing a contract for Hawkins on that property north of town. You keeping things safe for everyone, Jack?"

"Doing our best."

"Mother's considering selling her store to a Texan." The thing upper-most on his mind burst from his mouth.

"Is he going to live in town or be an absentee property owner?" Jack asked around licks of his ice cream.

"Not sure. I'd lay odds the buyer, a woman, won't get through the first winter."

His ex, Janice, had stayed only because of the babies. Ultimately, they weren't enough to make her fight the cold. It drove her away. Perhaps, honesty compelled him to admit, he'd played a part, because his work made him an absent husband and father.

He'd let one blonde bimbo sucker him. After that experience, he'd sworn off Texas women, and he'd never dated another blonde either. Not that he planned to date his mother's potential buyer. He sure as hell didn't.

"I better get back to the office," Jerrod interrupted Jack and Harold's argument over the merits of a sugar versus the waffle cone and threw his napkin in the trash. "Great ice cream, Harold. Jack, watch those two scoops. They'll show up over your buckle."

The sheriff laughed. "They do now." He patted the gentle protrusion over his belt.

By late afternoon Jerrod completed his work for Hawkins. On his way from the courthouse where he'd filed the papers, he passed his mother's store and considered her plan to sell the business. His hands clenched in frustration at what he couldn't control. If his jerk of a brother kept a job and stopped gambling his money away, Mitch could afford to buy the fool store.

Well, not a fool store. His mother had turned it into a nationally recognized establishment specializing in Vermont-made crystal What she'd accomplished made him walk taller. He'd go to her house this evening to make amends for his admittedly less than cordial exchange with Karen's friend. He'd take his mother out to dinner and talk her out of this insane idea of working with the Texan.

His mother should sell to someone who'd value a state-made product. Who better than a Vermonter? Not the woman from Texas.

At six-thirty, with a light breeze at his back, Jerrod strolled up the sidewalk toward the red brick Georgian with its black shutters and door. A short, white picket fence outlined the structure. Plenty of good memories resided in this house of his youth.

Colorful flowers filled the white window boxes he and his father had built together. Twenty years, and he still missed the man. Jerrod swallowed hard against the loss.

He swung open the gate and paused. Veterinarian Tim Livingston's car was parked in front of the house. If anything were wrong with Princess, his mother would be upset. She adored the white piece of fluff, despite the dog's bad habit of escaping.

Princess might be her name, but to Jerrod she was always Dust Mop. She greeted him with her usual yips when he unlocked the front door. Jerrod leaned over, rubbed her behind the ears before he scooped her up for the obligatory kisses.

"Mother," he raised his voice. "What's Tim doing here? Dust Mop seems fine." Where was she? "I want to take you to the Woodstock Inn for dinner."

He followed sounds coming from the rear of the house. Was Tim back there? Jerrod's mouth watered at the wonderful aroma of food. "We can eat here if you've already cooked something. What do you—?" His gaze bounced around the people gathered in the den.

Not only Tim and Karen, but also the friend. The Texan. His stomach clenched.

Normally great with names, Jerrod blanked for a moment. Oh, yeah. Barlow.

"You're welcome to join us here, Jerrod, if you promise to be on your best behavior." His mother's tone left no doubt of her intent.

Damn, caught now. Hard to beg off with another engagement when he'd made it clear he planned to spend time with her. Well, this couldn't be any more difficult than working with a jury already convinced your client had broken a contract. Everyone's gaze targeted him.

Jerrod pulled out his best "trust me" smile, the one he used for contrary juries, and set Dust Mop on the floor. The pooch made a beeline for her mistress.

"Of course, Mother." He turned to the new woman. Pretty, he noted. "I hope our visitor will accept my apologies." He glanced at the vet, who'd been his best friend since their days playing high school basketball. "Tim, tell her I've been out of line a time or two in my life, and I acted like a jerk."

Tim rose and rested a hand on Jerrod's shoulder. "You got that right, pal."

"No problem," Jill strung out the words using a conciliatory tone. A tone Jerrod had used a time or two when he wanted to keep the peace.

The woman's smile quirked up the corners of her mouth and displayed a dimple on one side. His stomach dropped.

"Everyone's entitled to a bad day. You should know, I don't intend remaining a visitor. I'm staying in Woodstock."

Double damn. Her warm brown eyes held a steel rod of determination, a trace of interest, and a ton of sadness. *What caused that?* His gaze scanned the Texan. He couldn't deny she was more than pretty. Little lines fanned out from the corners of her eyes, but were almost non-existent around her mouth and gave no hint of her age.

"What's the matter, Jerrod? Can't think of anything to say?" His mother scratched Dust Mop behind the ears.

"No, just wondering is all. Uh, how'd you happen to pick Woodstock? I mean I love this town, but people from other parts of the country don't move here without a good reason."

"I visited—"

"We're too rural for those who are used to big cities." He'd cut her off but wanted to make his point. "The weather is a killer for many others. Oh, summer is fine but short."

"Hey," Tim jabbed Jerrod in his arm. "Speaking for the Town Council, we'd appreciate you not bashing Woodstock."

Jerrod ignored the interruption. "Fall is spectacular. But the dark winter days often linger into May. Those who haven't grown up with the climate usually can't hack the hardships brought by the long cold." He stopped. What would she have to say now?

"During the fall a couple of years ago, I came to visit Karen and fell in love with the town." Jill turned to his mother. "Are you sure I can't help with the meal?"

"Thank you, dear, no. Everything's in one large cast iron pot. Roasted chicken with wine sauce, onions, new potatoes, and carrots from one of the local farms."

"We have Ben and Chuck's ice cream to go on top of the apple pie. I checked." Tim's grin spread across his face in obvious anticipation of another of the thousands of world-class meals he'd eaten in the Phillips' home.

All the talk of food and the aroma wafting in from the kitchen made Jerrod's stomach growl. Laughter filled the room and smoothed over the earlier awkwardness his sudden arrival caused.

"Speaking of ice cream, that's all I had for lunch today, so I'm hungry."

"Did you finish the project for Hawkins?" Tim slumped into a leather chair. Jerrod nodded.

"Good dear. I know he was pleased. You're returning to Montpelier tomorrow?" his mother asked.

"Yes, early in the morning. I don't want to miss a vote we have on a piece of legislation on gun registration."

"What's up?" Tim reached toward a bowl of almonds on the coffee table and popped a few in his mouth.

"Some bleeding heart liberal wants us to get a permit to purchase our shotguns and rifles. Surprised the hell out of me when the bill got through the committee, but it won't pass the whole body."

"You don't have a background check when someone buys a gun in Vermont?" The Barlow woman asked.

Her brows had drawn together, carving small creases between her eyes. Her tone, one of disapproval. Her Texas drawl wasn't strident like his former wife's had been, but Jerrod was surprised it didn't grate on his nerves.

"We follow the federal law which requires those checks for any gun if you're purchasing from a licensed dealer. That doesn't apply to private sales. What's the matter, Ms. Barlow, not a gun lover? And you a Texan?"

"I don't like what guns do, Mr. Phillips."

She spoke each word distinctly, hammering her point home like nails into a two-by-four. Her back straightened like an oak log ran up her spine.

What was behind her dislike of firearms? Well, it didn't matter. She wouldn't be around long enough for him to find out.

His mother stood. "Jerrod, come help me with the wine." She snapped out the words and started for the kitchen but paused for him to precede her out of the room. Didn't she trust he'd follow?

"What's the matter with you, Jerrod Phillips?" Her tone dripped with censure. "The woman's a guest in my home. I can't see a reason for your antagonism."

"I'm sorry, Mother. I'll get the wine."

He thumped down the stairs to the cellar. The musty smell tweaked his nose. The odor had always done that when he was a kid.

He must get a handle on his reaction to Barlow. Grown or not, his mother would kick him out if she considered him impolite to a guest. He hadn't meant to be rude. Something about the woman brought out his worst side.

Jerrod grabbed two bottles of his mother's favorite Merlot, went upstairs, and followed her into the dining room.

"Pour the wine, Jerrod, and Tim, will you light the candles, please? My husband said having them lit always added to his enjoyment of a meal." She glanced at Jerrod, and he nodded.

Her lips twitched as though she suppressed pain. "I'll be right back."

Not surprising his mother and he became emotional tonight over the loss of his father. Anniversaries were tough. She returned with a basket filled with homemade rolls. The aroma teased Jerrod.

The candle flames reflected in the crystal glasses before he filled them.

"The perfect touch. Let's be seated. Thank you," she said to Tim who then turned to seat Karen.

No choice but to seat the pretty Texan. *Damn. Stop thinking of her that way.* Her scent, a light floral mixed with vanilla, drifted upwards, stirring a longing he hadn't expected. *What the hell?*

"Thank you," Jill murmured, glancing briefly over her shoulder at him, the dimple barely in evidence.

He'd hated blond hair for years, but hers seemed different, not bleached, but more a soft, golden color like summer corn. She wore it pulled back in a low, loose ponytail reaching to the middle of her back, not puffed up in a hard bubble like his ex.

His mother, the consummate hostess, made the inquiries of her guest seem natural.

"Where's your family, dear? How do they feel about you moving to Vermont?"

Jill fidgeted with her fork and glanced at Karen, whose eyebrows slanted upward. Did the two share a secret?

After a moment, Jill said, "I have twins. My daughter Ellen's a marine biologist and lives in the Florida Keys, and my son Ethan's in the Army in Virginia. They both live busy lives. They just want me to be happy."

"No one else, dear?"

"No." Jill shot another look at Karen.

"Liz, Jerrod's daughter, owns a Pilates studio in town," Karen jumped into the silence. "She's great. I go twice a week. You'll have to visit."

"Thanks for the plug," Jerrod nodded toward Karen.

"I tried Pilates once in Fort Worth, but couldn't fit it into my schedule on any kind of regular basis. I'll have more opportunity here. I'll be sure to check out her studio."

"Might not have more time—if you buy the store," Anne said, an optimistic lilt in her tone.

"Mother." God, he sounded like Hawkins' thirteen-year-old daughter. What was the matter with him?

"I'm not pushing." She waved her hands in front, palms out. Her smile lit her entire face, and she arched her eyebrows at him, as though attempting an innocent expression. She leaned forward. "Don, my other grandchild, is an FBI agent."

Jill dropped her napkin.

"Spoken like a proud grandmother." Jerrod leaned over and retrieved the cloth for his mother's guest. She nodded her thanks, but didn't make eye contact.

"As if he's not special to you," his mother teased.

Jerrod's laughter boomed out. "You got me. Don works out of the Montpelier office, so we see each other often during the session, Ms. Barlow."

"The Assembly meets annually, Jill, unlike in Austin, where your—"

"The Texas Legislature meets every two years." Jill cut off Karen's words.

Damn. Jill's rude interruption of Karen, gave Jerod the impression she was afraid of what her friend would say. Well, count on a Texan to be brash. He'd better get out of here before he let slip a comment he'd regret.

"Mother, please excuse me. I need to be up and on the road early. The session has less than a week to run."

"You're skipping out on my apple pie?" He nearly laughed at the tone suggesting he'd mortally wounded her.

Jerrod nodded. "Afraid so. I promise to make up for the loss when I return." He punched Tim on the arm. "I'll be in touch. Karen, make sure he gives you enough time off from the clinic for your volunteer activities." Jerrod patted her on the back.

He held out his hand to their guest from Texas. "Pleasure to see you again, Ms. Barlow."

He'd barely begun speaking before she returned the shake, this time in a firm palm-to-palm grip. A zing from her hand ripped up his arm. She gulped in a short breath. Did she feel something, too?

What the hell was it about her that short-circuited his nervous system?

"Uh… Thank you, Mr. Phillips," she said in a breathless rush. "Hope the rest of the session goes well."

"Me, too. The dinner was up to your usual excellent standards, Mother." He kissed her on the cheek. "Promise you'll secure Dust Mop."

His mother patted his shoulder. "I'll try, and thanks for today's rescue, Son. I'm glad you chose to join us. Especially since we had company."

\* \* \* \*

Jill's hand tingled. She'd been determined to give Jerrod Phillips a proper handshake and not let him get away with the light-fingered touch he offered at the store earlier in the day. The electric-like charge took her breath for a moment. He'd be gone for several days, and when he returned, they didn't need to see much, if anything, of each other.

Jill normally displayed more self-control with desserts, but she ate every bite of Anne's flaky crust pastry with just the right amount of cinnamon. Tim had been right to be excited about this award-winning pie.

Despite her best efforts to stifle it, a yawn escaped. "Thanks for inviting me, Anne. I've had fun, and the meal was delicious, but this has been a busy first day."

"Come by the store tomorrow around ten-thirty. We'll talk about the business a little. We really didn't tonight." She slipped an arm around Karen's waist. "Thanks for stopping by with Jill. I'm excited to see what might come of this."

"I'll see you in the morning then." Jill went out the front door but waited for her friends. If she'd been using her brain, not one of her strong suits of late, she'd have had a conversation with Karen and Tim already. Stress, anxiety, and exhaustion apparently played havoc with most of the neurons in her head, an argument against making any business decisions now. Probably accounted for her odd reaction to Anne's son.

"I'm excited you're considering buying the store." Karen joined Jill on the sidewalk with Tim close on her heels. "People come from everywhere to buy Anne's crystal."

"I can't play tourist this time, though I loved doing so when I visited before. I want to do something useful." Jill twisted her hands around the shoulder strap of her purse.

"What's the matter?" Karen asked, her eyebrows rose. Her body angled forward.

"I'm sorry for interrupting you in there. I was afraid you'd say something about Dad, and I don't want folks learning the details about his or George's deaths. What would they think? I mean, who has two family members murdered?" Her attempt at gallows humor fell flat. Neither Tim nor Karen cracked a smile.

"Whatever you want." She squeezed Jill's hand. "You don't need people carrying on about it, and a few in town would. We're pleased you're here, and that's what's important."

Jill hugged Karen and tried not to cling.

"Anything you need help with, let us know." Tim patted her shoulder in support.

"Thank you. After Anne's meal, what I need is exercise before turning in. Will a walk around town be okay?"

"We're a tight community." Tim opened Karen's door. "You'll be safe."

Jill nodded. "Thanks. Talk with you in a day or two."

"We'll see the realtor when he gets back to town." Karen climbed into the car.

"Sounds good." Her friends pulled out from in front of Anne's house. Jill dragged in a deep breath of the clean, fresh air. She'd made the right choice coming to Vermont.

She set off down the street toward Crystal Rainbows. If anyone had suggested before she came to Vermont she'd think about buying a store in the first week she arrived...well, she'd have laughed him out of the county. But this particular shop called to her. Could she make this happen?

Her steps slowed, and her gaze traveled through the windows. This morning, the sun's rays had caressed the stunning crystal. Rainbows had floated around the room and fueled a hope she might find a new life. In the now closed store, spotlights focused on several pieces shooting brilliant colors in all directions. Her eyes brimmed, and her breathing hitched.

God knew her life needed some rainbows.

# CHAPTER TWO

*Friday, April 27*

"Good morning." At ten-twenty Jill smiled at the attendant who held open the front door of the inn for her.

"Have a good day, ma'am."

Hope filled every cell of her body. She walked with a spring in her step toward the shopping area of town. All good things seemed possible in this brilliantly clear, crisp air. A few puffy white clouds highlighted the blue sky.

"Oh." She dropped onto one of the benches in the small central green. Guilt gnawed at her insides. For a moment there, she'd almost felt happy.

What kind of person was she to forget how her husband was murdered? How her father was murdered? How her life was murdered? She dragged in deep breaths through her nose.

*This is the natural progression of grief.* The words of the counselor rang in her head. Jill could expect to drown in pain one minute, followed by a rise up into the fresh air until another wave of agony threatened her death. Ultimately, she'd experience more up times than down. Jill prayed the counselor was correct.

She pulled her lime green sweater close, the chill a stark reminder she wasn't in Texas any longer. Jill rose, straightened her shoulders, and walked on, ignoring the flutter in her stomach. Dread and anticipation mixed together at what she might discover in the next couple of hours. Was she crazy to consider doing this?

Maybe not any crazier than running away to Woodstock in the first place. Crazy defined her life of the last two years.

She waited for a stoplight to change. The cars, though many, moved at a leisurely pace. So different from life in Fort Worth. She scraped together a smile for the two young people passing by. Much like her own kids.

Jill never interrupted Ethan or Ellen's lives with frequent phone calls. They'd want to know what was up if her behavior changed. So no calls. She had to trust her father was right. With him gone, Richardson and his crew wouldn't need to come after any of them. The safest thing to do was to keep the flash drive stashed at the bank.

A sharp pain shot through the middle of her chest like someone pushed a hand in, took hold of her heart, and squeezed.

What if she were wrong?

Someone might be searching for her or her kids right now. The stiffening went out of her legs. The racing of her heart made her light headed, and she grabbed hold of a light pole on the edge of the sidewalk. Her jagged breaths didn't bring in enough oxygen.

If she hadn't been such a wimp, she'd have read her father's note in Fort Worth before leaving. If she'd done that, she'd have stopped using her credit cards. She'd have taken a less direct route here.

A shiver of dread ran through her veins like a Texas sleet storm. *Oh my God. Have I put them all in danger from the gambling consortium?*

Drawing in a few shaky breaths, she willed her heart to slow down and her brain to think logically. No one should suspect she had a copy of the flash drive, so they had no reason to search for her. Besides, she couldn't undo what she'd done. Her heart pounded less rapidly. Straightening, she pulled in needed oxygen. A few more deep breaths, and her heartbeat slowed. With determined steps, she proceeded to the shop and pushed through the door, curious to see what lay ahead.

"Ah, prompt, I see. Good morning, Jill." Anne's welcoming tone said more than just her words. "I want you to meet Sally Dickson, my assistant."

A tall gray-haired woman had a smile wide enough to take in the whole world. Her dark blue denim trousers and crisp white blouse looked comfortable and professional. The refreshing scent Jill remembered from yesterday made her relax, easing her breath and heart rate back to normal.

"Sally's been with me for twenty years, starting part-time. I've cut back and now she does almost everything. She knows as much as I do about how this place operates."

"Hello, Sally." Jill met the woman's outstretched hand with her own firm grip.

"Nice to meet you, Ms. Barlow."

"Oh, please, call me Jill."

Sally's smile grew wider in response to Jill's greeting.

"We'll be in the office for a while, Sally, so I can tell Jill about running this store."

"Maybe not *all* about it, Anne. You don't want to scare her off," Sally said in a conspiratorial tone. The two women were obviously good friends.

With Sally's laughter filling the air, Anne led Jill to a rear area, which appeared to be almost the same size as the front of the shop. "I told her I had a hot prospect on my hands. We've had a couple of people consider buying. One even drew up a contract, but he lost his funding."

To the left of the doorway, an antique desk accommodated a computer. A four-drawer file cabinet stood near the desk. Jill wandered up and down the aisles to the right of the doorway. "You keep a lot of inventory, Anne." Three large storage units held shelf upon shelf of labeled boxes of crystal.

"We keep duplicates of some pieces, but many are one of a kind. For our glasses, I always try to keep whole sets in case someone comes in and wants to buy that way. They can either carry their purchase with them, or we'll ship to their home."

Jill ended her brief tour of the stacks and sank into one of the chairs covered in rainbow-patterned chintz. The sitting area contained a second stuffed chair with a small antique-looking table standing between. The space welcomed visitors to sit down and enjoy a chat or a drink.

She rubbed her damp hands on her slacks and shook her head. What had come over her to think of taking on this enormous project?

"I don't know, Anne. This seems like more of an undertaking than I can handle." The words rushed out in an effort to slow down the scary process. "I know nothing about crystal, except I like it, and I love the name of your store. Crystal Rainbows. Perfect, but—"

"Don't panic," Anne held up both hands. "We're just beginning, and don't expect to grasp everything all at once." The low pitch of her voice calmed Jill. "Would you like something to drink?"

"Coffee, if you have some. I'll need a lot of caffeine to get through all the business specifics, and if I decide to take this on, gallons."

Anne chuckled again, and then made her way into a small kitchenette where she started a fresh brew. "While this is perking, tell me more of your life in Fort Worth. I bet you have useful talents for this job." She settled into the other chair, her smile bright enough to make the most uptight person relax.

But what should she tell this kind woman? Jill didn't want to lie, and she wasn't lying, because she used her real name. Best to stick with the basics.

"I was a society wife. Like my mother, I belonged to a number of organizations, many set up to help others, chaired boards, gave money, hosted large fundraising events, and never—" her shoulders hiked in apology— "held a paying job."

"It sounds to me like you made a difference in your community. Being paid isn't the most important thing. Doing something valuable and something you love is." Anne crossed to the cabinets, took down two cups and got the cream from the refrigerator.

"How did you come to own the store, Anne?"

"I'd shopped in here off and on forever. One day, I'd drove out into the country and stumbled on a glass blower. He was looking for a way to sell his product. I mentioned it to the storeowners, and one thing led to another. Before I knew it, I'd become the new owner."

Anne's story sounded a lot like what Jill was considering. Maybe it was a good sign that Anne had been so successful.

"My late husband, a judge and landowner, had considerable investments. Our families settled this area, so I didn't need to buy a shop." Pride glowed in Anne's face and voice for the family's heritage. "Oh. The gurgles have stopped." She filled two cups from the fresh pot. "He always laughed at my work, told me it was my inborn Yankee spirit of independence. Still, he appreciated what I did with the store and in Woodstock. It sounds like we've both been deeply involved in our communities."

*Mom would've said something similar.* A deep ache throbbed through Jill. The loss twelve years ago nearly broke her father's heart and hers too. Jill yearned to share the recent happenings with Anne but resisted and merely nodded. Better for everyone's safety.

"Wouldn't those skills you've developed serving in various organizations help you handle things around here?"

"Perhaps."

"What do you want in this, dear?" Anne held up a mug.

"Nothing, thanks."

"You and Jerrod. He says if it's good, you don't need to mess with coffee."

"Thanks." Jill accepted the blue pottery from Anne who turned back to doctor her own. So she had something in common with Anne's son. Jill would've lost money on that bet. She'd never experienced such unfriendly behavior from someone she'd just met before. Almost rude. Something about her offended him. Her cheeks warmed at the galling idea she was attracted to him. His negative reaction could create an awkward situation between his mother and her. She sipped the strong brew. "This is good."

Best address the concern now. Placing the mug on the table between them, Jill clasped her hands together and leaned forward.

"Your son doesn't seem to like me, Anne, or the idea of my buying the family store. Will that be a problem if we go through with this?"

The older woman appeared to take a moment to decide how to respond. She shook her head. "No, dear. I own the shop. Jerrod doesn't want any of this." She swung her hand to include the store. "If I died and he inherited, he'd sell. This has the same result. Except, I hope you'll love Crystal Rainbows the way I do."

Her voice wavered on the last words. She cleared her throat, set her cup on the table next to Jill's, and rose. "Now, no more worries about my sometimes irritating son. He really is a good man."

She drew Jill from the chair. "Let me show you the pieces so you can begin to get a feel for the stock. Don't try to remember everything I say. Absorb what you can, but mostly enjoy. If you choose to do this and want her, Sally will be with you all the way."

Jill recognized Anne's let's-get-down-to-business tone.

And they did. They spent several hours studying the works of the different artists Crystal Rainbows carried, pausing only for a quick break for lunch. When they moved about the showroom with cases holding gorgeous cut glass and crystal, the kaleidoscope of rainbows lifted Jill's spirit, and a peace she hadn't experienced in a long time filled her soul.

Because the shop sat on a corner, both morning and afternoon light played a part in making the shop special.

Magical even. Touched with fairy wings.

"Here, take these to peruse, Jill."

"What?" Jill jerked back to real life.

Anne held papers in her hand. "I warn you, they'll put you to sleep at night."

Jill took the pages and looked at them. "Oh, my gosh." She squealed and not in pleasure. A sea of numbers ran together from the end-of-year printouts.

"Well, I want to make sure you know exactly what you're getting into. You need to get this data to your accountant." Anne's tone brooked no disagreement.

"You're right, of course." A chuckle bubbled out. "Gary will have my head if I don't talk with him first. So will my attorney. Let me mull over them for a week or so at least."

Jill slapped the pages against her thigh. How to handle this? "They'll want to see them, but I—at this time, I don't want to return to Fort Worth." She hoped the last showed it was no big deal, but doubted it came out that way.

Anne looked at Jill with a question in her eyes, but she didn't voice it, just nodded. "I'm sure we can email anything either your accountant or attorney needs."

Jill turned away feigning an interest in one of the exquisite glass pieces to hide her trembling chin and damp eyes. Anne's kindness touched Jill. After a big gulp of air, and a quick wipe at the moisture, she turned around. "Thank you."

* * * *

*Tuesday, May 1*

Greg Richardson paced back and forth in his Austin office like a lion looking for a way out of his cage. He'd done everything possible to cover his tracks. He'd kept his hands clean, not even a traffic ticket. Sid Cranston, the Las Vegas kingpin, and Greg had only met once many years ago in the gambling capital where they set up the deal.

They'd been successful. The Texas legislature first set up the lottery and then legalized gambling on horseracing, and the money poured in. The next prize was expansion to casinos. The state's finances were in crappy shape, the perfect time to pass the casino bill. With Representative Bill Stevens dead, no one stood in their path. Greg rubbed his hands together, anticipating his riches. Except for one glitch.

Somehow, Stevens discovered documentation of Greg's phone calls with Sid and had turned that over to an FBI agent in the Austin office.

Fortunately, for Greg, the agent was one he had in his back pocket, or Sid and he would've been toast. Greg once tagged Special Agent Franklin in a compromising situation with his boss's wife. Because of that knowledge and the money Greg paid the agent, Franklin kept him well informed.

Greg fingered the flash drive on his key chain. Hell and damn. Franklin had reported that Stevens said he'd made a copy of the drive for safekeeping. Stevens had lived with his daughter Jill Barlow in Fort Worth when he wasn't in Austin, and the two of them had been very close. If he shared it with anyone, it would be her. Greg had sent Slade to check out the Barlow home.

Greg lit his electric cigarette. Stupid city leaders had made Austin a smoke-free zone. He stared out the windows. Searching Barlow's house could take a long time. He really shouldn't expect to hear a report from the man for at least another hour. Greg puffed and waited. Not his strong suit.

"Mr. Richardson?" his secretary's high-pitched voice interrupted his thoughts.

"Yeah."

"Mr. Slade is on line three for you, sir."

"Okay." Greg's heartbeat accelerated. He punched the button. "What'cha got?"

"Nobody was there, Mr. Richardson." Slade's nasal voice always sounded like he had a cold.

"Should've made the search easier."

"No, I mean, it looks like Barlow skipped town. Some pieces of furniture are inside, but a For Lease sign stands in the yard. I went through what was there but didn't find a flash drive."

Greg snapped the electric cigarette between two fingers.

"I'll be in touch, Slade."

*Shit. Shit. Shit.* Greg mentally kicked himself for not starting the surveillance of Jill Barlow sooner. Stupid of him. He'd underestimated the woman. Her children had returned to their work in other states right after the funeral. Now, she'd taken off.

When did she leave? Despite using electric cigarettes, Greg retained a lighter, which he pulled from his pocket and opened.

Where did she go? He flipped it closed.

Why did she take off? Greg flicked his lighter open and closed.

*Click. Click.*

She couldn't hide from them—at least not for long. Greg would order Franklin to track down the woman. Greg had to get his hands on the copy of the flash drive. His need to celebrate Stevens' death warred with his cautious side. The information on the device couldn't get out. Being poor wouldn't matter then.

His Vegas "friends" would ensure he was very dead.

\* \* \* \*

*Friday, May 4*

"Jill, you've found yourself a solid business," Gary Myers, her accountant, said in his folksy west Texas twang.

It had been a week since she'd emailed the statements to him and Michelle Smith, her lawyer. Gary's good ol' boy Texas speak misled many people into believing he didn't know what he was doing. From Jill's perspective, he held his own against the best in financial circles.

"The statements are in great shape. In my opinion, you'd be making a sound investment."

"So, what's the *but* I hear in your voice?" She clamped her hand around the cell.

"Hon, I'm concerned about you. What do you know about running a store?"

"Well, I—"

"And you want to buy one right after arriving in Vermont? Playing tourist during the fall or summer is one thing, but I hear the winters can be brutal."

"Yes, but—"

"You intend to come back home, right?" His words sprang like a lion after a gazelle. Pounced on the subject she'd been avoiding with him and Michelle.

"I don't know, Gary." She hated the sound of frustration in her voice. "You'd feel better if I could tell you I was a hundred percent certain I should do this—"

"Yeah, I would."

"I can't. All I know is how desperately I needed a change." She didn't share her concerns about her father's letter and the flash drive he'd sent her. "Nobody but Karen and her husband know me here or about George and Dad's deaths."

"Why not?"

"I've told people I don't have any other family than the kids, and no one pushes for more. I like that."

A long pause from Gary caused Jill's damp palm to clench on the cell before she switched it to the other ear. "What's going on? What aren't you telling me?" Despite her best efforts her pitch rose.

She paced to the window in her suite, seeking the peace she craved from the green grass, flowers, and trees outside. One hand moved to her chest to stifle the fluttering of her heart, whose beat grew faster the longer it took him to answer.

"Well, I've debated telling you this, because I didn't want to get your hopes up. It appears the legislature is going to kill the gambling bill."

"What?" She dropped into the straight back chair at the desk.

"A group of representatives is determined to stop the bill in your father's honor. At this point, the legislators have focused on paying tribute to your father's work. Pretty great, huh?"

Jill gripped the edge of the table so hard her knuckles turned white. Fear lodged a large ball of cotton in her throat, and she could hardly swallow. God, if the bill didn't pass, the kids and she could still be at risk.

"Jill, are you still on? Did I lose you?"

She unclenched her teeth before she answered him. "No, you didn't." She cleared her throat. "I'm here and yeah, that's great. Uh, listen, Gary, I don't know when I'll return." She made a sudden decision. "I'm getting a new cell phone. I'll call you with the number. Share it only with Michelle."

"What's going on? Are you all right? I can come up there."

She expelled a long whoosh of air. "I'm fine." She spoke louder than she'd intended. "And no, you don't need to come now. If the sale goes through, you can come then. How about that?"

"All right. If you're sure you're okay. Michelle said to remind you to send a contract before you sign anything."

"As if I'd do anything so foolish."

"Hell, Jill. You're looking at buying a store before you've been in town even a couple of weeks. How do you expect us to react?"

Jill recognized the tone of voice and envisioned the red face that usually accompanied it. He spoke to her like she was a pre-teen asking to drive. She ignored his dig, which was justified.

"Between my father and George, they had approximately seventy years of law. If I didn't get Michelle to go over the contract with a magnifying glass, they'd both come back to haunt me." She faked a chuckle and Gary joined in.

"You're probably right. If you need me to come, I can, or we'll handle everything by email and overnight express. Promise you'll take care."

"Of course, Gary." Jill disconnected, warmed by his support. She set up the coffee maker so in the morning she'd only have to press the button. A habit of hers she started after George died. He'd always been the first one up and made the coffee. Afterwards. . .well, now. . .this seemed easier.

She stomped her foot.

"Damn. I want that bill to pass."

She needed the bill to pass. The bill her father had worked for over ten years to defeat. Disloyal and weak. That's what she was.

"I'm sorry, Dad." She sank into the desk chair, dropped her head onto her arms and cried huge, gut-wrenching sobs. Her father had been a fighter. He'd be disappointed in her, but she'd do anything to ensure the children were safe, including praying the bill would pass.

The only sure way for her family to be safe was for Richardson and his bunch to get their damned casino gambling. Wanting the bill to pass went against everything her father and she believed to be good for the state. If it did, then Richardson and his people would have no reason to hassle them. If it didn't, she faced two more years of living with doubt and fear.

Was there any reason for them to suspect she had a copy of her father's flash drive? Her stomach cramped, and she rubbed the palms of her hands against her eyes, trying to stop the tears, but they kept falling.

Had she made a mistake not looking at the information her father collected on the damn data storage device? Did she want to know the specifics? Knowing would maybe make her more vulnerable. She paced the confines of the suite. Should she take the information to the FBI?

"Yeah, sure. A lot of good that did Dad." Her sarcasm sounded heavy enough to crush Austin limestone.

By the time she stopped the crying bout, it was almost one-thirty. The way her head pounded, she feared it might split apart. A sip of water helped her gulp down two aspirin. She hadn't eaten supper, but at the idea of food, her stomach roiled. Not bothering to take off her clothes, she stumbled to the bed, yanked back the covers, clicked off the light, and crawled in.

Doubts and questions rumbled through her brain like a train on a continuous loop of track. She ached for the release of sleep.

* * * *

*Saturday, May 5*

The piercing ring of the inn phone by her bed penetrated Jill's consciousness and shot lightning bolts ricocheting around inside her skull. She'd stopped using landlines. However, fearing the bombs exploding in her head more than whoever was on the other end, she snatched up the receiver in a shaky hand. "Hello?" God, was the scratchy sound her? She swallowed, and her raw throat indicated how much she'd cried the night before.

"Ms. Barlow? Jill?"

The deep voice on the other end startled her into sitting up. Her head spun and her stomach threatened to pitch. Might as well haul her off to the funeral home.

"Who's this?" She struggled to get the words out.

"Jerrod Phillips. If you have time, I'd like to visit with you."

Jill cut her gaze toward the bedside clock. Ten. The meltdown last night had taken a toll on her. She never slept this late. She pressed a hand to her forehead.

This was Anne's son. She had to make an effort. "When did you have in mind, Mr. Phillips?" She struggled from the bed toward the little coffee maker and flipped the switch.

"Please call me Jerrod, and how about now?"

"Oh, no. I couldn't." Desperate for caffeine, she glared at the pot to make it drip faster.

"You won't call me Jerrod, or you won't meet with me now?"

"I'll call you Jerrod, but I can't meet with you now." She pulled out the scrunchie she'd forgotten to remove last night. God, she needed her brain to function without breaking apart. "Aren't you still in Montpelier?"

The coffee aroma filled the room. She poured the steaming dark brew into a cup, and took a too hasty sip, burning her tongue. The pain was worth it to get the caffeine into her system.

"The session closed a couple of days ago, but I only got back into town this morning. How about lunch?"

No way. She found him entirely too attractive. Something about his voice sent tingles to her middle. Her reactions, so soon after meeting the man seemed disloyal to George. And completely inappropriate. That's what her mother would've said.

"Jill?"

She didn't want to offend Anne. She had to respond.

"How about five this evening? They serve coffee and tea here in the solarium."

\* \* \* \*

Jerrod waited in the Woodstock Inn library, pretending to read. He couldn't stop thinking how Jill had hung up on him. Click. The noise rang in his ears. Her voice had been just-woke-up-croaky when she first spoke. It wasn't until the end of the conversation she hit her I'm-awake-and-in-charge-tone.

"Jerrod."

He glanced up and rose. The magazine fell to the table. Jill wore black pants and a matching long-sleeved sweater hinting at curves. For such a small person, she had a great build.

"Sorry to keep you waiting." She raised her chin just a touch. Every bit the lady and no trace of a hoarse voice. Her hair was pulled back into the low ponytail she seemed to favor. Simple gold hoops hung from her ears. She wore no rings and only a watch on her left wrist. Nothing flashy about her. Used to judging potential jurors, it only took seconds for him to take in the whole package. His groin tightened. *What the hell?*

He had trouble finding words. Finally, he said, "No problem."

"Let's get something to drink, and then we can talk." She led the way to the Solarium where they both ordered coffee.

Jerrod settled into one of the large leather wingbacks in the library. Jill sat on the edge of the chair next to him. He stared at her rose-colored lips when she took a tentative sip and her throat when she swallowed. He jerked his gaze away.

"I'm sure you must be busy. Why did you ask to meet? Frankly, I've had the feeling I'm not one of your favorite people."

Well, she was honest about some things. "Let me apologize again for my behavior."

"Apology accepted. Now what do you want to discuss?"

The woman was all business. Jerrod leaned forward, his hands clasped between his knees. "I don't want you to buy Crystal Rainbows." Her eyelids batted the way they would if a gnat attacked. Before she could respond, he went on. "I know who you are."

Color drained from her face. Her hand trembled when she set down her cup. "Well, of course you know who I am." Her words came out in a rush. "Your mother introduced us."

Her voice rose to higher pitch than normal. He gave her credit for attempting the bluff.

"Did you assume no one would check up on you?"

She hopped up at his words, paced in front of the chairs. He went on. "You've had an interesting couple of years." He stood, stepped in front of her. "Did you leave Texas because you killed your husband and father?"

The sting from her hand slapping his jaw stunned him. He never saw it coming. She spun around and brushed past startled guests. She had quite a swing on her. He rubbed his face and then rushed after her.

By the time he got to the stairs, she'd reached the bottom and pushed open the door. She headed for the gardens behind the inn.

*No way out that direction, sweetheart.*

The air cooled his stinging cheek. His beard helped cushion the blow, but she'd let him have it. Halfway across the gardens, he caught up to her, grabbed her arm, and pulled her around in front of him. Pain-filled eyes and streaming tears grabbed his heart, but he held on. After fumbling for a handkerchief, he offered it, and she swiped at her face.

"Let go of me." She spat the words between clenched teeth. Struggled to pull away.

Jerrod tightened his grip on her arm and shepherded her toward the back part of the gardens to benches under tall oak trees. He needed privacy. When they reached the secluded grotto, he released her but blocked the path to the inn.

"What do you want with me?" Her breath hitched, and she rubbed her arm where he'd held her.

"Damn. I didn't mean to hurt you."

"Are you—are you going to kill me?" She backed away, her gaze darted around. Probably looking for a way to escape. She put the bench between them, her arms extended in supplication. "Please, don't hurt my kids. I'll do whatever you want, if you leave them alone. I beg you."

What the hell was going on here? He stepped away, his hands raised in front. "All I wanted was to talk you out of buying Mother's store. Your reaction makes me more certain I don't want you anywhere near her or settling in my town."

"What?" She blinked and seemed to come out of trance. Gulped air. Her body shook.

"You better sit. I don't want you fainting."

She slumped onto the far side of the bench. "What are you talking about?" Her voice was shaky, but her lips formed a hard straight line he'd seen on her a couple of times. No trace of her cute dimple.

"This is about the murders of your husband and father. Why leave your home? Why leave your friends, and their moral support? Why come to Woodstock? Unless you're somehow involved. Are the cops after you?"

"Where did you get those crazy ideas?"

"I did an Internet search and found several articles about their suspicious deaths. I discovered you had an alibi for both murders. But you could've hired someone to kill them."

He slammed his hand on the back of the bench, hoping his intimidating behavior would result in her getting the hell out of Woodstock. "You have another guy on the hook, Ms. Barlow? You couldn't wait for Daddy's money? Why'd you come here?" He shot the questions at her each one louder than the last.

Her right hand tightened on the arm of the bench, whitening the knuckles. Her left clenched in her lap.

"How dare you?" Her voice lowered in pitch. Vibrated with anger. "Who are you to accuse me?" The words flew from her mouth and marched through the air in bold capital letters.

"I'm taking care of my town and my mother." He straightened and crossed his arms. "Woodstock isn't the place for you."

"You can dictate where I live, and what kind of work I do?" She pushed herself off the bench, and straightened to every inch of her five feet two. Her hands clenched at her sides. "Being an Assemblyman gives you that kind of power?"

"Being from one of the oldest families in Woodstock, I have a responsibility to keep my family and the town safe."

"You bastard. You don't know a damn thing. The store belongs to your mother. If I have the money, which I do, and she wants to sell, which she does, then I believe we have a done deal."

She stepped closer to him and poked him in the chest with her index finger. "Now, you leave me alone. If you repeat your malicious lies to anyone, my lawyer will sue you for slander."

# CHAPTER THREE

*Sunday, May 6*

The night after the disastrous meeting with Jill Barlow, Jerrod escorted his mother to dinner. "You look nice." She'd dressed in a purple suit and a lavender silk blouse. The heels she wore were one of her vanities.

He'd driven them to a restaurant with windows overlooking a large waterfall near the Vermont and New Hampshire state line. She'd been unusually quiet on the ride. No matter. He had to make her understand the possible danger of doing business with the Barlow woman.

They'd taken their seats when his mother asked. "What's the occasion for us coming to one of my favorite places to eat?"

The waiter brought menus. "I can't take my lovely mother out to eat without an ulterior motive?"

They placed their orders.

"You're a politician, Jerrod." Her tone suggested he thought her dense.

The wine arrived.

"This evening has the trappings of a grand scheme. Let's take care of whatever is on your mind then we can enjoy our meal." She took a sip from her wine glass. "Nice woody flavor."

He swirled the dark liquid before taking a sip. He'd intended to put off the discussion until she'd had a drink or two and enjoyed her favorite veal dish. She'd have been mellower.

"Well? What's going on?" Her fingers briefly tapped on the white tablecloth then stopped.

"I ran an Internet search on Jill Barlow."

"You did?" She leaned back in an apparent attempt to separate herself from his action. Her eyebrows shot halfway up her forehead.

"Of course. We needed more information about her than knowing she had the money to buy your shop."

"Regardless of whether I want to hear or not, you're going to tell me what you found. That was the purpose behind this dinner tonight, or am I mistaken?" His mother's ramrod straight back and fingers of one hand drumming on the table shouted he was in trouble.

The soft buzz from the diners sitting around them and the clink of silver and crystal provided the backdrop for what Jerrod had hoped wouldn't be a difficult conversation.

He ran a hand around the back of his neck before he attacked the issue. "The store is important to you, and you'd be upset if you sold it to the wrong person."

"Wrong person. You think Jill is the wrong person?"

"At least, you should know more about her before you sell the store." He reached inside the breast pocket of his jacket and pulled out copies of two newspaper articles he'd printed. His mother read the first one about the death of Barlow's husband in Fort Worth two years before. Her only comment a short gasp. After reading the second, which recorded the murder of Barlow's father, Representative Stevens, in Austin almost a month ago, his soft-hearted mother wiped at a tear with one hand and bunched the paper with the other.

Before Jerrod could talk with her about what she'd read, their food arrived.

"Let's eat, and then we'll discuss this afterwards, Mother." What he'd intended in the first place.

Her short nod of agreement didn't bode well for later.

Jerrod regaled her with stories from the recently adjourned assembly. Something his mother normally enjoyed hearing. Despite sharing a couple of the more absurd incidents, he never pulled more than a partial smile from her. This endeavor was proving to be more difficult than he'd anticipated. When their desserts and coffee arrived, Jerrod, against his mother's wishes and at the risk of straining their close relationship, returned to the uncomfortable subject of Barlow buying the store.

"Mother, having read the articles, I'm sure you can understand why I'm concerned."

"If it were about what this poor woman has gone through, I'd say yes. Since I suspect that's not it, why don't you tell me?" She blended cream with the liquid in her cup to make a pale pretense of what coffee should be. Her steely blue gaze pinned him.

"I think she's running away. Because she killed one or both men." His brows knit together, remembering Jill's reaction in the garden yesterday. "Or—or she knows who did."

"Oh, Jerrod—"

"In either case, I'm certain she's hiding something. This has the potential to be a dangerous situation. I'm not comfortable with Barlow hiding out in our town, much less her doing business with you."

His mother glared at him in the same manner she had when he was a boy, and he'd disappointed her. Since becoming an adult, he'd only received the look once. When he told her he was getting married.

"I have failed somewhere in your upbringing, Jerrod. You have a blind spot about women. You married Janice when anyone of modest intelligence could tell she was only interested in our name and money."

"Mother, let's—"

"I can forgive you, because she gave us Don and Liz. All these years later and you've never found someone to settle down with. It wouldn't hurt your political career to have a wife. I've heard the rumors. They're talking about you for the US Senate."

"That's quite a speech, Mother."

She huffed out a sigh. "Now, when a woman needs your understanding and perhaps your help, you turn on her for reasons which I struggle to discern."

"I have very good reasons."

"The only reason I've been able to find for your dislike of Jill is she's lost loved ones in a tragic manner." She paused, leaned against the back of the tall chair and again tapped her fingers on the white cloth. "Or is it because she's blonde and from Texas—I assume that's because Janice was. You really should've moved on from that."

He had no answer for her.

"You've painted Jill as some sort of black widow."

"To be precise, Mother, 'black widows' kill multiple husbands. To my knowledge, she was only married to one man, George Barlow."

"Thank you for the clarification. Do you have one scrap of evidence to suggest she was involved?"

The waiter came toward the table, but Jerrod waved him away. The sounds of the other diners again filtered past his concentration.

Jerrod leaned forward convinced he could make his case. "The articles mention the police interrogated her."

"Wouldn't that have been normal? Don't they always question the spouse?"

He drummed his fingers on the white tablecloth but stopped after only a few raps. The action modeled his mother's finger gymnastics. He granted her a reluctant nod of agreement. Damn her and her mysteries, which she read by the car load.

"If they'd had anything, she'd have been arrested," his mother insisted in her determined manner.

"Maybe, maybe not. Could be they didn't have enough to arrest her before she took off. At any rate, Mother, she's been involved in sordid matters." Damn, now he sounded like his grandmother. He drank a large swallow of wine. "If she'd been honest with you, she'd have told you what happened."

"Son, we've not known her long—"

"My point exactly," he said.

"I was going to say, we've not known her long. Perhaps she didn't feel comfortable confiding in us at first. If a problem exists, I'm sure Karen and Tim know."

"If they know, they should've told us. Damn. Karen introduced Barlow to Liz."

"Don't swear," his mother admonished him. She picked up her glass, tipped it up, finished it, and then carefully set it on the table.

"Let me make something clear to you, Son. I can do whatever I want with the store, because it's mine. I like Jill Barlow. If we can come to terms on the financials, then I intend to sell Crystal Rainbows to her. You have absolutely nothing to say about the transaction. Do you understand?"

Jerrod nodded but ground his teeth.

"And what's more, I intend to spend time getting to know her better. If you can't, or won't tolerate her the result will be I'll spend a whole lot less time with you."

He couldn't think of anything else to say, and silence followed his mother's announcement. He'd make himself scarce, and see how long she held out. He'd miss her, but he'd win her over in the month or two before they could complete the sale.

He gestured to the waiter who hurried over.

"We'll take the check now."

"Yes sir." He laid the brown leather folder on the table. "I'll handle it when you're ready."

Jerrod glanced at the bill. After taking care of it, he nodded at the waiter. "Thank you. I don't need any change." He turned back to his mother. "If that's the way you insist on handling this situation then it's time we go home." He held her chair and took her arm to escort her outside. Neither spoke during the ride home. No doubt where he got his stubbornness.

* * * *

*Tuesday, May 22*

Jill hadn't seen Jerrod Phillips since the appalling evening he'd accused her of murder. She shuddered at the memory. If she never saw him again, it'd be okay by her. It was a wonder people at the inn talked with her after she slapped him. Damn, it felt wonderful, and he'd deserved it. Bigoted ass.

Her behavior shocked Jill. Something about the man aroused her emotions. Powerful emotions, which made her uncomfortable.

The lawyers were still negotiating with papers going back and forth. Michelle and Gary planned to fly up for the signing. Maybe they'd feel better about the whole thing when they came to see the store for themselves.

Jill and Karen with Mark Jennings, the real estate agent, found a perfect place. The move into the weathered frame house on Pleasant Street brought back memories of her old life. The smallest thing caused flashbacks.

Dreams disturbed her rest. Sometimes they seemed surreal and other times all too realistic like last night's.

*Detectives showed up on her porch speaking words, which hit her with the force of a baseball bat. Excruciating pain began in her middle and trembling spread outward. Her breath dissolved in her chest. Darkness closed around her vision. She stumbled backwards. "No."*

*Her glass dropped from her hand and shattered on the floor. The red wine puddled on the white tiles. Her legs gave out. The detective reached for her, but she slid down the wall. A long agonizing wail came from deep in her core. Her father, too, had been murdered.*

Jill shook herself free of memories and focused on the good things in her life now. One of those was being able to leave work and run home for lunch. She stepped into her sunny yellow kitchen and pulled the ingredients for a sandwich from the refrigerator.

After putting it together, Jill held the back door with her hip and picked up the plate and glass of iced tea. Mid-step, her cell rang. She backed into the kitchen, put her lunch on the table, and glanced at her new phone. Her accountant.

Maybe an unnecessary precaution, but she enjoyed a sense of control to know no one had the new number beside him, her lawyer, the kids, and a few choice people in Woodstock. She clicked *answer* before the message kicked in.

"Hey, Gary, how are you doing?" She popped a chip in her mouth.

"Jill. I've got bad news."

She gasped, nearly choked on the chip. What more could go wrong? "What is it? Tell me." She gulped a sip of tea and made herself pull air into her lungs to get past her tendency to hold her breath in times of stress.

"Your house has been broken into."

"Oh, my gosh." Her legs gave out, and she sank into one of the kitchen chairs. Property. Not people. She could deal with this.

"We discovered the problem when I took a prospective renter to see the house. By the way, we've probably lost him."

Even under the circumstances, Jill appreciated Gary's understated humor, and a smile pushed at one corner of her mouth.

"My first clue was the deactivated alarm. I'm positive I armed the system the last time I left the house. The police are walking around inside now taking pictures of everything. Officer Fletcher wants to talk with you. He's already made noises about you coming to check out what's missing."

"I'm not returning, Gary."

"I agree that's not necessary, but still you've got to talk with him."

"You have the inventory of everything I left in the house and garage, which should be sufficient to determine if anything was taken."

"That's what I'd expect, but I'm alerting you that Fletcher insists on talking with you."

"Okay, Gary. Get his phone number for me, and I'll call him. I'm sorry this is getting dumped on you."

"It's okay, I'm glad you weren't here when they broke in."

"Yeah, me too." Had it been a random break-in? Her heart skittered at the direction her thoughts ran.

"Fletcher is coming this way now. I'll get his phone number and call you back."

Her sandwich forgotten, she paced and prayed. *Please, God, don't let this burglary connect to George or Dad's murders.*

The store was on speed dial, and after one touch and a brief pause, she connected.

"Crystal Rainbows. This is Sally, may I help you?"

"It's me. Jill. Something's come up. I won't be returning right away. That okay?"

"Sure. It's quiet now. Everything all right?"

"Yes. Thanks, Sally."

Jill ended the call right before Gary got back to her with Fletcher's number. Putting off contacting him wouldn't accomplish anything. First, she pushed the buttons customer service promised would keep anyone from identifying her number. Guess she was about to find out if they were correct.

\* \* \* \*

*Wednesday, May 23*

Homicide Detective Mike Riley hung up the phone on his desk at police headquarters in downtown Fort Worth. Interesting. Jimmy Fletcher had called about a break-in at the Barlow house. Sharp cop to connect the B & E, Senator Stevens' recent murder, and George Barlow's death two years ago. One of Mike's unsolved cases. Damn.

Mike headed out to meet Detective Fletcher and Gary Myers, Ms. Barlow's accountant, for a walk through of the house. He'd been meaning to contact the woman again anyway. Kind of a courtesy call, to let her know they had nothing new on her husband's death. He kept in touch with family members when he had an open case.

Just before ten o'clock, he parked in front of Barlow's residence. While he waited for Fletcher and Myers to arrive, Mike flipped through his folder on George Barlow's murder. His death looked like a professional hit, although they suspected the real target was Representative Stevens, and he'd survived.

One of those flukes when someone moves unexpectedly, making a millisecond of difference. Bill Stevens dropped his phone and leaned down. The action saved his life. Had he been sitting up, he'd have been hit and not his son-in-law. And Jill Barlow wouldn't be a widow.

She'd been gracious at her husband's funeral despite her pain and the job he had to do. Her father and kids had surrounded her almost constantly. Still she'd played hostess, seeing to others' needs. She'd been dressed in a dark suit. The skirt had hit at her knees, setting off a great pair of legs. It made him uncomfortable he'd noticed.

Not the time, the place, or the woman.

Fletcher's car arrived derailing Mike's thoughts. A dark blue Mercedes pulled in next. A large man climbed from the sedan and walked toward him. Fletcher intercepted, and made the introductions.

"Riley? I remember you. The lead detective in the investigation of George Barlow's murder, right?" The man's Texas twang laid the words out like a casual meander through a prairie.

"That's correct." Mike shook Myers' hand. The accountant wasn't someone you'd want to tangle with. Mike could almost see the wheels whirring in his head. He had to wonder why a homicide detective arrived on the scene of a burglary.

Myers dismissed Mike and turned to Fletcher "I can help recognize whether anything is missing. Ms. Barlow's detail minded, and before she left, we went through the whole house listing whatever remained after sending boxes and several pieces of furniture to storage."

"Do you have a list, Mr. Myers?" Fletcher asked.

"Yep, and I've brought you a copy."

Two hours later, they'd gone through the entire place, but they reached the consensus nothing was missing. Lots of mess. The safe had been broken into. Myers reported that Ms. Barlow placed everything of value in her Fort Worth bank.

"What're you going to do with all this?" Mike glanced across the room with drawers pulled open and the contents emptied out.

"My guess is we'll box everything and add it to what's already in storage. The only one who can make sense of the file folders is Ms. Barlow, and she's not able to return right now."

"Do you know where she is, Mr. Myers? I've been trying to contact her." Mike asked.

After a pause, Myers said. "I'm sorry, Detective, I couldn't say."

Where'd that misdirected garbage come from? Not a simple, "I don't know." That would've been straightforward. But no, his response was, "I couldn't say."

Okay, if he wanted to play that way, Mike would track Barlow's credit card use. It would take a while, but then he could see for himself what was going on with the widow.

"Thanks, Fletcher." Mike shook hands. "Appreciate your help." He held out his hand to the accountant. "Nice to see you again, Mr. Myers. Keep me posted if you learn where Ms. Barlow is. I want to talk with her."

"Why's that necessary, Detective?"

"It's possible she could be in danger."

# CHAPTER FOUR

*Wednesday, May 23*

"I ran into Mike Riley at your house today." Gary's distinctive twang cracked through the air.

Jill tightened the hand holding the cell while she worked the late shift at the store. "The homicide detective?"

"Yeah. Says he's tried to reach you, but he keeps getting the 'no longer in service' message."

"Did he say why he was calling?" He'd contacted her several times during the first year after George's death but only twice this second year. He'd also attended her father's funeral. "What'd you say to him?" She hated the position she'd put Gary in, breathed in deep, lifted one finger at a time from the death grip on the cell. Michelle could at least plead client confidentiality.

"I told him you were dealing with your losses and needed time alone, but if I heard from you I'd pass along his message to call him. I wasn't about to give him your new cell number."

"Good. He wasn't more specific about what he wanted?"

A long exhale came over the line. Her stomach pitched.

"He seemed concerned about your safety, so please, hon, do me a favor and call him back. I'm sure he's worried about the break-in at your house, because I am. He was pretty close mouthed about whether anything else specifically troubled him."

Her heart rate kicked up, and one hand rolled into a tight knot.

"Jill?"

She forced herself to breathe so she could respond to Gary's question. "Yes." She looked across the store, wishing the rainbows were real, and she'd come to Woodstock on an extended vacation.

But that wasn't the case.

"Thanks for running interference, Gary. I'll get in touch with Riley soon. I promise. Sorry I've caused you this much trouble."

"Don't worry, hon. That's what you pay me for." He laughed at his joke. "Changing gears, how late do you stay at the shop? I don't like you being there by yourself."

"When you come up to the closing, you'll see why I love being here. I'm very safe."

"Okay. Glad you like the place, and I'll see you then. Take care now. Don't forget to call Riley."

\* \* \* \*

*Thursday, May 24*

The door burst open. Jill glanced up from wiping a glass shelf. Anne Phillips blew in on a gusty spring wind.

"Hi. Come to check up on me?" Jill asked smiling over at Sally.

"No. No." Anne walked up to the counter. "But there is something I want to share with you."

"Sure. Come on back. Coffee's fresh."

Jill and Anne went into the office area, and this time Jill fixed their drinks. Something must've gotten under Anne's skin, because the furrows on her forehead stood out more than usual. Jill handed Anne a cup fixed the way she preferred it— light and sweet.

"Thank you." She took a quick swallow. "I don't want you to think badly of our town folk. We really like you, Jill, but people are saying all sorts of things. Wild stories. You're a witness to a murder and in the witness protection service. One story even says you're a murderer."

Anne stopped talking and picked up her cup.

Jill supported herself against the one small cabinet in the kitchenette, not certain her legs could do the job on their own. God, had they found out about George and Dad?

"No one provides any evidence, of course." Anne set her cup down. "I don't believe any of this, but I'm concerned how these stories might affect the business."

Jill shook her head at people's inventiveness. "I should've told you." She dropped into the other chair and rubbed her index finger around and around the top of her cup. "At first it was too raw, and when I knew you better–well, I never found a good time to say anything." She shot a quick glance at Anne and back to the coffee.

Could she tell Anne the truth? Did Jill trust her? Would the knowledge threaten Anne's safety?

"If you want to talk, dear, I'm willing to listen." Anne spoke in a low, inviting voice. One which made you trust her.

Jill recounted the events of the last two years ending with, "A month-and-a-half ago in Austin, my father was murdered."

"Oh, my dear. How horrible." Anne laid her hand on top of Jill's. "Have they caught the person responsible?"

"No." Jill shook her head. "No. You can see why I'm vague and don't give details. I don't want to go into the whys and wherefores with anyone. It's safer, to say nothing else." Her eyes moistened. "If you decide you don't want to sell Rainbows to me, I'd understand."

"But I do—"

"Anne, I want you to be certain. Consider, and then let me know in a few days. We can contact our lawyers to stop the process if that's your decision." Jill squeezed her friend's hand once. She stood. "Now if you'll excuse me, I have a few errands to run." She turned, picked up her purse from under the desk, and went into the shop. Jill didn't want to cry in front of Anne.

"Sally, I'll be out for a couple of hours, but I'll be back in time for the evening shift."

"No problem, Jill. See you when I see you."

What lay ahead if she didn't buy the store? The idea of leaving Woodstock, Crystal Rainbows, Karen, and her new friends squeezed Jill's heart right out of her chest. She wanted the town to be her haven. Thought it was. Hadn't she lost enough already? Her husband. Her father. Did she have to lose Crystal Rainbows?

She stumbled toward her house. For the first time, the streets' quaint beauty didn't warm her spirit, but increased her sense of loss.

* * * *

Pounding sounds drew Jerrod from his office. Before he got there, his mother thrust open the front door. One he seldom kept locked, unless he was out of town.

"Jerrod, I'm so glad you're home."

"Come in, Mother. What's got you in a tizzy?" Despite their tiff, he greeted her with his customary kiss on the cheek,

"It's about Jill."

"And I, of course, want to hear?" He turned away, strode toward his desk. His mother's steps echoed on the hardwood floor.

"Yes, you do." Anne said. "You'll doubt her less when you hear. She told me about the deaths of her husband and father."

"I'd already told you." He plopped down, swiveling the chair back and forth, unable to control his agitation.

"Yes, but one of your issues was she should've trusted us enough to tell, which would've increased our trust of her." She perched on the edge of a chair in front of his desk. "Aren't you pleased? You don't have to worry about her now, or the sale."

"The woman has completely taken you in, hasn't she, Mother?"

"She did say something that concerned me." Anne looked down.

"And what was that?"

She raised her head and looked him directly in the eye. "It was *safer* for me to not know all the details."

He slammed his fist on the desktop, sending a pen flying. "That's exactly the kind of thing that gives me nightmares when I think about you doing business with her." He swung his chair away from her. "Damn-it-all-to-hell."

"She offered me an out on the sale if I wanted."

Jerrod swiveled back and hope sprang into his heart. He studied his mother. The hope flickered out. "You didn't take her up on it, though, did you?"

"I have several days to reconsider, but no, I'm not going to. I'm happy knowing someone will own Crystal Rainbows who loves the store the way I always have. I'm optimistic the shop can hold special meaning for her. It has for me."

His mother rose and made her way to the front hall before turning toward him. "I do wish you could see your way clear to give Jill another chance, Son. I'm afraid she may need our help."

Jerrod knew when he'd lost. She wasn't backing off her commitment to the woman. His mother and he had avoided each other since the dinner when he confronted her about Jill Barlow. Neither had been happy about the state of affairs. Their relationship was more than parent and child. They were friends.

"Okay, Mother. I give." He extended his hands, palms up, in surrender. "I'll play nice. How's that?"

"Thank you, Jerrod. I love you. Don't let me keep you from work. I'll take a rain check on lunch." She sailed out.

Jerrod closed the door and ambled into the kitchen. After fixing a sandwich, he grabbed a cold beer from the refrigerator. Taking another look at Jill Barlow would be a pleasure. She was easy on the eyes to use an old expression of his grandfather's.

Jerrod carried his meal outdoors to the patio, sat at a small wrought iron café table, and propped his feet on a chair. Birds sang from up in the huge old oak. He'd do what he promised his mother and give Barlow the benefit of the doubt, but…he wished he didn't have this crazy reaction to her. The blonde Texan was his worst nightmare. Why did she affect him this way?

His gut tightened. He remembered her reaction when he'd confronted her in the garden. To suggest he could kill her. She was afraid for her kids. An extreme reaction to say the least. He'd thought so at the time, but got caught up with other things and never pursued the issue.

Now, he had to follow up, because it appeared Ms. Jill Barlow planned to stay a while. At least until the first of the brutal snowstorms blanketed the area. She'd never handle the isolation.

\* \* \* \*

*Friday, May 25*

Jill concentrated on sounding firm and in control responding to Mike Riley's questions. "I've decided to lease or sell my Fort Worth house. Do you want to make me an offer, Detective?" She could almost hear him grinding his teeth. She remembered him being tall, with broad shoulders and wearing western boots every time she'd seen him, including at her father's funeral.

How odd she'd noticed. He and the Austin homicide detective Tom Catching, lead investigator of her father's murder, had been at the church, at the cemetery, at her house afterwards.

"No, Ms. Barlow, I was contacted by the head of non-violent crimes. He connected your father's recent death and my handling of your husband's murder investigation. I walked your house with him and your accountant."

Maybe if she didn't contribute much of anything, he'd get tired and hang up.

"Ms. Barlow, where are you now? No one here seems to know."

"Are you checking up on me?" So much for not responding. She pulled her ponytail and twirled the ends around her fingers.

"Ms. Barlow, in a relatively short period of time both your husband and father have been murdered."

"I'm aware, Detective. What's your point?" The strident tone jumped from her mouth displaying a mind of its own. Jill dropped into one of the wing-backed chairs in the living room and drew a long breath. No reason to be rude to the man. Wasn't like her.

"I'm sorry." The lower pitch sounded better. "I'm not telling anyone where I am, and that includes you. I appreciate how you handled the investigation when George was killed and your kindness when Dad was shot. I'm not in Fort Worth and don't plan to be any time soon."

"Are you—are you afraid for your safety, Ms. Barlow?"

At his words, spoken softly, shards of fear scraped along her skin. She fought the tremor in her chin, clamped her teeth together. Breathe. She had to remember to get air in her lungs.

"Ms. Barlow. We'd protect you if you were in Fort Worth."

His words brought her right out of her chair. One hand covered her mouth to keep in a scream.

Breathe.

Move.

She walked from the living room through the dining room to the kitchen before words tore from her heart.

"Right. Like the Texas Rangers protected my father. Nobody's supposed to be better than the Texas Rangers, but someone got to Dad anyway." She slammed her hand on the counter. Pain shot all the way up her elbow. "Oh." Stupid move. Absolutely stupid. She cradled the phone against her neck.

"Are you okay, Ms. Barlow?" Riley's voice was muffled by her shoulder, but full of concern.

She opened the refrigerator. Grabbed ice cubes she wrapped in a paper towel before forcing words through clenched teeth. "Yes, but I need to let you go, Detective Riley. I appreciate your interest." Before she could disconnect he went on.

"If you know a piece of information that could help us find the murderers of your husband and father, please tell me. I promise you, we'd keep the information confidential."

"If I knew anything, I'd tell you, Detective Riley. Good night."

Silence filled her house.

"Oh, God." She moaned, drowning in a bubbling cauldron of pain, loss, loneliness, fear. She slid down to the tile of the kitchen floor, leaned her back against a cabinet. Tears poured down her cheeks.

She pulled up her knees and hugged them. Tried to stem the flow. Searched for an anchor in the storm of emotions raging through her, over her, around her.

Since arriving in Vermont, she'd more often than not been able to keep her fears under control. But the Fort Worth break-in, the conversation with Riley, and arrogant Jerrod Phillips accusing her of killing two of the three men she loved best in the world combined to make her on edge and fragile.

How ludicrous she found the man attractive. Anger at herself and anger at him grew and pushed out everything else. Thank God. She could deal with anger. The other emotions left her weak and vulnerable.

Vulnerable. She could not, would not be vulnerable.

Had she made a mistake keeping the information on the flash drive to herself? Could she get in trouble with the law? She didn't know specifics of the content, but Dad believed he had enough to stop the legislation and the consortium.

If she shared the flash drive, and word got back to the gambling syndicate, she and the kids would be even more at risk. If she suspected the FBI was somehow involved, and she did, who would be safe to receive the information?

No one.

She pulled her hair loose and massaged her head with her uninjured hand. What was the best decision for the safety of her family? The answer seemed obvious to her.

Leave the flash drive in the bank safe deposit box where no one could discover exactly what the contents were.

She struggled to her feet, made her way to the cabinet, took down a glass, and grabbed a bottle from the wine rack. Her hand shook to the point the red liquid sloshed onto the counter, and dribbled onto the floor. She put the stopper in and grabbed a dishcloth to wipe up the mess. Using the mundane activity to push back fear. Flipping off the lights, Jill dragged her body up the steep stairs of the old house.

After a soak in the claw-foot tub, where the scent of lavender candles helped her relax, she walked into her bedroom furnished in antiques. The wrought iron bed with its white coverlet and blue pillows gave off welcoming, peaceful vibes. The soft pajamas wrapped her body in a cocoon. She sipped the comforting woodsy flavor of her favorite wine and read until her lids drooped. Turning off the lights, she snuggled under the covers, praying she'd sleep without any troubling dreams...

*Friends and wannabes packed St. Stephen Presbyterian Church. Loud organ music bulged out the sides of the building. A ten foot tall Greg Richardson spoke to her. His long arms reached to the ground then groped toward her.*

*"I'm sorry for your loss, Mrs. Barlow." His voice echoed from a deep well. "Your father and I didn't agree about casino gambling, but I considered him a worthy adversary." She slapped his hypocritical face. "You killed my husband and father. I hate you. I hate you." Screams tore from her throat. He dissolved in the mist.*

*Then she stood in her house. Each room burst with people reaching out to her, pulling on her, begging her to make the bad go away. Everyone vanished, and only Ethan and Ellen remained.*

*She tucked them in, but their legs draped over the ends of their small beds, their feet rested on the floor. The emptiness of the house terrified her. Pain exploded from her gut and shot in all directions. Tears flowed from her eyes in a steady stream, filling up the bottom floor of the house. God, would she drown?*

*What had she done to cause her life to career down this dreadful, dark tunnel? When the flood of tears dissipated, she gazed at the room. Her tears had gushed with such force they'd rearranged the furniture.*

*"I can at least do this one thing. Move the chairs." Magically, everything went back to its original place. Her body drifted like a ghost into her office where the mail stacked to the ceiling. Her hand reached out for a small package stuck in the middle of the pile. When she pulled on it, everything tumbled down around her, bruising her, making her ache. The box her father had mailed before he was murdered.*

*She picked up giant scissors with both hands and slit the tape and pulled off the lid. Snakes slithered out on the floor, wrapped around her, squeezed the breath from her, bit her. Several slid off after Ethan and Emily. She cried out to warn them, but she couldn't protect them from the serpents' sharp teeth. Terrified screams ripped from her throat.*

She jerked awake. Her heart beat at a frantic rate. Tears bathed her pillow. Morning light filtered in between a crack in the curtains.

So much for a restful night.

# CHAPTER FIVE

*Wednesday, June 13*

Jill raised her hand to her mouth, but the giggle bubbled out followed by another. Signing day finally had arrived.

Gary and Michelle flew into Hartford yesterday, rented a car, and drove to Woodstock in the evening. They were staying at the inn. Neither Ethan nor Ellen could rearrange their schedules to come. Overcoming her disappointment at their absence, Jill practically skipped up the steps to the Inn. Sparklers flicked along inside her veins. She wanted her Texas folks to like Woodstock, her store, her new friends.

"Good morning. Don't you love this place?" Jill hugged Michelle, a brunette, even shorter than Jill, and then Gary before they entered the restaurant for breakfast. "How were your rooms? Did you sleep well? Did you have everything you needed?"

"Fine, fine. Hey, have they hired you to be their new PR woman?" Michelle teased.

Jill laughed, and asked the hostess if they could have one of the tables overlooking the grounds. The woman nodded and led the way.

"You have to remember I've stayed here a lot. It's almost a second home to me. I eat here often, and attend meetings here. Sometimes I come to sit and stare at the visitors wondering what brings them."

She picked up the menu, her stomach so full of butterflies, she didn't know if she'd be able to swallow a mouthful, but she knew exactly what she wanted. The blueberry pancakes. "Everything is excellent. You'll be happy with whatever you select."

"You're sure they're not paying you?" Gary's mustache twitched, and part of a smile snuck out. "If I ever feel I'm falling short on work, I know who to enlist to bring in more clients." He turned his cup up, and the server came right over.

"Wait until you taste their coffee. It's the best."

At that, Michele and Gary laughed at her.

"Okay, okay. Perhaps I've been going on a bit much. Must be nerves. I can't believe we're going through with the deal today."

"Ya' think you've been going on a bit?" Gary shook his head at her then raised his cup. "Umm. This does smell good."

"I want you to love Woodstock the way I do."

"Honey, I don't think anyone can love it to the extent you apparently do." Michelle reached across the table and squeezed Jill's hand. "You seem happy. Are you? Really?"

"Yes. I am. Oh, I miss you two, and I hope we still visit the way we have while we've been getting the sale put together. I can hardly wait for you to see the store."

"How many—?"

"I get a warm, peaceful welcome whenever I walk in. All sorts of people come through the doors. You'll love Sally. She's been a Godsend."

"What—" Gary began.

"I probably couldn't have done this if she hadn't been willing to stay on. She's getting things ready so after we sign the papers, we'll all go over there for a celebration. It means everything to me you came."

Jill raised both hands in front of her mouth. "Oh, I'm so sorry. My excitement ran away with me. I haven't let either of you get a word in." She leaned back. "I didn't mean to be rude. Your turn."

"Well, I'm damned hungry." Gary placed his menu on the tablecloth and looked around for the server. "Are we going to order or not?" Jill and Michelle laughed out loud. They had almost finished breakfast when Gary cleared his throat. "I have an announcement to make."

"Please don't tell me I've lost all my money and won't be able to buy the store." Jill fanned her face in mock southern bell manner.

"No. That's not it. Today is a day for good news. Michelle and I weren't sure if you'd have heard already. No telling how much you get on the news about Texas way up here in New England."

"You're a crazy man, Gary Myers. What are you talking about?" Jill looked between her two friends.

"I told you it appeared the gambling bill might fail. Well, I was correct. It went down big time. It was the last item they handled before the end of session May 31. Many of the speeches proclaimed the reason was your father and his long years of work. Made me proud to have known him." Under his mustache, Gary's grin was wide. "Pretty great, huh?"

Her blood froze. She fought a physical tremble. She nodded. No words passed her tight lips. She dug deep for the resources to relax her muscles and unclench her teeth. "This is wonderful. I appreciate you making sure I knew. I hadn't heard."

She struggled to swallow the bile rising in the back of her throat. God, this was not the time or place to be sick. Her stomach pitched. "Excuse me for a minute."

Gary stood and held her chair. She flew out of the dining room and around the corner toward the women's restrooms. She barely made it to a stall before throwing up her all of her breakfast and half her stomach lining. After the heaves subsided, she rested her forehead against the cool of the stall door. She staggered out to the sink, rinsed her mouth, and put a wet paper towel across the back of her neck.

"Damn, damn, damn." Of all days to hear this. She never wanted to hear it, but today was supposed to be about celebrating her joy at the purchase of Crystal Rainbows. Somehow, she had to pull herself together. She couldn't let on how much this bothered her. Her friends wouldn't understand, and she wasn't able to deal with the questions they'd throw at her. Jill sure didn't want her Woodstock friends dragged into all of this.

She looked in the mirror. Her eyes were wet, but only slightly bloodshot. Color returned to her face. A few eye drops and a touch more lipstick, and she'd do fine. This was an important day to her, and damn it to hell, she wasn't going to let Richardson steal it from her. He'd taken so much already. She squared her shoulders and marched out to meet Gary and Michelle.

"Okay, let's go sign those papers." She linked arms with them and hurried out of the inn toward the title company office.

Anne and her accountant were already there, and Jill made the introductions. Almost everyone had talked to each other on the phone, but this was the first time they'd met in person. A title company representative asked them all to sit down. They signed and initialed the reams of paper required for the sale. Jill took a cashier's check from Gary, walked around the table, and handed it to Anne.

"I'll take good care of the shop for you."

Tears glistened in Anne's eyes. Jill understood how hard turning loose of something you loved was. "I promise you."

"I know you will, dear." Anne rose and held out her hand with the keys. "These are now officially yours, I believe."

Jill hugged her. She pumped her hand holding the keys high in the air and spun in circles. "Whoo Hoo! I'm a storeowner." Everyone laughed. "Please come over to Crystal Rainbows for the official celebration."

They'd decided against closing the store. If people came in, they'd join in the festivities. A couple of bunches of balloons filled two of the corners of the shop, but Jill had decided to let the store speak for itself. Sally had arranged delivery of those and a large cake. Though it was a few minutes before noon, champagne corks popped and everyone applauded.

"I want to make a toast." Jill raised her voice. "All of you were not initially thrilled by the idea of me buying this shop." She paused and her gaze picked out Gary and moved to Michelle, flicked to Jerrod and then settled back on her two friends. "So I'm especially grateful for how hard you worked to make this happen. Thank you."

She turned to the former owner. "To you, Anne, I lift this glass for all the years you've spent building the shop into a reputable establishment. I give you my word I'll do everything I can to carry on your tradition. You'll never have to be sorry you sold Crystal Rainbows to me. To Anne Phillips."

Responses of "Hear, hear!" and "To Anne!" filled the room. Jill moved through the crowd receiving pats on the back, congratulations, and enjoying the way everyone got along.

She caught Jerrod's look. He raised his glass to her and tipped his head. His lips curved upward in a nicely-done-smile. Maybe they could be friends. No question, he was handsome, and she'd observed he was a caring man. Could they get past their rotten beginning?

Despite the little trilling along her veins whenever she came upon him unexpectedly, she'd limit her dealings with him. Besides him being a politician, she was too busy with her store to have time to work on any kind of a relationship.

That's right. Her store. Crystal Rainbows.

\* \* \* \*

*Wednesday, July 4*

Jill breathed in the refreshing air. Could it be this gorgeous in July? The temperature had dropped to the mid-fifties the night before and that afternoon had only risen to the low eighties. The Livingston and Philips families were gathered in Anne's large back yard, and Jill told them about how she celebrated the Fourth in Fort Worth.

"How could you possibly stand to be outside much less picnicking when the thermometer reached 110?" Anne protested.

"Well, we slathered on tons of sun block and never strayed far from the pool, but yeah, I remember a lot of those days. The worst was climbing into your car when the inside thermometer read 116. It completely drained your energy. You can understand why I'm celebrating this sparkling July day."

"You're becoming a true Vermonter, Jill." Tim tipped his beer bottle in her direction. "On behalf of the town council, I thank you for your words of praise for our small part of America."

"We pay for this, don't forget, Tim." Jerrod said. "Our winters can be something else."

"Don't scare her, Dad," Liz punched her father on the arm. "We want her to stay."

"Every place has its highs and lows." Don leaned forward for more shrimp dip. "I was in Texas near Austin earlier this spring. Those blue flowers lining the highways mile after mile make up for a lot of your blistering hot summer days."

Jill swallowed convulsively then gulped in air, forced herself to speak. "Yeah, we're pretty proud of our bluebonnets. Everybody takes a stab at painting those gorgeous fields. Camera happy folks become a real menace when they stop along the roads to plop their small children and puppies into the middle of a blanket of blue trying for the perfect picture." She held her plastic cup out to Liz who refilled it with iced tea.

"Thanks. We took a photo when Ellen and Ethan were six and turned it into a painting. It used to hang in the dining room. It's in storage now."

Jill rambled on about bluebonnets, while one part of her brain chewed on Don's comment about being in Texas. Surely, he couldn't know anything about her father or have anything to do with the gambling consortium, could he? However, somebody in the FBI must have for her father's murder to fall so quickly on the heels of his turning over the information to an agent.

For a moment, sadness overcame her, a lump filled up her throat, and she had to get away before anyone saw the tears forming. "Excuse me. I'll be right back."

Jill hurried through the back door and got to the powder room before they flowed. She'd been so busy and excited about everything, she hadn't cried in quite a while. Tears fell for George and her father and their lost family. She had to pull herself together. If Don were involved, she couldn't let on she suspected him. Thank God, he wasn't around much. She'd pretend nothing was a problem. She'd be able to do that. Couldn't she?

Jill splashed water on her face, patted it dry, and refreshed her lip color from the tube she carried in the pocket of her white slacks. She moved into the hall going toward the kitchen. A dark mass appeared in front of her. She stumbled back.

"Oh." Her hand flew to her chest where her heart kicked up a thundering beat.

"Sorry." Jerrod reached out to steady her, his hands warm on her arms. "Didn't mean to startle you. I wanted to make sure you were okay. You seemed upset before you came in."

"It was nothing. Silly really. All of a sudden, I missed the kids."

He dropped his hands, but didn't back up. The hall appeared to have shrunk since she walked through earlier. Of course, she knew it hadn't. Jerrod's broad shoulders filled the space. She didn't care for the little fluttery feeling low in her middle his nearness caused. She was way past the age for this kind of reaction. He was the last person on earth she should be having these inappropriate feelings about. Way too soon.

Besides, the man didn't like her. He managed to be polite now, always polite, but she sensed a subtle hostility underlying every exchange. Not the way he'd been in the beginning, she admitted, but still... Why didn't he say something? Standing in the hall staring at each other this way didn't make sense. Damn her out of control breathing. The shallow breaths made her head spin a bit.

\* \* \* \*

As if under its own control, Jerrod's hand lifted, and he just stopped it from touching her golden blonde hair. His gut tightened. He yanked his arm away. Denying his feelings wasn't working. He wanted to kiss this Texan, who'd come to play a part in their lives. The woman he'd accused of murder. Her eyes opened wider, while he struggled to do what he knew he should, rather than what he wanted to do.

"I'll fix the strawberries, you start dishing up the ice cream, Don."

Sounds of Liz from the kitchen penetrated the haze of his lust, and he stopped.

"I don't want it to melt. I'll get the bowls. You get the fruit ready, and then I'll dish. Didn't Dad come in here?" Don asked.

Jerrod swallowed, pulled his gaze away from the temptation of Jill's lips. He raised his voice. "Yeah, I'm here. I can help." He turned toward the kitchen and left Jill in the hallway.

"Strawberries smell great. We can both cut. It'll go faster," he told his daughter.

"Oh, Jill, I think everyone wanted fruit on top, but can you double check for me?" Liz cut a large ripe berry into four pieces.

"Sure." Jill breezed through to the outside with hardly a glance in his direction.

His daughter cut a look at Don before she spoke.

"So, Dad, I like Jill, don't you?" She stared at him her eyebrows raised in question.

Don's mouth turned down, and he shrugged. "It's her deal. I'm scooping the ice cream, nothing else."

After a moment, Jerrod found words. "Yeah, hon. Jill seems to be taking good care of Mother's store." Seemed a safe enough response to make while he tried to tamp down the crazy desire he had to get into the Texan's pants.

The back door opened, and the woman in question reentered.

"Everybody but your brother wants strawberries. The last comment I heard was, 'Could you do this any faster?'"

Liz laughed. "What? Of course, no one has eaten anything this entire day."

The four people worked in tandem, cutting, scooping, and taking bowls outside until everyone had his own dish and had settled in the Adirondack chairs under the trees.

"What do you think of your first New England Fourth of July celebration, Jill?" Karen licked her spoon.

"The gathering at the Billings' Farm was pretty amazing. I loved the high school band playing patriotic songs. The best part for me was the reading of the Declaration of Independence with all the flags flapping in the breeze. Definitely a chill bump moment."

"We'll go back out for the fireworks later tonight. It's always spectacular." Liz finished the last bite of her strawberries and ice cream with a long sigh.

Gently the early evening turned into night. Jerrod couldn't remember a nicer holiday. Could his enjoyment be related to the Texan who'd bought his mother's store?

Deciding how to drive back to the farm for the fireworks in the least number of cars took a few minutes.

"Well, I can take our crew and one more. Why don't you ride with us, Mitch?" Tim asked.

"No thanks. I'm going to pass on any more red, white, and blue. Got enough of that earlier today. See you around."

Jerrod didn't say anything, but his brother probably had a game of chance waiting. The man was sick, not that Mitch would admit he had a problem.

"Grandma, you ride in the front with me. Dad, you, Jill, and Don take the back."

If his daughter hadn't questioned him about Jill earlier, he wouldn't have suspected she had ulterior motives for the arrangement of people in her vehicle. When he slid in next to Jill who was sitting in the middle, his thigh brushed against hers. Damn, he didn't know if he was glad the ride was short, or he wished they had farther to go.

They sat in the stands for the fireworks display. Everyone "oohed," and "ahed." He'd managed to keep Jill beside him, but maybe that wasn't such a good thing. When she shivered from the coolness of the summer night, he draped his jacket across her shoulders, reluctantly removing his arm. What he'd wanted to do was pull her close.

He was just nuts.

Close to eleven, they rolled up in front of his mother's. They'd told the Livingstons goodbye after the fireworks at the farm.

"What a terrific day, Anne. Thank you for including me." Jill hugged his mother.

"I'm glad you enjoyed yourself, dear. Now, Jerrod, you walk Jill home."

"It's not—"

"No arguing about this allowed. Don, are you staying here or bunking at Liz's?"

"I'll hang with her, Grandma. Need to make sure she isn't getting into any trouble."

His mother kissed both her grandkids and him, and gave Jill another hug. "Good night all. I had a wonderful day."

They stood on the steps, watched her go in, and waited until the lock clicked.

After brief goodbyes to his kids, Jill and he walked down Church Street and turned on Central. Festooned in red, white, and blue bunting, the old-fashioned streetlights cast a soft glow across the grounds of homes and businesses. Neither of them broke the companionable silence. Pleasant Street was just that.

"Thanks for walking me home, Jerrod." Jill stopped in front of her rental.

"Are you doing okay with this set up?" He nodded toward the house. What a lame way to ask to go in. Seriously crazy of him.

"It's nice. Not large. I use the second bedroom for a study."

He caught a slight blush hitting her cheeks. Was that because of her mention of the bedroom? Certainly had sent his mind in interesting directions.

"I'm lucky to have found this property." She glanced everywhere but at him. "If it weren't late, I'd ask you to come in. Karen thought I was crazy to settle on the first thing I saw, but I knew."

Her words tumbled over themselves. Could she be nervous?

She turned to open the door, but dropped her keys. Jerrod bent to retrieve them. He held them out. Her tongue flicked out to moisten her bottom lip and captured his imagination. One kiss would satisfy his curiosity, and he'd be done with this almost obsession.

He put the keys in her hand, but didn't let go. With the other, he cupped her chin, turning it up at the same time he leaned toward her. If she made the least move to push him away, he'd stop, but she didn't.

His lips found hers in the porch light. A soft gasp opened her mouth to him, and Jerrod slid his tongue in to find hers and begin that timeless dual. His stomach quivered, blood rushed to lower areas of his body. The intensity of the heat they generated made him jerk away to stare into her chocolate browns, in which, not only surprise, but passion flared.

"Jerrod."

"Jill." They both spoke at the same time.

He didn't apologize for what he'd done. He wasn't sorry and couldn't promise not to kiss her again, given the opportunity. Besides, it had been mutual.

"I, uh…" Jill stammered.

Apparently, she couldn't figure out quite what to say either.

"Here, let me." He retrieved the keys and opened the door. "Good night, Jill. Lock up." He pressed the keys in her hands.

She nodded, closed the door, and the lock clicked.

Jerrod spun on his heel.

"Damn. Damn. Damn."

# CHAPTER SIX

*Saturday, August 25*

Jill was over the moon, a grin permanently plastered across her face. Both Ellen and Ethan had arranged their schedules to come up to Woodstock to celebrate her birthday.

The big Five-O.

Karen tried to talk Jill into having a "to do," but she resisted. Neither Gary nor Michelle could come, but both sent flowers, and Michelle included a gift certificate for a massage at the athletic center in town. Jill looked forward to the experience. Massages had been a regular part of her routine in Fort Worth, but they weren't something she made time for anymore. The store kept her busy.

Ellen planned to stay a couple of days. Ethan had to get back to Virginia, where he was heavily into counter-terrorist training. Her daughter had arrived Thursday, the twenty-third, and Ethan came in the afternoon before her birthday.

In their family, the birthday person always chose the place to eat. Despite the many wonderful restaurants in town, for a special supper with her kids in town, Jill preferred the Woodstock Inn.

They'd finished their meal and had coffee in front of them. "This has been a delightful evening. It means a lot to me you both came." Jill squeezed a hand of each of her children.

"Mom, isn't that Anne Phillips leading a group this direction?"

"Well, yes it is."

"Even though it's been a while, I recognize Karen and Tim, but who are the other three people with them?" Her daughter craned her neck.

"The man with the beard is Anne's son Jerrod, and the younger man is his son Don. The gray-haired woman is Sally, my assistant."

"Jill Barlow, didn't you think we'd want to celebrate with you? My dear, certain birthdays demand we pay special attention. This one does." Anne hugged Jill's neck and straightened. "How wonderful your children got here."

She turned to Ellen. "Good to see you again, dear. And you must be Ethan." Anne extended her hand. "It's nice to meet you. I appreciate your service to our country."

"Thank you, Ma'am." Ethan had stood when she stopped at their table.

Anne made the rest of the introductions. "Now, you're all coming to my house, because you can't have a birthday without cake."

Laughing, Jill relented. Everyone gathered in Anne's kitchen. It was wonderful how they got along and had things to talk about. Pride at getting to show off the twins filled her soul. They were the best thing she'd ever done.

She bypassed Jerrod, whom she'd avoided since the July Fourth debacle. She pushed away thoughts of their kiss and the way his whiskers tickled her skin. Every time the crazy moment jumped into her mind, her cheeks heated. She didn't want to have to explain her reaction to anyone, least of all him, so she kept her distance. He did the same. Clearly, that night must've been an aberration of sorts on both their parts.

Jill walked home from Anne's with Ellen and Ethan. He carried the left over cake Anne had insisted they take. Jill's laughter tumbled out when her children horsed around fighting over the dessert. Turning fifty hadn't been the disaster she'd anticipated. Having her father and George with them, of course, would've made everything perfect. Since that was impossible, the night had been more than she'd hoped.

* * * *

*Friday, August 31*

Jerrod had a lot on his mind. He'd avoided being alone with Jill. But he couldn't seem to stop his mind from drifting back to "the kiss." He'd been wrong to imagine one kiss would take care of the odd yearning he had for the woman. It hadn't.

He could no longer pretend he wasn't attracted to the blonde woman from Texas.

In the kitchen, he poured himself a shot of whiskey. What the hell was the matter with him anyway? He'd broken off a years-long deal he had with a lawyer in New Hampshire. Sex with no strings. A perfect situation for two people with incredibly busy lives. No time to work on a relationship. While she was younger than he was, she didn't want kids, a complication they certainly didn't need. It had worked fine the way things had been. Until Jill Barlow arrived.

He'd changed since the night he kissed Jill. His fingers closed around the glass. He downed the drink. The burn flowed right down to his gut. He roamed through the house, while pictures of her filled his mind.

When she'd turned on her heel right after she slapped him.

When she'd stood up to him threatening to sue if he repeated to anyone his accusation she was a murderer.

When they'd run into each other in the hall at his mother's during the Fourth of July holiday.

His groin had clutched. Heat ignited within. The need to kiss her built. When he'd taken her home later that night, when he could no longer pretend a flame didn't burn, he'd given in to desire.

What was more incredible? Apparently, the fire smoldered within her, too, and she hadn't ignored it either.

What was he going to do now? Did he expect to get something hot and heavy going with Jill anytime soon? Not likely. She'd been a widow all of two years.

Yeah, she'd kissed him back, but she sure hadn't made any effort to be alone with him since. He hadn't tried to see her either.

They hadn't had an opportunity to talk about whatever this was between them. Maybe that was what he needed to do. Find a way to spend quality time alone with Ms. Barlow.

* * * *

*Wednesday, September 5*

Mike Riley scanned the report he'd received on Jill Barlow's credit card. Woodstock, Vermont. She'd driven across country in her car, stopping three nights along the way. He pulled up his notes from her husband's murder. Sure enough, she'd gone to New England about six months after his death and stayed for a week.

She must've enjoyed her visit a lot to return. She'd already been there longer this time than before. Did she plan to remain? Maybe since he knew where she was now, he could get something else from her accountant. Mike picked up the phone, and Myers' secretary put the call through.

"Mr. Myers, this is Detective Mike Riley. Do you have any time for me this afternoon?"

"Uh, yeah. But Detective, if you're still trying to find out where Ms. Barlow is, I can't help you."

"No, Mr. Myers. I'm not calling about that. How about one-thirty?"

Myers expelled a long breath of air, apparently resigning himself to the meeting.

"Sure, that'll be fine. I'll see you then."

Mike would convince the accountant to tell him why Jill had gone to Woodstock and what her long-term plans were. Promptly at one-thirty, he opened the door to Gary Myers' office in a small building on the west side of town. An attractive, slender young woman looked up from a reception area.

"May I help you, sir?"

"I'm Detective Riley and have an appointment to see Mr. Myers."

"Yes, of course. Have a seat, Detective. I'll tell him you're here."

Mike didn't sit. He walked over to the large windows with a view out onto I-30 and Camp Bowie Boulevard. Lots of cars passing by, but no traffic sounds made it through the walls of the well-made building bearing Myers' name on the outside. Obviously, the accountant did all right.

"Detective, he'll see you now."

He followed the secretary down a hall. She pushed open a dark wood-grained door. "Mr. Myers, Detective Riley is here."

The large man came around from behind his desk with his hand outstretched. Myers wore a dress shirt, but had the sleeves rolled up and his tie loosened. His suit jacket hung on a coat rack in the corner.

"Thanks, Missy," Myers said.

She went out and closed the door.

"Detective." Myers gestured Mike to one of the chairs in front of his desk.

"Appreciate you seeing me on such short notice." Mike sat. The accountant settled himself in his large desk chair, rocking back and forth.

"I trust you're not going to ask me again where Ms. Barlow is," Myers' tone emphasized his determination not to share that information.

"No, I'm not going to ask that."

"Well, great."

"Because the last place I've traced her to is Woodstock, Vermont."

Myers' chair came forward, and he jerked to a stop. He propped his elbows on the desk, and steepled his fingers. "Why do you think that?"

The man wasn't a good bluffer. "I checked out her credit card use."

"Maybe she was traveling through."

"Perhaps. If I don't pick up anything else, I'll contact the authorities there to see if they can tell me anything."

"Listen, Detective, wherever she is, Ms. Barlow doesn't want her location to get out to the general public."

"And is that somehow connected to her husband and father's deaths?"

"Now see here." Myers stood, stretching to his over six-foot height.

Mike's adrenalin kicked in, but years of experience allowed him to stay calm. Myers was too smart to attack a homicide detective in his office.

"Are you implying she was involved in those murders?" Myers voice rose. "Because if you are," He raised his hand and pointed toward the door. "You can march out of here this minute. Don't come back. I thought we got that idea squashed."

"She's lucky to have such a good friend." Mike leaned forward but kept his pitch low, the one he used with overwrought witnesses. "And no, I'm not, nor do I believe she was involved. So you can calm down."

Myers seemed to consider for a moment. He sat but didn't lean back or relax.

"I've got to weigh the possibility the murders and the break-in at Ms. Barlow's house are related. Has she mentioned that her father left anything with her?"

"Not to me. Look, Detective, I'm sorry if I got out of line. I've been the family's accountant taking care of tax returns and managing their property for years. Our families have been friends forever."

"I get it, Mr. Myers"

"Tell me more about what you're thinking."

"The way things were torn up in her house, it looked like someone was searching for a particular item. Not one of the appliances or electronics was touched. No paintings."

"That's true." Myers squinted. Was he picturing the chaos they'd found?

"When Ms. Barlow's husband was killed, we looked into his father-in-law's legislative work to see if we could get a clue to a motive for the shooting." Mike shook his head. "Frankly, while we had suspicions, we never found any definitive proof to conclude Representative Stevens was the target."

"Now you've pointed it out, I can see how you'd think the burglars were searching for something specific." Myers paused and tapped fingers on the top of the large desk. "To answer your question, no. Ms. Barlow hasn't indicated to me the Senator left her anything special." Myers frowned as if he were studying all the possible angles. His fingers tapped faster.

"If this is connected to the Senator's work, it will have to do with gambling. When that bill passes, and eventually it will, some folks will come into a whole pile of money. If there was a piece of legislation Bill Stevens would've gladly given his life to defeat, it had to do with keeping casino gambling out of Texas." Myers rested his elbows on his desk. "I'm speculating here, Detective, but if Bill knew anything to block passage for the foreseeable future, that'd be pretty powerful stuff."

"And provides a significant reason to stop him. If Ms. Barlow has information on that order, then she's in a dangerous position. I'd hate to see harm come to her. Losing her husband and father the way she did should be more than her share of trouble."

"If I talk with her, Detective." Myers seemed determined to stick with the story that he didn't know where Barlow was. "I'll ask her if she has anything from her father."

Satisfied, Mike rose. "I'd appreciate it, Myers. I don't want to frighten her, but I'd rather she be scared and prepared than ignorant and dead."

# CHAPTER SEVEN

*Thursday, September 27*

Mitch Phillips shoved his cards across the table at the black jack dealer before taking a belt of whiskey. The glass in his hand shook. The fire rushed down his throat but didn't give him the lift he'd counted on.

God, he'd hit a shitty run of luck. Down three hundred grand, and not a chance in hell of covering his debt. He glanced up. Two muscled men headed his way. Should he try to get out? He knew the Golden Tables well, his favorite Las Vegas casino, including a few of the back exits, but how would he leave town? He'd hocked his plane ticket days ago, and afterwards, he went up a hundred grand.

Why didn't he walk then? Because his luck had been running. He'd been certain this time he'd make enough, he'd never have to depend on his mother or brother again. He'd stayed in the game. Bad decision.

While he'd considered his options, the goons reached him. They looked like linebackers. His gut churned at the image of busted kneecaps.

"Mr. Phillips, come with us, please". The guttural tones in sharp contrast to the expensive looking silk suits. The "please" an afterthought.

As if he had any choice. He downed the last of his bourbon. "Sure." He got up, and they escorted him, one on either side. Not touching, but he got the point. The din from the casino penetrated his awareness. Never guess it was three in the morning. The jangle of the slot machines gushing money out for those lucky few.

The constant clang of coins poured into the flashing monsters by suckers sure they'd be the next big winner.

The men led him into a section of the complex Mitch didn't recognize. Sweat began to pool under his arms. Maybe he needed to worry more, but he'd been in this position before. They'd always given him time to come up with the dough. His welcome committee shoved him into a room. The door closed behind him with the two goons on either side. Mitch recognized the lone man behind the desk. Slicked back dark hair. Italian suit and matching shoes. He'd stand out in a crowd anywhere. Mitch waited to speak.

"How ya' doing, Phillips?" Cranston's heavy New Jersey accent raised hairs on the back of Mitch's neck, reminding him of characters in mobster movies.

"Okay." Hard to talk. Spit had dried up in his mouth.

"Sit down." Cranston indicated a place in front of him. "I hear you've had a run of rotten luck."

"Yeah, but you know me, Mr. Cranston." Mitch slid into the chair. "I'm good for it, just not right at this minute, but I've always covered my debts."

"You're right. You always have in the past. But I hear your brother cut you off, and he's encouraged your mother to do the same. How do you plan to pay us this time?"

Mitch swallowed with difficulty over the large knot suddenly filling his throat.

"I know you're an honorable man and would want to, but with what?" The steel in Cranston's voice sent chills down Mitch's spine.

Damn, how could he know about Jerrod? "Yeah, my brother's a hard ass, but I can get around my mother. Give me a couple of days to get home, talk to her, and I'll have your money." His hand trembled with the effort not to wipe the sweat beginning to bead on his forehead.

"Well, Mr. Phillips, your luck may have changed, because we're gonna waive your loss this time."

Shit. What was going on here? They never did that. He'd expected to get the crap beaten out of him whether they let him go home or not. They'd figure his smashed up body would be a convincing factor with his mom. "Waive the three hundred grand?" His voice cracked.

"Yeah, we need you to do us a small favor. When you do, we'll forgive the debt you owe, and you'll be welcome again in our casinos."

God, he hoped they didn't want him to kill someone, but he knew himself well enough if they asked him, he'd probably do it to keep his own head. "What's the favor?"

"We need you to find an item for us."

Whatever they wanted, he'd do his damndest to deliver. He nodded his agreement.

Cranston's cold expression filled with contempt, and he popped each knuckle on his hands. "You should find this simple. We believe what we're after is in Woodstock, Vermont. A place, you're familiar with."

Far from bringing him any comfort, that this guy wanted him to do a task in his hometown made Mitch's stomach tighten into a ball of nerves. He nearly gagged. But what choice did he have?

"Sure, what do you need me to do?"

\* \* \* \*

*Friday, September 28*

Cranston, an impatient bastard, had handed Mitch a ticket for later the same day plus several grand to tide him over. They wanted him to find a flash drive or another type of data storage device. They hadn't given him much more information. Except they believed Jill Barlow probably had what they wanted.

She was the woman he'd met at his mother's Fourth of July celebration. He might've been mistaken, but he suspected heat between his big brother and the woman. It'd be interesting to see how this played out. If he could somehow hurt his oh-so-perfect brother at the same time he handled his business…yeah, that'd be damn fine. One thing for certain, he'd do whatever Cranston wanted.

The airplane ride between Las Vegas and Hartford hadn't been too bad. The wind currents made both landings and takeoffs at McCarran International Airport a challenge for anyone with a weak stomach. Not a problem for Mitch Phillips. You couldn't be a gambler and have anything but cast iron insides and balls of steel. Mitch prided himself on having both of those.

When he got to Woodstock, he'd go to the store first. The best place to hide a flash drive would be in the back room. Or maybe the woman's house. He didn't know where she lived, but it couldn't be too far from the store. At the picnic, she'd talked about walking to work.

Several hours later after landing at the Hartford airport, Mitch pulled into a parking spot on the corner of Elm and Central Streets in Woodstock. He'd have a long walk, but this time of year finding a space was always a joke. He hated his hometown in the fall. The idiot leaf peepers came from across the country and acted like they'd never seen a tree covered in red before. God, they drove him crazy.

Maybe he'd get lucky and find what Cranston wanted right away. Then he'd take off for parts unknown until the tourists cleared out.

The large clock on the corner bonged out the quarter hour. The shops stayed open another fifteen minutes. He pushed through the door to Crystal Rainbows. That damned tinkling bell. It always drove him crazy. Shit. The store was busy for this late in the evening.

"May I help you? Oh, Mitch, hi."

He did an automatic sweep of her body. Not exactly hot, but not bad for an older broad. Brown skirt and boots with an orange colored sweater, which displayed a nice pair of knockers.

"Are you looking for a special gift, Mitch?"

He pulled himself together. "Yeah, something for Mother's birthday." He didn't remember when that was, but at some point she'd have a birthday, and he'd need a gift.

"Let me point you to her favorite artist. I've gotten in some new pieces by Andrews. I know she'd love one of these." She gestured toward several crystal flowers. "I've got to help a couple of other customers, and then I'll be back with you." She hurried over to another counter.

She'd gotten into this whole deal, hadn't she?

Smiling at the tourists. Listening to them.

Seeing to their needs. Ignoring him.

Like Mother.

Jerrod had already been in school with friends and activities to keep him busy, when she'd gotten into the whole store thing. Mitch had to hang out in the back room more times than he wanted to remember. Any wonder he had no use for the place?

At nine, Barlow turned the sign in the window from "Open" to "Closed," but she had one other person to help. Finally, the customer left, and she turned to him.

"Now, have you decided on which piece, Mitch?"

"These are nice, but I need to look around some more."

"Well, help yourself. I have a few things to do before I can leave. Let me know if you make up your mind before I'm finished." She walked toward the back room.

Mitch ambled around behind the counters, checking the sliding doors on them. Still kept locked like when his mother ran the store. If they'd been open, he could've pocketed a few things and made himself some money on the side. Nothing worked out for him.

He crept toward the back room, sticking his head around the door to see what Barlow was doing. She sat at the desk filing what appeared to be receipts. He slid up behind her. "Can't make up my—"

"Oh, my God. You startled me."

She'd jumped right out of the chair. Mitch swallowed a laugh.

She stood with a hand to her chest, while she heaved in short breaths. "I'm sorry, Mitch. I got caught up in the details and forgot you were here."

Yeah, good ol' Mom all over again. "No sweat. Decided not to get anything tonight. I'll probably be back later for one of those crystal flowers."

"Okay. Sally's usually here with me in the evenings. She had a cold coming on, and I convinced her to leave earlier than usual." She blew out a puff of air. "Let me get the door for you." She started toward the front room.

"When are you leaving?"

"Oh, I've got another five minutes." She stopped and looked back at him.

"How about I stay until you lock up and make sure you get home okay."

"Thanks, that's sweet of you. We're normally finished around nine-thirty when everyone else is, and all of us shopkeepers leave about the same time. We had such a large number of customers I've been a slow poke. If you're sure you don't mind, I'll take you up on the offer."

She turned back to her books. Mitch took the opportunity and wandered around the office and stock room. Sure enough, the spare keys still hung where he remembered them next to the restroom door.

"Mind if I use the facilities?"

"Of course not."

* * * *

Jill didn't look up when Mitch left the room to do his business. She hunched her shoulders trying to release the stress. She hated this part of the work. Her stomach twisted into knots. If Sally ever left her, she'd have to sell the store. Jill put the last info into the computer and was in the process of shutting down when the commode flush reminded her of Mitch's presence. Nice of him to offer to see her home.

She'd have to figure out a different system when she was in the store alone. By the time she was ready to leave the other shop folks were long gone, and only a handful of tourists remained on the streets. Given everything her family had experienced, she was amazed how safe she felt in this little town. Everyone seemed to watch out for each other. Comforting.

This late, aside from the couple of ice cream stores, everything else would've closed. The computer completed shutting down.

"You about ready?" Mitch joined her by the desk.

"Yes. I appreciate this. I feel perfectly safe when I leave earlier in the evening." She pulled on a jacket, grabbed her large satchel purse, switched off the lights, and pulled the door closed behind them. The tinkling sound of the chimes filled her heart with pride. She never tired of hearing them. After turning the key in the dead bolt lock in the front door, she set off down the street with Mitch.

He was quite different from his older brother. Taller, with at least several days growth of beard, but not neatly trimmed the way Jerrod's was. Mitch dressed the part of a biker gang member. In fact, if she didn't know who he was, she wouldn't want to meet him on a dark street at night.

*Terribly stereotypical of you,* she chided. Despite spending part of July Fourth with him and his family, Mitch and she hadn't had an opportunity to visit.

"So, Mitch, you weren't around much during the summer."

"No, I travel quite a bit."

"You travel for a living?"

"You could say. You know how some people gamble on the stock market?"

"Yeah." The word "gamble" shot adrenalin through her body. Her fingers tightened on the strap of her purse. What was the matter with her? This was Jerrod's brother, and he was talking about gambling on Wall Street.

"Well, that's what I do. I bet. Make my living from the cards."

"Oh, I see." She didn't, but they'd reached her house. She'd pursue whatever Mitch did with his life another time. Karen or Anne could fill her in if she remembered to ask them.

"Here I am. Thanks for walking me home." She pulled out her keys and crossed the grass to the front door. The porch light, set on a timer, provided its soft yellow glow and spelled home.

"I'm sure we'll see each other around, Mitch. Thanks again."

He nodded before he turned and walked back the way he'd come. A shiver ran over her shoulders and down her back. The click of the strong deadbolt made her feel secure.

She made her way to the kitchen, flicking on lights in each room. A nice glass of wine, a good book, soft music, and she'd be relaxed in no time. Exhausted every night, still she sometimes had trouble falling asleep. Running the shop seven days a week left her physically drained. How Anne had managed was a mystery.

Tomorrow Jill planned to ask Sally to find extra help for them, and then Jill could cut back on her hours. Sally could too, if she wanted.

Upstairs in her room, Jill got ready for bed. She hadn't made it to Liz's Pilates studio in a month, nor found opportunities to explore the town and countryside further. A disappointment, because she'd looked forward to discovering the area.

Walking to work provided glimpses of the glorious persimmon, ocher, and burgundy colored leaves. They lived up to the memories of her previous visit after George died. The different shades were truly amazing. Jill pictured an artist wielding a paintbrush to get the desired effect.

She wanted to burst into song at the sight of them. Silly, for sure. Particularly when she couldn't sing a note. These trees spoke to her soul. Her soul responded.

When Jill had run out to buy lunch for Sally and her earlier that day, she'd caught the scent of leaves burning. Truly, she experienced sensory overload. She abhorred the reasons for moving to Woodstock, but she found herself almost content, as if none of the awful events her family experienced had taken place. A counselor would say it was some sort of coping mechanism.

\* \* \* \*

*Saturday, September 29*

At nine forty-five, Jill let herself into Crystal Rainbows, but she left the closed sign in the window facing outward. She enjoyed a few moments on her own with the lovely glass creations. Some shaped like flowers, others like animals. Her favorite, the dove with wings spread and a sprig in his beak, sat in a prominent place on a pedestal. The artists had based some works solely on their imaginations, with no use or purpose existing other than to catch the light.

The lure of a medium-sized vase had been impossible to resist. She bought the Gerald Duff creation the second day she owned the shop. Filled with fresh flowers, it sat on one of the counters.

The sunlight, already streaming in the windows, cast rainbows around the room, soothing her spirit the way they had the first time she'd visited. She extended both arms over her head, stretched, and yawned.

Coffee. She needed more coffee.

Nightmares had plagued her sleep for the first time in several months, causing her to oversleep.

If she could get down another cup before the first customers arrived, she'd be all right. Not feeling well, Sally had taken off yesterday, but promised she'd come in today. Jill was glad. She'd missed a couple of sales because she couldn't get to the tourists quickly enough.

Just inside the office area, she stopped and looked around. Pride and gratitude for what was hers brought a tear to her eye. Running the store had built her self-confidence. Three years ago if someone had told her she'd be doing this, she'd have scoffed. She still made errors with the stupid credit card machine, and readily admitted Sally's skills kept them out of trouble. Overall, Jill had gotten back a sense of control over her life.

She knew all too well the falsity of that concept. Everyone was a hairsbreadth away from disaster.

She drew in a deep breath and admonished herself for being morbid, got the coffee going, and lit a few scented candles around the showroom. They provided the lovely, calming scent of lavender when Anne owned the store, and Jill had continued the practice. The chimes tinkled, and she looked up to see Sally enter. She flipped the card to "Open."

"You could've stayed home another day." Jill welcomed her employee.

"If I needed to, I would've, but the extra sleep and scads of Vitamin C put me in great shape. What time did you finish up here last night?" Sally hung her coat then got a cup down from the shelf.

"It was almost ten before I closed the door."

"I hope you didn't walk home that late at night by yourself."

"No. Mitch Phillips showed up looking for a birthday gift for Anne. He walked me home. When is Anne's birthday, Sally? I want to get a gift for her."

Sally opened her mouth to answer, but the front door swung in, the chimes rang out, and the first of many customers poured through the door. People weren't only window-shopping, they purchased. The day flew past with Sally throwing frozen dinners in the microwave oven for their lunch, which they ate at different times. Supper was the same thing, but by late in the evening things tapered off a little.

Sally started on the record keeping while Jill took care of the remaining customers. Finally, nine arrived and she turned the card in the window to "Closed," shut the door behind the last person, and propelled herself to the office through sheer force of will before dropping into one of the large chairs.

"Whew. What a day. I can't say you didn't warn me, Sally. How much longer do we have such a huge number of tourists coming through? I've counted four busses this week alone." Sally's laughter told Jill she must look like an old, dirty dishrag. Not far off from how Jill felt.

"We'll keep this up through the middle of October, at least three more weeks. I could ask the gal who worked with us in the past if she wants to return. Anne didn't get to it with the sale going on."

"Please do, Sally. See if she can come in three days a week for me. Gives me a chance to get back to Pilates with Liz. How about one day for you?"

"Okay, I'll do it first thing in the morning. But right now I'm finishing up the receipts."

"Good." Jill dragged herself out of the large chair. "I'll straighten the kitchenette and set up the coffee for in the morning." In twenty minutes, they were ready to leave, switched off the lights, and locked the door. Jill pulled her jacket around her, stuffing her hands in the pockets. "Burr. A definite chill in the air tonight."

"Yeah, we'll see more of that with each passing day."

"But the days are spectacular, Sally, and I'm missing them cooped up in the shop the entire time. That's why I want us to get some help."

"I hear you, and I'm certain we'll have someone ready to go Monday at the latest."

"Thanks, Sal." Jill hugged the woman without whom she'd be hard pressed to run Crystal Rainbows. "You're invaluable." She took a couple of steps away toward her house then turned back. "Oh, I forgot. You never told me when Anne's birthday is."

"In February. I can't imagine what Mitch was doing. You know to my memory, he's never willingly stepped foot inside the shop before. It always appeared to me he had some sort of aversion to the place. Odd, huh?"

Jill pulled her coat closer. "Yeah. Odd."

# CHAPTER EIGHT

*Monday, October 1*

Jill's heart kicked up in excited anticipation at the prospect of three days off a week. Sally was a miracle worker. She arranged for Mary Ann Sanders to come in four times a week until the last of the fall leaf peepers left. The retired teacher had made her Christmas gift money working at Crystal Rainbows, and she'd been worried the new owner didn't want her. Mary Ann was thrilled Jill did and started Sunday.

Jill had anticipated working with Karen in the historical society, but that hadn't been possible with practically living at the store. Other than checking on new inventory, she'd be unable to travel around the countryside to enjoy the scenery.

Walking to work, Jill decided if she were smart, she'd figure out how to bottle this glorious New England fall morning.

Sparkling, crisp, cold air.

Trees so brightly colored in red and gold and orange they almost hurt the eyes.

The quintessential fall smell of leaves burning.

She indulged in one long, last whiff before she unlocked Crystal Rainbows and pushed open the door.

No welcoming tinkle? Jill glanced up. No chimes. Something must have broken, and Sally or Mary Ann took it down to do repairs. She stuck her gloves in a pocket.

First on the list, turn up the heat and get the coffee on. The temperature had dropped to almost freezing. Before long, her black wool coat wouldn't be enough for the morning walk to the store. Setting her purse on a counter, she stepped into the back room, and then jerked to a stop. Her gaze flew around the office. File cabinet drawers stood open. Folders and papers strewn across the floor. Boxes of crystal dislodged.

Her heart rate kicked up. Breath froze in her throat. *Get out*, her thoughts screamed. Someone might still be here. She scrambled for her purse and dashed for the front door. What should she do?

Call the police.

Of course. Her hands fumbled the phone from her purse. *Come on. Come on.* Fear fogged her brain and turned her fingers to mush. The cell hit the ground. She couldn't function worth a damn. Breathing became almost impossible. She squatted down. Her stiff fingers scrabbled for the cell.

"What are you doing?" A man grabbed her cell.

She slithered away before looking up. Thank God. Jerrod.

He took her hands and pulled her to standing. She struggled to find any words, to keep her chin from wobbling. "Some…" She pointed toward the store. "Someone broke in." She hardly recognized her voice it was so much higher than usual.

"Okay, you stay here, and I'll check this out." He reached inside his jacket and pulled out a gun before he stepped into the store.

"Oh, my God." Her head whirled, her lungs hung like empty bagpipes. No air pumped. She'd pass out, if she didn't do something. Resting her hands on her knees, she leaned over. She gasped in a short breath and then a longer one. Yes. After the third time, she slowly stood up and leaned against the lamppost. Jerrod stepped out of the store, his gun no longer in evidence.

"Didn't find anyone, but I've called Sheriff Hardwick for you. He'll be here in a few minutes. We can wait inside if we don't touch anything."

"I'm glad you came along when you did. What I saw froze my brain. I couldn't figure out what to do." She stepped into what had been her haven. Trembling shook her body.

"No problem. I was on my way to Mother's for brunch."

"I'm making you late. I—I'm fine now. Go on. The sheriff will be here soon, anyway."

As if her words conjured the man, he walked into the store. Again, the bell hadn't tinkled. Maybe that's important. She'd tell the sheriff. A squarely built man with short gray hair, he looked to be in his late fifties. A badge and insignia prominently displayed on his jacket told of his job, and the gun on his hip told of the danger he sometimes encountered.

"Sorry to meet you under these circumstances, Ms. Barlow. People say you're doing a good job keeping up Anne's store." He said in his crisp speech.

"Thank you."

He walked into the back room. His gaze missed nothing. "Can you tell whether anything is missing?"

His words eerily reminded her of when she'd talked with Detective Fletcher after her house in Fort Worth had been broken into. Damn, not a pleasant memory, or one she'd ever wanted to repeat. "No, I'm sorry, I can't."

"You'll need to be closed for at least today. I'll get one of my deputies to come in and dust for prints. No idea whether we'll find any. Might've been kids trying to make a mess."

"They were successful." She pressed her fingers into her temples, trying to relieve the building pain.

"Good morning."

Jill jumped and spun around. Sally, of course. Jill's heart rate slowed, and she chided herself for being such a wimp when two armed men surrounded her. She stuck her head into the show room.

"Don't turn the sign to open. We're going to be closed today."

"Why in the world would we do that? The town is swarming with shoppers." Unbuttoning her coat Sally started toward the office but stopped when she saw Jill wasn't alone. "What's wrong?"

"We've had a break-in. Probably going to get worse when they dust for fingerprints." Jill hated the tremor in her voice.

"Well, damn, we've never had anything like this happen before." Sally looked around shaking her head. "Whoa. It is a wreck."

Sheriff Hardwick's tech came in adding to the crowd in the room. After a brief conversation, they began moving around checking the doors and the front windows.

"Jack, be okay with you if I take the ladies to Mother's? If we stay here, we'll only be in the way."

The sheriff nodded, and turned his attention to the scene.

"Jill, give your cell number to Jack."

"No. I don't want to."

"He can call you when he's finished."

"Couldn't he call you?"

Jerrod cocked his head at her and then nodded. His lips set in a straight line. "Sure."

"Do you have a spare set of keys, Ms. Barlow? I'll lock up when we're finished."

"They're hanging on the wall near the restroom." She crossed toward the shelf they hung under. Stopped. "They aren't here. Sally, did you give them to Mary Ann?"

"No." She shook her head. "She's never wanted them. Anne or I always opened and closed. Maybe they're under this mess." She gestured to the clutter on the floor.

"No signs of forced entry. Suppose someone could've used the keys. We'll follow up with you to see who had access to them. For now, Jerrod, go ahead and get them out of here. Give me your set, Ms. Barlow, and we'll lock up when we're finished. I'll drop them off at Mrs. Phillips'."

"Thank you, Sheriff." How she remembered her manners in this situation, she had no clue. Must be Mom's ingrained training. Jerrod ushered Sally and her outside.

"We can't burst in on your mother." Sticking to the formal society rules of waiting for an invitation, Jill struggled to pretend her life was normal. Yeah, like she could make the break-in go away.

"Jill, did you hear me?"

"What? Sorry, Sally. Mind must've wandered."

"Understandable with what's taken place. I said if we're lucky, Anne will invite us to stay. We'd be very fortunate."

Jill found herself sitting at Anne Phillips's kitchen table drinking coffee, and eating stuffed French toast with too many calories, but worth the extra pound she'd probably see on the scale tomorrow. Sally hadn't lied about the taste. "You never had this kind of trouble before, Anne?"

Her hostess shook her head. "In fact, we've had few thefts at any of the stores. An occasional hot check from a tourist, but other than that, we've been fortunate."

"Most of our local folks have a great respect for history. They share a sense of stewardship. We're taking care of the town for future generations—" The muscle in his jaw bunched and released. "Well, that sounded pretty corny." He got up and grabbed the coffee seemingly embarrassed by his words. "Anyone want more?"

"Not corny, at all." Jill found herself staring at the man. More to him than merely a handsome face. Warmth spread through her belly and lower. Awareness of Jerrod that way clearly made her certifiable given the circumstances. How could he arouse these feelings without his outwardly having to try?

"Well, ladies, I have an appointment at the courthouse, so I need to get out of here. I hope to help put things together at the store late this afternoon, but depends on the judge."

"Nice of you to offer, dear." Anne patted her son on the shoulder. "We'll call if we need you, but I'm going back with Jill and Sally, and I bet we can take care of whatever is needed."

"Always make sure more than one of you is in the store. I wouldn't expect you to have any more trouble, but no sense taking chances." He kissed his mother on the cheek and made his way toward the front of the house.

"If we get Mary Ann in to help, can we get ready to open tomorrow, Sally?" Jill asked.

"I intend to help too, dear. Between the four of us, we'll get it done." Anne's tone left little doubt they'd handle the problem.

Get it done, they did. Sheriff Hardwick's staff finished their work and removed the crime scene tape at noon. The locksmith showed up around two and re-keyed the front and back doors, presenting Jill with three new keys. Jill sent Anne home at five, not wanting her to over-do. They were finished by seven that evening, and ready for the next day. Jill thanked Sally and Mary Ann then headed home. She'd let herself in the house when her cell rang. She recognized Gary Myers' number and answered right away.

"Hey, Gary." Exhaustion rang through her voice. Accurate for how she felt.

"Are you selling a lot of crystal? You're in the height of the fall vacationers, aren't you?"

"Yes, but we've not done much of that today." She dropped her coat on a chair and headed for the wine bottle she'd opened the night before.

"What's going on?" Gary's voice held a strain, she hadn't detected when he'd first spoke.

She poured herself a large glass of Merlot. "We had a break-in last night. Between what the person did and the sheriff's staff with their dusting for fingerprints, the office was a wreck."

"What?"

"Hang on." She set the wine and cell down long enough to get the gas fire going in the living room. "Nothing was taken, and the speculation is someone lifted the spare set of keys."

Kicking off her shoes, she dropped into the closest chair, a long breath whooshing out. "Probably kids on a lark. We sometimes have young people come in, but generally, they're with their parents, so we can't figure how they got hold of the keys. We put everything back together, had new locks installed, and we're ready to go tomorrow. I have great help here." Damn she'd run on, not letting him get a word in. She sipped the calming garnet-colored liquid.

"Gary, did you hear me?"

"Yeah, hon, I did."

"Well, you called me. Must've wanted to say something."

"Jill, I've been meaning to tell you this, but a project had me flying back and forth to Colorado."

"What is it, Gary?"

"Detective Riley knows you're in Woodstock."

Her stomach clenched at the news. Her leg muscles quivered. She'd have fallen if she hadn't already been sitting. "How'd he find out?"

"He checked your credit cards."

"Can anybody do that, Gary?"

"No. Just law enforcement."

Didn't do much to make her feel more secure. If some FBI agent in Austin ratted out her father to the consortium, they could know where she was right now. In light of the information about the break-in at her house in Fort Worth, and the ability of the consortium to locate her, the store vandalism looked a whole hell of a lot scarier. She gulped her wine.

"Riley asked me if I knew whether you had anything belonging to your father. Do you, Jill?"

She swallowed the ball of fear in her throat and found the strength to speak. "Well, I have lots of Dad's things, but most are in storage." She didn't like the direction this conversation was going.

She forced her legs to work, rose, and edged around the room, checking all the windows in the living room. Locked. Of course, they were locked. A sigh edged from her tight lips.

"Did you bring anything of his with you, Jill? An item of value? "

Carrying her glass in one hand and her cell in the other, she pushed through to the kitchen. She wished Gary would say goodbye.

"What did you have in mind?" she stalled. God, she couldn't tell him. She circled the table. "Hold on a second." she set down the phone and her wine again, pulled up a small step stool, climbed on, and checked that the window over the sink was locked.

Gary's words vibrated from her cell before she picked it up again. "Jill, are you all right? What's going on?"

"Sorry. Just pouring another glass of wine. Now what did you ask?" She pulled her ponytail holder out and ran a hand through her hair, hoping to lessen the pain building in her head.

"Did your father leave you any papers or a file? Maybe a CD with information about one of the issues he spent a lot of time on?"

Damn. Her stomach twisted, and she fought the urge to throw up.

"Jill? Did you hear me?" Gary's voice had a hard insistence she'd never heard before.

"Yeah, Gary. I heard." She glanced frantically around her kitchen. Did her father tell Gary about the flash drive? What could she say to derail the conversation? "I'll go through what I've brought up here. How will that do? Uh, listen, I hear knocking at the front door. I'll get back with you."

She disconnected, without waiting for a response from him and slumped into one of the chairs. Her arms wrapped around her body, and she rocked back and forth. Whimpers escaped through her clamped lips. What could she do? Should she leave Woodstock? Where would she go? Maybe she should plug the damn flash drive into her computer and see what—

No, no, better not to know exactly what it contained. Make her denial more believable.

She popped out of the chair. A jack-in-the-box had nothing on her. Damn, did she think someone was going to grab her and force information from her? She ran a hand around the back of her neck to release tension. Not successful.

Her whole body quaked at the idea of coming in contact with the consortium goons. Too many trashy novels in her spare time. She walked through the house checking doors and windows again. The old time remedy of a chair under the handles of the front and back doors gave her a modicum of comfort.

After swallowing the last of the wine, she poured another glass. No more running back and forth in her brain tonight, or she'd go crazy. A soak in the tub was in order. Her muscles ached from the physical labor today at the store.

She prayed Gary wouldn't call back.

\* \* \* \*

*Tuesday, October 2*

"Detective Riley, this is Gary Myers."

"What can I do for you Mr. Myers?" Riley gripped his phone. Anticipation that Myers might have info for him rippled along his muscles.

"I got hold of Ms. Barlow last night. I tell you, I'm concerned about her."

"Why's that?" Riley sat forward, his pencil tapped on the desk. "Did she tell you she had an item of her father's?" He hoped the answer was yes, but dreaded to hear the words, for the woman's sake.

"Jill said she didn't, but she also told me the office in her store had been torn apart the night before."

Riley's pulse quickened. "What was taken? Do they have much robbery crime in the town?" He shot the words fast, impatient for a quick answer.

"If anything was removed, she couldn't recognize it. Files had been pretty much wrecked." Myers paused, and swallowed loudly. "Like her house here. Whoever broke-in couldn't gain access to the computer, because it was password protected. Riley, I'm worried this is related to her father and husband's deaths." Strain spiked Myers's voice and pinged across the connection.

"Suspicious certainly but could be random. Don't know what to make of this incident. Did Ms. Barlow seem worried?"

"No, not when she first started telling me. But after I mentioned the possibility of her father leaving information with her, she changed."

"How's that?" Mike struggled to keep his voice even, while wanting to jump through the line and pull the information from the accountant.

"She took a long time to respond, put the phone down a couple of times. Finally, said she'd look around and then mumbled about someone being at her door and disconnected. I'd have been worried if I'd thought she was serious. It seemed to me she wanted an excuse to get off the phone."

"Could Ms. Barlow have a boyfriend who'd be coming by at night?" Silence greeted him from the other end of the line. "Mr. Myers, did you understand the question?"

"Yeah. I understood, and I don't know if she does, to use your term, have a boyfriend. Frankly, I'd feel better if she did, contrary to being by herself."

"I understand her needing to get out of Fort Worth after suffering the losses she did, but how'd she decide on Woodstock? I don't believe I ever heard."

"She has a friend from high school who went to college in Vermont, married a native, and stayed. Visiting with her after George's death helped Jill start the process of getting back on her feet."

"Do you know the friend? What's her name? Can we use her to check on Ms. Barlow?" Again, he fired questions, not giving Myers a chance to answer. Mike wasn't sure where he was going with this, but knew he needed more info on Barlow's current situation.

"Karen Livingston and her husband Tim live a few miles out from town on a few acres, so they're not close geographically to Jill's store or her house. Are you familiar with Vermont, Detective?"

"No. I'm not."

"Well, it's very rural, but nothing's far apart by our standards."

"Have you seen the house? How secure is she?" Riley couldn't let it go. That gut feeling he'd learned not to ignore was kicking his insides around and raised his fear level for the widow.

"I went up for the store closing. It's an old house, quaint, but I don't remember seeing any security system."

"Can you convince her to put one in?" Mike asked.

"Don't know if she can. She's renting, but I'll damn sure try."

"Good. I appreciate you keeping me posted on this, Myers."

"If I can't convince her about the security system, what's the next step?" Myers' tone said he was determined to help Barlow. She was lucky in her friends. "Well?" Myers waited, but not patiently for an answer.

"I'll touch base with the local law enforcement."

# CHAPTER NINE

*Thursday, October 11*

"Any news for us, Phillips?"

Mitch swallowed what felt like one of the red potatoes served in local restaurants. Cranston's low guttural voice sent shivers across Mitch's shoulders even though the man was across the country. He'd wondered whether to call and report he hadn't found anything or wait until he had something good to report. Obviously, he'd made the wrong decision.

"I've taken steps, Mr. Cranston, but don't have the information you want. I checked out the woman's store but didn't find anything. I'm waiting for the right opportunity to go over her house."

"Don't *wait* for an opportunity. Make one."

It sounded to Mitch like Cranston took long puffs from one of those cigars he favored. "I want results. You owe me. You want me to take payment in another, more physical way?"

"God, no." Mitch's voice telegraphed his fear. It curdled his insides. If he didn't get off the phone quick, he'd crap his pants. "I'll get in her house, give me some more time. Please."

"All right. Don't disappoint me."

The buzzing sound was the only indication Cranston had hung up. Mitch disconnected and ran to the bathroom.

At seven-thirty that evening he walked by the store. Pausing at the window pretending to shop, he saw Barlow helping a customer. The other woman must be in the back. He'd walk over to Barlow's house now. She wouldn't go home for at least two hours. That'd give him enough time to search the house and get out free and clear. He ambled down the street, playing tourist, glancing in the windows, supposedly without a care in the world.

"Oh, shit." He sucked in a breath. Her friend, the Livingston woman, came out of the store ahead of him. He barely stopped himself from plowing into her. Maybe she'd not notice him, but she turned.

"Hey, Mitch. How are things?"

He had rotten luck. "Karen."

"I'm surprised to see you in town when we still have this many tourists here. Know you can't stand all the craziness."

"You're right. It's not my favorite time of year."

"Not to worry, though. In another week, the numbers will drop right off."

"Yeah, I'll be glad to see them go." Would the woman never stop talking?

"Where you going? I'll walk along with you. I'm killing time, waiting for Tim. He made a home visit to check on Mrs. Mortonson's cat."

Shit, shit, shit. What could he do now?

"I'm headed home, Karen. See you around." He took off walking fast toward the small place he had on the opposite side of town from Barlow's house. He didn't handle that well, but hell, who'd have guessed Karen would show up. Damn her anyway.

The extra detour would cut into his time, but he still needed to take a shot at this. He didn't want Cranston getting so pissed he'd send someone after him. The idea shot ice through his veins. He shivered and pulled his jacket collar higher.

He came up to Barlow's house from across a field in the rear. One light shone from the back window, but he had no reason to think she wasn't still at the store. He'd learned Thursday was one of the nights she closed. Inching up to the windows, he looked in, but didn't see her purse or keys lying around. Using a pair of latex gloves, he'd picked up at the drug store, he tried the back door. Locked, of course. He fiddled with a credit card. Such an old house maybe some muscle…a shove… sure enough the lock popped open, and he eased inside.

Palming a flashlight, he started with the kitchen, pulled out drawers, and rummaged through cabinets. No telling where a person would hide a flash drive. Maybe in the canisters on the counter. Nope. Would she put it in the refrigerator? He shuffled through the vegetables, fruit, even checked the butter dish. Nothing. Damn.

The dining room didn't have much but the china cabinet. Quick work through that and still no results.

In the living room, the curtains stood open, and he closed them. He didn't want a passerby to see him moving around. The bookshelf looked promising, but was a disappointment. He dug into the sofa between the cushions and in the stuffed chairs.

Nothing.

Halfway up the stairs, they creaked, and he nearly peed his pants. The first room he came to appeared to be Barlow's bedroom. Glancing at his watch, he hurried through dresser drawers. Nice lingerie. He held up a thong. Hmm. Maybe he'd give the old broad a thought or two. He'd like to get a looksee at her in that scrap of silk, and yeah…a matching black lace bra.

Get busy. He dropped the bra and panties on the floor and hurried to finish the bedroom.

With time moving, he upended the bathroom. Nothing. Then he pushed open the door of another room. Thank God. A flash drive lay right next to a laptop in her study. He rustled through the two drawers of the desk. No other storage devices. This must be the one. He grabbed it and her laptop to make sure he got anything she downloaded. He'd check it out at his place. He pulled in a deep breath, the first good one in all the days since he'd talked with Cranston in Las Vegas.

Nine-twenty. He'd better get the hell out. No time to straighten. He blamed Karen Livingston. Damn. Barlow could have fun picking up the mess. Mitch slipped out the back door and cut across the field toward his house. The car would've been faster, but too conspicuous, so he'd walked, which he hated. He raced toward his house, his hands itching to get on the cards again. Cranston would be grateful.

On entering his house, Mitch turned on the computer and plugged in the flash drive. Not password protected. Easy access. He searched one file after another. Then he checked the files on the laptop's hard-drive.

Damn. The flash drive and the computer held nothing but her personal correspondence and a couple of things about her business. He leaned back in his chair. All the energy drained from him, replaced by crushing disappointment. Shit. He'd learned his lesson last time when he didn't call right away. Not how he'd wanted to end the day, but he wasn't putting it off. He picked up the phone.

"You got me the information?" Cranston's voice formed icicles along Mitch's spine. He'd never heard anyone who sounded like evil, whatever evil might sound like, but Sid Cranston scared the crap out of him. Thank God, he wasn't in the same room with him.

"Yeah, but not what you want to hear, Mr. Cranston. I searched Barlow's house and found a flash drive, but it only had her personal garbage. Not what you're looking for. Are you sure she has the one you want?"

"I'm certain the flash drive exists. Have you checked her purse?"

"No. She's had it with her when I searched the store and house."

Again the sudden buzzing from the other end. The man gave Mitch the willies. Hell, how was he going to get into Barlow's purse? He poured himself a straight shot of whiskey and then another.

Disappear. He'd like nothing better than to disappear. No one here would miss him. He'd take the chance if he weren't positive Cranston would send his thugs after him. After a third shot, he sprawled across his bed. He'd figure something out tomorrow.

\* \* \* \*

"Whew." Jill stretched her hands over her head, leaned left and right, trying to get the kinks out. "What a day. I'm so glad you're here, Mary Ann. I'd have never gotten to everyone tonight."

"I'm happy to be able to help, Jill. I keep expecting the crowds to slow down. They normally do after the Columbus Day weekend. I bet you'll see a difference when we open Monday."

After locking the front door of the store, Jill pulled her knit hat low over her ears, thankful for the long wool coat and boots. She still needed to get something heavier. The wind had picked up, and the weather forecasters talked about the first snow.

"See you Saturday, Mary Ann. Stay warm." Jill started down the street in one direction and her employee in the other. Walking fast with her head down, Jill focused on getting to her warm house, the fire she'd build, and the glass of wine she'd sip curled up staring at the flames.

Anne had stopped by the other day and seemed pleased with the report Jill gave the former owner on how things were going at the store. The schedule they'd worked out for Sally, Mary Ann, and her was working well. Two people were always in the shop, and on Saturday and Sunday, when they had the largest crowds, their schedules overlapped so all three worked.

The good thing about staying so busy was that during the day, she kept at bay her concerns about the break-in. She wasn't so lucky at night. The worry often interfered with her sleep. Neither was she a hundred percent successful at the task of locking out the bearded lawyer either. Jerrod managed to creep into her thoughts with an unsettling frequency.

Tomorrow she'd call the number for the security company Karen gave her to see when they'd be available to address problems at the store. Maybe she'd do what Gary suggested and talk with her real estate agent to get him to check with her landlord. She'd pay to have something installed on the house at the same time she got the store wired. She had tomorrow to herself. Maybe Karen could make time for lunch. Jill could catch up on how plans were coming for the Historical

Society fundraiser scheduled for November. She'd looked forward to helping with the project, but she hadn't found a moment to spare.

Things were about to change if Mary Ann was correct about the slow-down in the number of tourists. They'd have to wait and see.

Jill walked faster the closer she got to the house, but the cold cut like a knife through her coat right to her bones. Shivers grew and seemed to take over. Oh, for the roaring fire. Her breath glowed in the porch light. Damn. The keys fell from her nearly frozen fingers, reminding her of Jerrod and the kiss.

Her stomach tumbled. Not thinking of that.

Finally, she unlocked the door and pushed into the entryway.

The powder room door stood open. She normally pushed it closed because of space issues. Turning toward the living room, Jill jerked to a stop in the archway. Her heart catapulted into her throat. Her breath fled. *Oh, my God. Not again.*

Her hand silenced the scream struggling to push past her lips. She turned and ran.

When she got to Elm Street, she stopped. Where was she going? Should she have gotten her car from the shed? She looked left and right and over her shoulder. Only a few people were still on the streets. Her feet began to move without a conscious decision on her part until she stopped outside Jerrod's house.

Her gloved hand knocked on the door. This was crazy. He might not be home. Or worse, she'd burst in on him and a woman. Before she pounded the third time, the heavy wooden door swung open.

* * * *

"Jill?" Surprise didn't keep Jerrod from drawing her into his home. He pulled her trembling body against his. "Damn, you're freezing, woman." He tilted her chin up to assess the situation. She was pink with the cold, and her lips quivered. He kept one arm around her shoulder, walked her into his living room, and seated her in front of the fireplace before he spoke. "What's wrong?"

She looked at him with the saddest expression he'd ever seen.

"They broke into the house." A tear slid from one eye. She appeared not to notice. He reached out with one finger and caught the moisture. Did she refer to some specific *they*?

"Don't move. I'll bring you a cup of tea."

When he returned he found her with her hands outstretched toward the fire. A large bag still hung on her shoulder. With one hand, he pulled the strap, letting the purse settle to the floor. He held out the cup. She grasped it, took a hurried sip, and wrapped both hands around the bowl. Still she hadn't spoken. "Talk to me, Jill."

"What?"

She appeared dazed. Was she going into shock? "Did you call the sheriff?"

"Huh uh. I ran. Ended up here. Sorry. I shouldn't impose."

Jerrod placed a hand on her shoulder to keep her from standing. "Don't worry, Jill. We'll get this straightened out. I'm glad you came." Later, he'd mull over the warmth in his middle because she came to him. Right now, she needed him to provide a safe base from which to operate. "Let me call Jack. You can tell him your story."

"Thank you."

"Drink some more tea." She took another sip.

"Let's get you out of the coat. You'll be more comfortable." After helping with her coat, he placed the call on his cell, but he wasn't certain she took in any of the conversation. Jack Hardwick had pulled a late shift and promised he'd be right over.

By the time Jerrod finished talking with the sheriff, she'd drunk all of the tea, so he took the cup and set it on a table. She leaned closer to the fire. Thank God, she was moving a little. He was afraid for a while she'd go into shock, either from the cold, the surprise she'd found at home, or both. He'd added a shot of whiskey to the cup, but she hadn't seemed to notice.

"I'd have you tell me about what you saw, but Jack will want to know the same thing when he gets here, and you'd have to repeat yourself."

She nodded once. The way her arms wrapped around her middle told him she was barely holding herself together.

"Can I get you some more tea?" He hoped she'd say yes, because he fully intended to splash in another jigger. At her nod, he hurried to the kitchen. When he returned he found her standing, staring into the fire. "Drink some, Jill. It'll help."

She'd taken several good sips when the sound of the doorknocker made her jerk. He placed a hand on her shoulder and gave a brief squeeze. "That'll be the sheriff."

When Jerrod returned with Jack in tow, Jill stood rigidly in front of the fire. Her eyes glazed over.

"Ms. Barlow, please have a seat and tell me what the problem is." Jack took her by the arm and gently eased her into one of the wing-backed chairs.

"After we locked the store, I said goodbye to Mary Ann and walked to the house. I was hurrying because it was so cold. My fingers had grown numb, and I dropped the keys."

Probably more info than Jack needed, but Jerrod didn't want to interrupt the flow of words, grateful she was able to talk, though she spoke softly, not in her usual strong voice.

"When I stepped inside, the first thing I noticed was the door to the powder room was open. I leave it closed generally, but I thought…then I turned to enter the living room…" Her hand reached up and brushed across her forehead. She rubbed a spot between her eyes.

"What did you see?" Jack encouraged her.

"Books off the shelves." Her chin quivered, but she went on. "Sofa and chair cushions scattered on the floor. I didn't say anything or go in any farther. I ran. I'm not certain I closed or locked the front door. God, this is a nightmare." She set the cup on the hearth and slumped forward, her elbows on her knees, holding her head in her hands.

"I'll get one of my deputies, and we'll see what's what. You stay here with Jerrod, okay? Can I have your keys, in case you did lock the door?"

She nodded, reached in the side pocket of her purse and held them out to the sheriff.

"I'll show you out, Jack." Jerrod headed toward the front door with Jack at his side.

"Oh, and Ms. Barlow." The sheriff stopped and swung around to Jill. "You did a good thing, to get out right away. Someone could've still been on the premises. Smart move on your part."

She nodded, and what looked like a smile touched the corners of her mouth, but faded quickly.

"I'll be right back." After seeing Jack out, Jerrod returned to the living room. "Can I get you something to eat?"

"No thanks." She held up her cup. "Did you put something in this besides tea?"

"I confess. Wasn't trying to get you drunk, but I worried you were going into shock. Between the cold and what you'd walked into."

"This helped." She tipped the cup in his direction. "I have a lot to thank you for… and to apologize for. I'm sorry I barged in on you this way." She got up and began walking around his living room, picking up family pictures and nick-knacks, before moving on.

"I'm glad you came. Guess we need to get Jack's phone number programmed into your cell." His laugh was hollow to his own ears. "Sorry, that was a lousy joke."

"No, you're right. Let's do it now." She held out her cell.

"Jill, I was teasing. You don't have to do this."

"Please, Jerrod. I want his number. I need his number."

He complied with her request, and returned the phone. "I also put in mine."

"Thank you." Her knuckles whitened from the tight grip she took on the cell.

They both jumped when his phone beeped. He read Jack's name. "I'm getting you more tea, and I'll be right back." He didn't know what to expect with the sheriff calling him so soon but suspected he'd be able to talk more easily not in Jill's presence.

"What'd you find?"

"My God, Jerrod, the place is a wreck. Drawers pulled out, stuff strewn around. In the bedroom, her lingerie is scattered all over. I hope we don't have us some pervert. It'll be a while before we're finished here. She won't be able to get in until maybe tomorrow. I've called Shirley to come dust for fingerprints. Can you take her to the inn? Isn't that where she stayed when she first arrived?"

"I'm not big on the idea of her being alone tonight. Mother's would be a possibility, but I can't put her in danger if this isn't random and someone's after Jill. I don't know how I'll convince her, but I'll keep Jill here. Talk with you in the morning." Jerrod disconnected and took a bottle of wine from the rack and poured two generous glasses.

She needed to get some sleep to have the energy to deal with whatever tomorrow brought. Staying awake wouldn't be difficult for him, regardless of how much wine. He'd only have to imagine the lovely blonde sleeping in the bedroom next to his.

When he entered the living room, Jill stood with her back to the fireplace and her hands wrapped around her body. Her eyes appeared more haunted than any he'd ever seen. She needed to tell him what was going on and what she was afraid of. If ever he'd seen a scared female, she stood before him now.

"Here, Jill, I've brought us some wine. It'll help warm you."

She raised the glass, taking a generous sip. "Appreciated on a cold night." She took another sip then sat down in the large wing back chair to the right of the fireplace, one leg over the other, swinging at a quick pace. "Was that the sheriff?"

"Yeah." He nodded and stalled with his own drink.

"Tell me. I can deal with whatever. Not knowing is the worst."

One gutsy woman. Nothing to remind him of his ex. Jill never would've walked out on her family, regardless of the circumstances.

"Jack reported the house was pretty torn up. Drawers pulled out with the contents spilled on the floor. He couldn't tell if anything was missing. You'll need to go through the house tomorrow to see for yourself. Often we don't notice losses for some time after a robbery. Stuff is so out of place, you don't recognize when a piece is missing."

"So I can't go back tonight?" Her voice sounded like a small child's. Her eyes seemed to contract, and the two lines above her nose deepened. She struggled to make sense of what he'd said.

He longed to reach out and gently rub the frown a way, to massage her shoulders, to hold her tight. He kept his fingers wrapped securely around the wine glass, the other hand in a pocket. She didn't need to deal with his libido, which was threatening to take control.

"Stay here tonight. You shouldn't be alone, and it's late to go to anyone else's house."

"I can't do that." The frown deepened. She jumped from the chair and moved around the room. He could almost hear her mind searching for an alternative.

"After considering other options, I've decided this is best. Come on." He held out his hand. "I'll show you where you can sleep." Her gaze darted around the room, stopped on him then skittered away.

"You'll be safe here. I'll keep you safe. I promise you that." His voice dropped into a lower register, one he hoped she found trustworthy.

He'd apparently used the magic word. She reached toward him and grasped his hand like a life preserver. Her hand in his made him uneasy. It felt too right. "Let me top off your wine, and you can take it with you."

On the second floor, he indicated the bathroom and the spare bedroom right next to his. Having Jill so close would trouble him, but he hoped the location would comfort her.

She stood in the middle of the room his mother had redone in silver, gray, and navy.

"It's lovely. The splash of bright yellow in the pillows a slice of sunshine, gives me hope. And a fireplace. Thank you, Jerrod."

"Let me get that going." Glad he'd installed gas. "Now I'll find something you can sleep in."

He turned and went into his room, grabbed a pair of his flannel pajamas, trying not to picture how she'd look in them. Nothing sexier than a woman wearing a man's clothing.

When he returned, she stood, one hand clenched on the drapes, peeking through an opening.

"I laid out towels in the bathroom for you." He handed her the blue plaid pajamas. "They'll be way too large but will keep you warm."

Jill took them and then surprised him when she threw her arms around his waist and rested her cheek on his chest.

"I can't thank you enough for this. Being alone tonight would've been… difficult."

She stepped back, a blush rising in her cheeks. For his part, the hug could've gone on longer.

"It's okay. Get some rest." He backed out and closed the door. He'd get little of that with her next door. In the morning, he had to get her to talk. Something was going on, and she wasn't being open with any of them.

He'd been right about not getting much rest. After he'd tucked her in, so to speak, he went downstairs and double-checked everything was secure. He went into his office and searched the Internet for more information on the lovely and desirable Ms. Jill Barlow. A couple of hours later he emailed Don to ask for assistance explaining a few things. About two a.m., Jerrod fell into bed but slept fitfully. A dream of someone breaking in thrust him into an uneasy wakefulness.

He got up, took his gun from the bedside table, and made the rounds of his house. Finding nothing, he went back up the stairs. When he reached Jill's room, he paused, took hold of the doorknob and gently turned.

She'd thrashed around during the night. Maybe the fire had been too high, because she'd thrown off the covers. The moonlight coming through the crack in the curtains focused his attention on her lovely pale legs coming from beneath his pajama shirt. She'd discarded the pants. Her hair lay across the pillow, all that lovely yellow gold.

His breath caught in his chest, his hands clenched, and he fought the crazy desire to crawl in with her. He crossed to the bed. After placing the gun on the bedside table, he pulled the covers over her. The opening of the shirt displayed the soft curve of one of her breasts. He yanked his hands from the covers, grabbed the weapon, and walked away from the desirable, but troubled woman.

# CHAPTER TEN

*Friday, October 12*

Jill woke slowly, stretched, and snuggled back under the covers. Hmm. Had she used a different scent in her dryer? This was woodsy, like she'd hung the sheets outside in the fresh air.

A picture of her trashed living room sprang full-blown into her memory. Her heart pounded loud enough to be heard in Texas. She shot up in bed and looked around. Her purse lay on the dresser, and men's pajama bottoms draped across the back of the armchair by the window. She lifted the quilt. She wore only the top.

Jerrod. She'd spent the night at his house.

That's right. He'd taken her in after someone broke into her house. The third break-in, counting the one at her home in Fort Worth. Her hand trembled when she brushed the hair off her forehead. She counted her breaths, slowed them down.

Surprisingly, she'd slept well. No dreams. Must've been the wine. And, she admitted grudgingly, the knowledge that Jerrod slept next door. It made her feel safe. He'd been gracious and understanding about her bursting in the way she had.

She didn't have any business leaning on him. That would be a trap entirely too easy to fall into if she weren't careful. She climbed from the bed and grabbed her clothes, which she'd hung in the almost empty closet.

A shower would sharpen her senses, but then she'd leave. Hoping not to run into him, she eased open the door and peeked into the hallway. Nobody. The wonderful aroma of coffee drifted up from the kitchen. She scooted across the hall. Maybe she'd take time for one cup before she left.

The bathroom had a gas heater with matches nearby. Sulfur tingled in her nose, and a blue flame danced. Ah, yes. Nothing better, unless perhaps a fireplace in the bathroom. A couple of women she knew in Fort Worth had those. They'd told her it did a lot for their sex lives. Not an idea she needed right now.

Jill slipped out of the top and stepped into the water relishing its warmth. Being careful, she showered without getting her hair wet. She had lipstick, blush, and some mascara with her. Better than nothing. After she dressed, she'd get her coffee, thank Jerrod for his kindness, and then go see the sheriff. She hated to deal with this. She'd come to Woodstock to get her life in order and escape the nightmares of Texas. God help her.

When she finished dressing, she headed for the stairway, but stopped at the top.

Jerrod stood at the bottom holding a mug. "How about a cup of coffee?"

"Absolutely. Thanks." Resting her hand on the banister, she descended. The scent of coffee made her almost light headed.

"Come in the kitchen. Mother says I make better oatmeal than our old cook Esther did. Of course, moms are partial."

"I need to get over to the sheriff's office to see what he can tell me about last night. Find out when I can go home and begin cleaning up."

He held out a chair for her at the kitchen table. "No ma'am. You need to eat a hearty breakfast first. I insist."

"Well—"

"Seriously." He took her by the shoulders and guided her to the chair.

She did need to eat to be ready for whatever lay ahead of her. She picked up the spoon and sampled the creamy cereal in her bowl. "I don't know what Esther's oatmeal tasted like, but this is…" She sighed and then took a couple of more bites. "What all do you put in this?"

He smiled in response to her praise, and she did her best to rustle up one in return.

His eyes twinkled. Maybe she succeeded. "I'd tell you, but then I'd have to kill you—Damn." His smile evaporated in an instant. "I'm sorry, Jill. Not a good joke today."

"No, it's okay." She pushed her bowl away with a trembling hand. "I've had enough anyway, and I've got to go to the sheriff's office."

"I talked with him this morning and told him I'd bring you around later on. So you do have time. Finish your oatmeal and have more coffee. One cup can't be enough for you."

A laugh bubbled out, surprising her. "No, you're right. I go through a pot by myself at home, and on work days at the store, we go through two at least." She picked up the spoon and scooped up another bite. "It's got the right amount of sweetness."

"Keep it quiet, but the trick is using brown sugar and letting it cook into the porridge."

She ate in silence for a while, her muscles losing the coiled tenseness from the strain she'd lived with since the break-ins.

Jerrod pushed his chair back from the table and rested an ankle on his other knee. "Anyone have something against you, Jill? You have any enemies?"

She dropped her spoon, and it clattered against the pottery. "What? What are you talking about?" Her heart wanted to jump right out of her body the way it was beating. A picture of one of those cartoon characters whose red heart springs in and out of its chest popped into her head. But those characters were in love, not scared out of their mind the way she was.

"In talking with Jack this morning, we both agreed it's too much of a coincidence to have the store and your house randomly broken into in the span of two weeks. Soon after you arrived, when I confronted you in the gardens behind the inn, you seemed to be afraid I'd try to hurt you or your kids. Those circumstances taken together tie this to you."

"No." She jumped from the chair and made for the front of the house. It couldn't be. She wouldn't let it be. She wanted to be safe. She wanted to be safe in Woodstock. She headed to the door, but Jerrod caught her, spun her around, and then pulled her close. Her head dropped forward and rested on his chest. His heart beat at a thunderous rate matching hers.

"We have to talk about this, Jill." His fingers gently raised her head, forcing eye contact. "You can't keep running. Because that's what you were doing when you came here, wasn't it? You can't ignore this anymore. You have to fight. And the way you start is by telling Jack and me what the hell is going on."

She wanted to say no to him. None of this had anything to do with her. The touch of his strong arms warmed her inside and out. She didn't want to move.

Without dropping his hold, he put space between them, his jaw firm and determined.

"Tell me. Tell me, Jill, and we can work it out."

He slid his arms around again and nestled her closer. One hand trailed from the crown of her head down her long ponytail and stopped on the small of her back. She felt herself weaken, melting into him. God, he made her feel safe. Not only safe, but cared for, desirable. This whole thing was making her a crazy woman. She shouldn't be reacting to Jerrod this way.

Could she chance telling him about the mess in Fort Worth?

Then he kissed the top of her head, and the rest of her reserves cracked. Tears gushed like they hadn't since the night she broke down in early May. Jerrod didn't need this. But she must, because she couldn't stop.

"It's okay, honey, let it out. Then we'll start fresh."

After a time the tears subsided, followed by a few hiccoughs. She struggled to get her breathing under control.

"Here." He handed her his handkerchief. "You need to talk to me."

She swallowed, looked at him, took a deep breath, nodded, and wiped her nose.

They walked to the kitchen with his arm draped across her shoulder, the weight and warmth comforting. She didn't know what it was about this man who hadn't cared for her when they first met—nor she for him—but she enjoyed being around him. He always made her believe he'd keep the bad stuff at bay. Figuring out strategies was supposed to be his strength. Guess she'd see how good he was. She stood in the middle of the kitchen, took a deep breath, and dove in.

"My husband was killed two years ago and my father this past spring before I came here." He nodded, but didn't say anything, so she went on.

"Despite their best efforts, the authorities found no proof against anyone for either of the murders." Her voice shook, but she kept going. "People speculated a connection existed to legislation Dad sponsored or tried to stop over the years, but nothing was ever proved."

Jerrod prepared fresh coffee.

She paced his kitchen. Touching this and moving that, trying to keep her hands busy so she didn't wring them. She stopped when he set the mugs on the table.

He held a chair for her, but she shook her head. Emotions boiled on her insides, forcing her to move.

He nodded and sat.

"Because the police don't have any proof against anyone, we're left in a kind of limbo. I came to Woodstock, really for an extended visit. I planned to stay longer than when I came after George was killed. Karen and Tim made me feel comfortable here." She paused, looked out the back window of the kitchen into the yard at the red and orange leaves on the trees. "Who can argue with the scenery?"

Then she turned toward him. "When I was unpacking, after I arrived, I found a small box my father mailed me not long before he was murdered. I hadn't been able to bring myself to open it earlier."

Jill crossed to the table and using both hands lifted her mug. She didn't want him to see the evidence of the fear smoldering in her middle, not needing any more incidents before it would burst into a conflagration. After drinking and setting down the mug on the table, she drifted around the kitchen, deciding what and if to say more.

"Did you open the package?"

Jerrod's softly spoken question stopped her in her tracks. Despite her best efforts her hands clenched around each other, her heart rate kicked in to high gear. She wanted to run. Where would she go?

"What did you find?" Still that calm, low voice.

She took a deep breath. Was he trustworthy? She had no doubt about his mother. What about Anne's grandson? Don worked for the FBI, and he'd been in Austin last spring. Before she went further, before she said anything, before she put her life in Jerrod's hands, she'd have to get his assurance he'd keep the story quiet.

She sat in the chair next to the Yankee she was oddly and definitely attracted to, leaned forward, and grasped one of his hands. The familiar lick of electricity whenever they touched zinged up her arm.

"I need you to promise me something, Jerrod. I can't say anything else, if you won't."

"What's the promise? The lawyer in me won't let me agree until I know what you want."

She dropped the clasp she had on him and pushed off the chair. Only his quick reflexes kept it from hitting the floor. "God protect me from lawyers and politicians."

A chuckle came from Jerrod. "You don't sound like you're joking."

Jill turned around and studied him across the room. "Here's the deal. I need you to promise you won't say anything to Don about what I say. "

"Jill, he's in the FBI. How could it possibly hurt to tell him whatever?"

"Do you promise?"

\* \* \* \*

Her hands on her hips, feet planted, and lips clamped in a straight line. He wouldn't get another word from her if he didn't give in. No way he'd tell her he'd already contacted his son.

"I hope I don't regret this, but okay." He nodded.

"Okay, you won't tell Don anything I tell you?"

"That's right. Yes." Her eyes, if possible, got larger. Jerrod saw the hesitation and the final capitulation when she let out a long breath of air. Still, she didn't move toward him, and he was afraid if he tried to approach her, she'd bolt. He continued to sit on the hard kitchen chair, an ankle of one leg resting on the knee of the other, hoping to gain her trust. Whatever she had to say was serious.

"The package contained a note from my father...and...a flash drive." One hand traveled up around her neck, and she massaged the muscles. Her lips turned down. Most people carried a form of tension in their neck and shoulders. She was apparently in that majority.

"You're doing fine, Jill." This was no different to working with a reluctant witness. "Tell me the rest. What did the note say?"

"Told me the flash drive had information on the gambling consortium." She clasped her hands together in her lap, as if reporting to the principal. "Told me Greg Richardson, the head lobbyist, was bad." Her voice cracked and her chin quivered. "Told me if Daddy were dead, the gamblers would've killed him."

"Okay. You can give the device to the authorities and get the bastards who killed your father and husband. Or have you already done that? Jill, I don't see why I couldn't share any of this with Don."

At her alarmed expression, he held up his arms, palms facing her. "Okay, okay. I've given my word." God, he hoped he didn't have reason to regret the communication with his son.

"My father wrote he'd already turned the information over to the FBI."

"That's even better. Have you heard if they've made any arrests, or are they still investigating?"

"You. Don't. Get. It. Do you?" She glared at him, her fists jammed at her waist.

"I guess not. Make me understand."

"Soon after turning over the information to the FBI, my father was murdered."

Well, shit. That wasn't good.

She swallowed and licked her lips. "It's possible someone in the Austin bureau office is on Richardson's payroll. To my knowledge, the FBI hasn't followed up on this. I've searched the newspapers, not in Fort Worth only, but Austin, too. The detective investigating Dad's murder in Austin and the Fort Worth detective with George's case kept in contact with each other. I'd have heard something from Catching or Riley if there'd been a break in the cases." The words tumbled from her mouth with increasing speed as she made her case.

"Detective Riley used my credit cards to trace me here. If he could do that, other law enforcement types could, too." She walked back to the chair and dropped down. "Do you see why I can't have you talking with Don?"

"Are you accusing my son of involvement in the murders? What's the matter with you?" Jerrod got up and stomped across his kitchen. His blood pressure skyrocketed, and he wanted to throw something. Here he'd given this woman shelter, and she attacked his son.

"No…not really, but he said he was in Austin in the spring. Consider this. Suppose Richardson doesn't already know where I am, and the break-ins are not related. I can't chance Don saying something to an agent, who'd speak to someone else, and word would get back to whoever in the Austin Bureau is responsible."

Jerrod clenched his fists, made himself calm down and use his brain rather than his emotions. That's what he did. How he made his living, using reasoning, logic, and studying the evidence. He was furious with her for bringing her problems and danger here to his mother's doorstep and his town, but he'd still help her. He spun back around.

Damn, what a mess. His gaze lingered on those soft brown eyes of hers. Did she already regret telling him? He crossed back and sat down next to her, took her hand in his. Waited to get over the shock he felt whenever they touched.

"Okay, Jill, we're going to work this out. I'm glad you've trusted me with this. I want to look at the flash drive, see if I can figure out what our next steps should be."

"No next steps, Jerrod." She jerked her hand free. "There can't be. I'm afraid they'll come after me or my kids. I won't do anything to put them at risk."

"They may already have come after you." He hated to hurt her, but she needed to face facts, even if those facts were bitter.

"No, don't say that." She jumped up, like a spring-loaded toy, and this time he couldn't catch the chair before it hit the floor. The crash resounded in the kitchen. "It's a coincidence. It has to be a coincidence. God, I shouldn't have come here, or at least I should've tried to cover my tracks." Her harried movements carried her around the room. "That's what I'll do. I'll leave. I'll just use cash. Neither the FBI nor anyone else will be able to follow me if I don't use my credit cards."

Words flowed from her like a burst damn spewing muddy water. Jerrod supposed she was talking more to herself than to him. He got up, stopped her in the middle of the crazy zigzagging around the room when he put both hands on her shoulders. "Jill, anyone can be traced. It's harder when using cash and takes more time. But if a person's willing to pay enough to find someone, he'll get his information."

She stared at him. Despair filled her eyes.

"What can I do then? I haven't told the twins. I wanted to keep them out of this. Should I just send Richardson the flash drive? Maybe then he'd leave us alone." Her hands squeezed his upper arms trying to drag the answers she wanted from him.

"How do you convince him you haven't made another copy?"

"My God, we'll never be safe." The pitch of her voice rose. She wilted into him.

Jerrod pulled her near and rested his chin on her head. How had he become so tied to this woman? The quiet sobs drenched his shirt and hurt him more than her earlier outburst.

He was not without resources. They'd figure out something. Primarily, he had to convince Jill she had to fight. The situation demanded she take a stand. Otherwise, she and her children would never be free. They'd never be safe.

# CHAPTER ELEVEN

*Friday, October 12*

Jerrod turned Jill's key in the front door. Jack had dropped it off earlier that morning. Based on what the sheriff told him, Jerrod tried to prepare Jill for what to expect. Yeah, she'd seen the office, but this was where she lived, where she slept. He pushed open the door, and the violation and helplessness victims of burglary experienced kicked him in the gut the way it had when he'd discovered the robbery in his apartment in Montpelier.

"Oh, my God, Jerrod. Oh, my God." Her hands covered her mouth. The scream didn't escape. They walked into the living room with the cushions awry and the books off the shelves. The dining room wasn't quite so bad with only the table and sideboard.

The faint smell of food beginning to spoil greeted them when they pushed into the kitchen, which didn't look much different than if a hurricane had blown through. Drawers pulled out. Cupboard doors stood open. Contents spilled across the counter and floor. "This is dreadful. Upstairs this bad?" she asked with a hitch in her voice.

"Sounds like."

She led the way to the second floor, keeping her hands in close to her body, trying not to touch the banister. Finger print powder coated everything.

"Oh." When she stepped through the door to her room, she sucked in her breath. Tears dropped unnoticed on her sweater.

Jerrod's hands balled into fists. He wanted to punch something or someone for causing her so much distress. Seeing her clothes strewn around the room, including her lingerie… Someone had touched every stitch she owned. Abruptly she turned around and bumped into him.

"Let's check the other rooms." Her mouth formed a tight, straight line. A muscle jumped in her jaw. Her eyes pulled into a squint.

He followed her into the bathroom, which didn't seem to be in quite such a state, maybe because he was looking at towels and sheets rather than silky thongs and nighties. Tops off the medicine and make-up containers. The contents oozed across the sink.

"I hate for you to have to deal with this, Jill."

"Yeah, and I'm sorry if I'm responsible for bringing this dreadful business to your town. And the Burton's lovely home. I'm sick for them, too."

He took her hand. "Jill this isn't your fault. You realize that, right? Whoever broke in is at fault."

She shook her head and jerked away from him. "Last room's the study." They walked across the hall. "Looks ominously like the office at the store, except I don't have quite the same amount of paperwork here." She walked to the desk then looked back at him. "My laptop's gone."

"I'll let Jack know right away." He stepped into the hall, pulled out his cell to fill in the sheriff about the latest, and hoped they'd found a sign this was a regular burglary. Then he called Karen, asked her to come over, and bring along some extra cleaning supplies. Jill came out of the study.

"This is going to take a while." Her voice was flat, no inflection at all.

"Yeah. But we're not finished with the discussion. For now, we'll focus on cleaning up. I'm bringing in reinforcements. Karen is coming and bringing Mother's housekeeper. We need dry cloths and damp ones. Do you have something we can use?"

"In the kitchen." She turned and headed back down the stairs.

"Until you get a security system put in, plan to sleep at my house."

Jill stopped halfway down shaking her head. She turned and looked up at him. "I appreciate you letting me stay last night. Clearly, that was the best thing to do, but I can't continue. What will people think?"

"That I'm a really nice man to help you out when you've had such bad luck?"

"Right." Jill rolled her eyes and continued down the stairs. "If you're serious about helping, I accept your offer. I'll show you where the rags in the kitchen are, and then I'll gather a load of clothes for the washer. Some things will go to the cleaners, but this is… Well, I better get busy."

"First, I'm calling a buddy who does home security. See how soon he can come out here." He grabbed the rags from under the sink.

"Jerrod, I'll need to check with the Burtons before I take such drastic steps.."

His glare locked with hers. "Well, normally I'd agree, but you can't stay here without a security system." He pulled out his cell phone and walked through the back door.

\* \* \* \*

The nerve of him. He didn't get the last word, nor could he ignore her opinion. Truthfully, she was grateful for his take-charge manner. To say this whole thing overwhelmed her would be an understatement.

In her bedroom she picked up her clothes, one piece at a time, and shook the powder from them, separating items into light and dark. Please, God, let this be random, some dreadful quirk in the universe. Not related to the evil in Fort Worth and Austin. A prayer she suspected God would answer in the negative.

Karen arrived in less than twenty minutes with Anne's cleaning-lady, Myrtle Bates. She stated they had to start on the top, because the powder would settle lower to the first floor when they dealt with the second. They divvied up jobs by location, so they didn't stumble over each other. Jill handled the clothes in her room, and Karen, the bathroom items. What a goopy mess. Jill hated to leave it to Karen. The scents from the various opened bottles and jars blended into a not altogether unpleasant aroma, albeit strong. Jill, focused on sorting and shaking clothes, jumped when Karen touched her on the shoulder.

"Sorry, hon. I wanted to get your attention, but didn't want the others to overhear me."

Jill's stomach muscles tightened at the expression on her friend's face.

"What?"

"No easy way to ask this. What are the possibilities the break-in here and at the store are connected in any way to what happened to George and your father?"

"What?" Jill was proud of the tone of incredulity she'd been able to infuse her voice with, but she couldn't make eye contact. That was too hard. She angled her body away from Karen and picked up more clothes.

"I've run the situation over and over in my mind. Woodstock has few burglaries. Tim and other town council members are always bragging about how low our overall crime rate is."

Both Jerrod and Karen seemed determined to see a connection to her life in Fort Worth, when all she wanted to do was pray none existed. Jill took in a deep breath and slowly exhaled, deciding to bluff. "I don't know what you mean."

"Come on Jill, get the blinders off. You're a smart woman."

Karen put her hands on Jill's shoulders and turned her around.

"Your father made some enemies during his time in the legislature. You have to consider the possibility one of those is responsible for his and George's deaths. You told me your house in Fort Worth was broken into, and here you've had two burglaries in two weeks. In all the mysteries I read, the cop always says sometime during the book, 'I don't believe in coincidences.' You know he does."

The low gruff voice she used for the cop's words pulled a smile from Jill. Leave it to Karen to bring some levity to this situation. "All right. It's possible. I haven't wanted to think that. I don't want to leave here, Karen. If I believed a connection existed, I'd have to, because I refuse to put y'all in danger."

"Have you talked with anyone about this?"

"Jerrod. This morning."

"Good. You probably should talk with the sheriff and maybe Don. Between them, they're sure to have ideas about what to do to deal—."

"Karen, don't suggest saying anything to Don." A slight hint of hysteria zinged through her tone, despite efforts to remain calm.

"Why ever not?"

"Well, you can't. I got Jerrod's promise to not say anything to his son either."

"So you're not telling me everything." Karen nodded. "Okay. You know if you need anything, Tim and I are here for you." Karen picked up her rag, her mouth tilted in a crooked grin. "I'd better get back to work before the boss fires me."

Jill worked for another half-hour before a brief knock preceded Jerrod sticking his head around the door. "Myrtle and I are going down. What's taking you so long? We're moving faster than you slowpokes." He disappeared through the opening.

"I heard that," Karen hollered from the bathroom. "He's issued a direct challenge. They're finished in the study. Why don't you start on the papers?"

"Okay. I've got the clothes sorted." Jill left her bedroom. Myrtle and Jerrod had done a good job in the study. They'd used both the dry and wet cloths, so she was able to get papers back into files. When she'd finished, she hit her bedroom again and scooped up another load for the washer. "I'm heading down, Karen."

"I'll be right behind you."

"Myrtle, I can't thank you enough for being here. Things are so much better." Jill set the basket of clothes on the floor next to the washer. She looked around the kitchen, which had two trash bags sitting in the middle of the floor. She notched her head toward them.

"Spoiled food." Myrtle was brief and to the point.

Jill nodded. "Thanks." She picked up one and carried it outside to the garbage can.

"Glad to help out." Myrtle said when Jill entered. "Mrs. Phillips wanted to come herself, but I discouraged her. Said if we got too many people in here, we'd be tripping over each other."

"Good. I wouldn't have let her help anyway. She did more than her share at the store." She looked around. "I didn't notice Jerrod when I came through the living room."

"He left a while ago. Wanted me to tell you he'd be back. Had an errand to run."

"Oh." Apprehension at what he was doing sent tension straight up the back of her head.

"I'll put that load in the washer for you after I move the things in there to the dryer. Do you have another load?"

"You are a jewel. Yes, I have several more loads. I'll be washing clothes for the next week."

Myrtle laughed. "Nah. It will just feel like that."

Jill joined in and pushed her concerns about where Jerrod was out of her mind.

* * * *

Jerrod would've preferred not to sneak out of Jill's house, but he didn't want her trying to talk him out of doing what he knew he must. He hoped she'd be able to forgive him for breaking his promise. While he valued his word above everything else, in this instance, her safety had to come first. Until this—whatever it was—got resolved, she'd never be safe. He pushed open the door to Woodstock Public Safety building, which housed the sheriff's office.

"Can I see Jack, Clara?"

"Just a minute." She checked with her boss. "Go on back."

Jerrod nodded his thanks before he headed toward Jack's office. He stuck his head around the door. "Hey, you got a few minutes?"

"Sure, Jerrod, come on in. You know it'll be some time before we get anything on those fingerprints we found. How's Ms. Barlow holding up?"

"About as well as can be expected. I left her with Karen and Myrtle. They have a lot to do before Jill can stay in the house again."

Jerrod pushed the office door closed and slouched into one of the chairs. "Jack, I wanted to talk to you without her around."

"What's going on?"

The worry about Jill's safety, the effect her nearness had on him, and what she'd possibly brought with her to Woodstock drained all his energy. He sucked in a breath. God, last night seemed a long time ago. He brought Jack up to speed.

"Jill made me promise not to tell Don anything, because she's convinced a bad apple hangs in the FBI's Austin office." Jerrod ran a hand around the back of his neck. Tension had burned from the moment she'd shown up on his doorstep last night.

"She didn't say specifically not to speak to you, although if she'd thought about it she might've. Before she said anything, I'd already asked Don to see what he could find out. Hope I didn't make the situation worse."

"Well, I'll be damned." Jack rubbed his jaw. "Pretty much of a mess, and you're probably screwed for saying anything."

"Yeah, and damn, I wish she hadn't brought her troubles here, if in fact, she has." Jerrod didn't analyze his statement, afraid he'd find he didn't mean what he'd said. "I got hold of Tommy Tomlinson, and he's going to tell Jill what she needs to do to make the place more secure. She's concerned about what the Burtons will say, but she has to put some sort of system in. If she's paying for the equipment, why would they mind?"

"Now, Jerrod, you're the lawyer. You understand that's not exactly kosher. Has she tried to get hold of the owners?"

"We've both talked with her realtor Mark Jennings, and he's trying to reach them, but they're on a cruise, and only sometimes have cell phone coverage."

"How is he with your plan?"

"Mostly okay. As long as Tommy can put in a system without affecting the architectural integrity of the house."

"Don't see how Jill has much choice. Town can't afford to put a deputy sitting outside her house twenty-four seven."

Jack's desk phone rang at the same time Jerrod's cell chirped. He gestured for the sheriff to go ahead with his call, and Jerrod stepped out of the office to answer his. Don's number showed on the call display. "How're things going? Quiet in Montpelier?"

"Yeah, Dad. Once you legislators take off, things settle down."

Jerrod didn't laugh the way he normally would've after the typical jab. "You have any luck, Son?" Jerrod held his breath hoping Don had found information to help them figure out what steps to take next.

"Not much. I confirmed what you already know. Unknown suspect killed her husband in an apparent attempt on her father's life which two years later was successful. Nothing else. The Austin Bureau isn't investigating anything to do with her father."

"I hope I haven't made a mistake having you check into this, Don." Jerrod's hand scraped across his beard. He considered that he was about to kill the possibility of any kind of relationship with Jill, but he had to tell Don the rest of the story.

"Why would that be, Dad?"

"Crap." As Jack said, he was already screwed. "Might as well go the rest of the way."

"What are you talking about?"

The determined insistence in his son's voice told Jerrod he wouldn't stop until he got the rest of the story.

Jerrod related to Don what Jill told him about her father's note and the flash drive. He shared Jill's suspicion the drive contained information to bring down Greg Richardson, the lobbyist for the Texas gambling consortium.

"Have you seen the note or looked at the flash drive yourself?"

"No. I don't know where or if she has it with her. Safe to say probably not in the store or her house." Jerrod stopped pacing. "God, she wouldn't be so stupid to carry it on her, would she?" Sweat broke out across his brow. He tapped his thigh with his hand.

"You know her better than I do, Dad."

"She's a smart woman, but up until her husband's death, her experience with certain elements of our society has been limited to TV shows. She's endured a lot of stress in two short years."

"But you don't think she'd carry the evidence on her person?"

"God, I hope not. Don, I'm concerned you didn't find any record of her father contacting the FBI. If he turned over information, some evidence of an investigation should exist. And for you to turn up nothing? Shit. Not good news."

"If I pick up anything at all, I'll give you a ring."

"Yeah, and we didn't have this conversation. This morning before Jill told me, she made me promise not to talk with you, because she was afraid any inquiries you made would get through to the alleged corrupt agent in the Austin office. But I didn't know any of that when I asked you to find out about her family."

"It'll be okay, Dad. I was vague with my inquiries. Probably a good thing I didn't know all the details. I would've asked more specific questions that could've tipped off an agent."

"Thanks, Don." A ball of worry the size of Maine filled Jerrod's stomach.

"Let me know if you need anything else."

"Sure thing." Jerrod disconnected. Needing to finish his conversation with Jack, he returned to the sheriff's office.

The sheriff ended his call and glanced up at Jerrod, a quizzical tilt to his eyebrows. "So, you'll never guess who that was."

"Probably not. Why don't you tell me?"

"Mike Riley is a homicide detective out of Fort Worth. This was something in the way of a courtesy call. He wanted to let me know he planned to come up here. He's concerned about Ms. Barlow's safety."

"Well, hell. Based on what Don told me, we may need to be concerned."

"He was your call?"

"Yeah. He found no record of any kind of investigation in the Austin office regarding Jill's father."

"Hum. And you expected he would?"

"If what Jill's telling me is true, yeah. Supposedly, her father handed over incriminating evidence about the gambling consortium to someone in the Austin office of the FBI. Of course, all we've got is her word." Jerrod dropped into the chair in front of the sheriff's desk.

"She seemed pretty upset last night at your house. What's she normally like? You know, is she prone to flights of fantasy? Or is she grounded in reality?"

"Well, she decided to buy Mother's store damn fast, which doesn't fit with the idea of her being a cautious person. On the other hand, both her children seem to be solid citizens. Daughter's a marine biologist. Son's in the Army."

"Maybe the result of an attentive father," Jack suggested.

Jerrod clenched his hands at the mention of Jill's husband and how they'd worked out the child rearing responsibilities. "If you talked with Mother, she'd swear by Jill."

"That's the best recommendation you can get in this town. I'll operate from that. Do you want to meet Riley when he shows up? We can pool our information. If people are after Ms. Barlow, we need to develop a plan so we'll be ready for them."

"Yeah. Let's do that. Listen, I've been gone longer than I anticipated, and my absence was already going to take some explaining." Jerrod stood and angled toward the door.

"I'm glad we've finished with the leaf peepers. Having fewer visitors around will make it easier to notice any newcomers. We've had so many people here I don't know how we could've picked out someone acting suspicious." The sheriff closed the file where he'd made notes.

"Maybe we'll be lucky, Jack, and none of this connects to the mess in Texas."

"I hope nothing else happens, but we've got to keep alert in case. Does she have a gun?"

"Don't know. Wouldn't think so based on some comments she made right after she arrived." Jerrod's hand held the door open.

"Find out. Keep in touch."

Jack Hardwick might be a small town sheriff, but he was a knowledgeable lawman. Depending on what info Riley shared, maybe they'd figure out this puzzle. Jerrod didn't like things or people who screwed with the tranquility of his town and family. At this point, Jill Barlow was messing with his ordered life.

It was almost one-thirty by the time Jerrod knocked on her front door. "Hey, anyone home?" he hollered when no one came right away. He pounded again, beginning to feel uncertain about having left them for so long, but the three women together should've been fine.

His imagination jumped into overdrive. All the stories of one man overpowering several women and slashing them to death flashed through his super charged brain. *Damn..* He'd raised his hand again when the door jerked open, and he looked into Myrtle Bates' steely gray eyes.

"You got a problem, Jerrod Phillips? I know your mother brought you up with better manners than to stand on a body's porch and holler loud enough to be heard in Boston."

"Sorry." He pushed past her. "Is everyone still here?"

"Yeah, we've still got a lot of work left. Not that you've been much help," she chided.

No one but an old family retainer could make you feel five-years-old again. "I'm sorry." He realized he was repeating himself, but it seemed needed. "Have you eaten yet?"

"Nope, we kept plugging away. Why? You got an idea to feed us?"

Jerrod laughed. Thank God for Myrtle. "Yes, that's exactly the idea I have."

"And what idea is that?"

Jerrod glanced toward the stairs where Jill stood part way down.

"I want to take the three of you to eat. If you haven't had a break, you need one."

Karen walked into the front hall. "I vote for that. Give us a second to wash our hands, grab coats, and you've got yourself a deal." She turned and headed for the kitchen with Myrtle.

"I can't stop now. We're a long way from being finished." Jill continued down the stairs with a basket of laundry in her hands.

"You're not staying here tonight if Tommy doesn't get some sort of security system hooked up. Frankly, I don't see how he can pull that off. He'll come by the house today, but it will be tomorrow or the next day at the earliest, before anyone can begin installation."

"And your point is?" She set the basket on the floor.

"You don't have to finish everything today because you're not staying until the security issue is addressed. Now go get your coat."

* * * *

Jill stared at Jerrod for a moment. She couldn't believe his audacity. "Listen, Mr. Phillips. I decide where I'm going to stay. You're not the boss of me." Jill turned and rushed up the stairs. Who died and made him king? She glanced in the mirror at the red staining her cheeks. She'd regressed to her four-year-old self.

Jill pulled her coat out of the closet. A sick feeling settled in her stomach at the idea of staying in her house before she got a system installed and the back door repaired. She should've followed Gary's suggestion about security. Maybe this wouldn't have happened. Maybe she needed to leave Woodstock. The idea popped into her mind at odd moments of unquiet. Followed quickly by a question. Where would she go?

God, she was exhausted. They still had a lot to do before they'd have cleaned enough for her to stay, no matter about getting a security system installed. Her stomach rumbled. She hadn't had anything since Jerrod's oatmeal. Excellent at the time, but long gone. She should eat.

When she descended the stairs, she found her helpers bundled up and ready to take off. "Okay, ladies, Jerrod's right. I'm taking everyone to lunch. Where do you want to go?"

"Mountain Creamery?" Karen suggested.

"No argument from me," Myrtle agreed.

"Mountain Creamery, here we come." Jill pushed everyone through the front door.

"What about me? Don't I get a vote?" Jerrod's words filled the emptying hall.

"No. You haven't helped to the extent they have. Let's take my car, because we've gotten enough exercise for today." She started around the house toward the shed in the back.

"I'll drive. Everyone pile in with me. My car's out front and already warm."

That made sense to the group, including Jill. "But I'm paying," she insisted.

"Whatever you say."

Riding with him provided its own problems. She felt physically safer with him, but being in the company of Jerrod Phillips for any extended time raised concerns for her emotional safety.

Last night she'd been exhausted, and maybe she'd be so tired tonight she'd be able to fall asleep. At some point, getting a restful night would be difficult if not impossible lying in the room next to his. She didn't need the added complications, the fanciful thoughts, the longings proximity to him sent surging through her mind and body. Damn. She should be able to control her reactions to the man. Reactions embarrassing in their inappropriateness. If her mother were still alive, she'd be mortified.

# CHAPTER TWELVE

*Friday, October 12*

Sid Cranston followed his ritual process of lighting his cigar knowing his actions would piss off his wife. She tried to limit him to one a week, but that was crap. What she didn't know wouldn't hurt her. His phone buzzed. Damn. Hadn't gotten the stogie going good. A few more puffs while the phone continued its annoying noise.

"Yeah?" Cranston answered.

"Sid, we may have a problem."

They didn't talk often, but the distinctive twang of the Texas lobbyist for the gambling consortium rang through the airways. Sid saw him on news reports when the Texas legislature was in session supporting casino gambling as a way out of the state's funding problems.

"Talk to me, kid." Cranston puffed out blue-gray smoke. Greg Richardson's recent call providing Jill Barlow's location had been the first one in years. A second contact so soon meant some serious shit must've hit the fan.

The sound of Richardson grinding his teeth at the nickname brought a smile to Sid's face. They'd first met when Sid caught Greg in a scam when he was just a boy. Sid, now sixty-five, loved reminding Greg of their history. It made the younger man squirm. Showed him who was boss. "Spit it out."

"I just got off the phone with my FBI guy here in Austin. He says he happened to catch a call from a man inquiring about whether any investigations around Representative Stevens had begun," Richardson said. "Makes me nervous."

"Could your friend tell where the questions came from?"

"He told me the guy had an accent—like a Yankee. Said his name was Tom Sullivan."

"Take it easy, kid. We've got a Vermont connection, and I'm on top of that." He rolled his cigar between his thumb and forefinger.

"You are?"

The doubt in Greg's tone insulted Cranston, but he swallowed his anger. "Richardson, you still got the original in your possession?"

"Yeah."

"Good. I was damn disappointed our bill didn't pass last spring."

"Me too. We had a done deal. Then several of the schmucks decided to *honor* their fallen comrade. Oh, they're saying for sure next time, but I was certain with the state's money woes and Stevens dead, this was our time."

Greg's whiney tone made Sid nearly gag.

"Another year and a half until the next session. We've lost a lot of money," Sid's voice became more guttural. "You gotta grow a set and get it done next time." How much firmer could he be with this message?

"Yeah, I know, Sid. What about the Yankee my contact talked about?"

"Don't sweat the New England thing, kid. I've got that covered." Cranston disconnected without another word.

He puffed on his cigar. Next steps? Phillips should have gotten back to him by now. He'd turned out to be a big disappointment. *One last chance, Phillips.* Almost time to send Judson to Vermont to extract a different kind of payment for the debt from the worthless welcher if he didn't produce.

Cranston leaned back in his large leather chair and punched in the numbers to find out where Phillips stood. He spoke sharply into the receiver. "Mitch boy, talk to me. How's the search coming?"

Phillips' gulp was audible. He'd obviously recognized Cranston's voice. The right reaction.

"I don't have her purse, yet."

"Get it. If you don't find anything in it, grab the woman and make her spill where she's hidden the God damned device." Cranston pinched the cigar between his finger and thumb. He'd squeeze Phillips' balls if necessary to get this job done.

"Are you certain she has the flash drive you're looking for?"

"What?" Who the hell was this little piss-ant to question his directions? "You do what I tell you. Understand?"

"Yeah. Sorry, Mr. Cranston, anything you say."

"Okay that's better. Once you've got the device with the gambling info, *off* her. I'm tired of messing with this bitch." Cranston blew smoke circles toward the ceiling. A trick his grandkids loved. His daughter, like her mother, ranted to him about smoking inside. "Did you hear me, Mitch?"

* * * *

Mitch's mind boggled. He tightened his grip on the phone until pain shot through his knuckles. *Off her.* As if it was that easy. "Uh, yeah. Besides locating the drive, you want me to get rid of Jill Barlow." What the hell had he just promised? His gut twisted into a mass of knots.

"Good. Let me know when you get it done. You'll be reinstated at all of our casinos, your debt forgiven, and a healthy amount added in your account."

The buzzing in his ear told Mitch the Las Vegas gambler had hung up on him. Shit. What was he going to do now? Could he kill the woman? It didn't take him long to come up with the answer. Damn, if it came to her life or his, the broad was toast. His skin crawled like snakeskin molting. Mitch paced figuring how to do the deed before he sank into a kitchen chair.

*Shit, shit, shit.* He cracked his knuckles. A situation with disaster written in red six-inch letters. Breaking in was one thing, killing someone entirely different. He grabbed the bottle, poured a slug of whiskey and then set about developing a plan.

Maybe he'd put a drug in her drink, but he needed to talk with her first. He'd get her to go for a drive with him for some reason. After he got the flash drive or she told him what he wanted to know, he'd hit her over the head with something like a baseball bat. Evidence. What would he do with the evidence? Maybe burn the bat and the body.

Or he'd could cart her up to the mountains, and let the snows cover her. Nobody would find her until next spring, if even then.

He was getting the hang of this, like being on a TV cop show. Only he was smarter than those stupid screw-ups who got caught. Not long now, and he'd be sitting pretty in one of those beautiful halls of chance, making so much money, he'd never have to come back to Vermont. Yeah, his luck had definitely changed.

The tricky part would be getting her to ride with him.

He needed to get to know her better so she'd trust him to go in the car. She and his mother seemed to be thick. Maybe he'd spend time with good, ol' Mom. He'd get some ideas of how to grab Barlow from her. Not that she'd know she was supplying him with them. He laughed then raised the glass in a toast to his changing luck and swallowed, the burn a welcome reminder he was alive and anything was possible.

At this point, his plans were hazy, and he needed to firm them up if he wanted to have a snowball's chance in hell of getting away with the whole deal. He picked up his cell.

"Hey, Mom."

"Mitch? How nice of you to call."

"Yeah, well, what's up?" Maybe she'd have a heart attack, and he'd inherit his fair share. Then he'd make tracks for Europe and disappear so Cranston couldn't find him.

"Have you heard about the break-in at Jill Barlow's house?"

"Break-in?" He played dumb.

She went on to share all the details. He clamped his jaws shut to keep from saying,

*Yeah, I know all about it.*

"I've invited everyone to dinner tonight who helped with the cleaning."

"That's nice, Mom." He hadn't helped, of course, but he'd contributed to the reason for the gathering.

After disconnecting, his laughter burst out at his own cleverness. He'd stop in tonight. She'd never send him away.

A few minutes after eight, he knocked once and let himself in to find the others already gathered in the dining room. "Hey, Mom. Got room for one more?"

"Well, of course, dear. I always have enough for one more, particularly when it's you." She approached him for a hug before going to set another plate.

Mitch hated being here. His brother and mother always made him feel he wasn't good enough. At this point in the game, he figured he'd put up with anything to do the job for Cranston and get him off his ass. It'd be awesome to have enough money to move on with his life and out of this tourist town.

One thing he could always count on—his mother's good cooking.

"You know the old saying when it rains, it pours?" Jill placed her coffee cup in the saucer toward the end of the meal. "My battery died today—or sometime. Don't drive the car enough anymore, I guess."

"That's the pits. Like you need any more trouble, especially with the car," Karen said.

"The mechanic's coming Monday morning to work on it, which wouldn't be a problem, but I'm scheduled to pick up a couple of Robert Dillon's latest creations. I'd hate not to go. I've already contacted Ms. Cooper, and she's driving in from Litchfield for them Monday afternoon."

"Peggy frequently met me at the front door of the shop when I let her know I'd gotten in one of his new works." Anne sipped her wine. "She knows what she wants and doesn't mind the price or the inconvenience of coming. I offered to mail them. She always refused."

"That's what she did with me, too. I hate to call and tell her not to come."

"I can take you," Mitch said, jumping in before anyone else spoke. He'd lucked into his chance. Damn, it was all going to work out. The fact everyone knew she'd gone with him provided an added alibi. No one would be stupid enough to attack a woman when so many people knew you were together.

Jill and his mother's eyes opened wide. Jerrod's head cocked to the side. Even Karen and Myrtle made eye contact. Mitch had surprised them all.

"Well...thank you, Mitch." Jill took him up on his offer.

That's all he needed. When she didn't show up afterwards, he could act upset like everyone else. Perfect.

"His store is out past Quechee, Son."

"Isn't that near the restaurant you like?" Mitch asked his mother.

"That's right."

"We can grab lunch there after you do your business with Dillon, and by the time we get back, your car should be ready to go."

"That's nice of you, Mitch. If you're sure you have the time."

Jill glanced around at the others. Was she seeking their approval for the arrangement, or hoping someone else would step in? It wouldn't be his brother. Jerrod had mentioned earlier in the evening a court date Monday, and he didn't know how long the trial would run. Big brother was out of the picture.

Mitch permitted himself a smile of congratulation for jumping on the opportunity to get Jill alone. He spent the rest of the meal figuring out what he'd do with her body after he'd gotten the flash drive or information from her.

"You've been quiet, Mitch," his mother said when she served the Ben and Chuck's ice cream. "Are you feeling all right?"

"Sure, sure." Damn, he needed to be careful. Couldn't give anyone a chance to say he acted funny. "Great meal, Mom, and this is my favorite." He picked up a spoon and dug in.

* * * *

"Do you want a glass of wine before turning in?"

Jill slipped past Jerrod who held open the door of his house for her later that evening. She ignored the fluttering in her stomach when her arm brushed his.

"Yes, thanks. Wine would be nice." Probably not a good idea, given what even one glass would do to her inhibitions around him, but she'd take it upstairs.

"I'll light the fire, and we can sit here." Jerrod got the blaze going and went for the wine.

"All right." Jill held out her hands to the fire. So much for the promise she made to herself to go upstairs. "I'm exhausted." She sank onto the sofa.

"With good reason." Jerrod handed her a glass. "You worked hard today." His tone sounded full of warmth and admiration. "Add in the emotional wear and tear of the experience, and it's not surprising you're bushed." He sat next to Jill on the sofa. "I'm sorry I can't help you out Monday."

"You've done so much already. Your brother was kind to offer."

"Yeah, wasn't he? Not his usual role. He's always been focused on taking care of number one."

The bitterness in Jerrod's voice surprised her.

"Should you talk about him that way?"

"Maybe not. Mother and I've tried over the years to help Mitch, but he has a sickness. He gambles. Not that he's admitted he has a problem, which is the problem." He took a large swallow of wine, and then another.

"I'm sorry to hear that, Jerrod. My uncle killed himself because of the trouble he inflicted on the family with his gambling addiction. He's the primary reason my father fought against extending gambling to casinos."

"At first everyone loaned Mitch money whenever he got in trouble. I stopped when I accepted I was enabling him and not helping. For the moment, I've brought Mother on board, but if Mitch came to her in a panic, she might give in."

Jill nodded. "Hard to tell your children no."

"We can't let them grow up expecting to get everything they want, whenever they want. Life doesn't work that way. I'm not saying Mother and Dad treated Mitch that way, but he was the baby of the family. He changed after Dad died. Mother did the best she could. In trying to make up to him for the loss, she probably gave in to him more than she should." Regret deepened his voice.

Jill couldn't say anything to make Jerrod feel better so she sat in silence and enjoyed the flames crackling and jumping in the hearth. She glanced at him. The expression in his eyes made a warm ache grow in her middle. She yearned to let go and let someone else control her body.

That wasn't right. She straightened on the sofa. Unbidden, the kiss they'd shared on July Fourth burst into her conscious like the fireworks shooting across the sky that night. She was so out of line to have kissed him. George had only been dead two years.

Her gaze drifted to Jerrod's lips.

Jill hopped off the sofa. She had to end this evening. Getting involved with Jerrod? Not a good idea. Between the wine, circumstances, proximity, that's where she was heading. The glass clinked when she set it on the coffee table. No more alcohol to weaken her resolve.

"Good night, Jerrod." She made for the stairs.

He moved quicker, and met her before she'd gone up two steps. The warmth from his body sharing the step with her made her insides quiver.

"Do you have to go up?"

"Yes." Her breath caught. More words weren't possible. She clung to the banister to pull past him, but his arm flashed across the stairwell, brushing her breasts. They jumped to attention, the nipples hardening. Damn. His other arm circled her waist.

"Sit with me on the couch for a while longer. It's not late."

His breath whispered across her ear. Chill bumps shot up her back.

"I...I..." Damn, why did she have such a hard time telling this man no? His midnight eyes drew her into their depths. She'd drown in them if he moved nearer.

Oh, my God, how she wanted him to kiss her again. Her gaze sought his lips. She caved and met him half-way.

A groan started low in her middle when their lips met. His tongue softly brushed against the corners of her mouth. He paused, rested his forehead against hers, and drew away.

The need throbbing inside her matched the need in his eyes.

His hands tightened at her waist, and he lifted her up and off the stairs. This time when she kissed him, she reveled in the sensations flooding her body. He carried her from the stairs to the living room, lowered her to the couch, and followed her down. His knee brushed against her thigh. His kisses left her neck and trailed to her breasts. She arched into his touch. Her core stained toward his erection.

She caressed his broad shoulders and kneaded the muscles layered across his back. Her hands moved lower toward his firm rear. He shifted to reach down between them. If he touched her anymore, she might climax right then. My God, what was she doing? She should stop this madness.

And yet, she returned Jerrod's kisses like her life hung in the balance. A feeling of security and rightness rushed through her.

His hand slid up under her sweater and caressed her through the lacy bra. It hazily crossed her mind she was happy she'd put on a pretty one. The sensations caused from the tips of his fingers gently squeezing the nipple of first one breast and then the other took her out of her mind. She focused on her body. Embers burst into flame in her lower regions, and she pushed her pelvis up trying to get closer to him. The man consumed her with kisses and filled her with passion in a way she hadn't experienced in years. Jill pulled the shirt from his pants to touch his bare skin. Then he pulled her sweater over her head. He made quick work of her bra. The slight roughness of his fingers was arousing.

"My God. You're beautiful."

His voice, husky with need, warmed her more than his hands did. She fumbled with the buttons of his shirt, and soon she brushed it aside. Her fingers stroked his strong chest with its light covering of dark hair.

Jerrod stood and cold flowed around her. He scooped her up and deposited her on the deep pile rug in front of the fire. Its warmth added to the heat rushing through her blood.

\* \* \* \*

"I want you, Jill." Would she tell him to stop? Frustration to the tenth degree, but he'd be a bastard to rush her with all she'd been through. His gaze met hers, willing her to say yes.

"I...I... Jerrod, I haven't done this for a very long time." Her breath came in short gasps.

He cupped her face with one hand and ran a finger along her jaw line. "It'll be okay. I'll take care of you." She was so little he was afraid of crushing her, and he supported much of his weight with the other arm. He wanted this to be wonderful for her, but he wanted Jill in a way he hadn't wanted any other woman.

He kissed her, inhaling her breath before moving to her neck and sliding down to each breast, giving them their own attention. Her sighs and moans encouraged him and turned him fiery hot. After removing her shoes, he slid off her slacks, revealing a scrap of silk, which matched the missing bra. Before getting out of the rest of his clothes, he slid a condom from his pocket and placed it within easy reach. Her gasp when he pulled off his boxers brought his gaze to her.

"Jill, you have to know how desirable you are."

She shook her head from side to side.

"Then let me show you." He took his time, careful not to hurt her, waiting until his kisses, tongue, and fingers pulled moisture from her. Her writhing body told him she was ready before her words.

"Oh, God, Jerrod. Now. I want you now."

He slipped on the condom, and entered her with care. God, her tightness nearly made him explode. He struggled for control, pulled back, and then pushed in farther. When he retreated the next time, her hands on his butt urged him to return, and he plunged deeply into her.

Their rhythm came together and grew more frenzied. Rising to the peak, they soared over together in a splash of colors bright enough to put the fall leaves to shame.

Later he gathered her into the circle of his body, their legs entwined. Jill was responsive and giving. Jerrod couldn't remember a time when a woman had so stirred him.

Her hand trailing through his chest hairs had him planning an encore, but not on the floor. "I'm taking you upstairs. No need for you to catch cold."

"Jerrod. I'm not in the least cold." A soft chuckle bubbled from Jill. Her lips quirked up at the corners, the dimple peaked out. Her blush was endearing.

He smiled at her, determined to have his way. "We're still going upstairs to the bed." He pulled her up, but couldn't resist kissing her once more.

The shrill ring of the house phone made them both jerk. Jerrod rested his head against hers. "Let's ignore the damn thing." He pointed her toward the stairs.

"What if it's important?"

"Right now I can't imagine anything more important than us getting upstairs to my nice warm bed."

The annoying sound stopped.

"See not important."

The noise crashed into their ears again.

"What if it's Anne? What if she has a problem?"

"Do you have to be so responsible?" He shook his head. "If it's my mother, and not a matter of life or death, I may kill her." He grabbed up the handset, stopping the incessant noise.

"Hello. Well, I was almost asleep." Jill's chuckle drew his gaze, and he winked at her.

Her cheeks heated while she pulled on her pants and sweater. She collected her undies and shoes. Jerrod never took his gaze from her.

"Yeah, I can do that. Thanks for asking me… See you then." He disconnected. Then he stretched both hands over his head. If he felt any better, he'd touch the moon.

"Everything okay?"

He leaned over and kissed her. "It was Jack." Jerrod grabbed his own clothes and with one arm around her shoulder herded her toward the stairs. "He was checking to see if I'd be interested in a trip to Montpelier tomorrow. He has an in with one of the techs there and wants to try his hand at hurrying along the fingerprint results."

"I hope he can." Climbing the stairs, her hand rested on the banister.

"Have dinner with me tomorrow evening?"

"I have to work at the shop all day."

"You have to eat. We'll have dinner around 6:30, and then you can go back to help Sally with the rest of the night."

"You don't have to do that, Jerrod."

Damn, was she beginning to have second thoughts?

\* \* \* \*

*Saturday, October 13*

Not being a patient man, Jerrod spent the day tapping his fingers, tapping his toes, and tapping his knees. Sheriff Jack Hardwick did his best to light a fire under the fingerprinting process, but the waiting made Jerrod nuts.

"Jack, how about we drop in to visit Don? We can pick his brain to help figure out what the hell is going on in our town." And with the woman who'd bought his mother's store.

"Good idea. The day won't be entirely wasted then." They piled into Jack's official SUV and drove toward Don's office.

In the beginning, Jerrod had lumped Jill Barlow into the same category he reserved for his ex-wife. What a colossal error he'd made. Jill was a giving woman, kind to her employees at the store. She'd jumped in with her friend Karen on the historical preservation bandwagon, and brought a fresh perspective and new enthusiasm to their board of volunteers. Liz reported Jill gave it her all in Pilates.

"Hey, Dad, Jack." Don came out from behind the closed-door of his office.

"Do you have time for a visit?" Jerrod asked after exchanging slaps on the back with his son.

"Can you give me an hour? I've got to finish up a report."

"Not a problem. We can entertain ourselves." Jack and he walked outside.

"I'm going to head back and check on the fingerprinting situation one more time. Something might've popped."

"Go ahead. I need to stretch my legs and will walk around town for a while. I'll meet you here in an hour." Jerrod parted ways with Jack, crossing his fingers the tech might have found a hit.

He strolled down the street. His mother, the best judge of character he'd ever known, trusted Jill.

Anne had never cared for Janice. His mother didn't realize he'd detected her reaction. Did some sort of mother's sixth sense tell her Janice would kick him right in the teeth? Just what she'd done.

While he hated his children grew up without a mother, he was secretly grateful she'd died in a car wreck a couple of years after leaving her family. That seemed less harmful to the kids' psyches than knowing she'd abandoned them.

"Hey, buddy, watch it." A man grabbed Jerrod's arm and kept him from stepping in front of traffic.

"Thanks." Woolgathering wasn't a safe activity. He'd better find a café and grab a cup of coffee.

Java Joe's had outdoor seating, which Jerrod chose. The chill wasn't bad right now, and the noise on the inside could sometimes be deafening.

"What will you have, sir?"

The young woman looked to be straight out of high school. Maybe a college student working part time. "Coffee."

"How about one of our blends? The special today is Mocha Caramel."

"No, thanks. Plain. Black. Coffee."

"Back in a jiff."

And she was. Jerrod's first sip burned his tongue. "Damn."

Ever since Don and Liz had grown up, he'd ceased to consider them with regard to his relationships with women. He didn't think they'd known anything about the New Hampshire lawyer. She and Jerrod had been a safe convenience for each other. He'd never been the type to sleep around with more than one woman at a time. Thank God, he'd ended things with her in July.

After last night…well, he was afraid he'd made an emotional connection with the Texan. It was not one he planned to tell his children about. He sipped his coffee, which was still hot, but not blistering. What had he been thinking last night? Only that she came in a hell-of-a sexy package and turned him on in ways no one else had. That's what. Jill was damned desirable.

And vulnerable.

She appealed to his need to take care of others. Had they been wrong to make love? Was it too soon? She'd brought danger to his town, to his mother, and maybe even to Liz. He'd never risk them.

Better put distance between the beautiful Texan and him. He'd cancel the meal tonight, but he couldn't in good conscience push her out of his home until he was certain she'd be safe in her house. He'd been so damn crazy about the kids' mother before they married he'd have done anything for her in order to keep her in his bed.

Well, he wasn't a twenty-year-old kid anymore led around by his dick. He'd be strong for two more nights and one more day. Then she'd be back at her own place. He'd slow this whole thing way down.

Jerrod finished the last of his coffee and left a tip. On the way back to Don's office, Jerrod placed a call.

"Hey, Jill, something has come up, and I'm not going to make it back by supper. See you at home around nine thirty." He exhaled a long sigh of relief. He got her voice message.

Better this way, even if it made him a bastard. Getting over Janice had taken many years. When he did, he swore never to be taken in by a gorgeous blonde, regardless the size of her boobs. He damn sure wasn't starting now.

He stopped beside the sheriff who leaned against the front of Don's building, his arms crossed, his lips in a straight line.

"No luck yet." Jack said.

"Damn."

"Yeah. It was a long shot. We'll have to be patient." They went inside and Don welcomed them into his small office.

"Thanks for waiting. What can I do for you?"

"Come out and grab supper with us." Jerrod invited.

"I can do that. Let me get my jacket."

The smell of French fries and burgers greeted them when Jerrod followed on his son's heels into The Grill. He clapped Jack on his shoulder. "This'll be some good eating."

"Yeah. Not telling my wife about this meal. She's on me about my cholesterol."

"Eat salads tomorrow, Jack, to make up for what we enjoy tonight," Don suggested.

They settled into a corner booth and placed their orders.

"Back right away with those drinks." The waitress scurried away, silent in her rubber soled shoes.

"Did you come up here for anything special?" Don asked.

Jerrod glanced at Jack and back to his son. "Yeah, but let's wait until we get our food and won't be interrupted."

Don cocked his head. "Okay." He dragged out the word.

Conversation turned to football and the weather until the server returned with their orders.

Jerrod's mouth watered at the aroma of the burger and onion rings on his plate. He'd eaten half his burger before he brought up the subject he wanted to talk about with his son.

"Jack knows about the situation with Jill Barlow, Don."

"I wondered if I could discuss that issue. I haven't made any more inquiries about Representative Stevens. After you told me Jill suspected someone in the Austin office was corrupt, I've held off. If she has a copy of the flash drive, our next step is to convince her to give it to us so we can access the information."

"Don't hog the ketchup over there." Jack said.

"Sure." Don passed the bottle. "If it's the way she says and someone in the Texas office should've followed up, I'll talk with my boss. Stan will know how to handle things without putting her at risk."

"Riley, the Fort Worth homicide detective told me her Fort Worth home was broken into before her store or house in Woodstock." Jack paused to stuff several fries slathered in ketchup in his mouth before he went on. "Whether we can find the connecting dots or not, it's too coincidental not to be related."

"Dad, you've got to find out where Jill has stashed the flash drive so we can look at it."

Damn it. Just when he'd decided to cut back on his involvement with the woman, here was Don pushing him into her path.

"Shouldn't be hard to get her to come clean with her staying at your house." Jack polished off the last of his fries.

"She's staying with you? Thanks." Don nodded to the waitress when she left their tab then pulled his billfold from his hip pocket. "I'll get this, guys."

Maybe the interruption will side track his son, and Jerrod could avoid a response.

"Why's she doing that?" Don lay down enough money to cover the bill including a generous tip.

Damn. Jerrod tried a distraction. "That's way over the customary percentage." He nodded toward the money.

"Yeah, but she's a good kid, goes to college part time, and struggles financially. I do what I can. You were about to explain why Jill Barlow was staying at your house, Dad."

One of the reasons his son was such a good FBI agent was his tenacity. He dropped nothing of possible significance, whether or not anyone else agreed with him.

He glared at Jack. Why couldn't the man have kept his mouth shut? Jerrod had to say something to satisfy Don, or he'd never let it go. "I was afraid for her to stay by herself at the Woodstock Inn. Karen and Tim are too far out from town. I didn't want to involve Mother and possibly put her in danger. That left me."

"Good choice. We could have some random thing going on, but hell, I've never known this many coincidences not to have meaning." He slid from the booth, and waved to the waitress. "When's Ms. Barlow moving back to her place?"

Jerrod and Jack followed Don out of the restaurant.

"Monday." Jerrod said. "Tommy Tomlinson will come then to install a security system. She should be set after he's finished."

"Has Jennings, the real estate agent, contacted the owners about this plan?" Jack asked.

"He's tried but hasn't reached them. If they give us static, we'll deal with it then. Since you don't have the staff to station someone outside her house full time, Jack, we're out of options."

"Sorry, Jerrod." The sheriff shook his head.

"That's it then." Jerrod nodded once. "Thanks for supper, Son. We've got to leave so I can meet Jill when she gets off."

"Good luck convincing her to give us that drive, Dad. If you can't bring it up here, I'll drop down. Jack, great to see you."

He walked in the direction of his office. Jerrod and Jack climbed in Jack's SUV.

"Will she give you the flash drive?" Jack steered down the road toward Woodstock.

"Don't know. I'll give it my best shot. She's still deep in denial any of this has to do with her father or her."

"Hard to admit someone is out to get you. If she doesn't take this serious, I'm worried about her safety, and Riley in Fort Worth is so concerned he's paying us a little visit."

"Yeah, so you said." Jerrod's tone was sharper than he'd intended. What was behind the detective coming?

They rode in silence. Jerrod needed to convince Jill that turning over the flash drive would go further to protect her and her kids than keeping it hidden. Safety was the key to bringing her around. He'd take advantage of her staying in his house the next couple of days to make his case.

Be tricky trying to gain her confidence at the same time he resisted his desire for her. Of course, maybe all the problems would be resolved when the big snows hit. So far, they'd only had a light dusting by Vermont standards. The big ones could drive her away. They'd done so to other people.

The idea of her leaving him sat like a wet log in his chest. The weather might not be the deciding factor anyway. After she found out that he'd shared her story, she'd never want to speak to him again.

Sooner than Jerrod expected Jack pulled up in front the Woodstock Public Safety Building. "Thanks for driving. Sorry we didn't get more information."

"Yeah, but Don paid for our dinner." Jack chuckled and slapped Jerrod on the shoulder. "Anytime you can get your kids to pay for a meal, you're ahead of the game."

Jerrod nodded agreement, waved, and ambled down the walk toward his mother's —no. It was Jill's store.

\* \* \* \*

"Thought you and Jerrod were eating out tonight, Jill?"

"We were, Sally, but he left a message on my cell saying plans had changed, and he'd meet me at his house." Disappointment enveloped her at the news. She shouldn't expect to lean on Jerrod. He didn't owe her anything. They had nothing between them, except maybe a little old-fashioned lust, which embarrassed the heck out of her. What had she been thinking?

While she was glad for the evidence her hormones still functioned, she'd be wise to keep them from influencing her decision-making.

Easier said than done was a major understatement of the year.

At nine, Jill walked to the front of the store and turned the "Open" sign to "Closed." A dark shadow appeared in the window, and the door pushed in against her before she turned the lock. She sprang back, her heart racing.

"Hello, Jill."

What an idiot she'd been. Jerrod. "Hey." The word came out a breathless huff.

"I didn't want you to walk home by yourself." He did a quick survey from her shoes to the top of her head.

Two different messages sent by this intriguing man. His words said he wanted to keep her safe. In the depth of those crazy dark eyes, she read a different story. Her breathing quickened. She'd be a fool to trust the second message, regardless of what they'd experienced last night. That way led hurt.

"Thanks. Sally and I will be finished in a few minutes. Come on back, while I fix tomorrow's coffee pot."

"Hi, Jerrod. You providing escort service? Our Jill seems to attract bad karma." Sally threw the words over her shoulder, barely taking her attention from the computer screen.

"Seemed like a good idea, Sal." Jerrod leaned against the door jam.

"I'll be done in about ten minutes. Business has slowed down."

"It always does after Columbus Day. Traffic tapers off, and the first big snowfall sends the rest of the early tourists running." He settled into one of the wingback chairs.

Sally and Jerrod talked about the tourists while Jill pushed away the picture of him standing naked, talking on the phone after they'd made love. Now he seemed relaxed, one leg crossed over the other, an ankle balanced on his knee.

Ripping off his clothes to jump his bones didn't seem an appropriate reaction. Heat flooded her cheeks.

"Okay." Sally shut down the computer. "Got it done for another day." She angled toward Jill. "You coming down with something? Your cheeks are flushed."

Damn. "No, I'm fine." Jill grabbed her coat, handed Sally's to her, and dashed into the showroom. "Let's go. We've kept Jerrod waiting long enough."

Not any too soon for her, they stood on the sidewalk in front of the store. The air, cold and crisp like an apple, cooled her fiery cheeks. She and Jerrod walked Sally to her car and waited until the engine pinged away before they turned down Elm Street toward his house.

The silence sparked between them. He didn't take her hand.

"Do you want to stop anywhere? You hungry? I'm sorry for bailing on you earlier."

"No need to apologize. You've done more than I can ever repay. And I'm not hungry." At least not for food. "Sally and I ate frozen dinners. Nutritious, tasty, and not too many calories. Perfect."

"How about a glass of wine when we get in?"

"That'd be nice."

Jerrod pushed open the front gate and took her elbow helping her over the uneven path. Inside, he let go.

"I'll start the fire in the parlor then get the wine."

"Be right back." She headed upstairs. She was one lucky woman. Odd she could say that, given what she'd been through, but she'd found such a supportive group of friends in Woodstock. Moving here had definitely been the right thing for her, if not for the town. Despite the way she jumped at shadows when Jerrod came, she was doing well.

She hung her coat in the closet and slid out of her shoes, flexing her toes in the socks. It had been a long day on her feet. Feet that welcomed her comfy loafers. She opened the bedroom door and jumped back startled. Jerrod stood there a wine glass in each hand and a bottle under one arm. *Oh my.*

"I hope you don't mind."

Jill shook her head. "We can sit by the window." Sitting on the loveseat, she pulled up one leg underneath the other, and wished she'd worn something more glamorous or sexy than her slacks and sweater.

Did she want Jerrod to see her sexy? She cast a glance at him over the top of her glass. Well, yeah. But did he? He'd followed to her room. That had to mean something. Lord knew sparks combusted in the living room last night.

He made quick work of opening the bottle and pouring the wine. She cupped the wine glass between her palms, rolling it back and forth.

Jerrod's eyes narrowed, a slight frown appeared between his eyebrows.

"Jill, we need to talk about a couple of things."

That didn't sound romantic. Get a grip, woman. "What about?" She was proud how strong her voice sounded.

"Tell me where you've stashed the flash drive your father sent you.

"Why? It's safe where it is, and nobody knows."

"If someone tore apart your house, your store, and your Fort Worth home, it must be important."

"What do you know about my home in Fort Worth?" Jill hopped from the loveseat, stumbling in her haste to get away from Jerrod. Went to show letting your hormones rule wasn't a good idea. How ironic if she'd taken shelter with someone who's FBI son might know who killed her husband and father.

"Jack told me."

"How'd he know anything about my Fort Worth house?" Was the sheriff involved?

"Detective Mike Riley filled him in on what happened."

She gasped, her legs gave, and if the bed hadn't been behind her, she'd have slid to the floor. "Mike Riley." She grabbed her glass, swallowed too big a gulp, and coughed. Pushing away from the bed, she turned toward the windows on the front of the house and gazed down Elm Street.

A lovely town. What a mess she'd brought with her, scarring its tranquility.

Jerrod came up behind her. Her took her glass and set it along with his on the dresser. Still she didn't turn around. His hands ran from her shoulders down to the tips of her fingers and back up. He massaged her shoulders. She couldn't keep the sigh inside. Tension ran through every part of her body at any thought of her father or the flash drive.

What was it about Jerrod Phillips that she gave him so much power? She should still hate him for accusing her of such ugly things when she first arrived, but she'd gotten past dislike a couple of months ago. Now she wanted to lean back against him, let him fix the things wrong with her life, the way his massage took care of the tightness in her neck and shoulders.

Jerrod dropped his hands and stepped back before forcing her around.

"We've got to talk, and then I'll do more of that."

"Bribery?"

"Does it work?"

She eased toward the door.

"You gonna run off, Jill? I'll catch you."

"Trying to scare me?"

"Just the truth, which is what I need from you."

"I haven't lied to you, Jerrod."

"You damn sure haven't been honest with me. Or with Mother. Does Karen know about the business in Fort Worth and Austin?"

"She knows George and my father were both murdered." She gritted her teeth to keep her chin from trembling. She wouldn't fall apart in front of him. He couldn't make her say anything to put his family and her friends in danger. If she had to leave to keep them safe, that's what she'd do.

Damn, but she wanted to stay in Woodstock. Traitorous moisture formed, and she blinked to keep tears from falling. She loved living here. Loved her store. Loved her friends. Yes, she even loved the idea of something developing between her and this grim-visaged Yankee. Guess it wasn't to be. She walked over to the dresser and picked up the wine glass. Took a small swallow before she faced him.

"I want you to leave now, Jerrod. I'm exhausted, and I have to open up the store in the morning. Thank you for letting me stay here. Two more nights and I'll be back at my place and out of your way."

"I can't let this drop, Jill. Sticking your head in the sand is not going to keep you safe. You've got to talk. Tell me where the flash drive is. Let the sheriff and me look at it, and we'll figure out what's the best thing to do."

Jill set the glass on the bureau with more force than necessary. It hit the marble with the sound of a gunshot. "No one is figuring out what's best for me, but me."

"Damn it, woman. Where's the flash drive?"

"What flash drive?"

# CHAPTER THIRTEEN

*Monday, October 15*

"Mitch, I appreciate you driving me around today." Jill climbed into his truck. "Have you been to Dillon's studio before?"

"Nah, but Mom gave me directions. I didn't have anything else to do today anyway. Funny how things happen." One edge of his mouth turned up in what passed for a smile from Mitch.

"You can drop me off at the store when we finish. It's been crazy of late. I sure need things to get better."

If the situation deteriorated, she'd decided she'd have to find somewhere else to live. She'd learned a lot from this move, enough so she'd make it difficult for someone to follow, despite what Jerrod said.

Though he didn't know the reason, Gary had set up an offshore account for her, so she'd have access to funds if she had to split. Money not easily tracked. It wasn't enough she'd blocked her cell number from anyone she called. She'd pick up some of those throw away, untraceable phones. The idea of leaving made her stomach clench and her heart ache. She pressed her hand against her chest.

Mitch had been correct. They had no trouble finding her artist. They spent longer than she'd expected, and a light snow began to fall. Dillon had wanted to show her some new pieces he was working on. Mitch didn't seem to mind. She paid for his gas. It was the least she could do.

When they got to the restaurant, Mitch and she walked around on the outside. The cold wind on the balcony blew straight through her. The awesome view made her heart pump faster. Large white flakes swirled in the air.

"What a beautiful and unique place, Mitch."

"Yeah. I'm going in. Too cold." He pulled at the door and went inside.

*Well, maybe he's seen this before, but I haven't.* The water crashed on the solid granite and shared its power with her. She stood taller. Confident she'd handle whatever came her way.

Jill drew her coat around her closer, reluctant to end the experience. But return she must.

"Sorry I kept you waiting." Jill settled at the table the hostess led her to.

"No sweat. I started without you." Mitch tipped a beer bottle in her direction. "Want one?"

"No thanks." They ordered and Jill made small talk.

"Well, I vote with your mother about what a great restaurant this is. Thanks for suggesting we eat here." She slid her empty bowl away. "The squash soup was beyond delicious."

"Yeah, it's an okay place. You about ready to shove off?" he asked.

"Sure," Jill said. "I've taken a lot of your day already."

He didn't protest when she paid the bill.

"Say, don't we need to head back south?" Jill glanced through the back window of his truck when he pulled out of the parking lot and headed north.

"We could, but I know a short cut."

"Okay." She looked out the front window, the windshield wipers making short work of the snow. "Don't you love living here, Mitch? It's so beautiful. We almost never got this kind of snow in Fort Worth. Ice? Oh, yeah. A couple of times a year." A long sigh escaped. "This may be my favorite place anywhere." The idea of leaving ripped at her insides.

"I'd rather be in Vegas."

His words, swift and hard, startled Jill. Of course, many people liked the place, and Mitch had told her he liked to gamble. Everybody who went there wasn't involved in crime. Still it troubled her when she remembered what Jerrod said about his brother's gambling problems.

"Do you see the shows when you go?"

"Nope."

"What do you do then?"

"Gamble."

"The whole time?"

"Yep. Nothing like drawing to an inside straight, making it, and having the dealer shove a large stack of chips your way. God, nothing better in the whole world." His fingers tapped on the steering wheel.

"Do you win more often than you lose?" She realized the car was slowing down, and then Mitch pulled onto a dirt road. "Is something wrong with the truck? Why are we stopping?"

He didn't answer.

"I've got to get back to the shop. Peggy Cooper is coming around three-thirty for her crystal. Mitch, what are we doing?"

"Be quiet, damn it. I'm tired of your game of twenty questions. Now, we're going to play mine." He popped the gearshift into park. "Get out." He shoved open the door on his side.

What was going on here? Jill's heartbeat kicked up, and sweat beaded on her hands inside her gloves. Adrenalin shot through her system, making her struggle to control her feet and arms, and she stumbled getting out.

"I'm sorry if I made you uncomfortable with the questions, Mitch. All I was doing was making conversation." She stepped in front of the truck, glanced around. The dirt path ran back the way they'd come. In front of them, it led into the deep forest, which surrounded them. Why hadn't she paid attention? But this was Jerrod's brother. She trusted him.

"Now you answer my questions. Let's start with you telling me where the flash drive is with the gambling information on it?"

Jill's mouth dropped open. She stepped back. My God. Had Mitch been the one tearing everything up searching for the device? No, it couldn't be. Her fingers clutched the strap of her bag.

Mitch's attention fastened on her movement. "Purse, huh?" He snatched it from her, jerking her shoulder in the process. Fire shot down her arm, and she screamed.

"You want something to yell about?" His punch sent stars streaking across the back of her eyes. She lost her balance, fell, and rolled down the embankment. She came to rest against a tree and clutched her head to stop the spinning.

She gulped for a breath. Keeping her wits was crucial. Breathe. She needed to breathe. Liz's Pilates training came into play. Centering herself, she pulled air in expanding her chest, let the breath out slowly, tightened her stomach muscles, and focused on her body.

When he didn't find what he was digging for, he'd come after her.

She must pull herself together to run or fight. She didn't think she was cut out for the latter. Items plinked on the ground when he emptied her purse. This was her only chance to take off while he searched through all the stuff she carried. She took stumbling steps away from Mitch. The direction didn't matter. What mattered was getting as far away from him as she could.

Tearing sounds like the seams of her purse ripping apart set her body trembling. Mitch was almost finished. She only had a short time before he'd realize she was gone. Her speed picked up, and she stumbled farther down the incline, ducking through the underbrush, clinging to tree branches for extra support. She searched for signs toward a road, or path, something to lead her back to civilization. One thing was certain. She needed to put all her energy into escape.

"Jill. You bitch. Where'd you go?"

He was too close. His enraged shouts sent her heart zinging to her throat. The rustling of bushes sent another shot of adrenalin rushing through her system like a wild fire during the west Texas dry season. Playing hide and seek when she'd been a child had terrified her. She never enjoyed the game with the twins when she was a grown up mom. Now her stomach coiled in a tight knot of fear. Oh, thank God, a path. She slipped and slid over rocks down the incline, hoping it would connect to a river or creek and lead her to a village or people who'd help.

What was that? A shot? She skidded to a halt and ducked behind a tree. My God, was he shooting at her? The thrashing of someone moving through the forest carried through the clear air. She couldn't stay here. He'd catch her.

She ran, scooting behind trees and pushing through bushes. Her face stung where the twigs won the battle against her dash through the underbrush. Soft snowflakes brushed against her face. The snowfall increased.

Already her side ached, and her breath came in big, heaving gasps.

Just ahead, large boulders dotted the hill. Thank God. Jill crouched behind one of them. Leg muscles pinged, and despite the cold, sweat trickled down her back.

Silence. Except for her breath and the pounding of her heart. They had to hear it back in Woodstock. Woodstock. Where the hell could she go now? Who could she trust? Jerrod couldn't be aware of his brother's involvement, could he?

What was that? Off in the distance, a truck's engine? Yes. The sound became fainter. The truck must be going away. Mitch leaving? Was he going to abandon her out here? She cast a look around her.

Woods. Nothing else. She was out of her element. Shivers ran down her arms and legs.

She listened so hard she feared her ears wouldn't have any hearing left, but there were no more indications of someone moving through the underbrush toward her. Aside from an occasional plop of snow from a limb when disturbed by an animal, all was silent. Thank God. The occasional bird or squirrel didn't scare her. A shudder ran through her body at what else might be out there. God, she wanted to stay hunkered down surrounded by the relative safety of the boulders and cry her eyes out.

Giving up wasn't going to do her any good. Tears would have to wait until after she found help, otherwise she could die out here.

Not the way she'd imagined her life ending. She hadn't met her grandchildren yet. Not that she had any. The cold turned her feet to unwieldy blocks of ice, unwilling to do her bidding. Had it also affected her mind?

Grandchildren? Dear God. She slipped and screamed, falling over a dead tree. Her hand covered her mouth. Had she given away her location? She lay on the forest floor, listened, and concentrated on controlling her breathing.

Her leg hurt. She inspected her torn pants and the bloody gash down her shin. "Oh." The word escaped as a whisper.

Several inches of white flakes covered the ground. Though lovely, they made walking difficult. Her boots made a crunching sound when she pressed through a patch of snow. Snow clung to her hair, coat, and pants. More attached every time she fell to the ground or brushed against the trees and bushes.

The dampness intensified the cold, permeating to the marrow of her bones. Nevertheless, she trudged on. Lying down and giving up wasn't an option.

What's that? She squinted overhead. The sun peeked through a break in the clouds for a moment.

Thank God. Maybe now she could figure out which way to go. She knew Woodstock lay south and west of where she visited Dillon. Surely she'd reach something before dark set in if she headed that way.

The idea of spending the night out in the woods sent her stomach into spasms. She didn't have time to be sick. She must keep on. With dusk setting in around four, and full dark by five, dawn would be a long time coming. If, God forbid, she remained here after dark, maybe she'd make out the lights of civilization and walk toward those. If there weren't any lights? She pushed the scary notion away.

Jill placed one foot in front of the other and kept going, resolving to find a way out of the mess. By golly, she'd make time to buy the good quality cold weather protective ware Karen always talked about. The clothes she wore now weren't cut out to handle freezing temperatures for extended hours.

She'd never be caught unprepared again.

Her breath filled the air in front of her, more and more labored. She expended more and more energy to keep going. The muscles in her thighs and calves screamed from the exertion. The gash in her leg ached.

Would this forest never end, or was she moving in circles? *Oh, please God, not that.* She must keep going. Couldn't stop. Couldn't stop. Couldn't stop.

She took the next step but found nothing beneath her feet. Jill's scream sent birds soaring from their perches. She tumbled, and rolled down a hill, landing in a pile of bruised knees and elbows on asphalt. A road.

*Thank you, God.* With care, she forced her trembling legs to support her and limped in what she hoped was a southwesterly direction. She strained her ears for the sound of a truck. She'd have to jump into the underbrush to hide. Her resolution strengthened. She'd get out of this. She would see Ellen and Ethan again and have a chance to meet those grandchildren.

After what seemed an eternity, she dragged into a gas station in the small village of South Stanton. The sign over the door identified the Post Office for what must be a tiny berg. The clock on the outside wall said four forty-five. She'd seen no one else on the narrow highway. Not that it would've been called a highway in Texas.

"You have car trouble, ma'am?" A white haired man in coveralls called to her from the doorway.

"Yes. Yes, I did. Do you have any water, please?" If she didn't get something to drink, she'd pass out. He looked her up and down. She must be a wreck but probably not threatening. He spat, nodded, and gestured for her to enter his store. "Sure. Come this way. Bottle okay?"

"You bet." She drank the bottle half down before his words stopped her.

"Hey. Take it easy."

She let out a long breath. "Right. I can't thank you enough for this. I'm afraid I've lost my purse, and can't pay you. If you'd consider making a phone call for me, I can get someone to come here with money."

She dropped onto an overturned crate sitting next to a wood stove. Trembling spread from her legs through her entire body.

"Who do you want me to call?"

A moan slipped out when painful tingling like sharp toothpicks driven under her nails hit her extremities. Feeling began its slow excruciating return.

She hauled her mind back from the pain in her feet and hands. Who should it be? If she called Jerrod, would he believe her about his brother's behavior? But would the sheriff be any better? If law enforcement was corrupt, was Jack Hardwick up to his neck in it, too?

Karen and Tim if he'd come with her.

"Here's the number." She told him the only one she'd memorized. The cell phone—her brain—contained every important number in her life, but it was with her purse, back with the truck or Mitch wherever he was.

She clenched her hands into fists. God, if she had a gun she'd want to shoot him. Certainly threaten him, at any rate.

After a time, the storeowner held the phone out to Jill.

"How are you? Where are you?" Karen demanded. "Everyone's worried. Sally started calling around when you weren't back by three."

"I'm okay. A little worse for wear, but okay. Honestly, Karen, I don't know where I am. It's called the Village of South Stanton. Don't tell anyone else.

"But everyone is worried about you."

"Karen, please." Jill gulped back a sob. "Can you come get me? I'll explain when you get here. The gentleman who called can tell you where we are." Despite her best efforts, her voice cracked and wavered, and if she weren't careful, tears would flood the store.

"Absolutely. Put the guy back on. Tim and I'll get there as soon as we can."

"Thank you."

"But you'll tell us what's going on when we get there, right?"

"Yes." She'd have to trust someone. If not Karen, who?

The owner of the gas station left her alone. She was grateful, because God knew she didn't have a clue what she'd tell him if he'd started throwing questions her way. He'd shown her the facilities, gotten her a cup of hot tea, and kept to himself. The downside was she had lots of time to think.

Why didn't Mitch keep coming after her? She was relieved when he stopped, but still his behavior was odd. Was Jerrod involved? His brother was up to his armpits with the gambling consortium and maybe the person in the Austin FBI. Was Jerrod's son involved? Would Jerrod believe her when she told him? He didn't seem close to Mitch, but did "blood is thicker than water" apply here?

Should she tell Sheriff Hardwick? He seemed to be a good man, but still, these were his people and his town. She was the interloper.

Mike Riley. That's who she'd call. He'd know what she should do. Despite him telling the sheriff about the murders, she trusted him. The sound of an engine and tires on the gravel outside made her jump. Rather than check who it was, she hid in the bathroom. Paranoid? Absolutely.

Knocks on the restroom door. "Jill, it's me—Karen."

Thank God. Jill unlocked the door. Fell into Karen's arms. Tears finally streamed like a Brazos

River waterfall in the spring.

"You're okay. I've got you. Tim's here, too." Karen comforted Jill like a baby. Exactly what she needed.

"Thanks," she said when she could force words through the slowing tears. "I'll owe you forever. Please pay the owner for a bottle of water, a hot tea, and the phone call to Woodstock."

"Sure. Tim." Karen looked over her shoulder. "Can you take care of that?" She set Jill a little away from her. "Let me see how bad it is."

Jill smothered a moan when Karen's hand squeezed her bad shoulder.

"Oh, God. You're really hurt."

"It's nothing. Scratches and bruises. I'll be okay." Doubt filled her when a crescendo of pain coursed through her body. From her hurting head, pain spread to her shrieking shoulders, past her knees to her aching ankles and feet. Feeling returned and it hurt like hell.

"I have a first aid kit in the car. I need to look at some of those gashes." The concern in Tim's voice said more than his words.

"Thank you both for coming." Damn, the tears flowed again. She gritted her teeth. No. She wouldn't cry any more.

"Come on. Let's go home." Karen led her out to the car.

On the dark ride back to Woodstock, Jill told them about the trip with Mitch, his attack, and how she'd fled through the forest. Frankly, she considered finding the gas station a freaking miracle, because she had no clue where she was.

"Mitch hit you?" Tim made Karen drive while he attended to Jill's hurts, fashioning a sling for her shoulder.

Jill found instant relief when he slipped it on, and breathed easier.

"That's how you got the bruise on your face?" Tim had bought ice from the service station. Jill held it against her cheek, while he treated the worst scratches she received coming through the forest. Constant stinging accompanied Tim's words. "We've always known he was the bad seed, but damn I've never imagined this. Did he tell you what he wanted?"

Ah. The million-dollar question and a decision to tell the truth or not. Did she trust these two people? She must. She had no other options. By the time they walked into the Livingstons' living room outside of Woodstock, Jill had shared the whole lowdown with them.

"I'm sorry I didn't tell you at first. It never entered my mind I'd bring trouble with me. I wouldn't have come if I'd suspected."

"Sweetie, this is not your fault." Karen took one of Jill's hands into both of hers. "You can't stop other people making bad decisions. Let's get you something to eat and figure out what to do next."

God, she was lucky in her friends. Surprised at her hunger, she gobbled down Karen's homemade vegetable beef soup while they discussed strategies.

"Jill, we need to call Sally to let her know you're okay."

She agreed and Karen told the assistant enough to keep her from worrying. The truck had broken down. The second call was to Fort Worth detective Mike

Riley. It took a while to find the number. They left a message, and almost an hour later, he called back. He promised to be on the next plane to Hartford.

What about Jerrod? What to tell him was the next giant question Jill needed to deal with, but before she decided what to do, a car rumbled up out front.

"It's Jerrod. Do you want to talk with him, Jill?" Tim turned to her.

Best to get this over with. She nodded. "I'm sorry to put you in this position, but will you stay with me, Tim?"

"If you want, of course."

"There's no *of course* here. He's your best friend."

"Yeah, but you're Karen's best friend. What she wants takes top billing in my family."

Jill hugged him and squeezed his hand. "Thanks." With the back of her hands, she wiped at the tears, still quick to fill her eyes. She would not cry in front of Jerrod.

The pounding on the door was loud enough to wake the neighbors if any lived close.

"Tim. Tim. You in there?"

No mistaking Jerrod's deep bass.

"Don't break it down." Tim opened the door. "Come in."

"My God, Tim. I've been crazy. Sally told me Jill's here. Is she all right? What happened?" The cold air blew through the room as Jerrod entered.

"I'm here." She stepped out of the shadows. "I'm fine." Jill pulled in a big breath, and released it slowly as she spoke the words. They were a long way from the truth.

When Jerrod started for her, Tim stepped between them.

"Hang on a minute, buddy. Stay where you are, okay?"

"What the hell's going on?" Jerrod stopped, and looked at Tim. "Have you lost your mind? Let me talk with Jill for a minute."

"Go ahead."

"Alone."

"No." Jill's heart constricted at Jerrod's look.

"What's the matter with your arms and your face? You're definitely not *fine*."

"It's nothing." Her hand covered the angry bruise the bathroom mirror had shown already turning blue and purple.

"I nearly lost my mind when Mother called saying Sally didn't know where you were. She'd expected you by the middle of the afternoon at the latest when Tommy brought by your new keys and the instructions for your security system."

He paced the living room, raking a hand through his hair.

"No one knows where my brother is either. We checked with Dillon and the restaurant. People at both places reported you'd come and gone." He stopped. "What the hell's going on?"

She didn't want to tell him his brother had attacked her and maybe shot at her. The words stuck in her throat. What if Jerrod were involved? She hoped not. Please, God, don't let Jerrod be a part of this.

"Talk to me." His legs spread. His arms crossed his chest, not a man to be ignored.

In a soft voice with little inflection, Jill told Jerrod about the day. How nice Mitch had been with the extra time at the studio. The lunch at the restaurant. The events on the small side road off the highway, including the fact she'd heard what might've have been a shot. She touched briefly on the hurt to her shoulder when Mitch grabbed her purse and the punch, which sent her rolling down the ravine and may have saved her life.

Jerrod blanched when she told him how Mitch hurt her, but maybe his reaction didn't mean much. Before he could say anything, his phone rang.

"Excuse me." He turned away to answer. "My God... That can't be... No, I'm at the Livingstons... She's here... Yeah, I'll wait."

Jerrod turned to them. His lips clamped into a grim line. He looked at Jill.

"What is it, Jerrod?" Tim asked.

"Officers found my brother. Dead. One bullet through the back of the head."

Jill's knees buckled, and before she knew it, she was sitting on the floor. Her stomach pitched. She fought throwing up. Mitch had scared the hell out of her out in the woods, but she didn't want him dead. My God. Had the shot she'd heard been the one that killed him?

Had someone else been in the woods? What was going on?

Karen helped her stand.

"Sheriff Hardwick is on his way out here and he doesn't want you to leave until he gets here." Jerrod said.

"Leave! Where the hell would I go?" She paced a tight circle. Her fingers clenched into fists. Her heart raced.

"I don't have an ID, credit cards, cash. Your brother took my purse and tore it up." Her anger exploded at him. "So you tell me, Jerrod Phillips. Where am I to go?"

# CHAPTER FOURTEEN

*Monday, October 15*

Jill morphed into a true damsel in distress, wringing her hands and pacing like a caged tiger in the Livingstons' kitchen. She wanted the sheriff to return her purse or what remained of it anyway. If not her purse, at least her phone. She needed to call Gary and Michelle.

She hadn't done anything wrong, but something didn't sit well in the way Jerrod worded Hardwick's request that she stay. Neither did the way Jerrod looked at her when he first heard the news about his brother's death.

Just as she'd feared. Blood was indeed thicker than water.

Jerrod didn't speak to either the Livingstons or her. Tim and Karen stayed close by her side. She'd hate if this situation drove a wedge between the two friends, but she wasn't responsible. Mitch was.

When Sheriff Hardwick arrived, he was nothing but business. Had she left this morning with Mitch? Did they go to the glass artist and to the restaurant by the waterfall? Questions he knew the answers to, so he must've been testing her.

Jill explained the best she could. They'd driven out north after lunch, because Mitch told her he knew a short cut.

Karen grew more and more agitated during the sheriff's questioning. Tim gave in the third time she pulled on his arm and muttered in his ear. "Okay. Hold on,

Karen. Excuse me for interrupting, Jack," Tim said. "I'm not sure we care for the tone of your questions. Does Jill need a lawyer present?"

"Not unless Ms. Barlow has something to hide."

"I resent your implication, Sheriff. I'm sorry to hear Mitch is dead, but he abducted me. Drove to a remote area, wrenched my purse off my arm, pulled some muscles in the process, and slugged me. Aren't I the victim?"

She touched the still tender skin. "The only good thing about him hitting me is when I fell down the ravine I dropped out of his sight and had an opportunity to run. Engrossed in searching my purse, he didn't notice." She threaded a shaky hand through her hair, pushing loose ends behind her ears. God, she wanted the interrogation over.

"Everything I need for my life is either in the purse or on the cell. Did you at least find the phone?"

"I'll ask the questions, Ms. Barlow."

Where'd the nice friendly law enforcement officer she'd dealt with on earlier occasions go? "Well, Sheriff, if you're going to act that way, I do want an attorney." She put her hands on her hips and planted her feet. He couldn't push her around.

"Damn," Jerrod muttered. "Jack, take it easy for a minute here. Jill doesn't like guns. We talked about gun laws when she first arrived. Karen, Tim, you remember? You were both at Mother's when I crashed the dinner."

"It doesn't matter, Jerrod. You better come with me, Ms. Barlow."

Jill shuddered and bit her lips to keep from crying. She wouldn't let on she was afraid. She had nothing to feel guilty about. She hadn't killed Mitch Phillips, and surely, any evidence they found would prove as much.

"Do you want me to call someone?" Karen walked over and put an arm around Jill.

"Yes. Michelle Smith. Tell her I need the best criminal lawyer she can locate in case the sheriff here decides to charge me with something. Try getting the number off Michelle's firm web site first. Contacting Ellen is a last resort. She's a walking phone book, but I'd rather not worry the kids about this unless it becomes necessary."

"Jack, she should see a doctor." Tim raised his hand to emphasize his point. "I only gave her minimal treatment. I know you'll see she gets what she needs."

"I'll take care of it, Tim." Hardwick turned to her. "You want to put your coat on before we head out?"

Jill slipped her free arm into the sleeve, but still a groan escaped. "I didn't make up the story, Sheriff." She noticed his gaze narrowing. "I took several spills out in the woods, not counting what Mitch did to me."

"Do you have to take her in?" Jerrod followed them out on the porch, his cell in his hand.

"She's the last person to see your brother alive."

"Only if she killed him, and I don't believe she did."

Relief coursed through Jill at the steel in Jerrod's tone and his words. She stood straighter, her heart a little lighter. This would work out somehow. Her natural optimism, having been tested, reasserted itself.

\* \* \* \*

Jerrod didn't say anything to Jill. She'd probably not want to talk with him anyway. He clenched his hands, determined not to care about her.

"You following along?" The sheriff looked at Jerrod.

"Yeah, I'll meet you back at the jail."

First, he had things he needed to attend to. He called Don and filled him in on the turn of events. Jerrod's voice broke when he described Jack driving off with Jill in the back of his car. *How'd that not-caring thing work for you?* Jerrod needed to pull out of the funk he'd fallen into, or he'd be of no help to his mother or Jill.

"I'm sorry to hear about Uncle Mitch, but frankly, we've known the chances were he'd come to a bad end if he never dealt with his gambling. Jack doesn't seriously consider Jill Barlow killed him, does he?"

"I don't know, but he's taken her to jail. He says he wants to talk with her. She made a request for an attorney."

"Good for her. Are you helping her locate one?"

"No, she wanted Karen to reach her attorney in Fort Worth and get a recommendation from her."

"Why didn't she ask you? You know everyone in the state who'd be best for this kind of thing."

Jerrod was too embarrassed to tell his son the details. "Let's just say, I'm not her favorite person right now." Jerrod envisioned a huge hole opening in his life if she never talked to him again. Maybe if he hadn't tasted the way things could be with Jill in his life...but he had. While he didn't regret their night together for a moment, the experience would make it harder to bear her loss.

* * * *

"Took care of Phillips like you wanted, Mr. C."

"Good, Judson. Good. Did you get the woman? What about the flash drive?" Sid blew smoke rings. He propped his feet comfortably on his desk, and contemplated how nice it would be to have this wrapped up,

"No such luck. She took off through the woods."

Sid's feet hit the floor. God damn. Surrounded by incompetents.

"I followed for a while, but lost her trail. Hell, Mr. C, the weather stinks up here. If you want me to stay, I gotta get some warmer duds."

"Did you leave any evidence?"

"Nah. Single shot to the back of his head. He didn't see it coming. I watched him go through the woman's purse, but he didn't find anything. I heard the sheriff took Barlow in to the jail."

"Looks like she'll need a lawyer. Stay in the state, but get out of Woodstock. Strangers are easier to spot in small towns. I'm sending Peterson to try something. If it doesn't work, you two have to grab Barlow. Make her tell you what she knows about the flash drive. Get the information any way you choose. She's got to tell us where the damn thing is.

* * * *

Jerrod held his mother while she cried. He hadn't wanted anyone else to tell her about Mitch. News of his death would spread quickly through their community.

"I feel such a failure. Somehow, I should've been able to help Mitch. It must be my fault. Did I not show him enough love or give him enough attention? Oh, God. Your child…your child is not supposed to die before you," she said through sobs.

He rocked her in his arms, at a loss for what to say to make her feel better. His mother wasn't to blame for his brother's bad decisions any more than Jill was. Mitch made his choices and failed to accept he had a sickness.

Jerrod suspected when everything became known, they'd find Mitch had been killed by someone to whom he owed money. He didn't tell his mother Jack had taken Jill in for questioning. He didn't see how that would make her feel any better.

Don was on his way down from the capital. Liz cancelled classes for the next week to be available to help, and she planned to stay with her grandmother. He was glad, because things were going to be grim for a while, and he needed to focus his attention on figuring out what happened between his brother and Jill and why.

"Hello, Dad."

He hugged Liz. "Thanks for coming so fast."

"How's grandma holding up?"

"About what you'd expect. If she asks for me, I'm going to the jail. I've got to talk with Jill." He kissed Liz on the check.

Jerrod reached jail faster than was legal. He pulled open the main door and stormed past Carla to the sheriff's office. "Jack, bring her out so I can talk with her."

"No. For all I know, you want to hurt her because you think she killed your brother. My duty is to protect her."

"You know that's shit."

"What I know is that, according to you, some scary guys probably want to harm her. This is the best place for her, and she's agreed. You're not her lawyer." Jack Hardwick walked to the door and held it open. "Go home, Jerrod. Look after your mother."

"Will you tell her I tried to see her?"

Jack nodded.

"I'll be back in the morning."

"Unless her lawyer's here, I'm still not going to let you talk with her."

* * * *

Jill's watch told her it was the middle of the night. Because of the bars on the window, the moonlight filtered through like something from an old gothic novel. A chill rushed over her. Despite the unlocked door, despite her agreeing with Jack to stay in the cell... My God. She was in a jail cell.

She stood, wrapped the blanket around her shoulders more snugly and began making the rounds of the cell, which she'd done earlier when the sheriff first put her in. Of course, it wasn't round. It was a square. Was she then making the "squares" of the cell?

God, she was close to losing her mind, but she needed to keep occupied. Moving would keep her from becoming stiff, but her shoulder ached, and her cheek hurt. The pain medicine the doctor left for her hadn't kicked in yet. True to his word, the sheriff made sure a doctor attended to her various cuts and abrasions, but they continued to sting. Bottom line, she'd hurt for some time. Great.

If she couldn't sleep, she'd play mind games to help the time pass.

Games and songs kept eluding her. The only image Jill's mind provided for contemplation was the way Jerrod looked at her when he first heard about his brother's shooting. For a moment, at least, he'd believed her capable of killing Mitch. Of course, that opinion fit with his first impression about her—she'd murdered George and her father.

How could she let herself care for the man after such an awful beginning? Jill faced the truth. She did care for him. During their night together, he snagged her heart with fingers capable of holding with a firm and gentle touch. Now he'd let go. The ache in her middle was physical, a hole she didn't know how to fill. She made her way back to the cot, doubled over with pain, and determined not to cry any more.

* * * *

*Tuesday, October 16*

The first of the morning light flowed through the window, making her blink her eyes, gritty from a lack of sleep. The night seemed exceedingly long. Lying on the cot, one arm thrown over her head, Jill remembered other long nights.

One when a raging temperature threatened to cook Ellen to a crisp. They'd rushed her to the hospital, blasting through stoplights. Adrenalin shot through Jill's system. Her arms jerked. Her fingers tightened on the remembered steering wheel.

The time Ethan fell from a tree in the park after George and she had expressly told him to stay out of it. He broke his arm in two places and required surgery.

The last night she sat with her mother before she died. Jill swallowed the tight knot in her throat. Crying wouldn't make it better.

The first night after George's funeral. Emotions suffocated her, and the room spun.

The night she learned of her father's murder. Despite pushing her hands against her eyes, tears welled. She hiccoughed against them.

All of them, exceptionally long nights. Jill dragged in one deep breath after another. Filled her lungs until they hurt. Exhaled the hurt.

Long nights she had survived.

When she next woke, bright sunlight poured into the cell. She sat, ran hands through her hair and stretched. Every muscle ached.

Did Karen contact Michelle? How long before her lawyer arrived? Had Karen reached her attorney without talking to Ellen?

Either way Jill accepted the time had come to let the kids know what was going on for their own safety. She didn't worry about Ethan. He was on an Army post and could use a gun. But Ellen was in the Keys, with lots of tourists. Easy for bad guys to mingle. Yes, she needed to talk with her children. What should she tell the lawyer? She told Karen and Tim everything. Well, maybe not everything. No one knew the location of the flash drive. The safety deposit box must remain her secret.

"Good morning, Ms. Barlow. I'll take you to the facilities, and then I'll bring your breakfast."

Deputy Clara Hicks had been kind last night, getting Jill an extra blanket. Jail cells were cold, and after her trek through the forest, Jill doubted she'd ever be warm again.

"Thanks. Do you know if Sheriff Hardwick heard from my lawyer?" She followed the deputy down the hall.

"I don't. When he does, I'm sure he'll let you know."

"Okay."

"Are you still hurting? Do you need more extra strength ibuprofen?"

"Yes, please." Jill planned to keep the painkiller in her system, so she'd be able to function without the pain overwhelming her. "Oh, and do you have a rubber band?"

"Sure. Be right back."

Hardwick had offered to let her stop at her house for anything she needed, but she reminded him her stuff was at Jerrod's, and they both nixed the idea. The deputy supplied a toothbrush and the requested band, which went a long way to making Jill feel almost human.

"Thanks, Clara." Jill ran her fingers like a comb through her hair and pulled it into a ponytail. No telling where she'd lost the velvet ribbon she wore when she set out yesterday morning. After breakfast, she went back to walking around in her cell. She tried different patterns, not content to "square" it the way she'd done last night.

"Ms. Barlow."

Jack Hardwick came through the hall door toward her cell. "Is my lawyer here?" Jill glanced at her watch, ten-thirty. Maybe it was still too early.

"A Mr. Charles Callahan called. You can expect him right around noon."

"Thank God."

"And Ms. Barlow, Jerrod Phillips came by last night and wanted to see you."

"Oh?"

"I wouldn't let him."

"Why?"

"Told him my job was to keep you safe, and I was afraid he'd want to hurt you for what he thought you'd done to his brother."

Jill stepped back. "He wouldn't do that, and besides I didn't—"

"No, I don't think you did either. But if what Jerrod told me about the lobbyist in Austin is true, and you're holding damaging information on him—well, this seemed the safest place for you for a while."

Jill's hands flew in front of her mouth, shocked to hear his words. A pain burned from her stomach up through her throat. Jerrod told Jack about Richardson. He'd promised not to tell. Well, in reality he promised not to tell Don. Her palms rubbed her thighs. She hadn't explained clearly enough she meant for him not to talk with anyone.

"Thank you, Sheriff."

"I'll be back." He left.

God, what a mess. Her fingers curled around the bars of the cell. She would have to leave Woodstock. She needed one of those non-traceable phones. Then she'd call her kids, tell them she loved them, was going away, and not to search for her. Disappearing would be the only way to keep them safe. Leaving was the hardest thing she'd ever contemplated in her life. Pain greater than all her body aches struck her heart. She sank to the floor.

She swallowed to keep from throwing up. A hole the size of Carlsbad Caverns, opened in her heart. Leaving her kids might well kill her. If it would keep them safe, it would be worth her agony.

Thank God Gary set up the offshore account. She'd have access to funds.

She rose and went back to pacing and planning what she needed to do to escape the lovely town. She plotted and brushed at the tears, which insisted on forming and sliding from her eyes.

She loved her life here. The store. Anne. Sally. The artists she'd met and other business owners.

The fall was beautiful, like she remembered. Her fists pounded on the back wall of the cell. Leaving before winter ended would prove Jerrod was right about her. Jerrod. She'd miss him, and the possibility of something developing between them.

How could anything grow when he thought her capable of shooting his brother? How could she ever trust him when he believed that about her? Was she responsible? While she didn't pull the trigger, if she hadn't come up here… If whoever killed Mitch wasn't connected to the gambling consortium, maybe his death couldn't be laid at her door.

Did anyone ever get killed in Woodstock, Vermont? In this idyllic village? She paced and chewed her lower lip.

\* \* \* \*

Straight up noon, a door slammed. Jill jumped up from the cot.

Sheriff Hardwick strode toward the cells. "You've got visitors, Ms. Barlow." He opened the door. "You can meet with them in one of our interrogation rooms."

"Thank you." She followed him down a hallway. He held the door for her to go through. Three men crowded the room—Jerrod, a stranger, and a man wearing a white western hat, which he removed.

"Detective Riley. You came." She flew across the room and flung herself at him.

Mike Riley's arms closed around her for half a second before he released her. "Yeah. I had some vacation time and have always wanted to see New England. Your friends in Fort Worth are concerned about you, Ms. Barlow. You look like you could use help." His hand rose toward her cheek. "That hurt much?"

Jill stepped away from the tall Texan, a blush rushing up her neck. She nodded. "I'm sorry about just now. It's heartwarming to see someone from home." Her gaze skittered across Jerrod to land on the stranger, a gray-haired man in a suit, carrying a briefcase.

"I'm Charles Callahan. Hear you need a lawyer."

She walked forward and met his outstretched hand. "Thanks for coming, Mr. Callahan." She glanced around uncertainly. "Have you all met each other?"

"As they arrived I made the introductions, Ms. Barlow," the sheriff said. "I'm assuming you want to talk with your lawyer first?"

"Yes, please." She glanced toward Jerrod and spoke to Riley. "I hope you don't mind."

"It's what I'd recommend, Ms. Barlow, and I don't mind at all," he said.

His Texas twang brought her a comforting reminder of home. She breathed a little easier.

"We can visit later." He placed his hat on his head.

She nodded.

"Let's give them space. Detective, Jerrod, this way." Hardwick ushered the two men out, closing the door behind them.

Jill turned to the lawyer. "How do you know Michelle, Mr. Callahan?"

"Please call me Charles, and may I call you Jill? How do I know, Michelle? Well, uh, I'm a first cousin twice removed or some such thing. You southerners are always more particular about that. We say cousins."

"That would be Michelle. She's always talking about her relatives."

"Why don't you sit down and tell me what's going on. Looks like you've run into some trouble."

Jill raised a hand to her cheek where a bruise throbbed.

"Anything you say will come under attorney-client privilege, so don't hold back. That's the only way I can help you." He settled in a chair on the far side of table, and pulled out a legal pad enclosed in what appeared to be rich brown leather.

Another decisive moment. Jill had already told Jerrod and Karen about her father's note and the flash drive. At this point, what was the harm in bringing in one more person?

She sat. In crisp, spare tones, Jill told Callahan the story starting with her father's note, break-ins in Fort Worth and Woodstock, Mitch's behavior yesterday, her escape through the woods, hearing the shot, and ultimately finding what stood for civilization in South Stanton. She concluded with the sheriff bringing her in, and his words about wanting to keep her safe. It appeared at first, Hardwick considered her a suspect in Mitch's shooting, but not now. She whooshed out a long breath, relieved to have gotten through the retelling.

Callahan listened quietly, made notes, and only a few times interrupted with a question.

"I don't see any reason you can't walk out, if you wish. Unless you want to stay here."

She couldn't spend the rest of her days hiding in the jail. Did she feel safe on the outside? Not exactly, but her house and work had new security systems installed.

"I want to go home. I know I didn't kill Mitch, but being in here makes me feel dirty."

"One more thing, Jill." He glanced down at his notes. "I believe I missed you saying where you put the flash drive."

He looked at her, his eyebrows raised, expecting she'd share the information. Jill should trust the man Michelle sent. And yet… Her breath stopped.

Paranoid. She was, with good reason, paranoid. Why did Callahan need to know where she put the flash drive?

She gulped in a quick breath, stood, and backed toward the door. Couldn't let him know she was suspicious.

He rose and followed her around the table.

"I didn't mention it, and you don't need to know, Charles. Thank you for coming. I feel so much better. Oh, by the way, do you know how Michelle's little dog is doing? The last time I talked with her, she was worried about him."

"Well, uh. He's fine. He was barking in the background when we talked."

"Good." Her voice betrayed a squeaky sound. Maybe he wouldn't notice. She turned from him. Her fingers closed on the doorknob.

Over her head, a large hand flattened on the door holding it closed. "You should tell me where the device is, Jill. You want to be safe, don't you?"

Callahan stood close to her. The heat from his body radiated outwards, threatened to burn her attempts at escape. Her palms grew moist, and she wasn't sure she'd be able to turn the knob. Her breathing hitched up. This couldn't be what she suspected. Michelle sent this man. Didn't she?

"Tell me where the device is." He whispered low in her ear.

The hairs on the back of her neck came to attention like cadets drilling at Texas A & M.

Damn, she should be safe in jail.

"Thanks for coming, Charles." By God, she'd bluff this out. Help lay on the other side of the door. She stepped back, turned the handle, and pulled. The door didn't budge. "Gee, it seems to be stuck. Can you help me open it?" She glanced at him, batted her eyelashes in a pure Texas simper.

Purple rage and frustration glared from his distorted face. "Damn it, woman, tell me where it is." He reached for her with both hands.

The moment he let go of the door, Jill tugged with every ounce of strength. It flew back against them. They lost their balance. She recovered first and dashed through.

"Sheriff, Sheriff." She yelled in her college cheerleading voice while she flew down the hall, aches forgotten. Where was everyone? She heard footsteps behind her, but didn't stop to turn around, raced through a door at the end of the hall, thankful it was unlocked.

Detective Riley and Jerrod sat on a bench with cups in their hands. They rose at her precipitous entrance.

"Thank God, I found you."

"What's the matter?" Riley stepped toward her.

"He's not real."

\* \* \* \*

Jerrod reached Jill first and couldn't resist pulling her to him. He didn't know what her relationship to the detective was, but, at the moment, he didn't care. When she'd run to the Fort Worth man earlier, a sharp pain struck Jerrod in the middle of his chest. Jealousy?

"What do you mean?" he asked. She leaned into him, breathing fast.

Jill didn't act as though she was involved with anyone else. She'd never have let them make love, if that was the case. He'd begun to recognize her fear of appearing to do something inappropriate.

He shoved his personal issues aside. She needed him focused. After barely touching the bruise on her cheek, he reluctantly set her a short distance away.

"What do you mean?" Jerrod repeated. "Who's not real?"

"Callahan," she sputtered, and tears began to pool.

"Didn't your attorney back home contact him for you?" Riley's eyebrows drew together.

She shook her head, wiping her eyes with the back of her hand.

Jerrod looked at Riley. What the hell was going on?

The door slammed open so hard, it cracked against the wall. Jill jumped behind Jerrod.

"Guys, we may have a problem." Sheriff Hardwick stopped. Drew in a quick breath. "Glad to see you're here, Ms. Barlow," he said in a calmer voice. "Where's Callahan?"

"I left him down the way." She gestured toward the hall.

"What alerted you, Sheriff?" Riley asked.

"A Mr. James Russell called, claiming to be her lawyer. He said mechanical problems with the plane delayed him, and he wouldn't arrive until late this afternoon."

"Send your deputies after the imposter." Jerrod's voice held an edge he normally used only in court.

"Already done. I'm glad to see Ms. Barlow in here. Neither of them were in the interrogation room, and I was afraid... Well, it's a load off my mind to see you here." He held out a cell in a plastic bag to Jill. "This yours?"

She nodded, and reached for the phone.

"My guys found it when they went back to search the scene in the daylight. I'd return it to you, but it's evidence."

Jill's arm dropped by her side in apparent resignation.

"We found it underneath the remnants of your purse. Snow shouldn't have affected any fingerprints. Do you want to call your lawyer friend in Fort Worth? Ask what the name of the guy is she's sending you. You can use my office phone."

They all trooped down the hall.

First Jill called Karen to get Michelle's number. Then she phoned her attorney. "Hey, Peg. Is Michelle in the office... Probate, huh? Maybe you can help. Do you know the name of the lawyer she contacted for me... James Russell. Okay... No. No problem. Thanks. Tell her I'll be in touch."

"Who the hell was Callahan, and how did he find out about this?" Jerrod searched the faces of those seated in the sheriff's office. "Did you tell him things about the gambling consortium?" Jerrod used his interrogator voice, demanding she answer.

Jill nodded. "But if they sent him he already knew."

"What made you suspect a problem?" Riley's fingers tapped a rhythmic beat on his leg.

"He was way too insistent I tell him where the flash-drive is, and he didn't know Michelle doesn't have a dog. She's allergic and can't be around them."

One of Jack's deputies stuck his head in the room. "No sign of the attorney, Sheriff."

"Thanks. Is Clara running his name through the Vermont Bar Association directory?"

"She's working that angle." The deputy closed the door.

"Can Jill go home?" Jerrod kept an arm around her shoulder, and she didn't pull away, for which he was grateful.

"Apparently my jail is no safer than anywhere else. You have my apologies, Ms. Barlow. I was trying to help. As you know, you've always been free to go," Jack said.

Jill nodded and sank against Jerrod. He kept his arm around her waist for support.

"This isn't over, Ms. Barlow. Whoever is after the flash drive is damned determined. If my department can do anything to help, please let me know."

He faced Jerrod. "We're continuing to pour through the evidence. We'll figure out what kind of gun the assailant used to shoot your brother. You know we'll do our best to bring in the culprit."

"Thanks, Jack." He looked over at the detective and down at Jill. "You okay if Riley comes along with us?" She nodded.

* * * *

Jill showered at Jerrod's house and changed into fresh clothes. With her head high and her shoulders back, she went down the stairs to see what was next. A "next" always followed.

The aroma of coffee and bacon led her to the kitchen. Jerrod and Mike rose, but she waved them back down.

"Can I fix you one of these?" Jerrod lifted in the air what looked and smelled like half a bacon and egg sandwich.

"It's good, Ms. Barlow, and you need to eat to keep up your strength." Riley suggested.

"After all this, you can call me Jill, and I'm calling you Mike. Yes, Jerrod, please, fix whatever you're having. I'm starving. After a gallon of coffee and something to eat, I'll be fine." If she repeated her mantra often enough, she might begin to believe her own words.

Jerrod lit a fire under the skillet, and Mike poured her a cup of coffee. Not bad being waited on by two attractive men. And they were. Jeez, where'd that crazily inappropriate thought come from? *Maybe because everything is in chaos.* She needed space between her and the walking nightmare her life had become. Who could help more than two handsome men?

"How much do your children know about any of this?" Jerrod skillfully flipped the egg.

The crackling sound made Jill's mouth water. She sipped her coffee. "Just how their father and grandfather were murdered." She shook her head. "I didn't find Dad's note or the flash drive until after I arrived here. I've only seen them once, when they came for my birthday, and I didn't want to ruin the visit by telling them. It didn't seem to be the sort of thing to share in a note or email."

"Mayo okay?" Jerrod held up the jar.

She nodded and watched him slap the sandwich together.

"Jerrod and I agree you should tell them, Jill." Mike got up and freshened his cup.

"Why? They'd only worry, and they can't do anything."

"I know my kids would want to know about this situation." Jerrod set the plate in front of her with potato chips piled beside the sandwich.

"I'm trying to keep them safe." She shook her head, released a long sigh, and made herself eat. "Um, good." Popped a chip in her mouth and followed with the strong, black coffee. "A couple of more bites, and I'll be a new woman."

No one said anything while she ate half the meal. "So what was your point about my kids?" She spoke into the silence.

"Knowledge is power, and if you want to keep them safe, you need to clue them in on what's going on. And why." Jerrod reached over and snagged a chip. "Thanks."

"You're welcome. Help yourself. I'll never finish all of them." She raised the cup, took a sip, and peered at him over the top. "So did you tell your son after you promised not to?"

Jerrod stood, walked around the kitchen, stopped, and leaned against the counter. "I'd already talked with him before you warned me not to. I was concerned about you. I believed, and still do, he could help." He looked at Mike.

"It's good he did, Jill. Because although we've run into some negative consequences, we've learned the Austin Bureau didn't investigate. And if your father turned over incriminating information, a record of that should exist—"

"What do you mean *if*?" She hated her screechy tone.

"Hear me out." Mike leaned toward her. "That they didn't is damning evidence something rotten has been going on."

Jill rested her elbows on the table and dropped her head into her hands. God, did everyone know about the gambling consortium? More and more her options were narrowing to one. She'd have to run.

Jerrod came over to where she sat, and he knelt down taking both her hands in his. "Jill, where's the flash drive? Let's look at it, because that'll help us determine who in law enforcement to give it to. Don's boss can give us some guidance with that."

She pulled her hands away, stood, and pushed her chair under the table. She picked up her plate. "Anybody want the leftovers?" The men stared at her. "No takers, huh?" Determined steps carried her to the sink, and she dumped the scraps down the disposal. The loud gurgle when she turned it on jarred the otherwise quiet kitchen. "Thank you for the meal. If I heard correctly, my house has a new back door and a security system. Do you have the keys?"

"Yes." Jerrod nodded.

"If you'll get them for me, I'll go on over." She left the kitchen. The men followed. "I appreciate you putting me up for so long." She turned toward the stairs. On the second step, Jerrod grabbed her arm. She looked down at his hand and met his gaze. Out of the corner of her eye, she saw Mike move closer.

Jerrod dropped her wrist.

"I'm going upstairs to pack my things, and if you'll get my key and instructions, I'll get out of your hair."

"What about the flash drive, Jill?" Mike stopped at the bottom of the staircase.

"It's safe where it is." She turned her back and climbed the stairs.

"Hell."

"Damn."

# Chapter Fifteen

*Tuesday, October 16*

"What the hell do you mean, it didn't work?" Sid Cranston's blood pressure zoomed. His head might explode at this report of yet another failed attempt to deal with the woman. Judson told him the scuttlebutt in town was that Barlow was at the jail and needed a lawyer. Sid had been certain Phil Peterson could carry off the impersonation.

"She told me everything about her daddy, Richardson, and the flash drive. Things were going great, until she got antsy when I pushed for the location of the storage device," Peterson said. "Mr. C, she's smarter than some broads. We were in one of the interview rooms in the jail, and I couldn't get away with strong-arming her."

"It's critical to get hold of her and the unit." Sid nearly bit through his cigar. Damn, did he need to go to Vermont?

"Judson and I have a plan, Mr. C."

"Tell me." Sid re-lit his cigar and took a deep drag.

"Nobody will recognize him, so he's going to play tourist in Woodstock and trail her, figure out where she's going and when. You know, what her pattern is. When we've got that, we can make a believer out of her. She'll give us the flash drive."

Sid hung up, feeling considerably better about the situation. He leaned back in his soft leather desk chair in his office. Blue rings circled upwards while he puffed on his cigar. No matter how his doctor told him he should quit, it wasn't going to happen. He reached for the phone again. Shit, he'd talked to Richardson more in the last couple of months than in all the previous years they'd worked together.

Greg picked up right away. "Hey, Sid. Got good news?"

"Yes and no, kid. We've eliminated several places Barlow could hide the damn flash drive. You had her Fort Worth house searched, and I've taken care of where she lives and works in Vermont. We've also eliminated her purse."

"Car?"

Damn he hated when Richardson was right. His people overlooked her vehicle. "Good idea, kid. I'll get my guys on that right away. We're still clear in the FBI office?"

"Yeah, we're square."

"Good." Cranston ended the connection. This was going to work out. He'd get Peterson and Judson to check out the car first. Maybe they'd find it there, and he could put this whole thing behind them. A little less than a year and half before the Texas Legislature would meet again in Austin, and they'd finally get their casino gambling bill through. He smiled in anticipation of the dollars rolling in.

\* \* \* \*

*Tuesday, October 23*

Mitch's funeral took place a week after his murder. Jill attended but she sat in the rear and didn't go to Anne's house afterwards. The whole town showed up at First Congregational Church, mostly out of respect for Anne, and the rest of the family. Mitch hadn't endeared himself to many.

After the services for George and her father, Jill couldn't face another funeral gathering. Every person in Texas behaved like the bereaved needed to hear from them. Well, she hadn't.

She sent flowers along with notes to both Anne and Jerrod. Nobody in the Phillips family would want to see her. She bore responsibility for Mitch's death.

Another light dusting of snow fell overnight. To hear everyone talk, the big one was only days away. The forecasters projected a storm headed their way before or right after Halloween. Jill looked through her winter clothes. The fabrics proved more than adequate for the short term, bone-chilling blue northers of Fort Worth, when temperatures dropped from sixty-five to twenty-three degrees in a matter of hours.

The deep freeze never lasted more than a couple of days, followed by moderate weather. But here? It was past time for a shopping expedition to get the right clothing so she could survive the long Vermont winter. Jerrod Phillips would learn she was made of tough stuff.

Jill walked out the front door of her house and toward the pitiful excuse for a garage. She seldom drove anywhere much and looked forward to taking Karen on a road trip. The shed door stood partially open. She pulled it back the rest of the way. Grey light didn't do much to illuminate the shed, but her driver's door stood open.

"Damn how careless. I hope the battery is okay." She peeked in the open car door. The seats had slits cut through the leather and stuffing was strewn onto the floorboards. Chill bumps pebbled along her spine. She gulped back a scream battering at the roof of her mouth. Her fingers curled into fists. If she hadn't worn gloves, she'd have cut her hands with nails digging into the palms.

Her stomach pitched. She pulled her cell from her pocket yanked off a glove, and punched in the sheriff's name.

"Woodstock Public Safety, Clara Hicks."

"This is Jill Barlow, Clara."

"Can you speak a little louder, Jill."

"I—I need to talk with Sheriff Hardwick, please." Silence. Damn. Hadn't she made herself heard?

"Sheriff here, Ms. Barlow. What can I do for you?"

"I think I've had another break-in, not that it took much to get into the old shed. My car door is standing open, and the seats have been vandalized."

"Where are you right now?"

"Still in the garage."

"I want you to get to your house. Do you think you can do that, Jill?"

"Umm." Could she leave the relative security of the shed?

"I'll stay on the phone with you."

"Okay." She peeked into an empty yard. With the cell clamped to her ear, she made a mad dash from the garage straight for her house, expecting at any moment someone would grab her. When would this stop? She let herself back inside.

"I'm in the house, Sheriff. I've locked the door and set the security system."

"Good. I've sent people your way, and I'm right behind them."

"Thanks." She disconnected, took several deep breaths and gulped a glass of water before putting in a call to Karen explaining they'd need to reschedule the trip.

"Oh, my God. Not again. I'm coming right over. I don't want you to be by yourself."

"No. Stay at home. You don't need to worry. Reinforcements are moments away, and I promise you I'm okay." Not that she could tell that by the speed of her heart rate. "I'm okay." She repeated the words to calm herself as much as Karen.

"How did this happen? Didn't Jack assign one of his deputies to drive by the house?"

"He did. I've seen the car." Noises outside drew her to the front window. "I've got to let you go, Karen. One of the patrols has pulled into the driveway, and the sheriff's right behind him."

"Keep me posted."

Jill went to greet the sheriff and his deputy. It would be an understatement to say she was relieved to see them. Because it was broad open daylight, this intrusion spooked her.

"Thanks for coming, Sheriff." She led them to the shed. A shiver ran across her shoulders. Jill relived the moment she stepped into the cold, possibly killing air. She'd felt like a spotlight focused a target on her back the whole time she ran to the house.

After a quick check, Hardwick showed her the disabled car alarm. "No telling when someone tampered with this."

"I drove last week sometime."

"You haven't seen anything suspicious, Satterfield?" the sheriff asked the patrol officer.

"No sir. I'll check with Burns who has the night shift, but he hasn't said anything." The young deputy went back to his car.

"Hope you've got good insurance, Ms. Barlow. I'd say repairs are gonna cost you a pretty penny. Damn." He hit his hat on his thigh. "I expected you'd be okay here with our official cars keeping an eye on you. I'm sorry."

"At least they didn't try to get in the house." She couldn't stop shaking.

"You know if someone tries that, we'll get him, because you authorized your security company to immediately notify our office if a breach occurs."

She nodded. Small comfort. Her stomach pitched with rapidly growing fear and dread.

\* \* \* \*

*Wednesday, October 31*

A week and a half had passed since Mitch's funeral. Liz said her grandmother was managing. Jill understood. Pain welled in her middle and shot up through her throat, where it gagged her. How you went on after the loss of a child, albeit a difficult one, she couldn't imagine. She'd only talked with Jerrod once. He was sticking close to his mother. He expressed relief at hearing the deputies continued to make drive-bys of her house.

Mike Riley returned to Fort Worth after the funeral, promising to keep in touch and requested she do the same. He was a nice man, a good man. She'd never told him how much she appreciated his coming to Vermont when she called. Despite

Mitch's murder and the business with the vandalism of her car, miraculously, things returned to normal, whatever normal was for her. She'd even been able to get Mrs. Cooper's sculpture to her. Officers found several pieces unharmed in Mitch's truck.

She went into work several days a week but never closed at night alone, and she developed a habit of frequently looking over her shoulder. Mary Ann came back to the shop. Jill found comfort in knowing if she left Woodstock, Mary Ann would help Sally. Jill resumed her Pilates sessions, which helped her deal with stress. The trick¬-or-treaters added to the ordinariness of her life.

Working with Karen on Historical Society events took on a familiar feel, a simple existence, similar to the "normal" life Jill lived in Fort Worth. Before all the tragedies struck. A lifetime ago.

She gave in and told her children about the break-ins at her Fort Worth house, the store, and her rental property.

"My God, Mom. What were you thinking? You should've told us when these problems first surfaced."

"I'm all right, Ethan."

"I can get emergency leave and come up there."

"Absolutely not. You already took time when your grandfather died and for my birthday. Wait for Thanksgiving. If you can only come one time, I want you here for the holiday."

"You can count on Ellen and me being there, Mom. In the meantime, I'll check with the sheriff to make sure he's doing everything to keep you safe."

Halloween night brought the snows.

* * * *

*Thursday, November 1*

After Jill opened the store and turned on the coffee, she called Karen. "Can we set out at noon today? I've got to get warmer clothes, or I won't get through this winter." Jill prayed staying the whole year proved a reality.

"Works for me, but then when have I ever turned down a shopping trip, particularly one involving spending someone else's money?"

Her laughter was contagious and Jill joined in.

"Sally comes into the store about eleven forty-five. We can leave after that, or do you think the snow will keep us from going?"

"No. It's already slowed down."

"Good. Can we lunch along the way?"

"Sure. I'll pull up in front at noon and honk. Be ready to run out, so I don't have to hunt a parking space."

"Great. See you then."

Jill was glad Karen drove. When ice came down in Fort Worth, which occurred more frequently than snow, literally, everything closed down—businesses, schools, courts, even trash collection. That left her with little experience handling a car in snow conditions. With education and practice, she'd get the hang of driving in the white stuff, which she'd heard was easier than ice. Karen could give her a lesson on the way back today.

At twelve, a horn blared in front of the store. Jill glanced through the window and waved. A delighted fluff of anticipation swirled through her. This would be a fun day.

"That's Karen. I'll check with you this evening, Sally, to make sure Mary Ann's still coming in to help close up." Jill grabbed her shoulder bag, buttoned up her coat, and headed for the door.

"Don't worry, Jill. You'll be exhausted after shopping with Karen. Relax and enjoy. See you tomorrow."

"Thanks, Sal." Jill pulled the door behind her to the tune of the chimes which she'd had replaced after the break-in. She hurried across the sidewalk and climbed into Karen's four-wheel-drive. "Where are we going?"

"I'm taking you to my favorite place to get winter clothes. It's in in Lebanon, New Hampshire."

"But that's another state."

Karen's laughter bubbled out. "Sorry, I couldn't resist. I knew how you'd react. I did, too, when I first moved here. Tim talked about going somewhere in the next state and plan to come back in one day. States are so small here in New England, it's no big deal. We're used to driving for the entire day and not getting out of Texas. Up here in that time, we've crossed four or five states."

"I need to get out on the roads more so I can get used to the difference in map scale. How long does this trip take?"

"Twenty minutes or so, depending on the traffic and the state of the roads. You'll love this store. It doesn't appear to be much from the outside, but they always have the latest and greatest in technology where warm clothes are concerned. Style's not bad either."

"This may be an occasion when warmth trumps style." Jill shivered and redirected the vent more toward her.

"We'll get you fixed up. You know you must always carry extra blankets, water, and gas during the winter. Tim insists on our cars having all that."

"I never gave it much thought, particularly since I haven't had time for many road trips."

"We're pretty rural up here, and you have to be prepared for whatever happens. You wait, we'll get you winterized."

When Karen and Jill left the store, both were loaded down with bags. Despite the new boots, one foot scooted out from under her. She caught her balance before landing on the parking lot.

"Be careful. We've had more snow come down. Those boots of yours are good, but you can still take a tumble." Karen opened the rear door and they loaded in their bags.

"Crank up the heat, Karen," Jill said as soon as they were on their way. "The temperature must've dropped."

"I wouldn't be surprised. Late afternoon, almost dark now, add the snow and—" Karen glanced at the temperature gauge, embedded in the rearview mirror.

"Wow, it's down to twenty-five. I didn't realize it was turning this cold tonight, but we'll be fine."

"Shopping was fun, Karen. A relief not to worry about anything for a while. Probably didn't need those fuzzy earmuffs, but they were so cute, I couldn't pass them by."

"You'll be glad you bought them. Just you wait. You know what they say about us up here? We owe more money on our snow blowers than on our cars."

Jill burst out laughing, and Karen joined in but her laughter died in an abrupt huff.

"What the hell is that guy behind us doing? The roads haven't been cleared yet, but he's driving like he's on a race track, for God's sake."

Jill looked over her shoulder. A large truck hugged their tail.

"I'm slowing down and pulling over a little, so if the stupid man insists on passing he'll have space."

The tires of Karen's car rumbled on the edge of the road. Jill grabbed the overhead door handle. Metal scraped. The truck hit them. Their SUV lurched and lost traction. Karen pumped the brakes, and steered into the slide.

They were too far-gone. Jill's heart rate ratcheted up. A scream surged through her clamped jaws. The car skidded off the road. Pain shot down her arm. The seat belt gouged her shoulder when they plummeted down an incline. A sickening crunch sounded as the hood crumpled against a tree. Had she passed out for a moment? Jill forced her eyelids to open. Thank God for airbags. Her door popped open. Rescue. No. A man in a gray ski mask held a knife in his hand. Oh, God. Was he going to kill her? Adrenalin shot fire down her arms and legs.

He hacked her out of the seat belt. She slid out and dropped on to the ground.

Another masked man hauled Karen out and half-carried her toward the front of the car. Jill closed her eyes against the horror. This couldn't be happening again. Not again. God help her, now she'd put Karen in danger. A moan slid from deep within.

The man holding her dragged Jill toward Karen and his partner.

"Barton's awake."

Damn. They knew who she was. A trembling began in her middle and worked its way toward her fingertips. She needed to pay attention to everything. The mask muffled his voice, but it sounded like he had a cold.

The man with Karen held a gun in his hand. Terror shot ice through every vein in Jill's body. She tried to yank away, but the man shoved a knife at her and sliced down her face. The warm blood welled, making a stark contrast to the cold of her skin. She whimpered at the sting and the horror of what was happening. Was he going to cut her to pieces?

"Now, you listen to me, Barlow," Gray Mask said. He coughed a couple of times. "Damn." His hand dug into her arm, cutting off the circulation. "My boss wants the flash drive. You'll turn it over." He glanced at the other man. "Show her what will happen if she doesn't follow our instructions."

The man in the black mask shoved Karen and aimed his gun. Her whole face grew white and filled with dread. She backed up, her hands held in front. "Please," she whispered.

"Don't." Jill yelled and struggled against the man who held her. She jerked at the sound of the blast. Her scream pierced the late afternoon air. The smell made her nostrils twitch.

No sound came from Karen before she slumped to the ground. Oh, my God. Had they killed her? Blood oozed from a wound in her arm. Jill stopped breathing for a moment. If Gray Mask hadn't been holding her, she'd have collapsed. Her legs unable to support her.

"You follow our instructions when we call or your friend's dead next time." The man said through a hacking cough.

He let go of Jill's arms. She collapsed on the snow-covered ground and prayed her lungs would start functioning and Karen wouldn't die. The two masked men left to hurry up the incline. She needed to see the license plate, but her legs refused to work, and she dropped back onto the ground. Doors slammed. Tires scrunched in the snow, and the engine revved before they sped away.

She crawled to Karen. Unconscious. A large bump swelled below her hairline. Jill gathered her wits. First things first. Stop the bleeding. *Damn, this looks bad.* Karen's upper arm oozed blood from the front and the back. Jill pulled the scarf from around her neck and twisted the material around the wound, tying a knot. Karen groaned. Was it too tight?

The stinging of her face got through to Jill, and she groaned. The slow drip of blood ended in stark red spots in the snow before melting. Her head spun, but she couldn't pass out. They needed help. She pressed her gloved hand to the place on her cheek.

Gritting her teeth, she fumbled in her pocket for her new cell, always kept on her body since losing the one when Mitch grabbed her purse. She pulled up Sheriff Hardwick's name. Thank God for coverage.

"Please come. A truck ran us off the road about ten miles northeast of Woodstock. I think on Highway 4." Her breath hitched. "Karen's been shot. Hurry." Tears clogged her throat. She couldn't say anything else. She'd kept in her terror, but now the sobs pushed their way up from her gut. What if Karen died?

"Ms. Barlow."

Hardwick's voice pulled her back from the darkness.

"Jill. Hang on. I'm putting on one of our deputies. She'll talk with you. We'll be there."

"Jill, this is Clara Hicks. Can you tell me where Karen was hit?"

"Arm." She bit her lip to get control. "Tried to stop bleeding."

Karen carried blankets for emergencies. This qualified. Jill struggled to stand again. Her legs didn't want to function. Up at last, but her knees wobbled.

"Clara, I'm putting you in a pocket… Want to get the supplies from the SUV."

"Be careful."

Clara, nice woman, kind to her in the jail. *Focus. I have to help Karen.*

Jill's breath huffed out in white vapor. Her legs gave way. They wouldn't support her. She crawled through the snow, slipping and sliding to the back of Karen's vehicle.

Had to get something to keep Karen warm. When she got the hatch open, the blankets lay in an open box. She pulled one from the car, carried it to Karen, and covered her. *Need the other one.*

Her muscles burned with the strain, but she stumbled and tumbled her way back to where Karen still lay unconscious and tucked the second blanket around her.

"Jill. Jill."

The muffled sound of her name. Who was calling her?" Damn. Her phone in her pocket.

"Yeah, Clara. Covered Karen with two blankets. She has no color at all."

"Good job, Jill. You rest, now. You've done everything possible."

The woman's low voice droned on, Jill must've passed out for a time, because the sirens seemed to arrive fast. Jerrod, Tim, Sheriff Hardwick, and the EMTs gathered around doing everything to make Karen and her comfortable.

"Karen, Karen, speak to me, honey." Tim's anguished cry tore at Jill's heart.

"I'm sorry, Tim, I'm so sorry." He never glanced her way. Perhaps her words were too soft for him to hear. A growl brought her gaze to Jerrod's grim face. She flinched when his finger feathered near what felt like a gash on her cheek. "Oh." She couldn't stop the moan.

"You're going to be okay, Jill."

"Karen?"

He didn't answer.

The EMTs lifted the stretcher with her friend's body and carried her up the incline to the ambulance. Jill was next. The movement almost made her sick. Maybe she had a head injury.

"Jill. I'll see you at the hospital. Hang in there."

Somebody patted her hand. Was it Jerrod?

The ambulance door slammed.

Then oblivion.

# CHAPTER SIXTEEN

*Friday, November 2*

Jerrod contacted Tim the moment he'd disconnected with the sheriff. Tim had mentioned over lunch Karen and Jill were out shopping together. He and Tim drove out to the crash site at speeds so high, only the very skilled or very scared would attempt on the snowy roads. Chills ran across Jerrod's shoulders at the picture of Jill lying on the ground next to Karen. He couldn't bear to think of what they nearly lost.

Repair to the two openings in Karen's arm took lengthy surgery. Her blood loss would've been a lot worse if Jill hadn't acted so promptly, or if the temperature had been higher. The cold had slowed the flow of blood.

Jerrod waited to bring his mother up to speed on the situation until he had positive news to give her. He leaned back in a chair in her kitchen. Mitch's death had aged her. The grooves around her mouth were considerably deeper than before.

"Any idea what's going on, Jerrod? This kind of thing doesn't happen in Woodstock." Strain raised the usual low pitch of her voice.

Jerrod shook his head. "Karen doesn't remember much. Jill reported a large, dark colored truck came up on their tail and ran them off the road. They didn't steal anything. No idea why they shot Karen. Jill has a mild concussion, is pretty bruised up, and her cheek was cut open." His mother flinched at his choice of words. He ran a hand through his beard. He needed to be more careful.

"Will she scar?"

"We won't know for a while, but Dr. Ludlow did the job.

"Good." His mother sighed. "He'll give her excellent care."

She was quiet for a moment before asking, "What is going on in Jill's life to cause all of this? We never have this level of crime. My God. Mitch killed. The break-ins. Someone ran the girls off the road and shot Karen. Can we stop this madness?"

The slight touch of hysteria in his mother's tone worried Jerrod. He sat forward, placed his cup on the table, and took one of her hands. Since he wasn't certain he said, "It's not clear, Mother." He answered her first question rather than the second. Not exactly the truth, but not an out and out lie either. "Neither woman got the plate number."

"Can Jill have visitors?"

"Want me to take you to see her?"

"Please. Can we go now?"

\* \* \* \*

"Jill, I've got some company for you." Her paleness, almost the color of the white bandage, took his breath.

"Jerrod." Her word a soft murmur. "Oh, you brought Anne."

Jill's smile, only on one side, played havoc with his heartbeat. Despite the obstacles against them, Jerrod wanted to keep this woman near him.

The memory of the smoothness of her skin when he'd touched her while they made love in front of the fire kept him in a perpetual state of unrest. It didn't matter that he was in politics, or she was from Texas and probably brought these bastards to his town. Jill Barlow touched something deep in his gut, and he'd fight to keep her.

His mother and Jill's soft words filled the room.

"You two be okay if I leave for a while?" They nodded, and he slipped out to check on Karen. Maybe Tim learned more from her about the wreck than he'd managed from Jill. At this point, Sheriff Hardwick didn't have a whole hell of a lot to go on.

When Jerrod neared Karen's room, the door opened and Tim stepped into the hall.

"They're changing her dressing again, but she's coming along well. I can take her home tomorrow or the next day. We're lucky the bullet didn't hit the bone, and we're hoping the scarring isn't too bad. She had quite a bit of damage. Who the hell cares about scarring, right? She's alive."

Jerrod hugged his best friend and slapped him on the back. "Kids get in?"

"Yeah. Nothing would do but for them to see her for themselves. We've loved having them here, and it makes them all feel better, despite Karen's early protests to the contrary. The kids ran home to pick up her toiletries."

"Mother's in with Jill, now. Want to grab a cup of coffee in the cafeteria?"

"Sure."

Tim fell in step beside Jerrod, and they walked in silence down to the cafeteria. They got their coffee and settled into straight-backed chairs.

"How's Jill doing?"

"Mild concussion. Dr. Ludlow is concerned about how bad the knife cut will scar. He took thirty-two stitches inside and out.

"Is she going back to the rent house when she's dismissed?"

"Not if I have anything to say about it." Jerrod gulped his coffee. "But we haven't had that conversation yet."

"This shit's connected to the other stuff that's gone on around Jill?"

"Don't know for certain, but yeah, I'd say so. Karen give you any other information?"

"Nah, she was focused on keeping control of the car."

Tim's hand squeezed the cup so tight his knuckles whitened, and the cup collapsed, sending the dark liquid everywhere. "Damn." He used a napkin to sop up what he could. A nearby attendant brought a wet rag and removed the mess.

"She doesn't remember the gunshot?" Jerrod asked.

"No. Thank God."

"That's a good thing."

"How's your mother doing?"

"Not too bad. She's resilient. Maybe in some ways, she feels she lost Mitch a long time ago." Jerrod finished his coffee. "We better get back." They headed upstairs and separated.

Jerrod stuck his head around the door of Jill's room. "Hey, ladies." The two women looked up, apparently surprised he'd returned already.

"Jill's heard rumors she'll be released this evening." His mother gave him a warm smile. "Good news, right?"

"Yes. And that means I'm going to run you home now, Mother, so I can return and help."

Jill frowned. Jerrod couldn't tell if it was from his insistence, or from the headache she must be suffering. "You don't have to, Jerrod. I have a rental and can drive."

"Well, you could, but it's at your house. And," he paused, "you're on some powerful drugs. Nobody wants you behind the wheel." He walked to the side of her bed, picked up her hand, rubbed his thumb along the back. "Let me do this. Please."

She dropped her gaze, and nodded. He hoped he was responsible for the slight flush, which put much-needed color in her cheeks. He squeezed her hand once.

"Let's get out of here, Mother."

"Thanks for stopping, Anne."

His mother leaned over and kissed Jill on her on the forehead. "You take care, dear, and do what my son says." Her eyes twinkled before she turned and walked out.

"You've got your orders." He smiled at Jill and followed his mother. He caught up to her at the elevator. "You trying to help?"

"Only if you want me to." Her eyebrows arched in question.

"Won't turn any away. Jill may be reluctant."

"Are you serious about her?" His mother took his arm on the walk to his car.

"Absolutely." They were quiet on the drive toward her house. Each wrapped up in thoughts.

Finally, she broke the silence. "I'm sure you'll manage, dear. You've gotten everything you ever wanted, or needed, and set your mind to. You'll win her over."

"And you'd be okay with that? I know she feels guilty about Mitch." He stopped the car in front of her house.

"Mitch made his choices a long time before Jill came into our lives."

Jerrod walked his mother to her door. She turned and rested a hand on his cheek.

"You go on. I'm fine, and if you were wondering, I'd love Jill to be a part of our family. She's good for you."

Jerrod returned to the hospital, and based on his mother's comments, nothing less than anticipation and hope rushed through his system. Because he'd been incredibly lucky—aside from the fiasco with his kids' mother—he'd tried to give back to the community and those less fortunate. Yeah, he'd worked his tail off, but he was born into a good family, raised with values. Others didn't have his advantages.

Did he have an explanation for why his brother turned out the way he did? No. Jerrod made it a point to try to help others. The way Don had done by leaving a large tip for the waitress at the restaurant in Montpelier when he and Jack ate dinner with him.

It was time to bring Don up on the latest, not that they had much, but still. After Jill went to sleep this evening, Jerrod would call.

He took the steps leading to the front entrance of the hospital two at a time, eager to see her. The overly clean, antiseptic smells assaulted his senses. Maybe the staff working here didn't notice it after a time. People could get used to almost anything, but right now, it annoyed him.

After a brief knock, he pushed open the door to her room. "Damn. Thought I'd catch you still wearing that sexy, backless hospital gown, and here I find you in real clothes. Nice, by the way." The pants hugged her rear in a flattering manner.

She turned from the window. He appreciated the sweater clinging to her breasts. The same pink stained her cheeks as when he left. He sure hoped he was responsible for the emotion behind the color.

"These were some of the clothes from our shopping trip. A deputy found them in the car and brought them to me."

"Well, that part of the outing was a success. You look great in that sweater. It matches the color of your eyes."

"Thank you."

"Ms. Barlow." A nurse pushed a wheel chair into the room.

"My chariot awaits, huh?"

"Best we've got."

"Come on, Jill." Jerrod walked to her, took her arm, and gently propelled her toward the chair. "Let's go home."

"Not to your home. To mine."

"We can discuss it on the way. You ride with the nurse, and I'll bring your things."

Her sigh signaled acquiescence. Lack of an argument on her part indicated she wasn't in good shape.

In the car, Jerrod couldn't stop himself from reaching for and patting the hands clasped in her lap. "I'm glad you're here." He let go of her hands, put his back on the steering wheel, and pulled out of the hospital driveway. "For now, plan to come home and eat with me. We can talk about other arrangements later."

"Okay. But I haven't agreed to stay with you," she said in a weak voice.

"I know." Jerrod fought the smile struggling to break through. She didn't know yet, but Jill Barlow was going nowhere but his house tonight. Afterward, they'd have to see. He wasn't averse to using his mother to keep Jill with him. All's fair, right? A cliché, perhaps, but if it improved his chances with this fascinating woman.

Jill was quiet on the ride from the hospital. He guessed she'd dozed off. Her lids lay closed against her pale cheeks. He stopped in front of the house. She jerked when he opened her car door, but she didn't rebel at his taking her arm to help her from the car and lead her through the front door.

"Lie down on the sofa while I throw together something to eat." He could tell she wanted to refuse, but her pallor worsened. The short trip obviously wore her out.

"I'd offer to help, but not sure I can be of much use right now. I'll take you up on the sofa proposition." A moan escaped when she lowered herself onto the couch.

The bright red of her cheeks showed she understood the possible double meaning of the words "sofa proposition." He certainly did and stifled a chuckle. Not fair to tease her now.

Jerrod went into the kitchen and reheated potato soup. He whipped up a salad and had it ready to go in around twenty minutes. After he put the rolls in the oven, he checked on Jill and found her asleep. He hated to disturb her, but she needed to eat. He sat on the edge of the sofa, leaned over, and kissed her gently on the lips. Her eyelashes fluttered.

"Ah, sleeping beauty awakes." Her lopsided smile warmed his heart. "Dinner's ready." He put an arm around her back, helped her sit and after a minute to stand. "Slow and easy." He kept his hold on her, and they walked to the table where he positioned the chair.

"No wine for you tonight, Jill. Your doctor wouldn't approve with all the drugs in your system."

"I know. Umm. Smells good, makes my mouth water. Wine would be nice, but oh well." After several bites, she looked up at him. "This is excellent. You do this or your mother?"

"I'd claim credit, but honestly, she brought over the soup, and after we got here, I made the salad. She wanted to make sure I had something she deemed good enough for you."

"She's a dear."

Jerrod wanted get her to agree to stay the night, but waited to broach the subject until they'd finished eating. "Sheriff Hardwick will probably stop by tomorrow. He has a few more questions for you."

* * * *

"I don't have any more answers." She hated the shrill sound of her voice, but she had nothing else she could tell him. "Why does he keep on about this? I've told him everything I know. A truck. Two men. One with a bad cough." God, couldn't they leave her alone? She pushed to her feet, her pacing unsteady.

She desperately needed some alone time to figure out what to do about the flash drive. Her nerves stretched to the breaking point waiting for the threatened call. At each trill of her new cell phone in the hospital, her heart had quaked. Her hand trembled every time she pushed receive wondering if this was the dreaded call.

Jerrod's arms came around her, halting her steps, pulling her from the maelstrom. He scooped her against his hard body, where she fit so well. He was solid, yet gentle. He rested his head against the top of hers. His breath feathered against her hair. Finally, he released her. Jill hadn't struggled, and in fact, she could've stayed in his arms a long time.

"Come with me."

Jill liked the way he took her by the elbow and led her from the kitchen. She didn't inquire where they were going. At the stairs, Jerrod kept an arm around her waist, ready to support her if she needed the assistance, but letting her do what she could. He seemed to understand her desire to do this on her own. By the time they reached the top, she was breathless and shaky.

Jerrod walked past the room she'd previously used and stopped at his, pushing open the door. "Come in here tonight. I'm not suggesting we make love, Jill. But sleep next to me."

Her heart tripped up to a heady beat. She reached a hand to touch his cheek, rubbing across his beard. He placed a soft kiss in her palm. Her insides melted, but she resisted. She'd brought so many bad things to his town.

"Please, do this for me. I'll rest better knowing you're safe."

She nodded, giving in, and let him lead the way. "My bag's here." She looked from it to him. "Were you so sure of me?"

"No, but former Boy Scouts are always prepared. Liz went by your house and packed a few things she figured you'd need. You change out of those clothes in the bathroom while I turn down the covers."

She took out the long-sleeved flannels she'd been sleeping in for a while and went across to the bathroom. Taking off the sweater made her wince. The doctors told her to expect to be sore for a while. The seat belt had done a number on her middle and shoulder. Bruising was already noticeable. Purple and red spread across her body like she'd fallen into two buckets of paint. The white bandage stood out on her pale face. How bad would the scar be? Would it bother Jerrod?

Jill yanked her gaze away. Looking at the injuries made her hurt more. She pulled out the twisty holding her ponytail and let her hair swing free then padded across the hall in her fuzzy slippers. The bed looked inviting. So did Jerrod standing near. He was still dressed. What had she expected? God she didn't know. Somehow, in its banged-up shape, her body still responded to the man.

"You climb in, and I'll sit here until you fall asleep."

He stood to the side while she slid in. Their hands reached for the covers at the same moment and pulled them up. A long time had passed since anyone tucked her in at night. Right now, it was what she needed and made her feel safe. His fingers feathered the hair falling across her shoulder. His lips barely brushed her forehead. Worried about what she'd dream, she nevertheless, closed her eyes.

"Sleep well."

Those were the last words she heard before she fell asleep.

\* \* \* \*

"Jill, Jill. You're okay. You're with me. You're safe."

She opened both eyes. Jerrod's leg was thrown over hers, and an arm draped across her stomach. She released a long breath of relief. "I was fighting with the man in the gray mask."

"I was afraid that might happen. Sometimes talking about a dream makes it less threatening."

She was quiet for a moment before she began in small voice just above a soft whisper.

"It was snowing. So hard, the road was a white haze in front of us. Then a monster-size truck, like an eighteen-wheeler, got on our tail. Karen tried to speed up, but the road was too slippery. The truck kept coming, getting closer, and closer. Then it rammed us and pushed us off the road.

"The car plunged down and down. It seemed it would never stop. A man pointed a gun, and I tried to get it away from him, but then he aimed at Karen. I lunged for his arm, shoved it down, but the gun exploded anyway. Karen fell. He threw me to the ground. Jumped on top. Cut me with his knife. Over and over. Karen screamed. Or maybe it was me."

She stopped. Dragged in several shaky breaths. A dream. Nothing more. She was safe. Safe with Jerrod. She exhaled and her shoulders relaxed.

"Thanks." She couldn't resist touching his cheek and running her hand through his soft beard. He turned his head and kissed each finger, making her yearn for his lips on hers. She ached in places she didn't know she had.

When—if they made love again, she didn't want anything holding them back— his fear of hurting her or hers of not responding to him the way she'd want. Stifling moans, she moved to snuggle against his warm body. She needed rest to face whatever chaos lay ahead.

# CHAPTER SEVENTEEN

*Saturday, November 10*

Sid paced the office in his house. Circled the desk. Looked out the window. Chomped on the cigar in his mouth. Not as good as puffing on the God damned thing, but his wife was a pain in the ass about cigar smoke in the house.

After the wreck earlier in the month, when Judson and Peterson ran the bitch off the road, Sid expected to hear what progress the guys were making. Patience wasn't his long suit. He wasn't waiting any longer. Sid grabbed his cell and punched in the number for Peterson.

A click indicated the call connected, but Sid didn't hear anything. "Peterson," he shouted. "Peterson. What the hell's going on?"

Shuffling noise.

"Mr. Cranston?"

"That you, Judson?"

"Yeah."

"Where's Peterson?"

"In bed."

Sid bit the cigar in two pieces. He spit it out. Shit. What was going on? Did he have the stupidest people in the world working for him?

"What's he doing in bed? Bonking some dame?"

"Doc says he's got pneumonia."

"Shit."

"They've pumped him full of penicillin. Said to take it easy for a couple of weeks."

"Why didn't you take care of the woman right after the wreck?"

"That's when Peterson started feeling rotten. We picked up stuff at the drug-store, but he got worse. When his fever hit a hundred and four, I took him to an emergency care clinic. They said pneumonia. Wanted to put him in the hospital. We didn't think that was a very good idea."

"No shit." Sid slouched into his chair. The fingers of one hand tapped on the desk blotter. His blood pressure rose as he swallowed bile. "How long till you think you guys can finish up this deal?"

Muffled sounds. All he could make out was muffled sounds. What the hell. His fist came down on the desk.

"God damn it, Judson. Answer my question."

"Another week. Maybe two."

The man's apologetic tone didn't mean much to Sid.

"You call me in a week and give me an update. Don't make me hunt you down or send someone to take care of you two."

"You don't have to do—"

\* \* \* \*

*Wednesday, November 21*

Despite many protests from Jerrod, Jill moved back to the rental. Her somewhat more conventional view of life reared its head when he'd suggested after the first night, she stay at his house. He'd argued she would be safer, and he would worry less about her.

How safe would it be with her hormones carrying on a wiggly dance whenever he was within touching distance?

Every morning, the question sprayed itself across her brain in bright red letters: Would this be the day she'd get the call about the flash drive? She'd never make it as a circus performer. Balancing on a tight rope brought out her worst.

"If you can't make up your mind about the crystal, perhaps you should look elsewhere," she snapped at a particularly difficult customer.

"Jill, I believe you have a phone call in the back." Sally stepped in. "Have you seen Joe Anderson's work?" she led the woman to the other side of the shop.

Jill huffed to the office. "Who does Sally think she is? The owner?"

"Can I get you a cup of tea, Jill?" Mary Ann asked, her hands wringing in front of her body, and her eyebrows nearly meeting over her nose.

Jill sank into one of the chairs. "Oh, my God. I'm so sorry. I don't know what's gotten into me." She dropped her head into her hands and fought to get her breathing under control.

"A lot's been going on, Jill. I know you prefer coffee, but this time how about tea?"

Jill nodded.

Mary Ann busied herself with the task. "Good thing we're closed tomorrow. Everyone needs a little rest now and then."

"Yes. A good thing," Jill agreed.

The occasional irritating shopper normally didn't bother her. She'd have to apologize to Sally. God, Jill couldn't believe she'd said that. No contact day after day drew her nerves into knots. A good night's sleep was something of the past. Even after drinking a half-bottle of wine for release, dreadful dreams disturbed her sleep. Sometimes she woke up screaming. Because of them, she insisted the twins stay at the Woodstock Inn when they came for the holiday.

"Mom, I can bunk with you, and Ethan can manage on the couch for two nights. He's sure slept in worse places."

Jill prevailed. No telling what her kids thought about her insistence.

She kept her ears glued to the sky and her radio tuned to weather reports, praying the recent snows wouldn't keep her children from traveling. Ellen and

Ethan were scheduled to arrive later that day. Jill had made reservations for them to enjoy the Thanksgiving meal tomorrow at the Woodstock Inn. She couldn't wait for them to get there.

They called when they drove into town on their way to the inn. They'd arranged their flights to the Hartford airport so they were able to rent one car between them. The sound of tires over the snow-packed driveway made her smile in anticipation. She turned the gas flame on low under the sauce she'd made earlier, and turned up the one under the large pot of water for the angel hair pasta.

Stomping on the front porch told her they'd arrived. Before the bell rang, Jill flung open the door and welcomed them.

"Hey, Mom." Ethan scooped her up and swung her around. "Happy Thanksgiving."

"Put me down, you crazy boy."

"Oh, God. I didn't hurt you, did I? Here let me see." He turned her face up toward the light. "Mom, this is worse than you let on."

"The mark is much longer than I expected." Ellen seemed to hesitate before hugging Jill. "Are you in any pain?"

"A twinge now and again. The doctors assure me it's the healing taking place, a good sign."

"Will this leave a scar?" Ellen studied her mom's face.

"Not much of one, if any. The plastic surgeon is well respected."

"Rub Vitamin E on the wound. That'll help a lot," Ellen said.

"Yeah, I do that morning and night. Liz told me about that trick." Jill raised a hand self-consciously to her cheek. "Is it ugly?"

Ellen hugged her. "No. And you look wonderful." Ellen pulled Jill's arms out to the side. "Maybe better than when we were here for your birthday. What's your secret? Have you found a man?"

Jill coughed and shook her head. "Let me take your coats, and y'all go into the living room while I hang these. Ethan, pour the wine, please. You'll find it on the side board in the dining room."

"So, Mom, you didn't answer your pushy daughter's question," he pointed out when she perched on the arm of the sofa.

She hoped her skin didn't flush and give her away while she tried to be nonchalant. "Pilates. I've been going two to three times a week. Liz Phillips has her own studio you know, and she's tough. Doesn't let me slack off. Pushes me when I'm sure I can't go any farther. But I do. She's always right. It's annoying." Her lips turned up in what she intended to be an I'm-proud-of-myself-smile. "Thanks to her workouts I'm wearing a size smaller in pants than when I arrived, and I still get to enjoy her grandmother's fabulous apple pie, which we're having for dessert this evening."

Babbling. She was babbling. Would it work to send them in another direction?

Her son's nose twitched. "Is that your spaghetti sauce?" He got up and wandered into the kitchen carrying his glass. Her rambling words probably didn't redirect them, but Ethan's fabled sense of smell did. "Umm. Nobody makes this the way you do, Mom." He stuck in a spoon and brought it to his mouth. "Can't wait to dig in."

"Need any help?" Ellen asked.

"Sure. Get the salad from the refrigerator, and, Ethan, pop the French bread into the oven. The pasta will be done in a few minutes."

Jill waited until they'd finished their meal and opened a second bottle of wine. They sat comfortably in the dining room, the candles burning low. They'd talked about Ellen's research, Ethan's training, speculated about when or if he'd be deployed, and how she and the shop were doing.

"There's something I want to talk about with you." She took another swallow of wine. The fingers of both hands entwined around the stem, while she searched for the right words. Lord, this whole thing had made her a crazy woman. "I don't quite know where to start."

"The beginning is best," Ellen said, always practical.

"You're aware your grandfather spent many years fighting the extension of casino gambling in Texas…"

Her children sat in stunned silence while she related what she knew of the situation. She included the likelihood gambling proponents had their father and grandfather killed. She only omitted the masked gunman's words to her right before he shot Karen. The memory made her cringe. So far, she'd told no one about his threat.

The only reason she'd been able to get away with her silence was Karen's amnesia. She remembered seeing the large vehicle in her rear view mirror, but nothing after that.

"You're sure your accident didn't have anything to do with what you've been telling us?" Ethan set his glass on the table.

He'd always been good at problem solving, going to the heart of the matter, which was the reason the Army trained him in the intelligence field. Jill had never lied to her children at any age, but the truth would cause them a great deal of worry.

Since they couldn't do anything about the situation, she opted for a half-truth. "We don't know." Later, she'd deal with the guilt of not being entirely honest with the twins along with the guilt of knowing she brought such danger to this lovely town and its people.

After the twins returned to the Inn, Jill got ready for bed. Had she made a mistake? Primarily she'd wanted to make sure they took precautions with their own safety. After she turned over the flash drive, it would be over. God, she prayed that was true.

Tomorrow was Thanksgiving, and she had a lot to be grateful for. Anne had invited her family to the house for the meal, but Jill wanted private time with her kids because she saw them so seldom. She'd agreed to stop by early in the evening for pumpkin pie. She'd skip the inn's excellent dessert offerings to make room for Anne's. Tomorrow would be a wonderful day.

\* \* \* \*

*Friday, November 23*

Jill reluctantly bid her children goodbye but hugged the memories of the special holiday close. If she weren't mistaken, she'd see more of Ethan whenever he found an opportunity to get away. He seemed to be taken with Liz. Well, Jill wouldn't be upset if something came of that. Liz was a great young woman.

How would her Pilates instructor feel about moving around the country? Jill hadn't inquired what Ethan and Jerrod had been in deep conversation about. She didn't want to know, but she was glad they seemed to get on.

Jill unlocked the store on Friday at ten o'clock. Sally and Mary Ann would come in later in the day. Jill had given them extra time off. Thanksgiving was her favorite holiday, but she was glad to get back to routine with the store again and was content after the wonderful, though brief, visit with her kids.

Maybe this business with the flash drive was over. She'd been certain they'd have called by now. What was going on? Shoving aside troubling thoughts, she smiled at an early customer. "Good morning, Mr. Slaughter. How was your Thanksgiving? Eat a lot of turkey?"

He was one of the town leaders, a contemporary of Anne's. Probably a little sweet on the woman.

"Oh, my goodness, yes. My daughter puts on quite a spread." He patted his stomach. "How was your day?"

"Perfect. My children came." Her phone vibrated in her pocket, a little tickle. "The Woodstock Inn's dinner is hard to match. How can I help you this morning?"

"I want something for my granddaughter's birthday, Jill. Found something for her here last year. She liked it a great deal."

"I can check the files to find what you bought then and see if we have any items by the same artist."

"Let me browse first then maybe I'll have you do that." He walked toward the display counters at the back of the store.

"No problem." When her phone tingled against her leg again, Jill reached for it. Maybe the kids had trouble getting to the airport. "Hello?"

"Where's the flash drive?"

The gravelly words sent chills across her shoulders and down her arms. Her stomach clenched like she'd taken a punch. She drew in a shaky breath.

"Tell me. Or don't you remember the episode on the road with your friend?"

Jill's fingers tightened around the small cell. Instantly her mouth went dry and swallowing became difficult. She licked her lips. "I—I remember. I'll tell you. Don't hurt anyone else, please." She prayed her children had made it to Hartford and were safely in the air.

"I can see the woman from where I'm standing, and unless you want her to take another bullet, spit it out, bitch."

"Citizen's Bank."

"What?"

"In a safe deposit box."

"Crap. How long until you can get there?"

"It's on the west side of the green. About fifteen minutes if I leave right now."

"Go. And, bitch, don't try to talk to anyone else. I'm watching you, too."

The buzzing sound in her hand told Jill he'd disconnected. "Oh, God." The muttered words slipped out.

"Is anything wrong?"

She whirled, startled. Mr. Slaughter. She'd forgotten him. He stood so close, he must've heard.

"Oh, uh, no. Would you mind checking back with me? I—I, uh, have a splitting headache, and I've left my medicine at home. I'm sorry to inconvenience you." The man's eyebrows rose with obvious questions she suspected he was too polite to verbalize.

"No problem. Can I run you home? I was lucky to get a spot right out front."

"No. The fresh air will do me good." She dashed to the back room, grabbed her purse and the long insulated coat she'd purchased in Lebanon with Karen. "I hate to rush you. Thanks so much for understanding."

She had to wait for Mr. Slaughter to leave, so she could open a display case where she hid the safe deposit box key. It sat in a purple glass container. She slid the key into her coat pocket, closed the shop door, and twisted the lock. Turning left onto Church Street, she pulled her hat and gloves out of her pockets and put them on. Brisk steps took her past the green between the Woodstock Inn and Anne's house, praying her friend wouldn't look out and want her to stop and chat. The road angled north.

Before she'd gone many blocks, despite her warm clothes, she was freezing. Her breath turned the air in front of her frosty white.

"Morning, Jill."

She didn't take time to place the voice and kept her gaze glued to the ground. She didn't even nod, intent on putting one foot in front of the other, taking safe, quick steps, praying to put this ordeal behind her. A quick peek at her watch told her it was now close to the allotted fifteen minutes. If the bastard watched her, he'd see she hadn't talked with anyone and was following his instructions.

She couldn't stand for anything else happening to Karen. Could it be a bluff? Maybe no one watched either of them, but Jill wasn't taking chances with her friend's life.

Jill slowed her steps when she neared the bank parking lot, and she paused. Because of the cold, no one stood around chatting in the parking lot, less than half-full of vehicles. She forced her feet forward. Dread built in her middle as though a load of wet cement settled there.

Her breakfast rose in the back of her throat. A large, black truck with a dented front right bumper sat in the middle of the lot. Everything in her wanted to turn and run, but she stepped toward the bank entrance, not knowing what to expect.

She jumped when a man grasped her right arm in a punishing grip. Her heart kicked into double time. Then someone moved close to her other side.

"So, Ms. Barlow, here's the plan." The man on her right spoke softly. "Don't look at us, and maybe you'll walk away from this in one piece."

She'd never had high blood pressure, but Jill guessed hers would be off the chart right now. Her heart thudded so fast she felt it thrusting up against her breastbone. She had to get a grip on herself or the trip into the bank was going to be disastrous, not only for her, but also the people inside. Gulping air, she breathed in for a five count. Liz made her do that at the studio. Jill let it out slowly, then again, and again. Better.

"We'll walk in with you. You explain you need to get into your safe deposit box, and you want us to go in with you, because we're family, cousins from… where, Judson?"

"How about Vegas?" The man on the left snickered after his answer.

Jill almost jerked her head up, but remembered the warning. The first man sounded so familiar, but she couldn't figure out why. The men who ran her and Karen off the road wore masks, which muffled their voices so much she'd never be able to place them.

"Okay, babe, you say we're cousins from Vegas. Not that's it's any of their God damned business who you take with you. You've got your key? Nod if you do. I don't want us getting this far and finding we have a problem. You don't want other people getting hurt."

Jill nodded. His statement confirmed her fears. She clenched her fists and focused on each crack in the pavement, each line of tar, each spot of bird droppings.

"Hey, Jill. How are you today?" A woman spoke when they drew near the building.

"Fine." Jill glanced briefly toward the woman, but didn't make eye contact, and kept on walking, proud her voice hadn't quavered. They moved inside, and the doors swung closed behind them. Jill looked around. The one security guard stood off to the left and rear where she remembered the vault to be. She walked over to the bank manager who handled the safe deposit boxes.

"Good morning, Mrs. Timmons."

The older woman with silver streaking her hair smiled up at her. "Hey, Jill, how're you doing?"

One of the things about a small town, everyone knew your business. People still inquired about her health, not in the general way, but with regard to Karen's and her car wreck.

"I'm doing fine, thanks." Could Mrs. Timmons recognize a faked smile? "I need access to my safe deposit box."

"Well, sure. You've got your key?"

"Yes."

Mrs. Timmons leaned over and pulled out the lower desk drawer. Her hand came up holding the master key. She stood. "Well, let's go then." She stopped when she got to the door leading to the boxes and looked inquiringly at Jill's escorts walking closely on either side of her.

"These are cousins from Las Vegas," she responded before the woman asked about the two men.

"I want them to go in with me."

\* \* \* \*

"Hey, Mother. How are you?" Jerrod spoke into his cell, but glanced at his watch. He had a few more minutes before the court hearing would begin. She'd have to make this brief.

"Hank Slaughter stopped by a few minutes ago, Jerrod."

He loved his mother, but she'd take a day's trip down a back road to get to the point. Unfortunately, he didn't have time for the ride with her today. One foot tapped on the floor while he tried to keep his voice even. "Listen, Mother, tell Hank hello for me. You need to have him over for dinner with us soon. I'll talk to you later." Jerrod moved the cell from his ear and was about to disconnect, when his mother's words froze his blood. "It's Jill. I'm worried about her."

"What?"

"Hank stopped at the store this morning, and she suddenly had to run out. Mumbled something about needing to go home for headache medicine."

"Okay. Go on." More had to be coming, because his mother was level headed and didn't jump to conclusions.

"Jerrod, she didn't turn toward her house, but in my direction. She didn't stop. Hank said she headed toward College Street."

"Thanks for calling, Mother. I'll check it out. Don't worry." He disconnected.

As he'd listened to his mother's words, he'd made his way back into the courtroom to find the judge's clerk to tell her he needed to reschedule. He placed a call to Jack Hardwick.

"Hey, Jerrod. You'll never guess who I'm with. Mike Riley's here, and we're on our way to Citizen's Bank. We got an odd heads up from the bank security guard. The message was about men Jill Barlow told Mrs. Timmons were her cousins from Vegas."

"Dear God. I'll meet you there." Dread shot adrenalin through Jerrod's body. He fought for a breath. He made the trip from the courthouse through downtown Woodstock faster than safety and the law allowed. What with the vacationers in town for the holiday, it was a miracle. He pulled up behind the sheriff and Riley and flung open his door almost before he brought his Jeep to a halt.

"Is she still in the bank? What do you know?" Jerrod spoke directly to the point without acknowledging the two men or commenting on when Riley had arrived.

"See the vehicle heading up the road?" Jack pointed north.

"Yeah." Jerrod's blood pressure exploded, making his hands tremble. He balled them into fists.

"She's in the truck with the two men who went into the bank with her," Riley stated.

"Well, why the hell are you standing here? Let's go after her," Jerrod demanded.

"I didn't want to be right on their tail. Hard to disguise my official Sheriff's Jeep."

"We'll go in mine."

Jack looked at Mike and they nodded. "You drive, Jerrod." Jack climbed in the front, and Mike got in the back.

\* \* \* \*

Jill's terror equaled the fear that had gripped her when the thug had pointed his gun at Karen and shot her. She'd hoped never to be in the same position again. Her heart parked in her throat, not simply because of the gun pointed at her.

The driver didn't have a clue about driving on snow. He drove worse than she did. From her position in the front seat, she couldn't miss seeing how close they came to going off the pavement at every turn. While it wasn't a mountain road, the incline was enough to cause the vehicle to turn over. Not fastening her seat belt increased her chances of injury in an accident, but it also gave more freedom of movement.

Hoping for a crash couldn't be good, but Jill considered it her best chance of escape. Despite her captors saying they wouldn't kill her if she didn't look at them, she suspected their promise was a crock. Whatever she needed to do to get out of the car, she would attempt. She glanced behind her and stared down the barrel of gun Judson aimed at her.

She didn't know where they were going, but the sooner she stopped the car the less distance she'd have to hike back to Woodstock. Optimism was her stock in trade. She couldn't—no, wouldn't—let herself believe she was going to die on this snow-swept road in Vermont. God, she wasn't a grandmother yet.

The turn ahead appeared rough. She needed to make certain the driver lost control then. She'd leap from the truck, hopefully, before it flipped and careened into the ravine.

"Hey, Phil, take it easy, huh? Unless you want me to accidentally shoot you. We're bouncing around so much; I don't know who the bullet would hit if the gun went off."

"Shut the fuck up, Judson. I'm concentrating here." The man white-knuckled the steering wheel.

His voice was familiar, but Jill couldn't place him. Okay, now or never. Her right hand grasped the "oh shit" handle above the door. In one quick movement, she tightened her stomach muscles, swiveled her legs around, and rammed them both into the driver's right arm.

A sickening crack. The driver screamed. At the same time, a flash came from the back seat. A burning pain exploded in her left shoulder, and the car crashed through the guardrail and plunged down the incline.

Desperate, Jill elbowed open the door and jumped. She rolled, coming to rest against the stump of a tree. Her world went black.

When she came to, the smashed truck had lodged among large granite boulders at the bottom of the ravine. The back tires spun in the air, steam rose from the front end.

"Jill, Jill. Oh, God, you're bleeding."

No voice had ever sounded as sweet as Jerrod's. A warm feeling curled around her heart. Wait. She had to tell him something. What? "The driver. The driver has the —"

"Don't worry. Let me take a look at you."

"No." She struggled to rise, but couldn't get her legs to function. Pain exploded when she moved an arm. "The driver… The driver has…memory stick."

"Shit, you've been shot."

"Get it, please." Her words came out a whisper. Not forceful. She'd intended forceful, because the action was important.

"Okay, okay. Take it easy." He raised his voice. "Hey, Jack, Riley, Jill says the driver has the flash drive."

"We'll grab it. You stay with her," the sheriff said.

Jill heard a ripping sound and pain tore through her. "Oh, God. Stop." She tried to move from Jerrod's hand pressed into her shoulder.

"Hey, be careful, Jack. We've got flames," said another voice.

The words floated toward her from a distance. Searing torture in her right shoulder, and another groan erupted from her gut. Why wouldn't Jerrod stop?

"I've got the driver."

Was that Mike Riley? She replayed the tape in her brain. Yeah. Jerrod had called his name along with the sheriff's.

At the thwunk of what sounded like a gunshot, Jill flinched. Had she been hit again?

"Jack, you all right?" Jerrod's voice rose above the fog of her pain.

"The other guy had been thrown from the car. He was taking aim at Jill. He's dead." The sheriff spoke in curt tones.

"We need to get back, Jack. The damn thing's about to blow." Riley's words filtered through a haze of pain enveloping her.

"This is going to hurt, Jill, but we've got to get away from here."

His strong arms cradled her, and he stood. Agony seared through her. Had he yanked her arm from her body?

# CHAPTER EIGHTEEN

*Sunday, November 25*

"We need to involve the FBI." His son glared at him. Jerrod crossed one leg, shifted, and then crossed the other.

It was damn uncomfortable sitting on the hard chairs in the hospital waiting room. They'd been here a long while. "Son, we still don't know who in the Austin office is the leak. Riley is right to work through his counterpart in the capitol police department. They can nail Richardson with the information on the flash drive, and hope to turn him so they can reach others involved." Jerrod rose to pace the confines of the surgery waiting room. "They've got nothing but two dead men now. Neither of those guys were worth a shit, but one of them needed to live to testify to make the case a slam dunk."

"Take it easy, Dad. She's a strong woman. She'll come through this."

Don's hand on his arm stopped Jerrod's frantic movements.

"We don't know that. Damn, I can't lose her before—"

The doors to the waiting room flung open, and Ethan and Ellen blew in. Snowflakes covered their heads and coats.

"How is she?" Ethan, his arm around his sister's shoulder, walked straight to Jerrod.

"Glad you got here okay. You're mother's been in surgery an hour. The doctor said it would last close to two." Jerrod reached a hand to the younger man and they shook.

"We were going crazy trying to get here, what with the airlines canceling so many flights because of the storms," Ellen said. "I'd barely landed in Florida when I got your call. Did she know we were on our way?" Ellen peeled a scarf from around her neck.

"Yes. I told her. Have a seat." Jerrod said to the twins.

Don jumped to help Ellen take off her coat. "Thanks," she said. "It'll be hours before I can sit again after the flights, delays in the airports, and the God awful drive from Hartford." She stared out the window.

Ethan hung his coat on a rack, next to his sister's. "Do you know why they waited to do the surgery?"

"They wanted to get her stabilized."

"Do they think she'll have permanent damage?" Ellen turned toward the men. Her arms wrapped around her middle, as if trying to hold herself together.

"Hang on, Sis. How'd you miss out on a healthy dose of Mom's optimism? You always see the glass half empty."

"Shut up." Her voice sounded sharp and piercing.

Jerrod made brief eye contact with his son, before Don spoke up. "Listen, I need coffee. The cafeteria's not half-bad here, Ellen. Maybe I'll get something to eat. Help me pick it out?" He held out his hand to her.

She looked from him to her brother and then toward Jerrod.

"Go on, Ellen. We'll call you if we hear anything." Jerrod patted her shoulder.

"Okay." She took Don's hand, and they left.

"She's exhausted and worried. She's been traveling for almost two days and one was bad enough." Her brother excused Ellen's behavior.

"So do both of you know what's been going on?"

"We thought we did. Mom told us when we were here for Thanksgiving, but obviously, she didn't share the whole story. She didn't mention she was expecting to hear from these men again. Damn, this is a nightmare." He rubbed his hands over his face and through his hair. "God, does it snow here all the time?"

For the first time in a long time, Jerrod smiled, relieved to tackle the normal topic of their winter weather. "You can just about count on it from late October through late March, sometimes later." He studied the snowfall through the window. The streetlights sparkled on the big, puffy flakes floating down from the night sky like butterflies on the wing. Jill had described them that way once.

"Mom must love this." Ethan walked to the window for a closer look. "When we were kids, the family went to Colorado every winter, stayed the two weeks of Christmas break. She acted a kid herself. Got out and played in it, you know. We had snow ball fights, and she raced us down the smaller hills on sleds."

Ethan's story made Jerrod ache to spend similar times with Jill. He needed to serve another year on his term in the Assembly, which would start again in January. People talked with him about taking a run at the US Senate in two years. He'd been giving the idea considerable thought. However, if he needed to give it up for Jill, he would. Politicians might never be her favorite people.

"Ethan." Jerrod waited until the young man pivoted in his direction.

"You should know I care a great deal for your mother." Clearly, his statement surprised her son, because his eyebrows nearly met his hairline.

"Okay."

Jerrod didn't flinch from the younger man's gaze.

"What are you trying to say?"

He closed and opened fists. Time to gut up. "I haven't done a good job so far, but I'll look after Jill from now on." Before Ethan had a chance to comment, the doors opened again, and Liz ushered in her grandmother.

"Have you heard anything yet?" Anne's voice was tight with worry.

"I tried to get her to stay home, Dad, but she has a stubborn streak."

Jerrod nodded. "Thanks for driving her, Liz. Everyone in our family is known for a strong streak of stubborn." He took his mother's outerwear and shook it to get some of the snow off before hanging it. Then he hugged her. Ethan had jumped to his feet when the two women entered. "Let me help with your coat."

Liz smiled at him and nodded her thanks. "How long have you been here, Ethan?"

"Not long. We came directly to the hospital. Don took my sister to the cafeteria to keep her from killing—damn. Probably not an expression I'll ever be comfortable using again except in the context of war."

Time stood still. Jerrod's mind spun toward chaos, not knowing how things were going. Ellen and his son returned and exchanged greetings with his mother and Liz. Every now and then, one of them mumbled something, followed by a few, flimsy responses. They all appeared to be in a weird time warp, swimming slowly through thick molasses.

The whirring of the heating system clicked on and clicked off, marking the passage of time in warm air flowing from the vents, followed by the growing cold until the heat kicked on again.

"I talked with Karen," Anne said to no one in particular. "She wants us to call her when we have news. She's keeping in touch with Sally and Mary Ann, too. They're taking turns with the shop."

Jerrod kept sneaking peeks at his watch at ten-minute intervals. He tried not to, but he prowled the room while the little hand made its slow trek around the clock.

"Dad, you can't make time go faster by checking every minute of two." Liz joined him.

He must be checking his watch more often than he was aware.

"She's going to be all right, Dad. She's strong and in good shape. I know." Her hand rested lightly on his back, rubbing small circles, attempting to calm him. Nothing would calm him but the news that Jill had successfully come through the surgery.

Finally, one hour and fifty-eight minutes after he began surgery, Dr. Sanders walked into the waiting room. "Jerrod."

He rushed toward the physician. Jerrod's heart-beat thundered in his chest. He made himself speak with calm. "Jill's children are here now."

The doctor glanced around. "I see we have quite a crowd."

"I'm her son, and this is my sister. Tell us. Will she be okay?" Ethan's tone of authority demanded the answer he wanted.

"She's going to be fine," the doctor said with a satisfied smile. "It will take time. She's in recovery, and family will be able to see her in a few minutes."

A cheer went up. Tears of joy fell, and they patted each other's backs and exchanged hugs.

Bleakness descended over Jerrod. The hospital wouldn't consider him family. They wouldn't allow him to go in. God, he needed to see Jill with his own eyes. She'd been so white when he carried her up the embankment only moments before bright red and yellow flames engulfed the vehicle. The explosion rang in his ears.

Ethan's hand on his shoulder made him jump.

"Come with us."

Jerrod took a deep breath and released it. "Thanks."

* * * *

*"Not all of you at the same time and only for a moment. She needs to rest."*

The words filtered through a fog. Rest. Why did she need to rest? Sleepy. She was so sleepy. Not tired. She wanted to look around, but her lids didn't cooperate. She concentrated. There. They batted open for a moment. Ellen's face shimmered in front of her. Jill frowned.

"Thought…you'd…" What's the word she wanted? Yeah. "Left."

"Mom, don't try to talk. I love you."

Ah, sweet. Sometimes grown kids don't use those words to their parents. Ellen picked up her hand. Jill wanted to squeeze. No movement. Huh. Must be more tired than she realized.

"Mom, you've had surgery, and you're in recovery. You're going to be okay. Ethan's here, too. We're coming in one at a time to keep from tiring you out. I'm leaving so he can come in and see you."

Again, Jill tried to squeeze her daughter's hand. Maybe more this time...and then her son's low tones warmed her heart.

"Hey, Mom. I'm the one who's supposed to have the dangerous job."

Danger? What'd he mean by that? She willed a smile in his direction, but wasn't certain it made it to her mouth before he faded out of sight like a cartoon ghost. Poof, he was gone.

"Jill."

Jerrod's deeper tones? Her eyes popped open again. Sure enough, the whiskered face she loved so much floated into view, and wavered before coming clear. She wanted to touch him, but her hand wouldn't do what she wanted. What was the matter with her? "Sick?"

"You're in the hospital, Jill, but you came through the surgery fine."

Was he kissing the palm of her hand? Her fingers slid through his whiskers, soft to touch. A tear fell from one of his eyes. Would he forgive her? The hope faded away, and she couldn't remember why she wanted him to. But it was important. Again, another kiss to her palm. Safe with Jerrod, she drifted off.

\* \* \* \*

*Tuesday, November 27*

Riley disconnected the call and leaned back against the headboard in his Woodstock motel room. His smile so wide it almost hurt. He'd followed his gut and returned to the New England town concerned about Jill Barlow's safety. He'd been right to be worried, but hadn't been in time or in the right place to protect her.

The phone call from the Austin homicide detective who'd investigated Bill Stevens' death had brought good news. Richardson cratered when faced with the information the authorities held a copy of his flash drive. He decided to turn state's evidence against Sid Cranston, the Las Vegas mob kingpin behind the push to legitimize casino gambling in Texas. Richardson wanted to escape the death sentence Texas so liberally handed out.

Maybe they'd get the evidence needed to seal the files on Jill's husband and father's murder cases. Finalizing those cases would be great. Give the woman some closure. Then she could move back to Fort Worth.

He glanced around his room. It was furnished in the traditional New England manner, according to the fliers he'd picked at the front desk. The fire crackling in the hearth did more than warm the body.

He understood why Jill ran to this town. But her roots were in Fort Worth. For God's sake, she was a Texan.

He didn't question why it mattered to him where she chose to live. It shouldn't matter at all. Yet it did.

Jill Barlow was on her way to a full recovery. Mike needed to make plans to go home. He'd put a dent in his stored up vacation days, but he was glad he'd come. If things worked out the way it appeared they might, solving two murders would be more than worth his efforts. He'd get his travel plans lined up and stop by the hospital to tell her goodbye.

First, he wanted to bring the local officials up to date with Austin PD information. Hardwick should know how to get in touch with Don Phillips. Mike slung on his jacket and hurried to the car. Damn. He was going to freeze his butt off if he didn't get out of this state. A spot near the Woodstock Public Safety building opened, and he slid in his rental. Thank God, he wouldn't be out in this snowy weather long. He walked in out of the cold and spoke to the deputy. "I'm Detective Jack Riley. If Sheriff Hardwick is in, I'd like to see him."

"Just a minute." The officer checked with her boss. "Go on back."

"Thanks." He nodded to the deputy. Small town law enforcement had advantages. He could get right in to see the headman without an appointment.

"Hey, Mike. Good to see you."

Hardwick held out his hand and Mike met his grasp.

"I didn't get a chance to tell you thanks for having my back out on the road." Jack said.

"No sweat."

"Have a seat." Jack gestured to a chair.

"I was glad Jill Barlow came through the ordeal okay." Mike slouched into the seat in front of Hardwick's desk.

"Yeah, everyone is." Hardwick, seemingly a patient man, waited to see what Mike wanted.

"Heard some news this afternoon. Expect you'll be interested."

"Yeah? What's that?"

Mike told him how the Austin cops turned Greg Richardson and expected to get the man from Vegas behind everything.

"That's great. Maybe the forward movement of the investigation will give us info on who killed Phillips. Mitch was screwed up, but he didn't deserve that fate. No one does."

"I'll be heading home to Fort Worth tomorrow. Got a late afternoon flight out of Hartford. When I learn more about the situation, I'll keep you posted." He stood.

"Appreciate that." Jack reached his hand across to meet Mike's. "If I don't see you tomorrow, have a safe trip. What kind of weather you got out there now?"

"Hate to tell you, Jack, but we had a warm front come through, and temperature's forecast to hit seventy tomorrow. If you ever get down our way, I'd be happy to show you around Cowtown."

"Thanks. I might do that." Jack nodded.

Mike shouldered his way outside into the frigid air. His warm breath rolled out in clouds. It might be good idea to stop off at the hospital and get the visit over. He'd pack tonight and leave early tomorrow morning. No telling what shape the roads would be in for his trip to Hartford. He wanted to give himself plenty of time to get to the airport.

He rode the elevator up to the floor in the hospital where Jill's room was and paced outside. This was probably a mistake. Maybe he'd leave without seeing her. He didn't have to. He stepped away from her door then stopped.

If she never returned to Fort Worth, this would be the last opportunity he'd have. He needed to see for himself how she was healing. She had so much family around, he'd not come before.

Mike never had feelings for anyone involved in a case, so this was a new experience for him. Not that anything was going to come of this... What? Crush? Damn the word sounded lame.

Anyway, he'd read the clear signs that Jerrod Phillips was in love with Jill. No telling how she felt about him. He straightened his shoulders and tapped on the door.

"Come in," Jill said in a stronger voice than he'd expected.

She sat up in the bed. The red line from the earlier knife wound made more visible by the pallor from her ordeal and surgery. A sling supported her left arm. Still beautiful to him. He swallowed. "Hey, how goes it?" Brilliant, man. Absolutely brilliant. His fingers gripped the brim of his hat.

"Oh, Mike. I'm so glad to see you. I was afraid you'd already gone home, and I hadn't had the chance to tell you..."

Was she crying? He stepped closer to the bed and handed her a tissue.

"Damn. Just when I think I've gotten the nasty effects of the anesthesia out of my system, I get weepy again."

"Don't worry. You've been through a lot." His heart skittered in his chest when she reached out a hand for his. He laid his hat on the chair. At the rate he was going, he was about to end up with a permanently bent brim.

"I will get this out." She dropped the twisted tissue before she clasped her hand over his.

Hers was cold. He couldn't help but wrap his other hand on top of it.

"You can't imagine what it meant to me to come out of that jail cell and see someone from home. Someone who knew me. Someone who believed in me. I'm forever grateful."

More than a little embarrassed by her gratitude, Mike tried to make light of the situation. "Oh, you know I'd never been to New England, and I had more than a few days of vacation time coming. Glad I could help. I'm heading back tomorrow. The temperature's gonna be seventy degrees. Want to come along?" He pushed what passed for a chuckle through his closed up throat. What the hell? She'd think he was nuts. Maybe he was.

She smiled as if at a private joke. "Probably can't quite make it yet, still hooked up to a few things here." She gestured to some of the monitors. "I'm sure I'll go back. Eventually. My house will sell. I won't make Gary and Michelle deal with the sale without me. Gary was executer for Dad's will when it was probated, but going through all the stored stuff? Nah, I'll have to return."

"Well, call me when you get back, we'll compare notes on what we know about the wrap up of this business with your husband and father."

"I'll do that, Mike. Take care and have a safe journey."

He patted her hand, grabbed his hat, and left her lying in the bed in the Woodstock Hospital. *Time to get yourself home, cowboy.*

# CHAPTER NINETEEN

*Monday, December 3*

Greg Richardson paced the perimeter of his office. He'd stashed enough money away he should get out of Texas. Maybe go live on one of those secluded islands where nobody would ever find him. He didn't have to stay here.

The thing was, he hated for anyone to screw with him as Cranston had done. Sid promised he had the New England deal taken care of. What a laugh. Sid's associates turned it into a real disaster. All they needed to do was steal the God damned flash drive from the Barlow bitch. Greg's anger increased his breathing rate. He began to hyperventilate.

That's all they needed to do. All they had to do. How many times did they try, and how many did they fail? Well, it didn't matter. Bottom line, Cranston didn't live up to his part of the arrangements, and now Greg's ass was about to be cooked. Well, he wasn't going down alone.

He glanced at his watch. He'd convinced Cranston to fly over to give them a chance to clear up a few issues. Yeah, they'd get things cleared up all right. Greg paused in front of the large mirror hanging on one wall of his office. A smile of satisfaction curled up a corner of his mouth. The wire Greg wore didn't show at all. He'd nail Cranston for everything.

The island Greg wanted was still a possibility. He'd spend some time in the pen, which was what he'd negotiated with the Feds. They couldn't get him on Barlow and Stevens' deaths. Greg fed the FBI Eddie Franklin, his jerk of an informant in their office. Now Franklin was going away for a long time. Greg would watch his trial with enjoyment.

*Buzz.* Greg jumped and flipped the intercom button.

"Mr. Richardson," a night security man said.

"Yes?"

"I've got a Mr. Sam Chalmers down here. You want me to let him come up?"

Cranston's usual punctuality helped with plans for tonight. "Yes. Direct Mr. Chalmers to the correct elevator."

Within moments, the soft swish of the elevator doors announced Sid Cranston's arrival. He strode into the office, his Italian suit and loafers, and the large diamond on his right pinky finger shouting his I'm-in-charge-persona.

"Glad you could make it," Greg said to his guest.

"Yeah, it seemed necessary."

"Want a drink?"

"Whiskey. Straight." Cranston looked around the office and opened the doors leading into other corridors.

"Nervous?" Greg poured them each two fingers.

"Cautious."

"You come alone?"

"Nah. Left my guys downstairs with the security man. Good system you have."

"Sit, sit. Let's figure out where we are after these fucking screw-ups."

Cranston took a sip of the drink. "I'm not making excuses for my men. They'd worked for me a long time. I figure they bit it. I haven't heard anything since they called to say they had Barlow and the flash drive." Cranston lowered his bulk into a large brown leather chair.

"We had a good thing going here, Sid. When your people got rid of Bill Stevens… God, we were home free." Greg settled on the end of the matching leather sofa.

"That should've taken care of any roadblocks. My guys did good work after that first misstep when they took out George Barlow. Goddamn, that was disappointing. If they'd killed Stevens then, we'd have been raking in the dough from those casinos for a couple of years."

"Past history. Can't do anything to change that." Greg sipped his booze, his hand steady. Nothing showed of his inner turmoil. "You did get him, and I worked my tail off twenty hours a day after that, trying to swing those votes so the bill would be approved last spring." He shook his head. "Damn shame."

"Sure as hell is." Sid took a slug of his whiskey.

"Next Legislative session enough time will have passed, and we won't have their stupid emotions working against us the way we did this year." Greg polished off his whiskey. "Tell me, Sid." Greg crossed a leg and straightened the crease so it lay flat. "Why'd you initially think you had the New England thing handled? When I first said where the questions were coming from, you didn't sound surprised. Gave me the impression you had it controlled."

"Should've been. The idiot I worked with disappointed the crap out of me. The amount of money Mitch owed should've motivated him to pull off the assignment. When he didn't, I had no more use for him. Sent Judson in to clean it up. Now he's gone, too." He finished his drink.

"Want another?" Greg stood to refill his own.

"Sure, why not?"

"So what do you suggest we do next?" Greg handed Sid the crystal tumbler with the high dollar liquor. This may be the last drink the man enjoyed for a long time.

"We lay low for a while. If the committee schedules meetings during the down time, attend, but don't make any public statements." Sid swallowed half the liquid in his glass. "Let things settle until the fall before the January session."

Sid stretched out his legs as if he didn't have anything to worry about. He'd see how wrong he was.

"That will be soon enough to start pushing these chicken-shit legislators to do what we want. An extra envelope or two of cash for some of the key players will ensure we get satisfaction."

"What about the flash drive? What are the odds the authorities got hold of the one Barlow had from her father?" Greg paced in front of his desk.

"If they had it, we'd not be sitting around drinking your good whiskey." Sid held the glass up to the light. He could be enjoying its color. "You've got the original, right?"

"I never let it out of my sight." Greg picked up his keys and leaned against the desk. A shiny device hung below the other items on the ring. He took a sip from his glass.

Sid stood, made his way to the sideboard, tipped his head, and downed the rest of the drink. He set the glass on the dark credenza and turned.

The silenced weapon in Cranston's hand pointed directly at Greg's chest. His breath stopped. His legs threatened to give out, but he pulled himself upright.

"Shit, man, what are you doing with that gun?" The fucking Feds better have heard him. They needed to make their move fast, or he was done for.

"Taking care of loose ends, kid."

Cranston's voice shot fear through Greg's blood like sleet in a blue norther. The booze that went down so smoothly rose in the back of his throat.

"What I should've done some time ago, when I saw the way this was going. Too many actions weren't panning out. So now you're one less piece of the puzzle to worry about."

Where the hell were the agents? Greg's heart pounded in his chest. His hands were so sweaty the glass fell but didn't make much sound on the thick carpet. Odd the things you noticed in a moment like this.

Sure enough, your past life did rush by. If the Feds didn't get in here soon, he was a dead man. The flash from the gun registered a second before the soft thwack. He grabbed his middle where a piercing sharpness threatened to cut him in two. His knees buckled, and he fell toward the floor. Guess he should've worn the vest like the Feds wanted him to. He'd badly misjudged Cranston. The door burst open, and gunfire popped. Cranston tumbled to the ground, a red bloom spreading across his chest. Well, at least Sid got his, too.

# CHAPTER TWENTY

*Tuesday, December 4*

"I don't want to be a bother to you, Ellen I'll be fine here."

Jill's daughter folded a sweater and shut the bureau drawer in her mother's bedroom. She hated doing nothing when others worked.

"But Mom, I'd love for you to come." Ellen said. Jill didn't know how she could desert her store or her friends. Or Jerrod. Her hands twisted while she paced. The thought of leaving gouged a giant hole out of her middle, leaving emptiness.

"The doctor said you'd heal better, faster, and with less discomfort in a warmer climate. You'll be able to exercise more in the Keys than here. Please come and stay for a couple of months until the worst of the winter is over. Isn't that what Ethan wants you to do?"

"Yes." God, she dragged the word out like a teenager caught in a lie. "He mentioned it before he left." Her son had more than mentioned the subject. He'd practically made her swear she'd go, but she didn't want to. Jill collapsed into a chair. No energy. Damn. Healing and regaining her strength would take time.

Ellen was right. Dr. Sanders did recommend she go to Florida when he learned her daughter lived there.

Jill hadn't seen much of Jerrod. The Assembly would begin in a few weeks, and he already had committee meetings to attend in the capitol. That's the way it had been with Dad. She should go with Ellen. Hadn't she had her fill of politicians?

Jill sighed her acceptance. Time away would be healing for more than her body.

"Ellen. Thank you. I didn't mean to sound ungrateful. I'll spend a couple of months with you, but promise you won't treat me like a guest."

"I'll treat you like a guest." Her daughter gingerly hugged her as if she were afraid Jill would break apart.

Ellen laughed and said, "But only until you're able to do more for yourself, then you'll have to carry your own weight. Okay?"

"It's a deal. I can't get out of here for a while. How much longer can you stay?"

"I have to go back to work right away, Mom." Her daughter's face scrunched into worry lines.

"It's okay, sweetie. I understand." Jill rubbed Ellen's shoulder. "You've already been here longer than I hoped. You head home, and I'll be on my way by next Tuesday at the latest. How's that sound?"

"You'll shake?"

"Yes, I promise."

Ellen huffed a sigh of relief, and the lines on her face flattened out.

Jill drew in a shaky breath. Trapped. No changing her mind now. She'd never gone back on a promise to her kids.

\* \* \* \*

*Friday, December 7*

The three days dragged for Jill. Getting out of bed took longer. The simple act of brushing her teeth took longer. And emptying the dishwasher? A non-starter.

She tired quickly and needed to rest often. She'd never been a person to take a nap, but promptly at three, she curled up on the sofa in her living room. The glowing embers of the fire added to the warmth of a multi-colored afghan thrown across her legs.

Stopping by the store for an hour one morning, she found nothing to do. Sally and Mary Ann handled things beautifully. Her plan, devised in case she had to run, worked. Thank God, she hadn't needed to. Leaving now was different.

Jill still blamed herself for causing Mitch's death. Had she not come to Vermont, maybe Jerrod's brother would be alive. Yesterday, Karen had stopped by to help her finish packing. Ellen was pleased when Jill called to say she'd arrive several days earlier than promised. The cold did make her ache more. Besides who could argue against the Florida Keys in December? Only someone who was foolishly in love with the snow. And perhaps Jerrod?

"You've made the right decision to stay with Ellen for a while." Karen drove them out of Woodstock early Friday morning, because the flight took off from Hartford at nine-thirty. "The warmer temperatures and swimming will be good for you."

"Yes. I get what you're saying in my head, but I was committed to staying the whole winter. Jerrod made such a fuss about my not being able to do that when we first met. I hate how my going proves him right."

"Jerrod, huh?"

"You know he was rude to me in the beginning, Karen, and went on and on about how I couldn't possibly get through a Vermont winter. I guess he had me figured out, after all." Jill looked out the side widow and fought the trembling in her lip. She'd cried enough in the hospital.

A social worker came to talk to her after the shooting and explained the emotional turmoil she experienced was natural. She'd gone through a traumatic event, and crying was a good way to cope. Well, not in Jill's book. It didn't do one damned bit of good. Still the tears seemed to have a life of their own and came when least expected.

"Did you?"

"Huh?" She must've drifted off. What had Karen said? "I'm sorry. Occasionally, I check out. Another side effect of the anesthesia, or trauma, or…something. What did you say?"

"I asked if you saw Jerrod before we left to tell him goodbye. Did you make plans when you'd see each other next?"

"I didn't see him, but I called. He didn't answer. I left a message." Jill clamped her hands together. "So, of course, we made no plans. In fact, I doubt we'll see each other again."

"But you're coming back, aren't you, Jill? I understood this was only a temporary trip, until your health improves."

"Yes." Jill's fingers had grown numb. She needed to relax the death grip on her hands. She carefully wiggled her fingers, flexing them in their leather gloves in front of the heater vents. Why couldn't Karen let this go?

"So how is it you two will never see each other again? Woodstock isn't a large town. You're friends with his mother and take Pilates from his daughter." Karen linked her arguments together.

"There's the sign for the turnoff to the airport."

"Got it." Karen smoothly swung into the lane leading to the departure gates. "I'm still waiting for an answer."

"Well, when I return, he'll be busy with the Assembly in Montpelier for the rest of the spring, and I'll need to spend a lot of time at the store, catching up. So…"

"If you care for this man, and you do, you'll have to deal with him and your feelings when you return. Jerrod's got those stubborn Phillips' genes. He won't be ignored."

Jill couldn't decide if Karen's assessment made her feel good, or if it scared her to death. However, after what they'd all been through, nothing would ever scare her to death again.

She'd experienced facing death, and she'd survived.

Karen's comments revived memories of the night Jill and Jerrod made love in front of the fire in his house. The warm tingling low in her middle must be a good omen. Something positive was possible where they were concerned. A part of her hoped he wouldn't let her ignore him. For now though, she'd put him out of her mind. She had a trip in front of her and a body in need of warmth, comforting down time, and healing.

She hugged Karen, thanked her for everything, promised to keep in touch, and headed to the baggage check-in. The plane took off into the gray, overcast skies. An ache filled the emptiness in Jill's middle. She'd miss the next snowstorm.

* * * *

*Monday, December 24*

Jill was frankly amazed at the improvement in her health in the two weeks she'd spent in Marathon. She walked every day, exercised in the pool, and soaked in the hot tub. Ellen's physician, Dr. Sullivan, told Jill she'd be able to take on the ocean in a couple more weeks. She was eating well, too. She and Ellen took turns grilling fish for their evening meal, challenging each other to outdo the offerings of the previous night.

For Christmas tomorrow, they'd planned a more traditional meal. Ethan hadn't been able to get away, so they were using a turkey breast instead of cooking the whole bird. They had the makings for all the rest, including the pumpkin pie made from her mother's recipe.

Because she'd limited her shopping trips to grocery runs, Jill ordered all of her gifts on line. Not the personal touch she liked to have, but for this year, it worked.

Jill dithered for quite a time about what, if anything, to get Jerrod. She hoped he liked what she'd finally decided on. They had no commitment to each other. Other than the one she was afraid her heart had made.

And to a politician. What was she thinking? She and the family had suffered enough because of their connection to politics. She strongly believed in the adage "to those whom much is given much is expected." Hadn't they given enough already? She hoped so. Jill considered the hours she'd spent mulling over the gift itself. Finally, she'd settled on a book, which seemed impersonal, but it was a listing of humorous "facts" about Vermont. The saying Karen had told her about the snow blowers was in there.

One of Jill's favorites was, "The driving is better in winter because the potholes get filled with snow." She also loved, "You know you live in Vermont if you have more miles on your snow blower than your car." She'd inscribed it simply. "Miss you all and the snow." The "all" was kind of a cop out, but—

"Hey, Mom. You okay? I've been trying to get your attention. If you need to stay home, we can."

Ellen hadn't always had the worry lines above her nose that seemed to have sprung out overnight.

*My Fault.*

Jill pulled herself to her feet, and pushed the corners of her lips upward into something she hoped would pass for a smile.

"Sorry dear. Your beautiful ocean view must have lulled me into a kind of stupor. I'm fine. Let's go." She looped her arm through her daughter's, and they set off together for the Christmas Eve service.

# CHAPTER
# TWENTY-ONE

*Tuesday, December 25*

Christmas Day dawned picture perfect in Woodstock, Vermont. Thirty-two degrees with no wind. Mid-morning, Jerrod trudged through the snow from his house to his mother's. Smoke from fireplaces filled the air and tweaked his nose. Don had arrived yesterday and spent the night at his grandmother's. Liz's call 15 minutes ago to see what was keeping "good ol' Dad" made Jerrod get his act together and head over.

It would be a bittersweet holiday. Mitch had seldom been home at Christmas, but this was the first one since his death.

Jerrod glanced down the street toward Rainbow Reflections. Much had changed since his mother sold her store. Dust Mop never got out any more. Maybe the only good thing. A long sigh blew white vapor in front of his face.

Jill was a good thing, but she was in the Florida Keys with Ellen. He couldn't imagine not having a white Christmas, but people in other parts of the country routinely celebrated without snow.

His mother's tree stood in its traditional place in the front window. The sparkling red, green, and yellow lights reflected on the white coverlet of snow in the yard. Snow flocked the evergreens, and the red bow on the mailbox at the sidewalk made the setting almost perfect.

"Merry Christmas, Dad." Liz threw her arms around him after he entered. "I was afraid you'd gotten lost." She helped him with his coat and brushed off the snow.

Her teasing brought an almost contented smile to his face. "Merry Christmas. I was enjoying our town this morning. Nothing like a brisk walk on a cold day to get my appetite ready for your grandmother's dinner. Well, Don. What are you doing?" Jerrod nodded toward the large chef's apron his son wore.

"Be careful." Don stepped away from Jerrod's hug. "Grandmother's got me helping with the dough for the rolls."

"Don." His grandmother's voice came from the back of the house.

"Guess I'm needed."

Jerrod laid a hand on his son's arm to stop him. "How does she seem to be holding up?"

"She's doing well." He winked. "Coming." Long strides carried him toward the kitchen.

"Nobody else is here yet, huh?" His mother had invited the Livingstons, but their car wasn't out front.

"No, but they're on their way. Karen begged so much to bring the sweet potatoes Grandmother finally relented. I suspect she wanted to do everything to keep busy."

"Yeah." Jerrod threw an arm around Liz's shoulder. "Let's go see if we can talk her into letting us help."

The day was great. Outstanding food, of course. Few cooks were of his mother's caliber. Tim, Karen, and their kids helped break the tension. The talk flowed smoothly through the meal.

He and Tim were in the middle of a conversation about a proposed bill's possible effect on veterinarians.

"Don't you, Dad?"

"I'm sorry, Liz. What?"

"I said it was thoughtful of Jill to send a Christmas gift, and I really wish she were here. Then I said, 'Don't you, Dad?'"

It seemed everyone at the table focused on him. His heartbeat skipped, his breathing got shallow. He'd give almost anything to have Jill sitting here next to him for this holiday. But she couldn't be, and he didn't know if she'd want to. His fingers clenched around the napkin in his lap. Hell, how was he expected to answer?

"Dad?"

Liz was nothing if not persistent. He needed to come up with an answer. He opened his mouth, closed it, and opened it again. "I'm sure she'd want to be with her children." He managed the statement in a flat tone, not giving away the churning in his gut about the woman.

"Ethan couldn't get away to spend the holiday with them. He'd taken so much time earlier this fall because of everything going on with the family." She turned back to her plate.

"And you would know that how, little sister?" Don leaned his elbows on the table and speared her with a speculative gaze.

"Because I've talked with him."

Despite Liz's attempt at nonchalance, the people at the table dropped their interest in Jerrod and moved to his daughter with much teasing from her brother and a few blushes on her part.

Jerrod sipped his wine grateful he avoided what could have been an awkward situation. He glanced at his mother. A smile emphasized the lines in her face, but she seemed to be enjoying the good-natured family banter. He was relieved at how well she was handling the holiday. Only once had she brushed away a tear.

\* \* \* \*

Later in the evening Jerrod propped his feet on the hearth in his living room, leaned back in the chair, and took a sip from his wine glass. Memories of sitting with Jill almost overwhelmed him——her scent, the feel of her soft skin, the way she sucked in a breath when he kissed her behind the ear.

Damn, he wanted to hear her voice. He should've called her earlier, but…
They were in the same time zone. Maybe she hadn't gone to sleep yet. The word
brought to mind the times she'd lain in his bed both before and after the truck
ran Karen and her off the road. He groaned. What the hell was wrong with him
to wait so late? He grabbed his cell and tapped her name on the list of contacts.
It rang once, twice, and he formulated what message he'd leave.

"Hello?"

Her voice sounded sleepy and strained. Hell, he should've realized his calling
this hour would startle her. "It's me, Jerrod. Sorry if I woke you."

"Jerrod."

Was that excitement he heard or was it wishful thinking on his part? "Thank
you for the book. I've had several good chuckles from it already."

"I'm glad you're enjoying it. The silk scarf is beautiful."

"It's to wear when you return and to remind you of me." Was he pushing too
much?

"Thank you. I love the colors and feel of the material."

"How are you doing? Healing going okay?" His gut clenched. He didn't
know if he'd ever get the picture out of his mind of her lying on the ground with
blood leaking from her body making bright red splotches before melting into the
white snow.

"Yes, the doctor here says I'm making good progress."

"I'm relieved to hear the report." He paused, and then said softer. "I've been
worried about you." He rubbed a hand through his beard, picturing how white
her skin had been in the hospital bed.

"Thanks, Jerrod. I'm doing fine."

Her soft breathing carried through his cell. Now what should he say?

"Do you have snow?" Jill's voice had a wistful quality.

"Yeah, great billowy flakes. Been coming down all day. Wish you were here
to see it." He pulled the curtains back. "Hang on a minute." He clicked over to
photo mode and shot through the window. Maybe if she wouldn't come back for

him, she'd come back for the snow. He'd take her either way. He sent the picture, and then he clicked back to her. "I'm sending you something I think you'll like. The family said to tell you hello, by the way, and they're eager for you to return."

"That's nice. Hang on... Oh, Jerrod. Thank you. It's lovely. I—I miss all of you, too."

Was that a hitch he heard in her voice?

Did she mean him specifically? He'd ask, but would he get an honest answer from her? She was polite. He couldn't imagine her saying, *"No, Jerrod. I only miss your family."*

"How is Anne doing?"

"Pretty well, considering everything. Only a few tears. Thanks for asking. Do you know when you'll come back?" He held his breath. If he had some idea of the length of this separation, he'd be better able to deal.

"Probably in the spring."

Spring was better than saying she wasn't returning, and for now, he'd take her answer.

"I'll let you get back to sleep. I only called to say Merry Christmas."

"I'm glad you did, Jerrod. Merry Christmas to you and the family."

A slight hesitation caught his attention. Was she going to say something else? No. Silence filled his ear. She'd disconnected. He wished he was in bed with her in Florida, or she was here with him in Woodstock. No matter where, as long as they were together.

"Probably in the spring." He repeated her words. Well, he'd see. When the doctors gave the okay that she was physically able, Jerrod wanted her home in Woodstock. He'd check with Ellen on Jill's condition. Maybe he'd have to skip out on the Assembly for a couple of days and go visit her. Could he do that? No, not really. He had a responsibility to his constituents. What about a responsibility to himself? Wasn't he entitled to find happiness? Deep down Jerrod accepted his happiness hinged on the Texan returning to Woodstock and him.

* * * *

*Monday, January 21*

"Ellen, if I get any more rest, I'll never be worth a damn thing again."

"Oh, Mom." She took her mother's hand and pulled her onto the glider. "What's going on? Aren't you happy here?"

"Yes, but I can't stay here, and if I were to stay, I'd need to find my own place. I don't want to keep sponging off of you."

"Yeah, like you're really doing that. What can I do to make you happy?"

Jill paused and took in the gorgeous ocean view, then looked at her daughter. "It's not your responsibility to make me happy, Ellen. Only I can do that." She used the toe of her sandal to keep the glider moving.

"I hoped after I got you down here, you'd decide to make this your home. You should be near one of your kids, Mom. With Ethan in the Army and set to move around, that means me."

"Oh, honey." Jill put an arm around her daughter's shoulder. "I've loved being here with you in this idyllic, movie-location spot. But this isn't my favorite movie scene."

"So where is that?"

"In Vermont, with the fall leaves in their riotous colors or the snow falling gently from the sky making a brilliant covering on the hilltops. Up there I have people I care about, and who I think care about me."

Ellen stopped the glider. "Maybe one person in particular?"

Jill took a moment, searching for the words to reply, but suspected the warmth spreading across her cheeks said more than she wanted. "I don't know, but I want the opportunity to find out. I've missed him more than I expected."

Jill leaned forward to pick up her glass of iced tea. She wanted feedback from Ellen, but felt presumptuous to bring up the hypothetical subject. The cold liquid cooled her throat. The hint of peach refreshed her. She'd better spit out her concern.

"I don't know if anything will develop between Jerrod and me, but if it did, how would you and Ethan feel?"

"Mom, your happiness is important to us. If you want Vermont, if you want Jerrod Phillips, we're with you a hundred percent."

"Thanks. Your support means a lot." Relief at her daughter's words rushed through her body like a fresh fall breeze.

Ellen pushed the glider to get it going again. "So do you have a plan? I'm sure you have a plan."

"You know me too well. While I haven't heard from Gary about a definite buyer for the house yet, several families are looking. I'll return to Fort Worth and attack the rest of the sorting, throwing out, and packing required before I can sell. When I'm finished, I'll head back to Woodstock."

"Good for you. How soon are you planning on this, and are you physically up to handling the heavy lifting alone?"

"The doctor gave me the green light when I was in yesterday. I'll return to Fort Worth next week. I won't do too much on my own. I'll hire people. Michelle can get those same folks who helped with the initial packing."

"But Mom, what if nothing comes together for you and Jerrod? Are you still going to want to live in Vermont?"

Talk about going right for the throat. Jill stopped the swing, rose, walked to the edge of the patio, and stared at the fading light over the bay. She ran her hands up and down her arms. She liked the lovely warm breezes and sun here. But it was January, and she wanted cold weather and, more importantly, she wanted snow. She wanted the seasons. Even if she didn't get what she most wanted. Jerrod. She turned back to her daughter. "Yes."

\* \* \* \*

*Tuesday, February 5*

It was late afternoon when Jill walked out of the terminal at DFW. Her Vermont coat kept the winds of the blue norther from touching her. She chuckled when her breath misted in front of her. It was a wonder she wasn't sick with the extreme temperature changes she'd experienced in the last two months.

The familiar sight of a tall man in a cowboy hat—boots and all—coming toward her brought a smile to her face. She did miss that look in Vermont. She'd left a message on Gary's phone when she'd landed. He'd promised her he'd pick her up, but his car wasn't in sight. Well, if he didn't show, she'd take a taxi.

"Ms. Barlow. Jill." The man lifted his hat.

"Oh, my gosh. Mike. How nice to see you." She hugged him. "I was planning on calling you after I got settled. You don't have any luggage with you. Are you picking up someone?"

"As a matter of fact, I am. You."

She must've looked the way she felt, startled. He laughed.

"I called Gary to give him some news, and he mentioned you were arriving this afternoon. I offered to come get you." He ran his hands along the brim of his hat. "Hope you don't mind."

"Of course, not. It's nice of you to offer."

"Let's get you into the warm car before I load the luggage." Before long, they were whizzing down the freeway toward Fort Worth. In an odd way, it seemed to Jill she'd been gone a couple of years, yet, it hadn't even been one yet. How flat the landscape seemed. It made her feel naked, and she longed for tall green trees.

"If you don't have plans, can I take you out to supper tonight?"

"That would be wonderful. You know what I'd like to eat?"

"No, but I'll take you anywhere you want."

"Mexican food. I've missed it. Nobody does Tex-Mex the way we do. And if you're allowed, you can tell me whatever you told Gary while we eat."

Later that evening over their chips and salsa, enchiladas, and rice and beans, Mike told her what he'd learned about the gambling consortium.

Jill gasped at the violent deaths Mike described. Not just George and her father killed, but Mitch, the two men who kidnapped her, and the bosses, Cranston and Richardson.

"We haven't quite worked out how they arranged the fake lawyer, but he was one of the guys who walked you into the bank. The other was Judson again."

"That accounts for why one of them sounded familiar, but I didn't place him. So he was the lawyer I met in jail." She took another sip of the beer and a bite of enchilada, the best comfort food in the world. She certainly needed it now, listening to Mike's story.

"We're narrowing in on exactly who shot your husband and your father, but we know it was the same crowd."

"That's a relief."

"Do you want to attend those trials when they take place?"

"I don't know. Maybe, if they happen pretty quickly, and I'm still here."

"Aren't you staying?" Surprise colored his tone.

"No. I'm going to finish getting the house ready to sell, and then I'm returning to Vermont. See for myself how long those winters they're always talking about are."

"If you're sure that's what you want to do."

"Yeah, I am."

"Then I hope everything turns out well for you."

# CHAPTER
# TWENTY- TWO

*Saturday, February 16*

Jerrod liked his small apartment in Montpelier, but he loved waking up in his own bed in Woodstock. Because of President's Day on Monday, he had a three-day recess. The Assemblymen and women raced home for a chance to touch base with their constituents. Jerrod's mother had promised blueberry pancakes if he'd stop by before making his rounds of the town leaders and citizens. It was hard to argue with her offer.

He carefully stomped the snow from his feet before entering the front door. "Hello," he hollered while Dust Mop jumped around begging for attention. "Okay, okay." He scooped up the little white dog and let her kiss him then set her down. She scampered toward the kitchen. "Bet that's where your momma is."

"Good morning, dear. I'm glad you stopped by." She gave him a quick hug and kiss on the cheek. "Help yourself to the coffee. These are almost ready."

The breakfast smells made his mouth water. You couldn't beat the aroma of fresh perked coffee, unless it was with bacon. Jerrod knew his mother loved cooking for others. He pushed away the thought of a time when it would become difficult for her. "Why'd you never open a restaurant or tea room? Everyone raves about your cooking."

"What a nice thing to say. Go ahead and begin. I'll be with you in a moment."

Jerrod plopped the butter on each of the steaming blueberry pancakes, causing a river of yellow to flow from the center. He followed with the warmed syrup, and then attacked the strips on his plate. "Yum. Applewood-smoked bacon."

His mother joined him. "Of course."

He dug into the cakes.

"Jerrod, I heard Jill returned to Fort Worth. Why don't you take a trip down there?"

"What?" His mother blew him away with her ideas. He'd only thought once about making a trip to Fort Worth, and he hadn't mentioned it to anyone, because he'd decided he'd wait until the session was over. "Why would I do that right now?"

"That police detective." She glanced once at him and away.

"Mike Riley? What about him?"

"He was kind of interested in Jill."

A sharp pain stuck Jerrod's middle. He laid his fork on his plate and shoved it away. "Why do you think that?"

"Jill mentioned him when I visited with her in the hospital. I didn't see them together much, but the way she spoke of him made me think she might reciprocate his feelings."

Jerrod's heart thudded against the wall of his chest. He'd expected to have more time where Jill was concerned. When she returned to Woodstock would be soon enough to work things out between them. What if she didn't come back? She'd said she'd probably return this spring, but...

"Mother, when you've talked with Jill, has she mentioned the detective to you?"

"She saw him at least once because he'd filled her in on what they'd learned from that Austin lobbyist. I forget his name."

Jerrod studied his mother and her wide-open eyes, but he knew this woman. He crossed his arms over his chest and leaned back in his chair. "So what's going on here?"

"Jerrod Phillips, do I have to draw you a map?" She jumped up, carried her plate with its half-eaten meal, and angrily scraped the leftovers into the sink then muttered under her breath, "All these years you've had me convinced you were such a smart man."

"What?"

Her huff of exasperation let him know he was in for it. She squared off with him. "Don't you care for Jill Barlow?"

"Well, yes." He nodded, and his head accepted the truth of the words he'd only accepted in his heart. "Yes, I do, very much."

"Well, go get her. Don't let that cowboy policeman have her. Jerrod, if you have feelings for her, you need to take action."

"We're in the middle of the session right now."

She walked toward him. Stopped. Planted her hands on her hips. "Seems to me you're in the middle of a three-day break. Fly to Fort Worth, Jerrod. At least let her know what's waiting for her when she returns." She paused. "Jill's talked about coming back." His mother's eyebrows crinkled into a frown. "What if she doesn't?"

Her lowered voice and words hit him like a baseball bat. His stomach roiled. For a minute he was afraid he'd lose her fantastic pancakes at the idea of his life without Jill Barlow. "God, I've been an idiot, just waiting for her to return." He hopped up from the chair, grabbed his mother around the waist, and kissed her on both cheeks. "Thanks. I'll be out of town for several days at least."

"I hope you're not too late, dear."

He raced home, barely escaping a fall on the snow, and made plane reservations. Best he could do was a flight from Hartford Sunday morning early. He packed one carry-on bag to save time when he arrived. He drove to Hartford that afternoon and checked in to a hotel near the airport.

Weather was so iffy this time of the year. He prayed nothing kept the plane from taking off. In his hotel room, he had arranged for a rental car in Fort Worth. He didn't want anything to slow him down when he arrived. Now that he knew what he wanted, delay was intolerable.

* * * *

*Sunday, February 17*

Six-thirty in the morning, and Jill's muscles ached from pulling her carry-on bag through the terminal. Michelle had dropped her at the curbside check-in where Jill left three bags. The movers had finished everything late Saturday afternoon, and she spent the night at Michelle's house. To say the week had been hectic would be a massive understatement.

Her days were long and the nights short, but she'd gone through everything, including Ellen's boxes. She got rid of a bunch of Ellen's things, per her daughter's instructions, and still Jill shipped five boxes to Florida. Ethan's were stored in Fort Worth. He'd have to come and deal with them himself when he had time. The storage firm was reputable, and his belongings would be fine until he got around to making arrangements.

She sent box after box of both George and her father's files to one of the numerous shredding companies that had sprung up around the Metroplex. The household items, knick-knacks, furniture, clothes, and a number of the books from the library she wanted with her in Vermont were on the moving van leaving sometime that morning.

The first thing she'd do next week was meet with her agent to get him to begin searching for a place to buy that would be entirely hers. Excitement licked through her veins at the idea of her own home in Woodstock.

While she waited for the boarding announcement, she took her phone from her pocket and placed a call to Jerrod's home. Answer machine. Oh, well.

"Hey, Jerrod. I'm about to get on the plane for Hartford. I'll drive from there and be in Woodstock this afternoon. Hope to see you and your family soon. I've missed you."

She disconnected. Had she said too much, not enough? God, she was a basket case where the man was concerned. Her emotions bounced around like one of those odd-shaped balls that careened off in all directions.

The attendant announced it was time for the people in the first rows to board the plane. Jill looked around the DFW terminal, and her eyes misted. She'd be back someday she was sure, but maybe not for a long while.

As the plane sailed into the air at that heart-stopping take-off angle, she gazed through her window one last time at the Fort Worth skyline. Considered less impressive than Dallas, it had been home for fifty years. She brushed away the tears before they had a chance to slide from her eyes.

This was a happy time, really, heading for her new life in Vermont. She was happy to move to the picturesque New England town. Happy. Even if she and Jerrod didn't work things out between them. Determination to have what she wanted tightened her jaw.

\* \* \* \*

Jill stopped at Henry's Groceries after driving in from Hartford and before going to the rent house.

"Oh, my God. Jill."

She recognized the voice and turned from the refrigerator units.

"Anne. How nice for you to be one of the first people I've seen since returning." She gave the woman a hug then stepped back. Anne bent over with her hands over her face.

"What's the matter? You're not crying are you?" Jill put an arm around the older woman's shoulders. "Are you ill? Do you need to sit?"

"No. I'm laughing. I'm so glad to see you." Another laugh bubbled out. "Oh my. When did you arrive?"

"Not long ago. I made good time from Hartford and came directly to the store."

"How was your trip, dear? How are you feeling?"

"Long, but uneventful, and I'm always glad when that's the case. I'm doing well, thanks. How's Jerrod? Still in Montpelier?"

"Actually, no." Anne chuckled again. "Listen, I'm going to let you go, so you can finish your shopping. We'll get together soon." The woman pushed her cart down the aisle at a dangerous rate and just missed running into another customer. Her apology sailed over her shoulder, and she kept on moving.

Jill shook her head. What had gotten into Anne? Jill continued in a more reasonable manner wandering the aisles. Why didn't Anne say where Jerrod was? Jill should've pressed, but she didn't want to appear pushy when Anne didn't answer right away. *I'll call his cell phone after unpacking.* He regularly checked his messages.

She had tons to do. Let Sally and Mary Ann know she'd returned. Figure out when to move into the rotation at the store. This time Jill would limit it to only two days a week, if that worked with them.

Too bad Monday was a holiday. She'd have to wait to call her realtor until Tuesday. Sorting lay ahead, even though she'd done some of that before sending things on the moving van. Probably more could go. Making mental lists kept her from worrying about what would happen with her and Jerrod. Her insides did flips of need and dread.

Tomorrow. She'd find out tomorrow.

* * * *

Jerrod slid his rental up to the curb in front of Jill's Fort Worth house. It looked like the kind of place she would've been happy. His gloved hands clenched the steering wheel. If he'd known Fort Worth experienced the kind of cold they had that afternoon—the wind chill making it feel like nineteen—he probably wouldn't have worried so much about her handling the Vermont winters.

Sitting here staring didn't accomplish what he wanted. He exhaled a long breath and made his legs carry him up the walk. He climbed the five steps to the porch and pushed the bell. It echoed. Anticipation curled a hard knot in his gut. He waited.

No response. He rang the bell again. Maybe she'd gone out for the evening. Maybe with Riley. Damn. Was he too late? He wouldn't accept the possibility. He tried to peek through the windows, but the drapes shut out the smallest view.

Jerrod walked around and peered in through the small glass slits at the top of the garage door. No car. Nothing. In fact, he couldn't make out any shapes at all. It was as if the garage were empty. Damn. Where was she? He went back to the porch, and feeling something like a fool, rang the bell again.

As he did, his cell beeped. "Hey, Mother. Everything all right?" Odd she'd call when she'd sent him down here.

"Jerrod, dear, I have some news for you."

"What's that? You okay?"

"Jill's home."

"No, she's not. I'm standing on her porch now, and no one's here."

"I mean Jill is in Woodstock. I ran into her at Henry's right before I called. How fast can you get here?"

He staggered at the news, leaned a hand against the brick to keep his balance. Jill had returned to Woodstock. He'd been prepared to move to Fort Worth if she wanted him to. But she'd gone back to Woodstock on her own, of her own free will. Hope surged through his body almost making him lightheaded.

"Jerrod? Did you hear me?"

"Yes, Mother. I'll get on the first flight heading east. Don't let her leave." He tore down the stairs, jumped in the rental, and headed for the airport. God, he hoped he wasn't too late to catch the next flight. He ran into the airport like a crazy person. A happy, crazy person. Purchased a ticket. The agent wasn't certain Jerrod could make the flight, but he got through security with a minimum of delay and made the four twenty-five from DFW going through Chicago.

He prayed he'd be able to catch the close connecting flight, a mere thirty minutes, between his arrival in the Windy City and departure for Hartford. As soon as he deplaned, he sprinted.

"Excuse me. Pardon me." He jumped over a piece of luggage in his way and carefully, slid a man to the side. Amazingly, the authorities didn't question him. He slowed when he finally reached the gate. He tucked his shirt in his pants and straightened his coat, trying to exhibit a semblance of normalcy. No other passengers were in sight. He handed his boarding pass to the older male ticket taker.

"Mr. Phillips." He smiled at Jerrod. "You nearly missed this plane. Get on down the gateway now. You're the last person to board."

Jerrod nodded and followed the man's instructions rushing toward the plane door, which the flight attendant closed behind him. He shoved his bag in the overhead and dropped into his seat. Better grab a few winks. He still had the drive to Woodstock after the plane landed in Hartford at ten thirty-five. It would be at least one a.m. before he got to Woodstock and Jill. Of course, that was only if the weather held.

After he landed, he drove his car to a late night drive-through where he bought a large coffee to help him stay awake on the drive home.

His desire to see her overwhelmed his normal, sane manner. Exceeding the speed limit, his car ate up the miles before the forecast snow hit. It was likely he'd lost his mind. He'd get hold of himself before he arrived on her doorstep in the middle of the night. Wouldn't he?

The rasp from his hand rubbing through his beard filled the car. Home and shower first. He'd been traveling for more than twenty-four hours. Maybe sleep some. No. He needed to see Jill, so he pushed on through the lightly falling snow, confident his vehicle could handle the roads. Only heavy snow would force him to slow down. His hands clasped and released the steering wheel. His fingers drummed the wheel in time with his heart.

\* \* \* \*

Jill stopped unpacking long enough to heat up soup. She set out French bread, Vermont cheddar cheese, sliced an apple, and opened a bottle of her favorite Merlot.

Jerrod still hadn't returned her call. Why hadn't she heard back from him yet? She sipped her wine and worried.

If she didn't hear from him by morning, she'd call Anne. Would she think Jill was a crazy woman? Maybe, but she didn't care. She nibbled on her lip, forgetting to eat. Surely, he was just busy and nothing was wrong.

She cleaned up her dishes and went back to unpacking and putting away. It was such a small house without nearly enough storage. She'd loaded her bags down so much she'd paid extra for all three of them. Finally, she stopped and wheeled them into the room she used for her office. The bedroom needed to be somewhat neat, or she wouldn't be able to sleep.

Though the hour was late, and her muscles ached, sleep didn't come. She rolled one way and then the other. She punched her pillow. She plopped one on top of the other. A warm bath hadn't helped. Jill recognized the churned-up and excited feeling for the one she got in Fort Worth when the weather forecasters first mentioned the possibility of snow. Snow that came so seldom, she never wanted to chance being asleep and not see it fall.

*This is nuts.* Snow had been coming down steadily in Woodstock for some time. Double-checking the security system before getting ready for bed, she stood by a front window and stared at the large white flakes floating through the air. Only the chill forced her upstairs. A glance in the hall mirror showed the silly, snow-induced smile she always got in Fort Worth.

The clock said almost one-thirty. One-thirty, and she lay awake, staring at the ceiling. She checked her phone for the hundredth time to make sure the battery was charged. No word from Jerrod.

He probably wouldn't try to get hold of her now until morning. Maybe another glass of wine would help her get to sleep. Maybe she was just nuts.

She slid on her fluffy house shoes and pulled on the royal blue chenille robe she'd found to be the best defense against the cold. Her plaid flannel pajamas, a long way from the silk nightgowns she'd always worn in Fort Worth, kept her toasty under the down comforter.

The unexpected ringing of the doorbell startled her into sloshing the wine she poured. Adrenaline kicked through her system—lightening shot down her arms. Her stomach knotted, and she fought the urge to throw up. She barely held in the scream clawing at the back of her throat. She reached in her robe pocket. Damn. She'd left her phone upstairs.

Hold it.

She drew in several deep breaths. Calm down. Overreacting here, to say the least. Everyone who'd been involved with the scary stuff in Texas was dead or in prison. Nevertheless, she shuffled toward the front of the house, her hand securely grasping a rolling pin.

The bell sounded again. "Jill, it's me. I saw the lights were on, or I wouldn't have stopped."

The voice sent electricity through her body, but for an entirely different reason. "Jerrod," she whispered.

She hurried through the living room, turned off the security system, struggled with the lock, and flung open the door. Cold air swirled in. Along with Jerrod. Snow coated his uncovered head and his coat. Dark circles surrounded his bloodshot eyes. His beard was a scraggly mess.

He looked wonderful. He stepped in and shoved the door closed with his foot. Grabbing her around the waist, he lifted her off the floor and out of her slippers for a kiss that stole her breath.

Both her arms went around his shoulders. The rolling pin slid from her fingers, making a loud crash on the hardwood floor. She groaned when he pushed his tongue into her mouth deepening the kiss, sending flashes of fire to her core. Her hands barely registered the bite from the snow covering him. Finally, he lowered her until her bare feet touched the cold floor.

"God, I've missed you." He set her less than an arms-length away, as if he couldn't stand to separate completely from her.

"I've missed you." She ran her hand along his bearded cheek. "Did you get my messages? When you didn't call back, I worried."

"I haven't looked at my cell. I drove directly here from the airport in Hartford."

She brushed at his snow-covered coat. "Let me take this." He shuffled it off, and she hung it on the hall coat tree. "Come into the kitchen. Would you like a bowl of soup? And I have a bottle of wine open." She shivered. Snowflakes had traveled from Jerrod's coat and hair to her. She tied the belt on her robe more securely. Lipstick would help her looks, but the tube was upstairs. She ran fingers through her tangled hair, hoping to help her cause.

He took her hand. "Don't." He pressed a kiss to her palm. "You're beautiful the way you are. And wine sounds great."

She sent him ahead of her into the living room with the bottle. She carried the glasses and savored the look of him. "Will you light the fire?" The emptiness in her middle grew smaller with each glance or touch from him.

Jerrod got the fire going quickly, while Jill lit the candles she kept handy. With only one lamp on, the atmosphere was warm, subtle, and seductive. He settled on the sofa beside her.

"I thought you'd be tied up in Montpelier."

"We have a three-day weekend because of President's Day."

"Oh. Well, I left Fort Worth this morning and arrived around mid-day."

"Yeah. I bet our planes passed each other in the air. Mother called me right after she ran into you at the store. I caught the next available plane out of DFW this afternoon."

Jill clenched the stem so hard, she feared she'd break the glass. Could he possibly have gone for her? Her heart rate increased with hope for the desired answer.

He looked away from her, took a sip of his wine then placed their glasses on the coffee table. He gathered both of her hands in his, pulling her around toward him. "Mother said something that set me to thinking. I couldn't take a chance she was right."

"About what?"

"I couldn't take a chance on whether you'd return."

"What in the world did she tell you? I've been talking about coming back."

He didn't answer but stared into her eyes. Then he feathered a finger gently across her cheek, tracing the area where his brother had hit her, and where later the knife sliced through her skin. Her mirror told her only a hint of the wound still showed, but maybe it was too much of a reminder to him of all that had happened. Her role in his brother's death.

"She told me about Mike Riley."

"Mike?" She frowned. What was this about?

"Mother suspected he was interested in you. Said I'd be stupid to let you get away. I'd decided if I couldn't convince you to come here, I'd stay with you in Texas."

"Oh." The word left her mouth on a sigh. Jill's gaze dropped, and warmth spread from her neck upwards. She licked her lips before she spoke. "Even if Mike cared for me, Jerrod, it takes two."

\* \* \* \*

At her words, his heart leapt in his chest before taking a nose dive, making him almost light-headed. Because she wasn't interested in Riley didn't mean he had a done deal here by any means. Groveling time.

"I've been a real jerk where you're concerned, Jill. Right from the beginning. I can't apologize enough for…" *Shit.* Bile rolled up in the back of his throat. He hated to repeat what he'd accused her of in his mind and said to her with his words. She helped him out.

"Are you referring to the time you accused me of murdering my husband and father?"

He shifted away, ashamed to look at her. His stomach twisted into a corkscrew.

"Or the time when you first heard of your brother's death." She reached up and pulled his face around to her. "You didn't use the words, but I saw your expression. For that one moment, you thought I'd shot him."

Jerrod dropped to his knees. His arms tightened around her waist, his head buried in her lap. "God, I'm sorry, Jill. I'll do anything if you'll forgive me. I want—no—I need you in my life."

Her hand touched him on the cheek, and then she raised his head. "Jerrod, can you forgive me for causing Mitch's death? How can your mother stand to be in the same room with me?"

"Honey, we can't control other people's decisions. Mitch made many bad ones before you ever came to Woodstock. I'm so sorry he hurt you." He touched her cheek. His chest ached for her pain.

He stood and pulled her from the sofa into his arms, kissing her deeply, with everything he had in him. He loved the way she melted into his arms and the low moan coming from deep within her. He pushed the robe from her shoulders, burying his face in her neck. Her breath hitched in a gasp. Jill's hands flowed over his body, pushing the sweater up and touching his skin. His stomach quivered under her fingers.

"Let's go upstairs." He reluctantly pulled her robe back over her tempting body. She kissed him and nodded.

She slid an arm around his waist. One of his went across her shoulders. When he was away from her, he forgot she was so small. His heart swelled in his chest at the chance he had with this woman. They made their way up the stairs, stopping every couple of steps to kiss. Each kiss longer and more heart stopping.

By the time, they reached her bedroom, Jerrod's desire for her had heated his blood, and he wanted to make love to her at once. But he loved her so much, he wanted to take his time showing her.

Kissing every inch of her face and neck, he walked her back to the bed and gently lowered her. He paused to kick off his boots.

"Wish I'd known you were coming I'd have put on something nicer."

"It doesn't matter." He quickly had the buttons of her top undone to reveal her breasts. He stopped. The angry red scar from her bullet wound drew his focus. "Does it still hurt?"

"Occasional twinges."

He pressed a gentle kiss to the mark. "I'm sorry you had to experience all of this. I should've been able to keep you safe."

"Jerrod, we did what we had to do. I'm sorry it's ugly, but I'm fine, and you were and are wonderful." She pulled his sweater over his head.

Her hot gaze seemed to inhale him.

"Never doubt that," she said in a breathy whisper.

He kissed the wound again and then let his hands roam freely over her breasts and followed with his mouth. First one nipple then the other, letting his tongue roam over each one. They perked beneath his touch. She moaned. Her reaction made him catch his breath. She moved beneath him as though to get closer. He slid one hand down her stomach reaching lower to her mound.

She arched against him and writhed beneath the pressure. "Oh, my God, Jerrod."

He slid off her bottoms and delved his fingers into her warm, moist center. Then his mouth quickly followed his hand. He toyed with her nub before his tongue plunged in and out, followed again by two fingers while he searched for and found her hot spot. She bucked off the bed, her cries a deep explosion of ecstasy. He let her slide down and held close her trembling body. He couldn't keep a smile from spreading across his face. Pleasuring her made him feel like he was a young stud.

Jill rolled and leaned forward to kiss his nipples each in turn. Each one pebbled beneath the tip of her tongue. Fire shot through his whole body.

He'd never seen anything more beautiful than this woman. She unhooked his pants, never taking her gaze from his, while she searched for and found a condom in his pocket. She placed it on the table and completed her task of getting off his clothes. Then she moved her attention to his tented boxers, where his erection strained for release.

With a feather-soft touch, she ran her fingers across his penis from the bottom to the top and then the boxers were gone.

"Let me keep you warm, Jerrod." She chuckled deep in her throat.

He moaned when she snaked her way up his body touching and tasting every part of him. She took him in her mouth, and he flew into a whirlwind of fire and ice. When she rolled the condom on, he went out of his mind. He pulled her up, kissed her, tasting himself in her mouth. His breathing hitched. Inside. He needed to get inside.

He positioned her, and with his hands on her hips, pulled her down bit by torturous bit. His hands shook, fighting for control on the heart-pounding journey.

"Oh, God." He held still while her warm glove squeezed him. He pulsed and quivered. His heart might explode he loved her so much—"Don't move."

"I kind of thought you liked it when I moved," she whispered in a husky voice. Her head thrown back, her eyes closed.

He placed both hands on either side of her head. "Look at me."

Her lids flew open.

"I love you, Jill Barlow."

From her beautiful brown eyes, one tear escaped. He caught it with his thumb, and a smile trembled its way onto her face.

"I love you, too."

Joy. Absolutely no other word described the feeling washing over him. Everything in the world fell into its proper place. He kissed her lips, her eyelids, and her cheeks. Then he flipped her underneath him and proceeded to drive them both out of their minds.

* * * *

*Monday, February 18*

The next morning Jill awoke tucked next to Jerrod, her rear against his growing erection. An arm draped across her middle, his hand on a breast. One of his legs was across hers. She smirked. Did he think she'd try to get away? Truth was if she died right here, she'd be happy. She was the luckiest of women to have this second chance for love. And with such a wonderful man. She gently moved his hand, bringing it to her mouth, tickling the dark hairs on the back with a kiss.

"You ready to start again, woman?"

She reached a hand behind her to touch the bulge pushing against her backside. She knew she'd never get too much of this man, who made her feel every inch a desirable woman.

"If you are…" She stroked him, and he jumped in her hand. "I'll take that for a yes." Jerrod rolled on top of her and showed her he was indeed ready.

\* \* \* \*

"It's almost noon, and I'm starving. We should consider getting up, Jerrod." Her stomach growled to make her point. "See. Besides, we don't want anyone to worry."

He leaned on one elbow and looked down at her, a finger trailing across her middle. "Tell you what, let's hop in the shower, and then we'll go see Mother. She can cook us something fantastic, and we can tell her we're getting married."

"Are we?"

"God, I hope so. How soon will you let me make an honest woman of you? I want you living in my house—*our* house. I want us to share the rest of our lives."

"What about Don and Liz? I mean, have you ever brought anyone but their mother to that house?"

"No, and they don't remember her. She left when they were hardly more than toddlers. Mother's been more to them than Janice ever was." He trailed his thumb lightly across her cheek and down her nose before he sat up and leaned against the headboard. "If you can tolerate it for several more months, I'll get out of politics at the end of this session. I'd leave now, but I have an obligation to my constituents."

"I couldn't, wouldn't ask you to do that. My father helped lots of people while he served in the Texas House. Yes. Bad people devastated our lives, because they hated Dad's actions. But good stuff resulted from his service, too."

She twisted around, kissed him, and then poked him in the chest with her index finger. "And I've heard those rumors about the US Senate. I'll stand with you, whatever direction you want to go."

"You amaze me." He threaded his hands through her hair, held her gently, and kissed her, soft as butterfly wings.

"What about your kids? I hinted pretty strongly to Ethan when he was here last what my feelings for you were."

"You did, huh? I guess that's why when I mentioned the subject to Ellen, she was quick to say they both wanted me to be happy. They were behind me, even if that meant Vermont and you."

"Is that what will make you happy?" His hopeful smile said he wasn't quite convinced even after the night and morning they'd spent.

"Yes, I want more than anything in the world to be your wife."

He enveloped her in his arms. "Thank you, God."

"Not that you're getting off easy for that half-baked way you proposed. Wait until I tell your mother and the kids." She leaped from the bed and ran to the shower, where he easily caught her. But then, that was her intention all along.

Finally dressed, Jill stepped into a glistening snow-covered world. Hand-in-hand with Jerrod, she walked toward her future mother-in-law's house for a celebration Jill expected would be the first of many. Celebration of her love for Jerrod. Celebration of his for her. Celebration of the success of her escape to Vermont.

*Did you enjoy VERMONT ESCAPE? If so, please help spread the word about my books. It's easy:*

*•Recommend the book to your family and friends*

*•Post a review*

*•Tweet and Facebook about it*

*And follow me at*

http://www.marsharwest.com/category/blog for Thoughts on Thursday

www.facebook.com/#!/marsha.r.west

@marsha.r.west http://www.twitter.com/Marsharwest @Marsharwest

I'd love to hear from you.

# ABOUT THE AUTHOR

Marsha R. West, a retired elementary school principal, is also a former school board member and theatre arts teacher. She writes romantic suspense where experience is required. Her heroes and heroines, struggling with life and loss, are surprised to discover second chances at love.

Marsha, who loves to travel, lives in Texas with her supportive lawyer husband. They've raised two daughters who've presented them with three delightful grandchildren, all who live near.

She's currently writing the second book in the series about four friends that follows SECOND CHANCES which releases in the Winter 2014/2015.

Below is a preview of my second book, available in all e-formats. Buy links are on my website. www.marsharwest.com

# PREVIEW OF TRUTH BE TOLD

**Chapter One**

*12:30 pm, Friday, December 18*

Meg Bourland jerked to a stop before she reached the bottom of the stairs in her parents' house. Her fingers tightened on the banister. The spit in her mouth dried up like the Texas fields in August. A figure in a long overcoat skulked through the study doorway. Meg reached toward her waist.

Damn.

Her weapon lay in the lock box in her Atlanta condominium. Packing it in her bags with the clear marking on the outside, begged someone to steal it. Too great a risk for a flight to Fort Worth for Christmas with her family.

Hindsight is everything.

Meg sucked in a deep breath before she eased her head around the study door. Relief buckled her knees, and she staggered back into the hall. She whooshed out the breath she'd held.

"Stupid. Stupid. Stupid." Meg slammed her hand on her thigh in time with the whispered words. The psychologist was right. She was close to losing her grip. Not as fine as she claimed, or she wouldn't have over-reacted. Her father, in the shape of the tall dark figure, came home earlier than expected and hadn't taken time to remove his coat.

She rubbed a hand over her eyes, sucked in more air before she stepped through the doorway into the study.

"I suspected for a moment someone had broken in, Dad. Glad it's just you." Her voice wasn't as strong as she intended. Her father didn't respond. Didn't he hear her? He threw a crumpled paper across the room, and then he sank into the chair behind his desk. His head cradled between his hands.

Adrenalin kicked through her system again shooting lightning spikes down her arms.

"Dad, is something wrong?" Again no response. Meg moved further into the study. The pipe smoke smell dimly registered. Was he having a heart attack? She stopped in front of his desk. "Dad?" Almost shouted the word.

"What?" His gaze lighted on her for a moment before darting around the room. Didn't he recognize her?

"Meg?" He shoved his hair off his forehead and dragged in a breath. "When did you arrive?" He asked in a voice tight with strain. His gaze never connected with hers.

Not a heart attack. Thank God. She let out a huff of air. "A while ago. Are you all right?"

Her father placed his hands on the desk and straightened into the ramrod posture she'd seen all her life.

"Everything's fine."

He used the same word Meg did when things were the opposite of all right.

"Glad you got home okay." His voice was stronger now. He shuffled through files on his desk. "I. . . uh. . . came to pick up this folder." Unusual for her father to stammer. He was always self-assured. He waved the file in the air and shoved others into the center drawer. "I'm heading back to work now."

He threw an arm around her shoulder, hustled her out of his study, and closed the door with a distinct thud.

"But Dad—"

"Don't mention to your mother that you saw me."

He glanced toward Meg, but still he made no eye contact. All her cop instincts shouted this was trouble.

"She'll tease me about my memory and try to stick one of her damn pills down my throat. See you tonight." Her father brushed past her in his rush to get out of the house.

Meg stood for a minute in the open doorway, but then a blast of cold wind skittered in and disturbed the rug lying on the hardwood floor of the entry. She shivered, turned the lock, and straightened the rug before entering the living room. She could just make out the taillights of his car as he wheeled down the street.

The flickering flames from the gas fire delivered welcome warmth. She rubbed her hands up and down her arms. What just happened?

The scent of the fresh evergreen enveloped her in the essence of the holidays. As long as they'd lived here, a real tree took center stage in the bay windows of the living room and her father's study. White lights and ornaments bedecked the tall firs. The cheerfulness clashed with her father's odd behavior.

"Dad," she whispered the word. They hadn't seen each other since the incident resulting in the loss of one the officers on her team. The incident that almost took her life. Scenes slashed through her mind, and her heart pounded faster than a woodpecker's beak against a tree.

Gritting her teeth, she shoved the pictures into the black hole of memory. She clenched her fingers around her forearms and muttered under her breath. "I'm fine, I'm fine. Not my fault." She leaned over with her hands on her knees and drew in big gulps of air. Each breath came out more slowly, her heart rate slowed, until she had herself under control.

Dad had barely hugged her. And don't tell Mom? His words made Meg determined to speak to her.

On the other hand, she'd suspected her father was a burglar. As much as she resented the psychologist in Atlanta suggesting she go home for two weeks, this may be for the best. She wasn't as fine as she kept telling people. Or herself. She headed toward the study to see what the paper was her father threw away.

Loud clumps down the stairs drew her attention, and she returned to the entryway. Sure enough. David. He always rushed to eat their mother's cooking. Meg raised a finger to her lips. At this rate, he'd wake up Scott McClaine, his LAPD partner who'd come to recuperate with their family.

Her brother slowed his descent. "What?"

"Scott's sleeping."

"And you know that how?" David joined her at the bottom of the stairs.

"Because I peeked in on him before coming down. His forehead furrowed, and he moaned, not a peaceful sleep at all."

"Personal experience?" David's voice dropped in pitch, and he placed a hand on her shoulder.

"Yeah." She nodded and then shoved away her own demons.

Certainly, Scott deserved a happier life after what he'd sacrificed saving David's life. As a cop herself, she understood the risks her brother and Scott took serving and protecting the city of Los Angeles. "Come into the den with me a minute. I'd like to ask you something before we eat lunch."

"Sure. I can survive a few more minutes if you can talk louder than my stomach's growling."

Her brother, always the jokester. They reached the TV room, and Meg yanked him down next to her on one of deep leather sofas. "What's going on with Dad?"

"What do you mean?"

Meg told him about the incident in their father's study. David, never one to sit still long, hopped off the sofa and paced in front of the fireplace.

"He didn't give you one of those giant hugs of his, crushing your ribs?"

Meg shook her head. An ache grew in her middle. Did health issues keep her father from lifting her off her feet? Had she disappointed him, because the psychologist suggested Meg take off and encouraged her to meet with a colleague here in Fort Worth?

David stopped walking and pinned her with one of his interrogator glares. "He asked how you were doing after Hank's shooting, right?"

She shook her head. A small twinge took up life in her left temple.

"Odd." David shoved his hands in his pockets and returned to crisscrossing the room.

Pain blossomed in both of Meg's temples. She pressed her palms to the sides of her head, hoping to limit its growth to a less than debilitating level. If the pounding didn't recede, she'd have no choice but to resort to meds, and she hated the way they made her feel.

"Anything else?" Her brother's eyebrows rose in question.

As if with a life of their own, her fingers dropped to her lap and twisted together into a knot about the size of the one in her stomach. "He told me not to tell Mom he'd come home."

"The hell you say." David stopped walking. "One of their cardinal rules is 'Never keep secrets'." He dropped onto the sofa next to her.

"Yeah. They always said if someone tells you not to tell, you probably should. It's the advice I always gave kids I mentored."

David had talked her into volunteering with Big Brothers and Big Sisters in Fort Worth when they'd both lived in town. Her brother mentored a boy now and again in LA. In Atlanta, Meg had dropped the activity. Too many times, she'd disappoint her little sister because of spur of the moment assignments.

"What about the paper he crushed and threw away?"

"I didn't have a chance to look. You came down."

"What are we waiting for? Let's go." He rose, grabbed her hand, and strode toward the front of the house.

"Hey, aren't you two hungry?"

*Mom.* Meg glanced at David. He shrugged and faced their mother.

www.ingramcontent.com/pod-product-compliance
Lightning Source LLC
Chambersburg PA
CBHW071255170626
46809CB00001B/225